I0818292

THE STREETZ

ALEXIS TAYLOR

The Streetz

Printed in the United States of America

First Printing, 2022

ISBN-13: 978-1-7357901-5-2

eBook ISBN-13: 978-1-7357901-6-9

Cover Design by Murphy Rae

Alexis Novel's Logo by Cartoon Logo Studio

Published by Eat My Lyrics Publishing Company, LLC

https://brittinydmorehead.com/publisher

THE STREETZ
CONTENTS

THE STREETZ ACKNOWLEDGEMENTS

Davon T. Matten
Valencia D. Lucas
Harmony A. Taylor
Kaiser A. Marshall
Irene K. Marshall
Tyrome Taylor
Monique Mcmillion
Damaria Jones
Jazmine Bennett
Zsa'keyriah Ashford
Michelle Collins
Brittiny D. Morehead
Murphy Rae
Sandra Hatter
All Family & Friends

This project would not have become what it is without each of you. I love and appreciate you all.

Thank you all for giving me support, helping me through my tears, showing me the way, and believing in my vision.

Each one of you has played your own role in helping me bring this novel to light, and I can't thank you all enough. Enjoy!

-Alexis Taylor

Naomi's Prologue

The Start of a New Beginning

May 15th, 2019

Hitting the locks on her car, Naomi tiredly yawned and pulled her bags up on her shoulder as she slowly walked towards her apartment. Her feet were killing her, and she could feel a slight migraine approaching-causing her to sigh. Words can't explain how exhausted and beyond tired she was from working two jobs.

Trying to make ends meet and balance her personal life became more than she could carry.

It was almost one o'clock in the morning, all she wanted to do at this moment was take a peaceful shower and just go straight to sleep.

However, she knew the chances of that happening were slim to none, but a girl could dream right?

When she opened the door to her one-bedroom apartment, that she shared with her boyfriend Deandre, she instantly sensed that something wasn't right. The place was dark, clothes were scattered across the living room floor, two empty wine glasses rested on the coffee table and then suddenly the sound of another woman's voice haunted her ears.

A part of her wanted to cry, but sadly this was not his first time inviting a woman over and cheating on her. The old her would have run up the stairs crying, ready to fight the next bitch for sleeping with her man, but at this point she was just numb to it all. It was clear; it didn't matter how many times he would see her break down and cry, he was still going to continue to do whatever he wanted, regardless of the pain he caused her- so she stopped reacting to it.

He also knew the chances of her leaving him were slim to none, which at a time was true. However, over the years her feelings have changed, she wanted nothing more than to gather her things and start over.

What's stopping her, you ask? Fear. There's a lot of things about Deandre many people do not know. He has a way of playing this certain "role" in front of others, but he's got a dark side in which has yet to be exposed.

Releasing a deep breath, in attempt to control her anger, she put her things down and began cleaning up the living room, as she reflected to herself on how and when things between them had gotten so bad. She used to love Deandre more than anything in this world. At first just the thought of him brought a smile to her face, but now, shit was just different. When they were kids, they met at her family's barbecue, their connection was almost instant. There was a point in time when you wouldn't have been able to convince her that he did not love her, all bets in, now- she would believe it for free. Sadly though, here they are four years later in a relationship, and it's like she doesn't even know who he is anymore. Most days it feels as if she's laying with a stranger every night, and every day, she must face him.

During the course of their relationship, Deandre has managed to instill fear within her, manipulate her mentally, and tear her away from her family and friends; all to gain full control over her, needless to say, his plan worked.

In the beginning, her family and even a few friends tried to warn her, but she ignored and excused every red flag he's thrown at her, and sometimes she feels as if what she's going through is all her fault. She had many opportunities to leave and walk away, but she didn't. Instead, she stayed in hopes of him one day changing and becoming the man she once loved, more than anything in the world.

"I never felt so alone in my life" She thought to herself.

Hearing voices coming from their bedroom, she listened in closely pressing her ear against the door. "We have to hang out more, I really enjoyed you." She heard the mysterious woman say, followed by a flirtatious laugh. The tone of her voice sounded very familiar, but she couldn't figure out where she had heard it before. Continuing to listen in, she began to hear Deandre's voice.

"Most definitely ma, just keep me posted whenever you're free." He responded using his smooth Trig Suave voice, the same voice he got her with. Becoming fed up, she had heard enough, she opened the door to their bedroom and froze at the sight before her. She could literally feel her heart shatter and break into a million pieces as she stared directly in the eyes of someone she thought she could trust.

Blinking a few times to make sure her eyes weren't playing tricks on her, and that she was actually seeing her close friend, Janelle, laying in their bed, butt ass naked, perfectly propped up against their pillows, relaxing as if this was *her* home. She yelled-

7

"What tha fuck?!"

Janelle immediately hopped out of their bed and began grabbing her clothes.

"Naomi, I am so sorry." She pleaded with fear laced in her voice, but Naomi wasn't trying to hear none of that.

Before she could even utter another word, Deandre entered the room shirtless, while sporting an olive-green towel wrapped around his waist.

Even though this was not Deandre's first time cheating, and probably wouldn't be his last, she never would have thought- or even suspected him to sleep with her so-called friend.

Shaking her head in disbelief, she scoffed. "I can't believe this shit."

When Janelle started to walk towards her, Naomi took a step back. "Naomi, I promise you I can explain. It wasn't supposed to go this far—"

Although Janelle 's lips were still moving, Naomi toned her out and just felt herself becoming more and more pissed off. She continued to analyze the room and saw remaining parts of their clothes scattered relentlessly, along with condom wrappers in *their* bed; she felt her blood begin to boil some more.

Janelle was the first person Naomi befriended when she and Deandre first moved there, and unlike her family and friends back home, Janelle was the only one who knew the severity of their relationship.

Janelle became Naomi's human diary; she confided in her about everything she's gone through with Deandre. So, to see that she has been having an affair with him after all that she has shared with her about his cheating, and the abuse- this was the last thing Naomi ever expected to happen.

Reverting back to reality, Naomi followed her first instinct and launched towards Janelle, allowing her rage to take over her body. Naomi repeatedly threw punches her way, not fazed by Janelle trying to get a good grip of her hair to gain leverage.

Tripping over one of Janelle's heels, the girls were now on the floor, Naomi on top of her as she swung nonstop, taking out every bit of built-up anger on her.

Deandre watched as they fought and began throwing on clothes, in case the laws got called. He came out of their closet, dressed in a pair of basketball shorts, and attempted to toss on a shirt. Deandre immediately tossed the shirt and ran over when he saw Naomi was now choking the shit out of Janelle.

Feeling Deandre try to snatch her away made her grip even tighter, as she watched Janelle struggle to breathe. Naomi looked down at her and felt no sympathy for bitches like her. She hoped in this moment, she got the message that she was not one to be fucked with, if you ever betrayed her trust.

Finally, after pulling Naomi off Janelle, Deandre slammed Naomi up against the wall, pinned her in a corner, and yelled. "You need to chill the fuck out bruh!" As if she would even listen to him; all of this is his fault in the first place.

"Just get that bitch out of my house Deandre!" She screamed as tears began to fall from her eyes.

She watched Janelle quickly gathered her clothes from around their room, before she vanished completely, never once looking back. Naomi felt absolutely humiliated. Here she was, confiding in this woman about the way this man has made her feel, and she slaps her dead in her face by sleeping with him.

"How long!?" Naomi yelled at Deandre, while he still held her arms against the wall.

She could tell he was trying to control his anger, but she knew it was all for show; he just needed Janelle to believe his innocence. Naomi knew the moment he heard that front door close, signaling that she left, somehow all of this would become her fault, and he'd take his anger out on her physically.

"Just shut the fuck up and sit your ass down." He demanded without a single trace of sympathy or nothing in his voice.

When he let go of her hands, Naomi had half the mind to charge after Janelle once more, but at this point she was over it. She knew she'd get exactly what she deserved for doing this to her.

Taking a seat at the edge of their bed, Naomi impatiently waited as her leg shook uncontrollably.

Hearing Janelle finish putting on her clothes upfront, too scared to be in the same room as Naomi, she mentally rolled her eyes and let out a scoff when Deandre left the room to escort her out; he's no fucking gentleman.

She stared at Dre long and hard wondering where the hell she went wrong, she felt herself going crazy mentally as her body started to shake against her will.

This was not the life she wanted for herself by far. It seemed as if she always found herself crying due to the deck of cards life gave to her. She craved for the love of her family and to possibly have one of her own, but that was now something she was starting to feel would never happen.

When Dre returned, Naomi just stared into space; completely out of it. "Get your dumb ass up and get in the shower Naomi!" Dre yelled as if he had any room to be making demands. Instead of arguing, she did what he wanted in hopes of saving herself from another possible fight.

Although she is extremely pissed and wants to go off, she knew a fight with Deandre was one she wasn't going to win. To keep her anger from rising, a nice shower followed by a good night's rest is just what she needed to relax her nerves.

Reaching their bathroom, she turned on the water to the shower and began to undress herself. She heard him enter the bathroom and she instantly did not want to shower anymore. She used to love and crave their intimate showers together, but now it does nothing for her. She wanted his hands everywhere else, except on her body.

Now when he touches her, all she feels is dirty and disgusted. The thoughts of him with other women and constantly raising his hand to her would haunt her mind each time he laid a finger on her.

"Damn, I missed you all day." He mumbled as he came up behind her and began placing kisses on her neck and shoulder. This is what pissed Naomi off the most about him. He does bullshit to her then turns around and acts as if nothing just happened moments ago.

The mind games he continued to play were becoming draining; one minute he acted as if he cared then the next, he acted as if she didn't even matter to him.

When she turned to try and get up to run away, Deandre grabbed her by her leg and dragged her back into their bedroom as she screamed.

Throwing her up against a wall, Naomi hunched over in pain watching as he started pacing the room and smacking his head ever so often.

As he began talking to himself, Naomi backed up against the wall and tried to look for something to knock his ass out with. She knew her hitting him would build up his anger to another level, but if she didn't defend herself, she could be as good as dead.

"You think you're running shit or something now Naomi? Huh? That must be it." He laughed. "This new nigga of yours clearly got you tripping if you're bold enough to put your fucking hands on me! I know one thing; you can tell that nigga who got your mind gone that the next time he kiss you that's my dick he tasting." Dropping the shorts he wore, he walked up towards her and reached down and pulled her up by her hair forcing his dick into her mouth as tears continued to fall from her eyes.

"One day you'll realize that man is no good for you, you need to leave while you can." The words of her mother were all that continued to ring throughout her mind, and it was at this moment she made a promise to herself to leave him for good. She wants to be free so badly that she's willing to die for it.

She no longer wanted to spend her nights covering up bruises with make-up, crying and healing for weeks in her bed, feeling alone. Along with having to come home to multiple women enjoying her man at any moment they desire. Or having to hide out from the people she loves because she has a jealous and abusive man.

Then having to constantly lie to coworkers about the different marks or scars that appear on her body and constantly frightened every time a man attempts to interact with her. She was fed up with it all and wanted better for herself before it was too late.

Looking up at him she bit down hard on his dick until she felt the bitter taste of his blood, as he hollered out in pain. When he shoved her off him, she used that time to escape into their bedroom. She panickily opened the top drawer and grabbed her 9mm quickly and let off 5 rounds as he charged towards her, barely even having time to think and process what just happened.

As those bullets ranged out, sending him flying back onto their bed before he slowly slid off. She watched as he struggled to breathe, still in shock at what just happened. Just from his screams and cries for mercy she could tell he was scared.

However, mercy didn't live there anymore.

Walking towards him with her gun still aimed and cocked, she watched him begin to choke on his own blood, just hoping that in this exact moment, he felt everything he had put her through, along with all the pain he's caused all these years.

She continued to watch, as his eyes began to roll back. He took his one last breath, she dropped to her knees and let out a loud cry that she didn't even know she was holding in.

Naomi heard the bedroom door open; she saw it was their neighbor Kim. Quickly scanning the room, Kim knew exactly what had just transpired; so instead of asking Naomi a million and one questions, she just hugged her tightly while she continued to cry.

Naomi was so completely out of it mentally, she didn't even realize how long she had been sitting there crying in Kim's arms, until the cops along with the ambulance arrived. Before she knew it, she was being read her Miranda rights, handcuffed, and placed in the back of a cop car.

Watching as they carried Deandre's body out in a body bag, Naomi began to cry even harder as everyone stood outside being nosey, watching everything unfold.

The red and blue lights flashed across the faces of many of Naomi's neighbors who never came to her rescue when she needed it; somehow, they were all front and center now, being nosey.

Noticing one particular face in the crowd, she squinted her eyes as she began to analyze where the familiar face was from. To her surprise it was Deandre's cousin, Trig, she hadn't seen him in years and when they locked eyes, he gave her an unreadable expression. She knew it meant nothing good, so she broke the stare by looking away and catching the tears that dripped down from her eyes. She wasn't crying because she killed the love of her life and was saying goodbye to a life that has caused her nothing but pain. Naomi was crying because she was finally free from the hold he had over her heart; she was finally able to say "Hello" to a new beginning.

"I'm finally free," was all that continued to run across Naomi's mind. Killing Deandre wasn't something she wanted to do or even enjoyed, but it came down to her or him and she finally chose herself.

Cartier's Prologue

September 4th, 2008

The sound of glass breaking followed by screaming and the voices of someone yelling, woke up a young Cartier out of his sleep. Letting out a deep sigh, he sat up and flipped the covers off himself to see what was going on. Stepping out of his room he faintly heard the voices of his parents and finally realizing what was happening.

"I'm so sick of this shit!" He thought to himself.

Every day it seemed as if there was always something going on between them; there was never peace within their home and Cartier was becoming fed up with it all.

Walking towards the stairwell, he noticed pieces of broken glass and stains of blood scattered across the living room floor. Trying to mentally prepare himself for what he was about to witness, he took a few deep breaths and closed his eyes.

Jogging down the steps to follow the sound of where the noise was coming from, Cartier stopped dead in his tracks at the sight before him.

Looking over at his older brother Quentin who was laying down in the corner of their kitchen holding his waist as he cried out in pain, he quickly reverted his attention to his mother who was pinned up against the wall being choked to death by his father.

Cartier watched his mother struggled to pry his father's hands off her as tears streamed down her face. She plead for him to stop. Cartier's blood started to boil, and his anger continued to rise. Every day his father came home drunk out of his mind and in full rage, at this point Cartier just wished things could go back to how it used to be.

Their father wasn't always like his though. It seemed as if the moment the drug game was introduced into their lives, shit changed. When it came to the money and the lifestyle, he was now able to provide it, everything was all good, but the real shit went to worst.

Every day they watched the money change him and morph him into this heartless cold-hearted monster.

Becoming fed up with everything now, Cartier grabbed the nearest item he could find, which happened to be a mason jar. He immediately lunged the jar towards his father, missing his head by an inch but it caught his attention.

"Nigga have you lost your damn mind!?" He yelled.

Although Cartier feared his father, he knew he had to do something to protect his mother. "Get the fuck off my mama!" Tears threatened to fall from his eyes as he stared back at his father with his fist clenched and eyes full of hate and anger.

Stunned by his son's outburst, Carter let go of his wife, Joyce, and ran towards his son in a drunken rage. "Carter! Stop, please leave him alone, he's just a kid!" His mother yelled as she fell to the ground holding her neck where his hands once were.

Not wanting to show that he was scared, Cartier stood up firmly, despite him only being fourteen years-old, five-foot three inches tall, and weighing about 112 pounds; he was ready to take on his father.

"Please don't hurt him!" Joyce cried out between gasps of air.

It was clear just by the way his dad was stumbling over his own feet, he was too drunk to even focus, and Cartier was going to use that to his advantage.

"Mama I'm good." Cartier replied, not once taking his eyes off his father. Cartier didn't really care about what was about to happen to him if his mother made it out okay.

He would rather take a thousand beatings if that meant his mama never had to struggle or experience any type of pain, ever again.

When his dad swung at him, Cartier ducked causing his dad to lose his balance when he missed. Barely even having time to catch himself and stand up straight, Cartier started sending punches his way repeatedly until he was on the ground before stepping back.

"Beat his ass C" Quentin yelled trying to encourage his brother.

"Getcho bitch ass up! You so quick to put yo muthafuckin' hands on my mama, hit me bitch! Hit me!" He yelled, hitting his chest repeatedly.

Struggling to get up, Carter laughed as he wiped his mouth and spit blood out becoming even more angry.

Cartier was very brave at heart and wouldn't bow down to anyone; he often felt as if his pride would be the death of him, but he honestly didn't care.

Slowly waking back up, Cartier started listening in on the two men's conversation. He silently prayed to himself that his brother would be okay.

"I thought the boss said there were four of them?" One guy asked, glancing back at the three of them.

"It is, but the other little nigga was fucked up so bad, I figured he wouldn't even make it out the driveway alive. He would've been dead weight literally." The other guy joked.

"This is one fucked up ass family, but you better hope ole' dude don't find out you left one of them behind."

"He ain't! I'm telling you that nigga is not gon' make it through the night. I'll simply tell boss man he got to running that mouth of his, tried to jump stupid and I popped his ass right then and there. Simple." He shrugged, feeling accomplished with the lie he made up.

The other guy simply laughed as they continued driving to their destination. Little did they know, back across town Quentin was a fighter, and he wasn't giving up until he got his family back.

After laying there until the coast was clear and he knew for sure that the men were gone, Quentin slowly sat up ignoring the pain he was in and used the kitchen counter as leverage to help him stand.

Holding onto his side he mumbled inaudible curse words as he slowly limped over to where his phone was. He quickly dialed up his Uncle Pernell's number.

Feeling his nerves get the best of him as the phone continued to ring, Quentin tried to control his breathing in hopes that he'd answer. When he finally picked up on the third ring, he let out a sigh of relief.

All that could be heard was the sound of movement, before he heard his uncle cough and clear his throat. "Hello?" He answered in a groggy voice.

"Unc... I'm sorry to call you so late but some niggas just came and—and they took mama and Carti!" Quentin managed to get out in between the bulging pain he was experiencing from when his dad stabbed him. He tried applying as much pressure as he could to his wound, but he worried about how much longer he could hold on.

Immediately sitting up in his bed, he reached over and turned on his nightstand light. "Wait—What!? Where are you!?"

"I'm at home," Pernell could hear the strain in his voice and could only imagine what all went down tonight.

Getting out of his bed, he motioned for his wife to get up as he quickly threw on some clothes. "Get up baby, we got some shit to handle real quick at C and Joyce nem house." He explained, causing her to get up as well in a hurry.

"We're on our way right now!" Not saying anything else he hung up the phone.

Sitting his phone down on the counter, Quentin slowly sat down and felt himself becoming slightly lightheaded. He was trying to hang on for the sake of his brother, but it was becoming pretty damn hard.

When Pernell and his wife arrived, they noticed their front door was broken off the hinges and when they stepped inside, it looked as if a tornado ran through and destroyed the place. "Que? Where are you at baby?" Pernell asked as he walked further inside the home.

Spotting him on the kitchen floor, their aunt immediately rushed over when she saw he was now slouched over. Checking for a pulse, she sighed due to how faint it was. "We have to get him to the hospital now." She explained as she choked back tears.

"You take him to the hospital, while I take care of this shit. I already know who's behind this shit, these muthafucka's have lost their mind kidnapping my sister and my nephew!" He snapped, punching a hole into the wall. "I'm done playing games with these niggas!"

Pernell knew it was time to handle business once and for all with the Howard family.

Once his wife was gone with Quentin, Pernell started making phone calls getting the boys loaded up. He already knew the exact location of their hideouts and where they possibly took his sister and nephew.

He was willing to burn the whole city down behind them, and he hoped like hell that they got the message that he was not one to fuck with.

When his boys all arrived at the house, Pernell wasted no time hopping into one of the all black SUVs that pulled up; they jumped onto the expressway and pushed 100mph the entire way there.

Glancing in the rearview mirror at his boys cleaning off and loading up their guns, Pernell looked down at the semi-automatic that rested in his lap, he was ready to knock some heads off.

Pernell had been plotting to take out Giovanni for a while now, especially when the beef he had with Carter started to progress and word on the street was that he was planning on taking out his whole family. Pernell was already aware of the ins and outs of his entire business; he just needed the perfect opportunity to strike, and this felt like the one.

When they arrived at the spot, Pernell parked right next to his brother Rome and their team of men, who had already been there scoping out the scene. "They took them all around back. We pulled up maybe ten minutes after them." Rome explained to Pernell as they both hopped out of their cars together.

Pernell simply nodded, "Let's go!" He told everybody, cutting the small talk.

Splitting up and going in different directions towards the abandoned house, Pernell placed his silencer on his 9mm, letting off two rounds at one of their guards.

Stepping over his body, Rome motioned that there were two niggas on the porch as they slowly crept up on them. One of the guys was oblivious to his surroundings because he was too occupied on his phone. He appeared to be having an intense conversation; Pernell wasted no time sending a shot to his head just as Rome killed the other one before he could react to what just happened.

Ducking real low, Pernell and his men managed to get to the side of the house, making their way towards the back. He could faintly hear voices, so he motioned for the guys to hold on, so that he and Rome could continue scoping out the scene.

Glancing from the side of the house, Rome saw it was about four niggas standing around smoking and drinking. "It's four of em, if we come through blasting on they asses, we'll get em all." Rome whispered.

Looking over at his brother Rome, Pernell nodded before counting to three. They stepped from around the house and let off rounds, killing them all instantly.

Pernell heard the house come alive; he knew a war had officially begun. Stepping inside the house from the back door, he could hear people loading up their guns, so he quickly scoped out the scene and shot a nigga right in the head; he saw him making his way from the kitchen.

Soon Rome and the rest of the guys all made their way inside, "We finna search this bitch high and low until we find Giovanni bitch ass and locate where my nephew and sister are!" Pernell ordered before taking off; showing no remorse, he killed whoever he came across.

The guys all knew by now Giovanni was aware of what was going on and they knew they needed to find him and quick, before it was too late. Spotting a young female who was hiding behind a couch crying, Pernell walked up to her. "If you want to make it out alive tonight, I'ma need you to start talking! Where tha fuck is Giovanni!?" He whispered-yelled, while holding a gun to her head.

Shaking her head no as more tears fell from her eyes she pleaded. "Please..."

Shoving the gun against her head with his finger on the trigger, she tried controlling her breathing so could talk. "They're—They're downstairs in the basement."

Signaling one of his guys to come over, he helped the girl stand before roughly shoving her into the guy's arms. "Take her ass to the car but watch her."

Doing as he was told, Pernell spotted Rome across the way and motioned with his hand where they were located.

Reaching the door that led to the basement, Pernell had his gun drawn and ready. Descending the stairs, Pernell could faintly hear the sound of someone groaning.

Once they reached the basement, Pernell mentally cussed to himself at the sight before him. Giovanni had managed to get away and all that was left was a bleeding out Carter, a badly beaten-up Joyce, and a traumatized Cartier who sat in the corner crying his eyes out as he stared down at his mother's body.

"I'm actually doing a lot better. I have my days of course, but I really assumed that I would be a lot more depressed and just moping around, all sad and shit; but girl I have never felt so free in my life before. For once I feel so at peace with myself." Naomi expressed.

"That's good, I'm so happy for you. But you know I have to ask." She started giving her a look.

Staring back in confusion, Naomi frowned. "Ask what?"

"Well for starters, why didn't you tell anybody what was going on, or come back home once things got really bad? You know we all love you and would have done all that we could to help you." She asked, causing her to sigh.

Although she didn't want to hear this, she knew Lanay was right. If she had told her family and friends the truth about her relationship with Dre, they would have come and rescued her in a heartbeat. The only person that knew the severity of their relationship a little was her mother, but she promised to stay out of her business unless it got too bad, but once it did Naomi cut off all forms of communication with her and her family.

Naomi's mom knew nothing about the abuse, only about the constant cheating. When they talked, she would always tell her how she deserved better and wanted her daughter to leave him, but she knew Naomi would only leave once she got fed up with the disrespect and that she couldn't force her to do anything she wasn't ready for.

Truth was, Naomi had it made up in her mind that eventually Dre would get his shit together, and that he loved her enough to change and bring back the man that she once knew and grew to love deeply.

Sadly, she was wrong.

"I wanted to tell everybody, but honestly I was too scared and thought he would change and that things would have gotten better between us." Naomi confessed feeling her eyes begin to burn. "I was stupid and too in love to let go."

Lanay soon got up from her seat and sat next to her giving her a much-needed hug.

"Don't call yourself stupid! This isn't on you; we've all been there before girl. I love you and all that matters now is that you're here and we're going to get through this together." She reassured her.

"Thanks, Lanay, I can't explain how sorry I am for cutting you off behind him. I vowed to never be that type of friend; to let someone come in between my friendships and I did just that."

Lanay waved her off, "I knew when you cut ties with me, that was nothing but Dre filling your head up and controlling you. He knew how close we were, and he knew the moment I caught wind of what was going on, I would have swooped in, beat his ass, and taken you away; he didn't want that."

"You're right, but I'm still sorry."

"We're good boo, I'm just glad to have you back and to celebrate your return. We should go out just like old times, did you have any plans for tonight?" She asked.

Shrugging her shoulders, Naomi shook her head no. "If you call binge-watching All American plans, then yes."

"Well, All American, gon' have to wait, there's this party tonight for your brother's birthday! Were you not planning on coming?"

Face palming herself, she sighed. "I completely forgot all about that, I've been so focused on getting settled in that it slipped my mind. I haven't even seen him since I got back, but yes, I was planning on going. I need to get him a gift though, did you want to come to the mall with me to find him a gift and an outfit?" She asked her, while standing up from her seat.

"Girl yes and I'll invite my homegirl, Sheree with us, I've been wanting you two to meet." She answered before pulling out her phone.

"Okay bet, well just give me about twenty-minutes to shower and throw something on real quick." Naomi told her before taking off to her room.

Walking into her bathroom Naomi turned on her shower to let the water warm up and started brushing her teeth. Once she was done, she got in the shower and began washing her body with one of her favorite body wash scents. It always made her skin feel so smooth and soft, and left her smelling good. The product itself is great, however, it being from a black owned company just made the product ten times better.

Turning off the shower once she was done, she stepped out and grabbed a towel to wrap around her body. Walking into her room, she tossed her hair into a messy bun before taking a seat at the edge of her bed to dry off and lotion up her body.

In the midst of putting on her bra, Lanay came walking in. “You’ve got to be the slowest person ever; will you hurry your ass up?” She asked while taking a seat on Naomi’s bed.

“Oh, shut up, don’t rush me I’m coming, bitch.” Naomi replied in laughter as she walked into her closet to grab a simple white Givenchy t-shirt that spelled the name out horizontally in black, and a pair of cute, distressed jeans.

Once she was dressed and ready, Lanay looked over at her and sighed before standing to her feet. “About damn time.”

“You know I have to make sure I look good everywhere I go.” Naomi replied, while sliding her feet into a pair of her Givenchy slides.

Lanay simply shook her head, seeing that much hadn’t changed about Naomi, which she was grateful for. Since they were younger Naomi and her brother stayed dripped in designer clothes; Lanay always wished that one day she could afford the finer things in life.

Nudging Lanay’s arm, Naomi playfully rolled her eyes as they walked towards the front door. While grabbing their purses and car keys, Naomi also made sure that all lights were off, and that everything was locked up before heading to the mall.

As they walked around the jewelry store, trying to find Naomi’s brother a gift, she became slightly frustrated because they still couldn’t find him anything. It’s so hard trying to find the perfect gift for someone who has everything. “I’m really about to give up and just be like fuck it.” she sighed. “My presence alone is a gift within’ itself.”

Laughing, Lanay looked around. “Girl, I’m sure it's something in this store that your brother would like!”

Glancing around herself, she shrugged before spotting a watch sitting inside a glass display box.

Smiling to herself, she walked towards it, falling in love with it already. “If you’re thinking about getting that, you got my vote. I think he would really like that.” Lanay said as they both stared at the luxurious watch.

"You really think so?" Naomi questioned looking back towards her.

Smacking her teeth, Lanay nodded. "Girl yes, you know how flashy your brother is with the gold chains and watches, this is right up his alley forreal."

Naomi laughed knowing she was right; her brother's favorite type of metal was gold and the longer she stared at the watch the more convinced she became to get it for him. The watch had just the right amount of diamonds inside and the numbers were in roman numerals.

"You're right, I'll get it for him."

Flagging down one of the salesmen, he quickly made his way over to them. "Yes, how can I help you ladies?"

Turning back to the watch, Naomi pointed. "I would like to buy this watch."

As he fetched his key to take the watch out of the display case, Lanay and Naomi made their way towards the check-out counter.

Once he started packing up his gift, Naomi took this as the perfect opportunity to ask Lanay about this Sheree girl. She's not against making new friends and meeting new people, she just hates being mixed in with drama and her city can be known for it.

Back when Naomi was in high school, she had a friend named Bianca. Her and Naomi were so close to the point where she could literally come and talk to her about anything. Bianca knew all of her deepest secrets and vice versa, she was honestly more like a sister to Naomi but that all changed one day. Their fallout happened over a guy Bianca knew Naomi had a crush on that attended their school, and not only did she betray her by sleeping with him, but she also posted all her deepest secrets online for the whole school to see. Her trust towards people hasn't been the same since. She never wanted to put all her trust in someone like that, only for them to turn on her one day.

"So, give me the scoop on your friend, what is she like?" Naomi asked.

"Oh, girl she's really cool, I think y'all will click well. She was raised here in Buckhead, and I already know what you're thinking, but I promise she is not like most of these girls around here. She stays out of the way and puts most of her focus on school." Lanay reassured.

"She's in college?"

"Yes mam, my girl is in her third year of nursing school and is killing it." She was proud of her friend's accomplishment.

Naomi nodded in approval, already starting to like her. Around here you don't meet too many girls that's all about their money and in their own lane, minding their business. You had everybody trying to do whatever they can to reach a certain lifestyle or trap a baller for a quick come up.

Once the salesmen finally finished wrapping his gift, she paid and headed to this new and upcoming store. They were known for selling all the latest and trendy fashions and just from what Naomi was seeing, she loved everything about the store. She was so amazed by the cute layout and the clothing pieces displayed within the store; the store was truly like every woman's dream closet.

"What do you think about this jumpsuit Naomi?" Lanay asked, holding up an all-black off the shoulder jumpsuit with gold chains wrapped around the midsection.

Naomi nodded in approval. It was exactly what she was looking for, something simple but sexy.

"Yes, I have some black booties that will look sexy as hell with this." Naomi said looking for her size.

"Hey girl." They heard from a female voice approaching them. When Naomi looked up to get a look at her, she saw that she was about the same height as her, had beautiful brown skin, and an amazing figure with a pretty face to match.

"Hey Sheree! "Lanay exclaimed, hugging her then turning to Naomi. "Naomi this my girl Sheree and Sheree this my best friend Naomi."

"Hey, it's a pleasure to meet you." Naomi greeted after finally finding her size in the jumpsuit.

"Hey, it's nice to meet you as well and I hope you plan on getting that jumpsuit. It's really cute." She complimented.

Naomi looked over it once more and decided it was a go. After she paid for her outfit and got some accessories to wear tonight, they all began searching for an outfit for Lanay picky ass.

Rummaging through multiple racks of clothes to choose from, Naomi came across a silver glitter, low cut V-neck body dress with spaghetti straps that she knew would fit her very well.

"Come look at this girl!" Naomi told her as she walked up to the dressing room.

"Ooh yes this is cute Lanay." Sheree agrees, just as Lanay comes walking out from the dressing room becoming slightly frustrated. However, once she saw the dress her eyes lit up with excitement.

"I don't even need to look anymore; I'm going with this!" She said as she held the dress up to her body in the mirror.

Once she found a pair of heels to match along with some accessories, they checked out then headed to the food court to eat and talk more before they left to get ready for tonight.

"What y'all in the mood for?" Naomi questioned as she scanned her eyes over the different food options they had. She felt her stomach begin to form a hole in it.

Everything looks soo delicious! She thought.

"I think I'm going with Chinese food." Lanay answered, looking over at this spot called The Li's.

"Ewww girl you know that shit ain't real chicken!" Sheree exclaimed, twisting up her lips.

Naomi laughed, "I heard that too."

"Fuck y'all, it's gon' be real chicken today." Lanay said as she headed over to the Chinese station ignoring their comments.

Naomi looked over at the Philly cheesesteak spot and decided to go with that for lunch.

"I'm heading to the Philly spot sis." She told Sheree before walking off, but not before she heard her say she was getting pizza.

The line wasn't that long so that made her stomach happy. As the smell of the food hit her nose, her stomach started to rumble once again. She laughed to herself then walked up as the girl in front of her finished.

"Welcome to Charley's Philly Steaks! What can I get you today?" The lady over the counter greeted dryly. She had a slightly annoyed tone in her voice, but it didn't really bother Naomi. Sometimes you just never know a person's life outside of work, so Naomi always tried to be nice regardless of how rude someone may be towards her.

"Can I get your Philly cheese steak sandwich with onions and fries on the side and for my drink I would like a large lemonade." Naomi said, pulling out her wallet.

When she was finally able to get a good look at the girl, she noticed a bruise on her cheek that she clearly tried to cover with makeup. Seeing that brought Naomi back to those times she spent trying to cover her face with makeup to hide her bruises.

Thinking of what all she could possibly be enduring made her almost want to break down, but she pulled herself together.

"Did you want this to be to go or dine in?"

"Dine in please."

"Okay, your total is $15.46 today. Just swipe or insert your card if you don't have cash." She explained.

Reaching into her wallet Naomi pulled out two twenty-dollar bills and told her to keep the change. Watching as her eyes lit up, she immediately tried to hand it back. "I can't take this." She whispered.

"Yes, you can, this is just a kind gesture in hopes of making your day better." Naomi replied politely, pushing her hand away to keep the cash.

After she thanked her and handed her the receipt Naomi stepped to the side and let the next person in line order. While she waited, she decided to check her phone and to her surprise she had a text from her mama.

Mama☺👵: Hey baby, just reaching out to check on you. I hope you're doing alright! When are you coming by to see us? We miss you.
Delivered at 3:57pm

Naomi sighed to herself, not really knowing how to respond. She avoided her parents as much as she could, so she wouldn't have to discuss Deandre. Her therapy sessions were almost to an end and her life is just starting to get back on track. The last thing she wants to do is relive everything and have to sit and listen to her parents' lectures on how she should've left sooner.

Naomi:
Hey mama, I'm doing okay just taking it all one day at a time. I'll come visit you guys soon, I miss y'all too.
Sent at 4:48 pm

After she texted her back, she put away her phone and grabbed her order once they called her number. Walking back to their table she saw Lanay, and Sheree already seated and enjoying their food.

"I'm telling you this shit slap!" Lanay boasted as she dug in her food. She laughed and sat next to her.

"Girl, whatever there's nothing you can say that will convince me to eat that shit." Sheree replied with disgust before taking a bite out of her pizza.

"Yeah, I'd rather make my own." Naomi said, agreeing with Sheree. Lanay simply waved them off and continued to eat her food.

"So, tell me more about this party we're going to tonight. What's the special occasion?" Sheree asked them both.

Using a napkin to wipe her mouth as she chewed her food, Naomi took a sip from her lemonade to help wash it down before replying. "Today's my brother's birthday and he decided to throw a birthday bash for himself." She shrugged.

"Damn, well I hope it's some cuties tonight I'm tryna get snatched." Sheree laughed.

Taking another sip of her drink, Naomi simply shrugged her shoulders again. "It probably will be, but I won't be checking for anybody tonight."

"Girl, she said that shit all nonchalant and dry only because it's her brother. It's most definitely gon' to be some fine ass niggas at the club tonight, her brother alone is fine as hell, and so is all his friends- so we definitely gon' have to come out steppin'." Lanay boosted being extra per usual.

Laughing at her dramatics Naomi shook her head, if Lanay didn't do nothing else, she was going to overhype Naomi's brother at any chance given. Don't get Naomi wrong though, she knows her brother is very nice looking, but he is not as heaven-sent as Lanay thinks.

Tossing a napkin at her, Naomi laughed. "You do too much!"

"So, are he and his friends not cute?" Sheree questioned, seeming a little disappointed.

Lanay and Naomi both yelled out "yes" and "no" in unison causing them all to laugh together.

"Well, I'm going to just get cute anyway, because I need a boy toy or something. It's been so long since I had sex, I'd probably have an orgasm just from a nigga touching my hand right about now." Sheree confessed jokingly.

"You'd think with you working in a hospital, you would run across some fine ass doctors or nurses." Naomi said, stuffing some fries in her mouth.

"Chile please! That's if you want a damn grandpa." She replied followed by a sigh. "It's so hard to find a nice man that actually wants exactly what you want. Like, I ain't gon' lie, there are some younger, attractive doctors where I work, but they're all just some horny hoes. These doctors sleep around so much with different nurses and other doctors, I'm choosing to stay away at all costs; last thing I need in my life is drama."

"I felt that!" Naomi agreed.

"See, I told y'all this would go well!" Lanay said excitedly.

Laughing, Naomi smiled. "*Lanay actually was right this time. Sheree isn't so bad.*" She thought.

"It really did."

"Yeah, you're cool people forreal." Sheree complimented.

After they finished up with their food, they stayed a little while longer to enjoy more girl-talk and laughter, then they headed out to get ready for tonight. Although this is Naomi's brother's day, she needed this night out with the girls.

Chapter 2

While getting dressed to go and handle some business in the streetz, Cartier felt a hard stare from one of the girls he messed around with burning a hole in his back. Checking his pockets in search of his keys, his eyes scanned the room but came to a stop when he saw an annoyed Porsha.

"What now man?" He snapped, while continuing his search for his keys to his Bentley.

When he heard her smack her teeth and let out a frustrated sigh, he rolled his eyes, not in the mood for her attitude at all today. Here lately, every time he got ready to leave after fucking on Porsha, she would catch an attitude, which always led to them arguing.

He didn't understand where the change in her demeanor came from, or why she was acting the way she was- nor did he really care to sit down and attempt to either.

Porsha watched Cartier continue to look for the keys she purposely tossed and hid from him. She sat forward completely annoyed with him at this point. "Is this all we are now?" She asked before folding her arms across her chest, as he glanced over at her.

"I mean I really thought we shared something special between one another and that I meant more to you. Things between us have changed and I'm tired of you treating me this way."

Smacking his teeth, he waved her off. "Treating you in what way? What have I done to you Porsha?"

"You treat me like I'm just one of your bitches! You just come through whenever you want, fuck me, and leave. We don't even talk unless you're in the mood and I'm sick of it! I thought we were more than that, I *want* to be more than that." She expressed.

Finally landing his eyes on the location of his keys he quickly grabbed them.

I need to hurry up and get the fuck up out of here. The last thing I'm about to do is argue with this bitch and have this conversation. He thought quickly, checking the list of things he brought with him.

"Hello!? Do you not hear me talking to you?" She yelled, snapping her fingers.

Taking a deep breath trying to compose himself, Cartier looked away. "Every time I come over, it's always some bullshit with you, this is exactly why I didn't want to come over here in the first place man!"

Cartier and Porsha's relationship wasn't always this toxic, nor did they ever really talk to each other like this. In the beginning, Porsha had become a close friend that he could come to about his problems and vice versa.

However, one night after drinking, their friendship turned into a little more and their situation turned into more like friends with benefits. At first, things were still cordial between the two. They would hook up occasionally and still chill and talk as friends, but it was like once feelings and emotions got involved, things changed for the worst.

Once Porsha realized that the feelings she had weren't being reciprocated, she started to question the status of their relationship and soon opened up to him about how she felt.

When Porsha opened up to Cartier about her feelings towards him, he honestly didn't know how to respond to her, besides with the truth. And the truth was that Cartier just did not see her in that way, nor did he feel anything towards her. He felt Porsha was good for sex and conversation, but that was all. A relationship just wasn't something he envisioned with her, nor did he want one.

So, after he confessed his feelings to her, as well as his outlook on what was happening between them, a switch flipped from her being cool to turning bat shit crazy. In result, due to her switch up, the two fell off big time; they talked a lot less and the only time they ever saw each other now was for sex, and even that was rare.

Becoming fed up with his nonchalant responses and attitude, Porsha hopped up from the bed and started walking towards Cartier. One thing Porsha hated was to be blown off, especially when her feelings were involved. She wanted Cartier to see that she wasn't just some broad he could have whenever it was convenient for him; she was more than that and she knew she deserved better.

"I'm so sick of you using me when it's convenient for your dick. I understand that you may feel differently about me, but shit Capone I have feelings as well. So, either you treat me properly and give me what I want or leave me the fuck alone!" She yelled.

"Then I guess we can just be done, because you were the one who kept hitting me for dick, even after I told you how I felt! So, in all honesty I only still came around just to do your ass a favor." Cartier said, brushing by her heading out the door.

Cartier knew within their situation he made a lot of mistakes, but he wasn't about to let Porsha put the blame all on him when she already knew what it was between them.

"A favor!? Nigga please, first of all, the dick ain't even all that! I'm so sick of you egomaniac ass niggas; get a little money and start thinking you the shit, but quick to forget all a woman has ever did for you." She snapped back, shaking her head, hurt by his comment.

Without uttering another word, Porsha locked the door behind him once he stepped out, and then broke down crying. She felt so stupid for allowing him into her heart when she was warned serval times; Her mama always told her to never fall for a man like Cartier, yet here she was, head over hills behind him.

ო

Walking outside to the sound of loud music blasting, Cartier laughed when he saw his best friend pull up in his new car. "What up bitch!?" He yelled out, not giving a damn if the neighbors heard him or not. "Man, I'm telling you now, the bitches are going to be all over me tonight." He boasted out the window about his new whip he just paid for straight off the lot, before turning up his music.

The car was an all-black 2019 Lexus LS and it was truly a beauty with the custom rims he had added on earlier that day, along with the 5% tint on his windows.

"Whew. That bitch is pretty." Cartier complimented slapping hands with him. "I see that stash is treating you right."

"Yeah, it is, but it won't hold a nigga long though, especially with my sister being back in town. Gotta make sure she forever straight."

"About damn time, I was becoming fed up with yo bitch ass moping around, crying about yo sister." Cartier joked as the two laughed.

When Naomi first left town it took a toll on Nassir, considering how inseparable the two were prior to her move with Dre. When she cut off all forms of communication with him and their family, it hurt him deeply.

Every day he worried about her because he knew Dre had to be fucking with her head for her to cease contact with her entire family. Once word got around that Naomi's time in Detroit wasn't as cracked up as she made it seem, he felt some-type-of-way that she wouldn't/didn't come to him for help.

However, now that she's back, he wasn't letting her leave his side ever again, and he was going to keep her as close as possible.

"Fuck you nigga, what you call me over here for anyways though?"

"We gotta talk about this nigga Trig." He sighed, already becoming frustrated at the thought of that nigga.

Slightly frowning Nassir shut off his car, being sure to lock it up behind him as he followed Cartier back inside the traphouse.

Bypassing a few dudes, Nassir gave them brief head nods as they made their way to the kitchen where nobody was. "What's up with Trig? What did he do?"

Cartier leaned up against the island that sat right in the middle of the kitchen, while Nassir took a seat in one of his bar stools, Cartier sighed.

"I think we need to stop fucking with him, he bad for business." He shrugged. "I'm hearing too much shit about him in the streetz."

Smacking his teeth, Nassir sat back. "Nigga like what? What the fuck happened?"

"That nigga been getting too wild out here and he coming off sheisty as hell here lately, so I already been on his ass. Our money being shorted, his product becoming ass now, so we are losing business. Then word on the street has it that his bitch ass just made a deal with the fucking devil by ratting out one of his partners as a way of ruling out the competition." Cartier explained everything he just discovered to Nassir. "He clearly on some other shit and he just not the type of nigga I wanna do business with anymore. He can't be trusted whether that rumor is true or not, I don't need no fake shit around me."

Shaking his head, Nassir looked away. "Damn man, this why I be hesitant with putting niggas on game. It's always some bullshit and if what you heard is true, how do we know he ain't finna target us next and try to rat us out to the feds?"

Cartier shrugged while pulling at his chin hair, "That's the thing, we don't know, so we just gotta get on it and watch his ass and slowly back away from him. I'm done telling that nigga anything, because any information we give him could possibly be used against us."

Listening to what all Cartier was saying, Nassir sat there in deep thought thinking of a way to save their slowly sinking business.

Ever since the two made their pack of becoming blood brothers, their undying loyalty towards one another has yet to be questioned. They started this shit together, selling dime bags for quick money, and soon their business just blossomed into more, and along the way they used their resources to bless other niggas by putting them on game.

However, nowadays it just seemed as if niggas just weren't as loyal and would turn on you quick behind some pussy, money, or both. Cartier and Nassir were lowkey ready to just cut everyone off and go back to how it was before, just the two of them running the streetz.

Becoming slightly frustrated Nassir pulled out a Newport from his pocket and lit it before glancing over at Cartier who was looking down. "Have you come up with anything yet, as far as a plan?"

Cartier looked up at him, giving him a certain look before shaking his head in disbelief. He couldn't believe how naive and careless he had been, two things his uncles and father never raised him to be.

Failing to do their own research on Trig, they managed to let a snake get in close with them; he could possibly ruin everything they've built so far if they didn't think of something quickly.

Cartier was lowkey disappointed in himself because he trusted this man way too fast. It fucked his mind up to know that their money was being shorted, their product was being watered down, and Trig was making shady business decisions behind their backs.

It was clear Trig let the money get to his head and felt that since he was the supplier, shit was going to go in his favor, but that was all about to change.

Cartier sighed, realizing that they needed to make a move and soon. He always dreaded that this day would come. "We gotta find a new supplier first." He mumbled nonchalantly, causing a smirk to appear on Nassir's face.

"So, we're meeting with your uncle?" Nassir asked just to confirm his assumption.

Nassir had been pitching the idea of going into business with Cartier's uncle for a while now, but Cartier was too bullhead to ever acknowledge the possibilities; he wanted to do things his way. So, Nassir had hope that today was the day Cartier would finally come to his senses.

Cartier's uncle was just the type of connection they needed. He was big time. Everybody knew and respected Pernell in the streetz. With that type of ally, they would be pulling in triple of what they make now at a minimum. Nassir was itching for that type of payday, so it excited his pockets at the thought of him finally coming around.

"It's the only way at this point, I don't trust anybody else, and he's been wanting me to connect with him for a good minute." Cartier replied lowkey upset.

Cartier never wanted to go into business with his Uncle Pernell simply because he didn't want to play by his rules. His uncle always told him that the only way he would do business with him is if he listened and legitimized himself, but back then a vengeful and angry Cartier wanted to do everything but listen.

Growing up, Cartier actually wanted nothing more than a one-way ticket out of their family business, but with having a big brother that didn't really possess what it took to be a boss, and their parents not having another child after him, he was the only option. Cartier was forced to take over, so his uncles applied the pressure and groomed him for the role to carry on their family's legacy.

Cartier's family's name was like royalty in the streetz, but their name was almost tarnished by a few bad deals his father, by the name of Carter Semaj Williams, better known as Bones, made back in the day. It took his Uncle Pernell years to gain back that respect.

So, with not much of a choice of his own, the pressure of being forced to choose this lifestyle made Cartier want to do things his way, so that he could make a name for himself.

Simply something his father could never accomplish.

However, it was clear that certain things one just couldn't do alone, especially when there's still so much you don't know or haven't learned yet.

Cartier knew he could've easily taken the quickest way to the top; but he honestly felt he wouldn't have appreciated a lot of the things he had been blessed with the way he does now since he worked hard for it.

So, when he partnered up with Nassir, he did it to prove to himself that he could do it on his own with no handouts.

"Well, come on then nigga, we need to hurry up and get this shit over with, so I can start preparing for my party tonight." Nassir urged as he hopped up off the bar stool, he was sitting in.

Laughing at Nassir's eagerness, Cartier leaned up off the island and grabbed his car keys. "Hold down the fort." He yelled, letting his workers know he was heading out.

After twenty-five minutes of driving with Spliffs being passed and minor conversation being held. They finally arrived at Uncle Pernell's house, which resided in Buckhead.

Looking out the window as they approached the house, Nassir stared in disbelief. "Yo uncle lives in Tuxedo Park!? This nigga definitely eating." He spoke out, admiring the view of his uncle's ten-bedroom, nine-bathroom mansion.

Pulling up in their driveway, Nassir sat back in pure amazement. This was exactly the type of lifestyle he always wanted for himself and Naomi, and he wasn't stopping until he achieved that.

Admiring all the cars that were parked out front- ranging from different styles of Bentley, Rolls Royce and Lamborghini. Cartier shook his head while laughing, his uncle was such a car junky, he knew they were only seeing about half of his collection.

Looking at two guys cleaning his Aunt's Porsche who he assumed was their butlers, Nassir shook his head. "Man, this shit is unbelievable."

"This is going to be exactly how we gon' be living one day, as soon as we straighten out this shit and get back on it." Cartier replied shutting off his car.

Getting out of his car, Cartier spoke to a few of the workers who stood out front on guard before making their way towards the front door. Not even getting the chance to knock, the door suddenly opened revealing one of his uncle's butlers who escorted them inside.

"Good afternoon gentlemen, Mr. Pernell is in his private office, follow me, please." He greeted them before turning on his heels and leading the way to where his uncle was waiting for the two.

Approaching the door, the butler softly knocked twice before opening the door. "Sir, your nephew and his friend have arrived." Pushing the door further open he revealed Cartier and Nassir so his uncle could see.

"What's up Unc?" Cartier briefly waved.

Adjusting his glasses, he glanced at his nephew, he waved for them to come on in. "Can you bring us three glasses and something from my secret stash in the kitchen, please Raul?" Pernell asked.

"Yessir, anything in particular you want me to grab?"

Leaning back in his seat, he smiled as he stared directly at Cartier. "Nope, surprise me! This meeting calls for a celebration, my nephew has finally gotten his head out of his ass and has come to his senses." He laughed.

Smacking his teeth, Cartier rolled his eyes as he slouched down his seat.

"Yessir, anything else you need before I go?"

"Nah, just inform my wife we have a *very* special guest here and to come home as soon as she can."

When Raul left out, being sure to shut the door behind him, Pernell pulled at his goatee while playing with Dice in his other hand. "I can admit that I'm happy you called, I knew one day this day would come. So, tell me what's going on, what really brings you two here?"

"We got mixed up with this nigga who we used as our supplier, he been on some snake shit, and we need to get out and find a new one, quick." Cartier answered, getting straight to the point. He loved his uncle, but he still kept business and their personal life separate to keep it professional.

"Who was your supplier?" Pernell asked, becoming interested in this new information even though he already knew.

"This muthafucka named Trig, he's been running around snitching on competition, supplying us with watered down product, and making deals with niggas behind our backs. He's playing a dirty game and we don't want any parts of it." Nassir spoke up for the first time since they got there.

When his office door opened, in came Raul with a tray that consisted of three glasses full of ice and a bottle of Jack Daniel's Tennessee Honey.

After filling their glasses and placing the bottle back on the tray, Raul quietly sat it on the table stand near the door before exiting out.

Grabbing his drink, Pernell took a sip of it shaking his head. "What Trig is doing now isn't anything new, he's been playing you." He smirked. "I'm not surprised though, I knew those muthafucka's would eventually come out of hiding one day." He scoffed followed by a laugh.

Looking at each other in confusion, Cartier and Nassir frowned. "Whatchu talkin' bout Unc? Do you know him or something?"

"I don't know him personally, but I am very familiar with his family." He started. "I heard on the street's that you were doing business with this Trig cat and although at the time I wasn't too familiar with who he was, after doing some snooping of my own I quickly found out and hired more guards to be on lookout for you."

Shaking his head, Cartier looked down. "Why didn't you ever tell me? You knew dude was a snake and never said anything? I could've been killed!"

Pernell smirked. "That was a risk you were willing to take, C! You didn't want to do business with your own family and decided to trust another muthafucka' and that almost cost you your life but see as always- family was the one who helped save your ass then, and family is the one who's about to save your ass now! You felt you were grown enough to do it on your own, so I let you. I only made a promise to my sister to keep you safe and I did just that! But until you wanted my help, I wasn't going to do anything other than that!" Pernell started raising his voice a little.

Cartier said nothing, because he knew he was right. He was so obsessed with proving that he was much more than his father and that he could operate on his own; He didn't realize the way he moved was jeopardizing everything. He grinded his teeth growing more upset with himself by the minute. He knew it was time to start maneuvering better.

"Well, who the fuck is Trig anyways? Is he somebody we should really be worried about?" Nassir questioned since it was clear Cartier was too in his feelings to speak at the moment. He wanted to know what type of nigga they were dealing with.

"Trig's family and ours have had this ongoing beef that goes back years, way before Cartier and his brother were even born. Him playing you wasn't by mistake; he knows you're William's blood. His father is the man that took down Cartier's!"

Looking up at his uncle, Cartier frowned. "What!?"

Laughing, Pernell continued to sip on his Jack. "Don't act too surprised now son. This is the exact shit I tried to warn your ass about Cartier, but nah you just knew you had everything all figured out. You fucked around and let a muthafucka who wants you dead get that close to you!" He semi-yelled chugging the rest of his drink before getting up to fix himself another glass.

Pernell wasn't trying to be too hard on Cartier, but right now he was all the family had as far as leaving the family business too. Although he and his wife have tried on many occasions for a son, they were only blessed with three beautiful girls by the names of Genesis, Jewell, and Aubrey Williams.

Pernell loves his girls, but he always yearned for a son to hand over everything too. He believed the business needed to stay in the hands of the blood line, but he never wanted to put that type of pressure on his daughters. So once Cartier was born and showed the family he had what it took to be a leader, the family imprinted and instilled everything they knew to groom and prepare him for the responsibility of being the next Heir.

They knew it would all take time but seeing Cartier today making rookie mistakes worried him. He needed to get him back on track, it was only a matter of time before it was Pernell's turn to retire, and he wanted to be confident that the moment he turned the business over to Cartier he was truly ready for it.

"I fucked up, I can admit that and I'm sorry. I'm sure seeing me down brings you a lot of joy. You've been saying since day one I couldn't do this shit on my own and here I am on the verge of possibly losing everything I worked so hard for, all because I wouldn't listen." He sighed. "So go ahead and say you were right and that you told me so."

Shaking his head, Pernell sat his glass down before walking back over to his desk. "Honestly nephew, I hate I was right, but I knew that your stubbornness would soon get you caught up. You're just like your damn daddy at times. Due to your dad's malicious ass ways, he had to learn the hard way what comes with that shit, and it cost him his life. You really think I want that for you?"

Taking a seat on the edge of his desk, he made the two of them look at him. "Cartier, I know you and your dad never saw eye to eye and he was far from perfect with the way he treated you, your brother and your mom. But he saw something in you that we all see, you have it in you to take over the game and dominate this shit. All I ever wanted to do was help guide you so shit like this wouldn't happen. I made a promise to your mom that I would look after you and your brother, but I can't do that if you don't let me."

"So, what's next? Where do we go from here?" Nassir asked, looking back and forth between Pernell and Cartier.

"That's up to Cartier, where do we go from here nephew?" Pernell asked while folding his arms.

When both Pernell and Nassir stared at him awaiting his response, Cartier playfully rolled his eyes before grabbing his glass and holding it up. "I guess we're business partners now."

Smiling, Nassir grabbed his glass, holding it up as well, before clinking their glasses together, Pernell said, "Alright, well let's talk business then fellas."

Retaking his seat behind his desk, the three of them sat in his office for a few hours discussing business strategies, product, pricing and the new way that the three of them would start conducting business together.

Cartier knew it was time for him to get back on his game; with this new information he found out with Trig secretly plotting against him, he knew he needed to do something fast to get Trig before it was too late.

However, what Cartier didn't know was that this was only just the beginning of the problems that were soon to come his way.

Chapter 3

It was pushing almost nine o'clock pm the girls and Naomi had finally made it to the club, "The Gold Room." Naomi was infatuated with how much the city changed since she left it years ago, it was a good change though. The women were dressed in the latest fashions, with their hair slayed to the gods, flowing flawlessly down their backs. The men were sporting Burberry, Gucci, Saint Laurent, gold chains, Rolex watches and even grillz.

Watching folks roll up in Bentleys and Rovers, Naomi admired everything, hoping to achieve this type of lifestyle one day for herself. It was clear this club was upscale and only a select few of certain people were allowed here. When the girls were all escorted inside the club, Naomi was amazed with how her brother went all out for his birthday. The decorations were really nice, and the club was packed full of people, including a few celebs. He had big banners, balloons, and even sparkling bottles carried by bottle girls.

"Damn yo brother must be paid! You see the type of motherfuckas in this party!?" Sheree said after checking out each baller that they passed by; she wasn't money hungry, but she wasn't one to say no to a nigga with money either.

"I see. Lanay, do you see him anywhere?" Naomi asked, unfazed by all the men and their flashy chains and designer clothing.

Naomi of course liked a man who had something to bring to the table other than their good looks; but after everything Deandre put her through, she was cool with holding off on relationships for a while. She quickly learned first-hand, not every man is all they present themselves to be.

"Are you Naomi?" Looking back at the voice, they were met with some big buff black man who appeared to be security.

"Depends on who's asking." She frowned.

"Your brother sent me down to escort you up to his section," He pointed, which made them all look to see her brother and others on the top-level drinking and partying. The girls all strutted behind the guard toward the VIP section, the bouncer let them right in as soon as they reached the area. It was set up nicely with royal black and gold sofa couches and furniture, and near the back rested a table with all his gifts and a private bar with another banner across it that read, "Happy Birthday Snoop!"

The room was filled with all his real close friends and family that Naomi hadn't seen in a long time, she didn't realize how much she missed being in the mix until now. After speaking to a few folks and sharing hugs with cousins she hadn't seen in years, Naomi wondered where the hell her brother had run off too. She managed to speak to almost everyone in the section, being sure to introduce Sheree and Lanay, but had yet to actually speak to the person this whole night was for.

Scanning the room with her eyes in search of him, she shook her head when she spotted him on one of the couches with some woman on his lap as he whispered things in her ear. She could only laugh because despite all these years passing, he had not changed at all when it came to the ladies. Once he noticed her, he quickly removed the woman from his lap and walked up to embrace her with a big hug.

"Damn, I almost thought you weren't going to make it. I missed your ass girl." He stated.

Smiling as they swayed back and forth. "You really thought I would miss your birthday? And you know I missed you too Nassir." Naomi said, purposely calling him by his government name since in the streetz he went by Snoop.

"Aye chill with that government name shit in public Nao, I don' told yo ass about that." He replied, pushing her off him as she laughed.

"Nope, that's what's written on your birth certificate so that is what I am going to call you. But anyways here, I got you a little something."

Handing him his gift, she watched as his eyes lit up. "Nao, you know you ain't have to get me anything. Just you being back home was all I ever wanted but thank you forreal."

Embracing him into a quick hug again, Naomi smiled to herself. "You're welcome."

Quickly kissing the top of her head, he pushed her off and started brushing off his clothes. "Ight enough of all this mushy shit, you gon' introduce me to your friend?"

Rolling her eyes, Naomi glanced over at both Sheree and Lanay who were already staring and shrugged. "Introduce yourself big pimp."

Checking his breath and rubbing his hand over his waves, he rubbed his hands together before walking over towards them.

"What's up Lanay? How y'all ladies doing?" He greeted, going in for a hug with Lanay. His focus was mainly on Sheree who stood off to the side trying to seem as if she wasn't paying him any mind.

Before anybody could respond their conversation was cut short when the sexiest man Naomi had ever seen approached them. Naomi was sure she looked like a whole creep with the way she was eyeing him down. Just with the way he towered over her, he had to be at least six feet and some inches tall. It was clear he had a nice fit body from what she could see through the tight dress shirt he wore. His hair was freshly cut, his waves were neatly intact, and his facial hair was freshly lined up around his nice set of light brown, plump lips, that were tinted with a light smoker's black.

To say the man was fine was an understatement; he was what you would call heaven-sent. His style was an extra bonus, as she noticed names on him such as Louis Vuitton and Gucci. She even checked out his jewelry, it shined too nicely to be anything close to fake.

She watched him slap hands with her brother, as they began talking. Naomi found herself staring right at his lips, following every word but not listening at all.

Feeling herself get roughly nudged out of the trance she was in; she snapped her neck in the direction of Lanay who was motioning for her to turn back around. She saw the guy slightly laughing with his hand extended out for her to shake.

"I'm sorry, were you talking to me?" Naomi questioned shyly, feeling slightly embarrassed.

"You good ma', you must be Naomi, right?" He asked as Naomi placed her hand into his.

Swallowing the lump forming in her throat, Naomi nodded her head nervously before tucking the loose strands of her hair behind her ears. "Yeah, and you are?" She responded, catching the gaze of his pretty brown eyes.

Damn this man is sexy. She thought. The scent of his Dior cologne traveled up Naomi's nostrils intriguing her even more.

"My bad sis, this my bro Capone." Nassir Interrupts.

"Nice to meet you." Naomi replied, trying not to come off too eager, even though she was ready to throw her life away for this man.

"Likewise." When Capone brought her hand up to his lips, the bitch almost melted. "Snoop has told me so much about you. It's nice to finally put a face with a name."

This was Cartier's first time ever seeing Naomi in person and he understood why Nassir was so protective over her. She was beautiful with a bang'n body, her smile was contagious, but her eyes were something dangerous. She had the type of eyes that'll have you sucked in and hooked on her every word when she spoke.

Cartier already knew with Naomi being Nassir's younger sister that every nigga in this club was probably looking at her, but he knew they would have no chance with Nassir cock-blocking ass in the way.

However, Cartier already had plans on shooting his shot with her, regardless of how Nassir may feel about it. He was always taught to go for what he wanted and not even Nassir could step in the way of that.

They held a brief gaze into each other's eyes, but their moment was interrupted when Nassir pulled Cartier away to introduce him to some folks. Lanay and Sheree pulled Naomi towards the bar to go and get drinks.

"Bitch I saw that." Sheree giggled, sitting to the right of Naomi. She joined her laughter and glanced over her shoulder at Capone who was chatting with her brother and another guy.

"I mean can you blame me? The man is fine as hell." She confessed, turning her attention back to her.

"You definitely have a point there." Lanay agreed, while looking over the drink's menu, debating what it is she wanted.

"I'm not going to say that I do because just as much as you were checking him out, I was eyeing your brother." Sheree admits.

Naomi's face instantly turned into disgust; she honestly didn't know what these women saw in her brother. Don't get her wrong she knows her brother is a nice-looking man, but far as relationships go, he doesn't act anything close to right.

Her brother is the true definition of a fuck nigga. He believed in having multiple girls at once. Due to his lack of trust towards women, he never got too attached to anyone since he didn't believe in love.

“Girl ew. Do yourself a favor and don’t even waste your time.” Naomi waved off.

“Exactly, because we might have to fight about that one.” Lanay jokes, followed by a laugh.

However, as Naomi looked at her slight smile, she didn’t believe she was joking. When they were younger, Lanay always had a thing for Nassir, but he just didn’t see her in that way; he looked at her more like a little sister, especially with Lanay being Naomi’s best friend, he tried not to ever overstep that boundary.

When Naomi was gone, the two did get closer, but they were more like best friends. They would chill and hang out at each other’s places, but it never went further than that. Nassir felt like Lanay was very beautiful and he had a lot of love for her, but he knew at the end of the day she deserved someone better; someone who was willing to give her the love she desired.

After they got a few drinks in their system, they all let the liquor take control of their bodies and started dancing together. It has been such a long time since Naomi was able to have a night of fun with her girls and just be able to cut up; tonight, she made a promise to herself to do just that.

Using the rail to hold herself up she began throwing her ass in a circle to the beat of the song playing as Lanay and Sheree hyped her up, fueling the sudden urge of confidence she had gained. Naomi felt her confidence grow the longer she danced, gaining the attention of others around her who joined in on hyping her up.

Dropping it low and picking it back up, Naomi spotted Capone out the corner of her eye, he watched her every move from across the room while sipping on whatever he was drinking. The intense stare he had on her made her nervous, it was as if he was undressing her with his eyes, so she decided to give him a show.

When the song changed, she began swaying her hips and sexually caressing her body, being sure to never once break the eye contact Capone and her shared. She watched as he bit at his lip ever so often. He’d also occasionally rub his hand up against his print; for a moment it seemed as if it was just the two of them there, she imagined herself dancing directly in front of him on stage.

Cartier knew he had no business looking at Naomi, especially with the way Nassir was behind her, but she wasn’t making it easy for him. It was clear they were both attracted to each other, and Cartier was tempted to test just how much they were.

A little casual flirting never hurt anybody, right?

Snapping out of the daze she was in at the sound of a bottle poppin', she looked to see it was her brother standing on top of one of the couches getting lit with his friends.

Naomi watched as he made a few girls drive the boat. She shook her head because she knew by the end of the night, he was about to be drunk off his ass.

When she noticed Capone was no longer seated where he was before, she looked around in search of him but eventually gave up after not locating him anywhere.

Deciding to take a break from dancing she walked over to the bar where Lanay and Sheree sat sipping on some drinks and talking amongst themselves.

"We see you out there showing out for Capone." Lanay teased, causing both Sheree and her to laugh.

"I'm just having a good time and enjoying myself," Naomi shrugged, playing it off even though she knew they were right.

"Speaking of having a good time, your brother is probably gonna need a ride home after this." Sheree pointed out laughing. Looking back over at him, she facepalmed herself when they saw he was now doing body shots off one of the bottle girls' stomachs.

"Girl, he'll probably crash at my place tonight. But I'ma let him have his fun for now, if he gets too out of hand with the drinking, I'll stop him." She shrugged, turning back to face them.

"Naomi?" A familiar voice calls out from behind her.

Turning her head slightly, she tried to hide her smile when she came face to face with Capone, her nerves began to kick in once again.

"Yes?" She answered kind of low. He had a way of making her get butterflies and becoming all shy.

A feeling she hasn't felt in so long.

“Is it okay if I could talk to you for a minute? Privately?” He asked with his hand extended for her to take.

Looking back at her girls they nudged for her to go. Naomi's nerves began to intensify and everything in her wanted to curl into a ball and hide, but she knew she needed to shake off her anxiety and finally do something she wanted without her fear trying to stop her for once.

“Uh, sure.”

She gave her girls a nervous smile and they both gave her a corny thumbs up followed by giggles. She took his hand and followed him to a secluded couch ducked off in a corner. Naomi took a seat and he sat directly beside her with a smirk plastered on his face.

Trying to avoid eye contact, Naomi nervously played with her hands causing Cartier to laugh. “Why are you so nervous? I ain’t gon’ bite.” He joked before waving one of the bottle girls over.

“What’s up C? Whatcha need?” The bottle girl greeted them warmly.

“We’re in need of something to help loosen this beautiful woman up here, anything you would suggest?”

Placing her hand on her hip, the girl smiled, “Depends on what she likes, what do you have a taste for sweetie?”

Giving Cartier the side eye, Naomi sighed. “Anything sweet and sour will be fine.”

“I know just the thing; I’ll be right back.”

Watching the girl walk over to the bar and whisper something into the bartender’s ear, Naomi used that time to try and relax herself without coming off weird. It’s been a minute since she’s been single so flirting and getting close with someone who wasn’t Deandre was new for her and it lowkey scared her.

“If being over here with me makes you that nervous, we can move somewhere closer to other people.” Glancing over at Cartier who was already staring at her, she let out a sigh.

“I’m sorry, it's just been a while since I’ve actually been out so it all just feels a little new and different.” She briefly explained.

Cartier nodded, "No need to apologize I can understand that. The club ain't really my type of scene either. It makes me money of course, but it ain't something I run out and try to do every weekend. But shit, if the women gon' be as beautiful as you up in here, I might need to." He flirted.

Laughing just when the bottle girl came back with her drink, Naomi thanked her before taking a sip instantly falling in love with the drink. "Oh my god, what is this?"

"That's a cherry vodka sour, what do you think?" The girl asked, smiling big.

"I love it, thank you!"

Waving her off, the girl started grabbing the empty cups folks left sitting around. "You're welcome, call me if you need anything else."

When she walked off, Naomi turned her focus back to Cartier whose attention was already on her. "So, what made you pull me to the side?" Naomi curiously asked even though she knew why. It didn't take a rocket scientist to see the attraction they had for each other.

"I mean if it wasn't obvious before, I'm clearly attracted to you." He answered honestly. "So, what's up? Whatchu on?"

Choking a little on her drink, she quickly grabbed a napkin to wipe her mouth. "Um, excuse me? What do you mean what am I on? I'm not on anything." Naomi asked, a little taken back but more so shocked at his blatant response.

She didn't think he would be so upfront and bold about what he wanted, but then again, she figured with the way he looks he's probably used to women throwing themselves at him, so it was easy for him to have this type of approach with her.

"Yes, you heard me correctly. I'm the type of man that if I see something I want I go for it and I saw the way you were dancing for me so it's clear the feeling is mutual." He slightly smiled, causing Naomi to frown in disgust but she played it off with a forced smile.

"How can you be so sure of that?" She retorted back, deciding to play a little with him, just see where it would go.

"Regardless of it being true or not, just know that one day I will have you and you will be mine." The confident tone in his voice made her feel a certain way, but she knew she couldn't fall for any of his words this soon.

She saw where that led her last time, it all sounded good now, but she knew some men will literally say anything to get what they want, and she was not about to be fooled again.

"Oh really? And how exactly do you manage to achieve that—Capone, is it? Hm, yeah I really hope you don't think a couple of sweet words and a little dance is all it is going to take to get me baby, you're going to have to come way harder than that." Naomi replied, smartly, getting close to his face so their lips were just inches apart.

As if she was about to kiss him, she smiled. "I'm on to your game Capone, I see the way these women look at you and you probably think I'm just one of these regular ass females looking for a nigga to trap. That weak ass game you may think you have might work on them, but news flash sweetie, I am not, nor will I ever be one of those females, so either approach me correctly or not at all."

Naomi was all for a man or anybody in general going after something they wanted, but she honestly felt he wanted her for all the wrong reasons. He didn't know much about her, but was ready for her to be his so she already knew what his motive was, and she was not with it at all.

When he noticed he lowkey upset her, Cartier knew he had to switch the mood back. He honestly never had anybody talk to him like that and if he really offended Naomi with his approach, he wanted her to know that wasn't in his intentions.

"I wasn't trying to upset you with my approach, and yeah you're right I notice the women who look at me and throw themselves at me constantly because of who I am and what I can possibly do for them financially, but truthfully, that shit doesn't spark my attention the way it used to back when I was younger. Having all the women and money felt like a dream at first, but the older I got, I began to realize folks were just leaching to get close to me because of what I have, that type of shit doesn't excite me anymore." He started as he took a sip of drink and glanced around the club.

"I know when most females see me, they see money and that's all they really want from me. I know just from how highly your brother talks about you all the time that you aren't anything like that." He went on to explain. "Plus, shit, trust me, I know with a woman as beautiful as you are, I'ma have to come hard and apply that pressure. I'm up for the challenge though and I know we just met and all, but I kinda wanna see where this could possibly go, and I am willing to go as slow as you want and willing to do whatever it takes to show you how serious I am."

Staring at him for a brief moment, he gently rubbed his thumb over her knuckles in a soothing motion as she searched his eyes for some form of dishonesty. Usually, Naomi would get uneasy by the touch of man, but his touch gave her feelings she hadn't felt in a while.

However, this was still a little too much for Naomi. She had only been in the singles' club for a good five minutes and it was already somebody ready to take her off the market. She was flattered nonetheless, but she was in no rush on getting with someone anytime soon, she really hoped Cartier would stand by his word on taking it slow.

After a moment of silence, Naomi let out a sigh, giving in, deciding to let her guard down just a little for now. She knew she couldn't compare every guy to Deandre and at this point what they were doing was harmless. "How about we start with your real name first?"

"What makes you think it isn't Capone?" He questioned followed by a laugh.

"Because I know your mama had to have better sense than to name you Capone." She teased.

Smirking, he sat back in his seat as he stared back at her. "It's Cartier."

Naomi smiled, "So, Mr. Cartier, how many other women have you said that infamous story to?" She giggled to hide her blush that was screaming to be released.

"I swear to you Ms. Naomi, you're the second one truthfully."

She nodded. "At least you're honest. Who was the first? If you don't mind me asking."

Before he could fix his lips to reply to her question, a woman approached them standing directly in front of Cartier with her arms folded.

When Naomi looked up at the girl, she had to admit she was very pretty; her hair was in a slick back low ponytail, and she sported a hot fitted black dress that matched a pair of sexy heels. The accessories she wore were simple, but still had enough shine to blind anyone. Naomi noticed right away that she shopped at the high-end designer stores because she saw that exact dress at one while window shopping. She had to give the girl her props for her taste in fashion.

"Hey baby." The unknown woman greeted with an attitude, giving Naomi a quick glance over before rolling her eyes in disgust.

Due to the death glare she was giving Cartier, it was clear to Naomi that the two shared some form of connection but something indeed was off about the girl as well.

Letting out a low chuckle to herself in disbelief, Naomi went to excuse herself. Cartier quickly looked her way and shook his head to stop her before looking back at the unknown woman.

Naomi knew his game was too good to be true, she knew a man as fine as him with a slick tongue definitely couldn't be a man on the market. She had to applaud him for it though, his words were almost believable.

"Don't come over here talking about some, hey baby Porsha. I told you we're done so move around." He replied harshly, slapping her hand away.

Porsha looked at Naomi and stared her down. Naomi did the same wondering what the hell her problem was. She honestly didn't know the two of them or their situation to even feel some-type-of-way, so she hoped the girl stayed cool, because at the end of the day she wasn't an enemy here.

As she listened to them argue back and forth, a part of her wanted to get up and be done with the situation altogether. But it was clear the longer she listened to them talk the girl was delusional and just wouldn't leave him alone.

"So, I'm guessing this is the bitch that got you acting funny on me? Huh?" She snapped.

When Porsha came out to celebrate Nassir's birthday, she expected to see Cartier but not with some other female already smiling and laughing. She was so fed up with Cartier stomping over her heart and emotions.

Although she knew Naomi hadn't done anything to her personally, she was an accessory to his poor decisions; so, in Porsha's eyes, she was a bitch and she didn't like her.

"Bitch!? Who the fuck you calling a bitch?" Naomi questioned standing up from her seat. Cartier stopped her once again.

"Are you really about to do this shit right now? Like you really tryna cause a scene at my homeboy's birthday bash?" He questioned and Naomi could tell from the look on his face he was getting frustrated.

Glancing over at Sheree and Lanay who were already looking over at the scene before them, Naomi gave them a look to reassure them that everything was okay. The last thing she needed was a big fight to break out and ruin her brother's night.

"Yes, I don't give a damn about your homeboy's birthday! I've called and texted you multiple times Capone and you ignored them all; so I showed up in hopes of working things out and here you are up in the next bitch face." She yelled.

Standing up, he grabbed her by the arm roughly. "I didn't want to embarrass your ass like this, but since you insist on being a little ass girl about the shit here it is. Porsha, yes, we fucked, we had a few good conversations and yes, I enjoyed you. But I told you the moment you confessed your feelings to me, that I do not feel the same way about you that you feel for me. I apologized and we broke shit off. Let it the fuck go." He said in a serious tone.

Porsha gave him a look from hell and if looks could kill Cartier would be six feet under right now. Laughing to herself, she nodded before stepping close to his ear. "Remember that baby, please know that karma's a bitch and that bitch is like my best friend." She whispered before stepping away.

When she left the club, everyone went back to partying as if nothing ever happened.

Letting out a deep sigh Cartier directed his attention towards Naomi with an apologetic look on his face. "I'm truly sorry for that shit. She's an ex, well I can't really call her an ex because we never technically dated, but regardless of the fact, she can't seem to take the hint that the relationship is really done." He quickly responded hoping this didn't turn her off.

Naomi simply shrugged, ready to go home already. "I understand, it's cool." She lied.

Just from this incident alone, it was obvious to her that Cartier came with a lot of drama and that was the last thing she needed. At this point, she didn't see shit going anywhere further than where they were right now.

“Well, I know I ain’t making a good first impression,” He nervously laughed.

Laughing as well, she finished off the rest of her drink. “Yeah, you got that right.”

“Let me make it up to you by taking you out one of these days.” He suggested. “I promise you, it ain’t gon’ be like this.”

“Are you sure none of your exes are not gonna pop up trying to fight again?” Naomi jokes, to help ease the tension.

Laughing, he swiftly licked his lips. “Nah, it would just be you and I, no interruptions whatsoever.”

Naomi smiled, “I’ll think about it, let’s see how the rest of this night goes.”

“For all my lovely couples in the building tonight, or for all the fellas who got they eyes on a beautiful woman up in here, we gon’ slow it down a bit- this next song is for you.” The Dj stated into the mic.

When the song changed to Zapp and Rogers hit song I Want to Be Your Man, Naomi couldn’t help but laugh since the song really fit her and Cartier’s current situation. “This seems like fate to me; would you like to dance?”

“I would love to dance.”

Taking Naomi by the hand, Naomi spotted Lanay and Sheree getting up to dance with some guys as they made their way closer to where everybody else was dancing in the section.

The sweet voice of Zapp and Roger rang throughout her ears as she threw her arms around his neck. He placed his hands around her waist. As they danced, she felt herself relax within his arms. She soon closed her eyes and laid her head on his chest to simply take in this moment, even if it only lasted for a brief second.

When his hand slightly touched her butt, Naomi looked up at him and he immediately apologized but she wasn’t fazed by it. The longer the two danced Naomi finally exhaled, releasing that breath she didn’t even know she was holding.

This was the closest she's been to a man in a while, and it felt good to be held like this. "Are you from around here?" She asked, deciding to make conversation, in hopes of getting to know him better.

Looking down at her, he nodded. "Yup, born and raised."

She nodded, "Have you ever thought about leaving here?"

Cartier shrugged at the thought, after everything that went down with his parents when he was younger, Cartier always planned on moving away, but there was still some unfinished business he needed to handle first.

"Sometimes I do, I mean it would be nice to get away for a fresh start somewhere to kinda escape some shit you can't outrun around here, but it's a lot I gotta do first before even considering that as an option." He briefly explained.

"I feel you on that, sometimes a fresh start is all a person really needs for the betterment of themselves and figuring out what their next step may be. That's kinda where I am right now in my life, simply tryna figure out who Naomi is and what Naomi wants to do with her life."

Smiling, Cartier looked down at her before using his hand to move a loose strand of her hair out of her face. "I'm sure you'll figure it all out,"

Not saying anything else in response to that, Naomi just smiled and laid her head on his chest as they danced to the rest of the song.

Over on the other side of the section, Nassir came walking back up the stairs from using the bathroom immediately noticing Cartier and Naomi dancing together.

At the sight of them together, Nassir didn't really know how to feel. He always had a rule for his homeboys that his sister was off limits, he knew most of his friends weren't shit and the last thing he needed was for one of them to ever hurt her because then he'd have to kill their ass.

Deciding to let it go for now, Nassir focused his attention on Sheree who was dancing with some nigga. He had been eyeing her all night and a part of him wasn't even sure if she was attracted to him since she barely paid him any mind.

Taking a sip from the bottle of Dussé he had been nursing all night, he walked up on her and the guy, deciding to shoot his shot anyway. "Do you mind if I steal this woman for a quick minute?"

At the sound of his voice, both Sheree and the guy looked back at him. Giving the guy a certain look, Nassir and him both slapped hands before the guy walked away going straight to the next available female.

Looking back at Sheree who was already staring, Nassir smiled. “So, what’s up? You tryna dance with the birthday boy?”

Laughing, Sheree shook her head. “I guess, but only because it's your birthday.” She joked.

Acting as if he was hurt, Nassir placed his hand over his heart as he passed his bottle of liquor off to one of his homeboys. “Damn, so it's like that? Are you saying any other day I wouldn’t have a chance?”

Shrugging her shoulders, she laughed. “Maybe, who knows.”

“Well shit, lemme soak in this once-in-a-lifetime opportunity then. Come here girl.” Pulling her close, he securely wrapped his arms around her waist as they danced. Sheree laughed at his dramatics, despite him being drunk off his ass, he was cute in an obnoxious kind of way.

After dancing to a few songs together, Naomi and Cartier decided to take a break and head over to the bar to get some food in their system. “Whatchu got a taste for? I can tell you now their hot wings are bussin’.” He suggested with his arm resting around her waist.

Looking at the menu they had, she squinted her eyes debating. “Hot wings do sound good, I guess I’ll take that.”

Nodding his head, Cartier waved for the bartender to come over to place their order. “What’s up C? What can I get you?”

“Hook us up with an order of your infamous hot wings and tell Chauncey bitch ass to not be stingy with the sauce back there either, and throw in two shots.”

Laughing, the guy entered what they wanted on his tablet, shaking his head. “Anything else?”

Looking back at Naomi, she shook her head. “I’m good, did you want anything else?”

"Nah, I'm straight but keep my tab open in case I change my mind."

"You got it; those wings will be out in about 10 minutes. Nice seeing you C." He slapped hands with the Bartender before walking away to start on their shots. Cartier turned his attention to Naomi who was staring off, looking at all the people in the club.

"You good?" He asked, capturing her attention.

Nodding her head, she simply smiled. "Just thinking,"

"About what? You don't like the vibe?"

Shaking her head, she laughed. "No, this night actually turned out to be amazing. I'm just thinking about where I once was in life and where I am now, and it just sometimes doesn't even feel real. But I am grateful, and I feel so blessed to even still be here honestly. There were days I didn't even think I would survive." She expressed.

Naomi knew the liquor in her system was pushing her to openly talk about this, she soon felt her emotions start to try and get the best of her, but she quickly got herself together and forced a smile. "But I'm good forreal."

Grabbing the two shots the bartender made them, Cartier smiled as he grabbed one of the shot glasses and handed her the other. "Well let's take a shot for this night turning out good for you and let's take a shot for you overcoming all that bullshit in your past."

Clinking their glasses together, they both threw back their shots and instantly started hissing as it burned their throats. Laughing at their own reactions, Naomi sat her glass down as she stared at him. "Are you always like this to women you barely know?" She questioned.

"Eh, only to women I really find interesting and actually want to get to know and not just fuck, which is rare." He replied followed by a shrug.

"What makes me special?"

He shrugged. "Ion know yet, but it's something about you and the way your brother talked so highly of you; I was lowkey anxious to finally put a face with the name, and honestly you were everything I imagined and more."

Not knowing what to say back to that, she just looked up at him and smiled, getting lost in his eyes. "Thank you, it's been a minute since I've last gotten a compliment."

"Well, you should get compliments all the time, you're beautiful." The intense stare he was giving her and the small buzz she was feeling had her ready to risk it all with Cartier right now.

She felt herself lean forward and focus in on his lips. He pulled her in as close as their bodies could possibly get, their lips only vibrating inches apart.

Just as Naomi began to close her eyes, the sound of gunshots ranging out caused them and everyone else to jump apart from each other as a group of men came running in shooting the place up.

Cartier quickly grabbed Naomi and pulled them towards the bathroom. "Don't move, stay right here."

Reaching in his waistband he pulled out a 9mm and started firing back at the shooters before disappearing in the crowd of people. Naomi was taken back and confused at how much shit was popping off, all she wanted was to go home now.

The sound of the gunshots began triggering the memories of her shooting Deandre. She instantly started to feel sick to her stomach as a lump in her throat formed, her breathing began to pick up.

All that could be heard was people screaming and yelling, along with glass breaking. Her eyes searched the club for her girls, but she couldn't see them anywhere. She instantly began to worry, her body started to shake from all the sudden commotion.

In the midst of her searching for them, she felt her heart drop to the pit of her stomach when she witnessed Nassir get shot in his shoulder and fall down to the floor as another bullet pierced through his arm.

Without thinking, Naomi immediately ran over to him screaming, she had to check on him. She did not need their first time meeting again to end up being their last; there was so much more they had to accomplish together. Snatching some tablecloths down from the tables, she immediately started applying pressure to his bullet wound as she fought back tears.

Watching him groan in pain, hurt her. “I’m good sis, just call someone for help.” He managed to get out. She pressed harder as he winced in pain while her eyes were searching for someone that could help.

All that could be seen was people running over each other trying to dodge the bullets. The place was being destroyed and Naomi’s vision was becoming slightly blurry as she tried to process all that was happening.

Once the shots eventually died down, Lanay immediately ran over to where she saw Naomi and Nassir. When she noticed the look on Naomi’s face she began to worry since she looked so out of it. “Naomi, you good baby?” She asked, but her voice had an echo, which made it hard for Naomi to understand what she was saying.

Damn near falling over, Lanay caught her just in time, and when she did, she noticed blood was oozing from her side, which instantly worried her. “I think she’s been shot.” Lanay barely whispered.

At the sound of that, Nassir instantly perked up and pushed Sheree (who was trying to help him) off. “Check to make sure Lanay!” He yelled unintentionally.

Laying her limp body on the floor, Sheree immediately went into nurse mode checking for any signs of where she could have possibly been shot.

Letting out a sigh of relief when she discovered it wasn’t her blood, Sheree directed the guards who were still there to lay her on the couch and to get her some water. “Nassir, she’s fine. I think she just had a mild panic attack due to what was happening.”

Laying his head back as the tears that emerged in his eyes fell, Nassir sighed gratefully, relieved that she was okay. He then continued to let Sheree aid his wounds until the paramedics arrived.

When Naomi was back stable, the ambulance arrived along with the cops to report events of what went down tonight. Sitting off to the side on the floor close to Nassir, Sheree and a Paramedic attended to him, Naomi slowly sipped on a gingerale, just wanting this night to be over.

Glancing over at his sister, Nassir felt guilty. He hated the fact that their first time seeing each other had to end like this. His goal was for her to be able to come back to peace and he hoped like hell this didn’t drive her away again. “Nao? Talk to me, baby girl. We gon’ be straight.”

Getting up, she sat directly beside him, being sure not to be in the paramedic's way, before leaning over and kissing him on the forehead. "I really hope so, Nas." She whispered softly.

The paramedic kept assisting Nassir, and Sheree also continued to assist to ensure that he was okay. Naomi peeped the way Sheree and her brother kept looking at each other, and she knew she wasn't the only one that picked up on it. Glancing over at Lanay, she could see the look of hurt on her face before she eventually stood up and took off to the girls' bathroom.

Shaking her head, Naomi sighed not believing how fast the night had gotten ruined.

Throughout all this commotion she didn't even realize that Cartier was nowhere to be found. Looking around in search of him, she wondered where he disappeared off to and she hoped that he was okay at least.

"I'll be right back, please call me when they get ready to take him to the hospital." Naomi told Sheree, while looking down at her brother.

"I'm good sis, this shit ain't nothing!" He replied through gritted teeth due to the pain he was feeling.

"Leave it to my brother to still try and be hard with a bullet inside him." Naomi thought to herself.

Giving her a reassuring look, Sheree smiled as Naomi stood up heading to the bathroom to check on Lanay.

Walking inside she saw her sitting on the bathroom counter crying as she used a tissue to wipe her eyes. Realizing that she wasn't alone anymore, Lanay looked up at Naomi and broke down even more.

"I already know Naomi and if you are here to lecture me, just please save it ok?" She sniffled.

"I'm not. I just came to provide you some comfort." Naomi replied, taking a seat next to her on the counter.

Wrapping her arms around her waist, Lanay laid her head on her shoulder as she released her emotions. "I just don't understand! Is there something wrong with me? Am I not pretty enough? Every guy I actually find attractive end up going after my damn friends!" Lanay sobbed. "What is it about me that doesn't make me good enough?"

“There is nothing wrong with you! You're so beautiful Lanay and I don’t want to ever hear you question yourself like that again! My brother is a dumbass, and he doesn’t deserve your tears, you’ll meet the perfect guy for you one day and when you do, you’ll never have to question your worth again. Plus, any man that’s attracted to any of your friends isn’t the kind of man you want anyways.” Naomi told her, handing her more tissue.

Lanay simply rolled her eyes, “Then why am I still single Naomi? You don’t understand how hard it has been out here to actually find a decent guy who actually wants more from than just sex. All I ever get out of a man is sex, decent conversation and then it’s over; I want more than that. I deserve more than that.” Lanay sniffled.

“Did you and Nas ever do anything?”

Looking up at her, Lanay sighed. “No, but we kissed one night at my place. Nothing else happened, I think we just sorta got caught up in the moment and it just happened. I thought the kiss meant something for the both of us, and that it was the start of something between us, but after a few days passed he came over and we talked and that’s when I discovered he didn’t feel the same way as I did, so we decided to just stay friends.” Sniffling, she wiped her eyes.

“It just really sucks because as long as I’ve known Nassir, he never saw me like that once, but he meets Sheree for one night and he’s all over her. I mean I get it, Sheree is beautiful, so I understand.” She shrugged.

Realizing that she was tipsy, and, in her feelings, Naomi decided to keep her mouth closed and just provide her with comfort. Even though this night didn’t go exactly as planned, Naomi still enjoyed herself tonight with Cartier and was just grateful that everybody was safe.

Looking up at the sound of the bathroom door opening, Naomi became alert when she saw it was Sheree. “Hey, they’re getting ready to take him to the hospital.”

Thanking her, Naomi quickly hopped off the counter and helped Lanay freshen up so they all could head out to the hospital before going home.

What a night.

Chapter 4

A few weeks have passed since Nassir's party and things were slowly going back to normal, Naomi couldn't be happier. Nassir's shoulder was healing well, and he seemed to be doing better, despite not only being shot but also after losing a friend that night.

When the news broke that their friend Meech was shot and killed, both Nassir and Cartier took it pretty hard. Naomi never had the chance to properly meet him, but she remembers seeing him around a lot and just watching them both grieve was hard, despite how tough they tried to act. It's always hard losing someone you care about.

Even though all of this was happening, life for Naomi was going great; she had recently landed a job at this salon that Sheree hooked her up with, Serenity's, owned by a girl named Tamara.

Tamara grew up in the city, so her salon was well-known and she's truly a beast at what she does, which is what keeps folks coming back to her shop. All you had to do was give her some heat, a comb, and some edge control and she can turn a messy head into a masterpiece.

With Naomi still being new, her clientele had to grow, so business wasn't all that great money wise, but she was still very grateful for Tamara taking a chance on her, and for Sheree who put in a good word for her. Witnessing all the other stylists' work she knew Tamara could have easily gone with someone else who had more experience, but she saw the potential Naomi had and for that, Naomi was doing everything in her power to fulfill whatever she saw in her.

Looking up from her booth to glance at the clock that hung right above the exit, Naomi mentally cursed in her head when she saw it was almost one o'clock. She had completely forgotten all about her plans to meet up with Lanay and Sheree for lunch and knew she needed to leave right now to make it in time.

Quickly cleaning up her area, she made sure she had all of her belongings before heading out, she also made sure to say bye to everyone.

Luckily, the spot they were meeting at was just down the street, so Naomi decided to walk to save herself from having to find another parking spot when she returned. The restaurant was called South City Kitchen and since she's been home, she has heard everybody talking about it, so Naomi was excited to finally give the place a try to see the hype.

Walking inside the building, Naomi looked around in search of Sheree and Lanay and spotted them seated at a table in the middle of the restaurant.

Approaching their table, Naomi took her seat with a huge smile on her face. “Hey y'all, how is everyone doing today?” She greeted them before she quickly picked up the menu to scan over all their food options.

At this moment, Naomi had a taste for just about anything; she was starving and regretted that she skipped out on breakfast. Having to work on an empty stomach since seven this morning was no joke; her stomach was ready to do a backflip.

“Well damn hello to you too, somebody must be hungry.” Lanay joked at how fast she grabbed the menu.

“Hey girl.” Sheree giggled.

“Hungry ain’t even the word, I’m starving!” She groaned. “But anyways what are y’all two talking about?” Naomi asked, sensing the tension in the air.

“Girl nothing, Lanay is just mad about Snoop asking me out on a date and that I accepted.” Sheree admits shrugging her shoulders.

“I just think it’s kinda fucked up when she knows how I feel about him.” Lanay interjects.

“But y’all never even dated Lanay.” Sheree retorted back. “I don’t see the issue; I mean Naomi do you think I’m wrong?”

Naomi was stuck in between the middle about the whole situation since she saw both sides. She felt Sheree had a good point when it came to the point, she made about them never dating. Nassir and Lanay were always just friends, and nothing ever happened besides the kiss they shared. But then again, she knew if a guy she had feelings for made a pass at one of her friends, she would be hurt about it too.

“Y’all have been friends way too long to let my no good ass brother have y’all into it. I personally wouldn’t go after someone I know a friend of mine has deep feelings for, despite them never dating, but Lanay you know my brother ain’t shit. I say just let it go.” Naomi said, attempting to mediate the situation. She already had four more heads to do right after and she was about to enjoy her lunch without any drama.

“Whatever, it's the principle of it all. I would never even allow myself to get close to any guy I know either one of you had feelings for. What am I supposed to do when I see y’all out and about together, kissing, and shit? Feelings just don’t go away overnight, and I just feel like at this moment you aren’t even trying to consider my feelings at all.”

“Lanay it’s just one date, this might not even go anywhere between us. It’s not like I’m about to walk down the aisle and marry him anytime soon, but you’re right, I wasn’t considering your feelings. It’s just been a minute since I’ve actually clicked with a guy like this and I’m sorry, so if it bothers you that much I won’t go; he’s not worth possibly ruining our friendship over.” Sheree expressed.

Staring back at her, Naomi looked in between the two wondering what Lanay was going to say in response to that.

Letting out a sigh, Lanay shook her head. “I guess I’m being unfair as well. If he likes you, I can’t be mad because it’s not me, so don’t let me get in the way of what could possibly turn into something good for you.” She half smiled.

Reaching her hand over, Sheree grabbed Lanay’s hand. “Thank you.”

“Aww, so we're good now y’all?” Naomi questioned as she glanced back and forth between them.

Laughing, Lanay nodded. “We’re good, but anyways, speaking of good, I meant to ask, what’s been going on between you and Capone?” She asked, raising her eyebrow.

Blushing at the thought of him, Naomi was saved by the waiter coming to take their orders in which she was grateful for.

“Hello ladies, are you guys ready to order yet?”

“Yes! I would like to try your strawberry salad with grilled chicken and a glass of your Clarendelle Rosé.” Naomi ordered.

“Okay, and for you?” He asked, glancing at Sheree.

“I would like the chef's chicken chopped salad, but I would like to replace the dressing with the raspberry vinaigrette instead, and for my drink I’ll take a water.” Sheree requested before handing him her menu.

“Alright, and for you ma’am?”

"Can I get your smokey beef brisket with a side of double fries, and for my drink I'll also take a glass of Clarendelle Rosé." Lanay ordered.

After reading their orders back to them to make sure he wrote down everything correctly, he quickly walked off to place their orders and to get their drinks ready.

As soon as he was gone, Sheree laughed. "It's not even after five o'clock yet and y'all bitches already drinking." She points out shaking her head.

Naomi laughed, "Hey, it's five o'clock somewhere and I need a drink right now."

"Exactly, but anyways back to the topic at hand." Lanay says touching back on the topic of Capone.

Sighing, Naomi looked out of the window, hating to be put on the spot like that.

Although Cartier does intrigue her, she's just not ready to pursue another relationship right now. She was cool with the way things were going between them but right now she just wasn't sure.

They hadn't talked in almost a week, and he stood her up on a date that he planned. At this point she was lowkey over him and his games. He was already starting off on a bad foot and it was clear his words meant nothing, so Naomi was ready to just be done with him for good.

"Y'all, I honestly don't even know what's going on between us. I mean, he's really sweet and funny- for some odd reason, I sorta like him but it's already been a week since we last talked, and we were supposed to go out, but he ended up standing me up. I still haven't heard from him. I'm already a little scared to even start back dating again and with me still getting over Dre and all that he put me through, I don't think I'm ready to trust a man or even be with a man in general this soon again. He's already starting off bad, so I think this is a sign that I need to wait and give myself more time to heal." She expressed.

Reaching her hand over, Lanay squeezed Naomi's. "I can understand that sis, well the best thing for you to do in this situation is to take it slow and work on yourself first and if Capone wants to continue to play games he can simply move around because we don't have time for that."

Naomi nodded, "You're right, I just need to take this slow, give myself time to properly get over Dre and time to feel him out before jumping into anything too soon. Plus, I mean I know him and my brother have been going through a lot, but he could have just simply reached out and apologized at least ya know?"

"Exactly." Sheree replied.

"As of right now he hasn't given me a reason not to trust him, so I don't want to just flat out think the worst without giving him a chance to try and explain himself; but if I don't hear anything by like Sunday then I'm done for sure."

Nodding their heads in response, the girls all agreed with what she was saying.

Naomi's life is starting to get back on track and the last thing she needs is another man dragging her back into a place she fought so hard to get out of. Naomi wanted a type of love that came easy, she wanted the life of marriage with kids, but she didn't want to have to go through hell and back with a man just to get that.

"So, Lanay what's been going on with you?" Sheree asked, putting away her phone.

Naomi looked over at Lanay as well, curious to know her answer. Since Naomi has been back here, she hadn't heard Lanay speak about any man or anything she's involved in, other than her brother which isn't usually like her.

She sighed, avoiding eye contact. "Honestly, I'm not talking to anyone right now. I've just been working and focusing on myself." She shrugged.

"You say that like it's a bad thing." Naomi spoke, trying to uplift her mood.

Naomi knows how much Lanay wants a man, but she often feels like at times Lanay forgets that sometimes having a man isn't all it's cracked up to be. Like she knows love is beautiful and having a man is a good feeling, to know you have someone you can count on for whatever, but there's just also more to life than having a man.

"That's easy for you to say when you always have a man or some guy that's interested in you Nao. All I hear every day from my friends are stories about their men and how much they connect and the dates they go on; all I do is go home to an empty bed with not one man to even text or call when I'm bored." Lanay confessed. "Like here lately, I've just been feeling so lonely and depressed."

The table fell a little quiet and both Sheree and Naomi felt bad for Lanay. They really didn't know this was how she was feeling until now and they wished they could do something to lift up her spirits.

Leaning over, Sheree just pulled her into a hug and soon Lanay started crying as she became overwhelmed with her emotions.

"You will find the perfect guy, made just for you. Until then just enjoy Lanay, like you said, focus on yourself, travel, live your life, and one day when you least expect it, someone will come into your world and add onto your newfound happiness." Sheree told her as she pulled away from the hug.

"And you will always have us to lean on." Naomi reassured her.

Wiping her tears, Lanay smiled at the both of them. "Thank y'all, I've just been very emotional these days." She laughed. "I wasn't tryna kill the mood with my issues."

Waving her off, Naomi shrugged. "Girl, we understand how you feel wholeheartedly, but I think we need to plan like a girl's trip or something. I'm in need of a vacation and I'm sure we all could use one as well." She suggested.

"I'm down fasho, this semester has been kicking my ass. I need a break too." Sheree replied just as the waiter came back with their drinks.

Nodding her head, Lanay agreed. "Yeah, I'm down for that as well. It would be nice to get away for like a weekend or something and just have fun with no worries."

"Well then it's set, let's start planning a girl's trip." Naomi smiled.

Shortly after their orders finally arrived, Naomi wasted no time digging into her food like it was Thanksgiving dinner. As they enjoyed the rest of their lunch together, the girls all discussed future plans as far as suggestions of places to go and when the perfect time to go would be.

The longer they talked the more excited Naomi was to go on the trip, she was ready for a weekend of peace in an unfamiliar place, so that she could let loose and have fun with her girls with no worries.

Across town, Cartier's house was dead silent. All that could be heard were loud sounds of his moans and the bed squeaking. Beads of sweat dripped down Cartier's face as he sped up his strokes with her legs raised above his head, the feeling of her walls clenched around his dick, Cartier knew he was about to bust soon.

Moans escaped both of their mouths as their bodies connected as one each time he slid in and out of her.

"Damn I love this pussy", He thought to himself, letting the sound of their bodies slapping together consume his ears.

Chardonnay's moans began to grow louder when he slowed up, wanting her to feel every inch as he repeatedly hit her spot. Cartier bit his lip at the sight of watching her breast bounce while she used her free hand to play with her clit, rubbing it in a circular motion.

Stopping her movements, Cartier tapped her and motioned for her to get up. Doing as he wanted, she watched as he began to move himself before he got out of the bed completely.

"Bend over." Was all he said, Chardonnay quickly followed his command, ready to receive some bomb ass back-shots.

Getting into position; she arched her back mid-perfection, her ass was tooted up in the air on full display, causing Cartier's dick to throb from how hard it was. Stepping a little closer to her, Cartier slowly stroked himself with one hand while using his free hand to play with her pussy from the back.

"Cartier..." Chardonnay whimpered out, not really wanting to be teased, which only amped Cartier up.

He wanted her to beg for it.

"What?" He questioned as he continued rubbing his thumb over her clit and sliding two of his fingers in and out.

Trying to muster up her words, Chardonnay couldn't help but bite her lip and moan out from him finger- fucking her. Building up the strength, she looked back as they locked eyes, but he didn't stop his movements- instead, he sped up. "Whatchu want me to do?"

When her eyes began to roll, she dropped her head into the bed and moaned into the sheets. "S-stop playing and fuck me already." She moaned out but all Cartier did was smirk since he wanted to have his fun first.

Sliding his fingers out, he grabbed his dick and rubbed it up and down her slit, teasing her even more before roughly entering her. He almost caused her to lose her arch, but he held her in place by her waist then slid out. Chardonnay took a deep breath, gasping for something to say.

Repeating his motions a few times, Chardonnay yelled out inaudible cuss words into her pillow to silence her loud moans a little. Cartier soon reached forward and pulled the pillow from up under her and tossed it.

She hated but loved the way he was teasing her, it felt so painfully good. She wanted so badly for him to fuck her already. She was craving the dick at this point and her pussy was leaking from how wet he had her.

He slammed into her a few times before stopping all together and Chardonnay couldn't help but wonder about what he was about to do next.

When she felt him grip and smack her on the ass, she smiled to herself, knowing the time was coming, but when she felt the coldness of his tongue swiftly lick her pussy, she tried to run. He held her tightly in place and continued eating her out from the back.

Dipping his tongue in and out, Chardonnay began throwing her hips back and forth, fucking his tongue as she moaned out his name. His dick ached even more from how sexy it sounded leaving her mouth.

It didn't take Chardonnay long to cum since Cartier had a way with his tongue but if he had to admit, it was almost taking everything in him not to bust. He had to constantly think of other shit to keep him going but it was a few times he almost just said fuck it, but he didn't want to stop.

As she lay there sprawled out on the bed, Cartier stood up straight and laughed to himself, catching her attention. "Don't laugh at me, I don't know what you're doing to me, I ain't never had it like this." She stated as she tried to regain her breath and strength from how crucial that orgasm was.

Hovering over her as she turned on her back to face him, he stroked himself a little before leaning down to kiss her deeply, allowing her to taste herself while sliding in at the same time. He caught her completely off guard as she moaned into his kiss.

Wrapping her legs around him and intertwining their fingers together, the sound of his headboard hitting the wall along with their moans could be heard throughout the room as he slowly, but roughly fucked her.

Raising up some, he grabbed her legs and held them up as he placed them on his shoulders before going deeper as he felt himself about to release. Speeding up his strokes, her titties soon started to bounce as she began to scream and cry out.

"Slow down." She moaned and he did as she wanted but he rode out his nut, still slowly stroking her walls being sure to hit that certain spot repeatedly.

Releasing all his seeds inside the condom, he laid there for a moment to catch his breath as she did the same before they started kissing again.

Pulling away from the kiss, Cartier rose off her and got out of the bed to go and get her a towel from the bathroom. Taking off his condom, he threw it down in the toilet and watched it flush before he grabbed the washcloth. He wet it a little bit and entered the room to see her still stuck in the same position.

“You good?” He asked, followed by a laugh as he stared down at her.

Smacking her teeth and rolling her eyes, Chardonnay grabbed a pillow and threw it at him. “Shut up, don’t talk to me until I can feel my legs again.” She groaned.

Chardonnay was beyond impressed with the performance Cartier just put on. Sex between them was always good but this time however was amazing and almost brought tears to her eyes at the thought of it; felt like he made love to her.

Cartier and Chardonnay have been together going on three years now, and within those three years the sex has never felt like this. Chardonnay wasn’t complaining though, she felt maybe this was finally a start for them to get back on track within their relationship.

Like many relationships, they have had their fair shares of ups and downs and in the beginning, Cartier really thought Chardonnay was the one for him, but over time his love towards her faded and it was very obvious.

So, in hopes of saving their relationship they were currently trying different things to gain that spark they once had back, but it just wasn’t working, at least for him it wasn’t.

Majority of the time Naomi was on his mind, even when they would be having sex. No matter how hard he tried, she would not leave his mind and Cartier already knew if Chardonnay found out that he was thinking about another woman while they were having sex, he would never hear the end of it.

Cartier couldn't deny that Chardonnay was a good woman, as long as they've been together, she has held him down and supported him through whatever; he appreciated her beyond words.

In the beginning Chardonnay was like Cartier's best friend, she was truly like his heaven on earth and with her being an elementary teacher, she always had like this calm and beautiful spirit- which is what attracted him to her in the beginning. In a weird way she was like the calm to his crazy, she kept him sane.

But it seemed like time went on, things changed within her. Cartier witnessed another side of her that many people didn't know about, consisting of her bad attitude and bipolar mood swings.

Cartier never thought someone so damn beautiful could have you ready to kill them within' a matter of seconds.

"Don't be mad at me because I did what needed to be done." He smirked as he walked over to place a kiss on her lips. "I love you."

Blushing, she held onto his chin, pecking his lips a few times before laying back. "I love you more, are you staying in tonight?" She asked, wrapping her body in the sheets while holding her head up in her hands.

"I honestly wish I could stay baby, but me and Snoop got some business we need to handle." Cartier lied.

It was something they did have to handle, but it wasn't anything that needed to be done right away. He just needed to get out and clear his head. Lately he's been in a different world mentally and it seemed like nobody around him even understood or was looking to help him with that.

A lot of his of past demons were resurfacing and it was really fucking with his head. Every day it seemed as if he was having some sort of a battle within his mind, he was over it all. He often wished he could escape the shit he went through as a kid and everything he's endured with this lifestyle, but he couldn't and every day the shit was slowly killing him inside.

Scrunching up her face, Chardonnay smacks her lips. "Yeah right, whatever."

Letting out a sigh, Cartier rolled his eyes. "What Char?"

"You act like staying in for one night is gonna kill you, who tha fuck is she?" She snapped. Chardonnay may have seemed like your typical naive, spoiled girl on the outside, but she was beyond stupid. She could read through Cartier's lies with each one he told. It disappointed her even more that each one was getting sloppier than the last, signaling his loss of care for her.

"Who is who?" He frowned, acting clueless.

"Don't play stupid Cartier, I know there's some other bitch out there you been creeping around with on the low. I mean why else would you be staying out all night?" She questioned.

Cartier shook his head before walking away towards their closet to get dressed. He couldn't afford to fight with her right now, he didn't have the energy for it. With all the shit surrounding Trig and his uncle, and mourning the loss of a fallen soldier, he just didn't have time to go back and forth with her.

"We are not about to do this tonight Char." Cartier said as he slid on a pair of his Nike sweatpants and a pair of socks he found.

Watching as he threw on a shirt and began putting on his shoes. Chardonnay quickly hopped out of the bed and stood in front of their bedroom door.

"I'm getting real tired of you treating me like this Cartier!" She screamed. "You don't think I haven't noticed the change in the way you look at me, the sex, how we never go out, or actually talk like we used to?! I mean who do you think you're fooling? There's clearly someone else who has your attention. I've put in way too many years with you, just to come second to someone else."

Rubbing his hand down his face, Cartier sighed. He couldn't admit that it was someone else, because he knew that would hurt her. Although he's had his fair share of affairs with other women behind her back and his feelings towards her have changed, he still had a soft spot for her. The last thing he wanted to do was hurt her. Chardonnay may not have been the best girlfriend to him, but she was still his friend.

When he didn't say anything, Cartier could see her eyes start to water up. "Do you even still want to be with me, Cartier?"

"Char—"

"Just answer the question, do you or not?"

"I don't know Char." Cartier replied. "I love you, but I just feel like our relationship has run its course and I feel like with everything that has happened, certain things we just can't come back from."

"How many times do I have to apologize for what happened? What can I do to make this right?" She asked. Chardonnay felt her heart breaking into a million pieces, she couldn't lose him. Especially not at the hands of another woman.

"Apologizing isn't going to bring the baby back; you always think shit can just be fixed because you apologized but it's more to it than that."

"I thought we agreed to never bring this up, I thought we got past this Cartier."

Shaking his head, Cartier laughed. "No, you agreed never to bring it up because you still don't want to face the reality of you aborting our child and not telling me. Like, how can we get past something if we never actually sit down and talk about it?"

Waving him off, she walked over to the bed. "I don't want to talk about this."

"Why? I really don't think you understand the damage you have caused within our relationship. Do you not remember how you put your career and everything else before our relationship? Do you not remember the nights I spent alone waiting for your arrival and you never came? Your selfish ways caused the split in our relationship and led to you aborting our child! I was hurting too!" Cartier yelled, finally releasing all the emotions he kept bottled up for so long.

Wiping her eyes. "You can't put the blame all on me Cartier, you've had your fair share of mistakes as well." She argued back.

"Nay, I know I've made my mistakes, but at least I own up to my faults. You still try to run from your mistakes rather than face them and each day we try to ignore the big issue within our relationship. It pushes me further away."

"Yeah, pushing you right into another woman's arms huh?" She laughed, but he didn't say anything back.

Nodding her head, she stood up from the bed and walked into their closet and began throwing his clothes and shoes out. "Since it's clear you've been feeling this way for a while, get the fuck out and go to wherever that bitch is!" She yelled.

Picking up all his things she kept tossing out, he sighed. "Char, really? You—"

"Save it Cartier, I don't want to hear any more of your excuses. I've heard way too many of them throughout our relationship and I'm tired of having to defend myself over something I've apologized numerous times about. I don't know what else to do at this point, it's clear you don't want me anymore." She sniffled.

She still doesn't get it. Cartier thought.

"I never said that."

"You might as well have, if you can't move past what happened then what exactly are we fighting to save this relationship for Cartier?"

He shrugged. "I don't know, but you can't expect me to be over something you lied about for so long. Were you even going to tell me if I hadn't found your discharge paperwork?"

Chardonnay knows Cartier is not one to forgive easily and she really wasn't sure what to do to make things right. Since that day their relationship has not been the same, it was like when she confirmed she aborted their child, she lost a part of him as well. But she just couldn't be honest and tell him the real truth behind it because she knew that meant possibly losing him forever. That was a risk she wasn't willing to take.

"Yes, eventually I would have! But baby, I knew how bad you wanted kids and I just wasn't ready. My career was just starting to take off and a baby would have slowed me down." She tried to explain.

"Who do you love more? Me or your damn career?"

"I never had to worry about my career creeping into another woman's bed, so what does that tell you?" She shrugged. "I can't apologize for wanting to be more established within my career first, before popping out a kid. Do I regret doing it? Yes, every day of my life I regret it because I see how much it hurt you, but I can't change the past."

Walking towards him, she grabbed his hands. "I want to fight for our relationship, but until you're sure this is what you want, maybe we just need some time apart."

She let go of his hands and walked into their bathroom slamming the door shut, Cartier sighed. The last thing he ever wanted to do was hurt Chardonnay, but he knew with him being dishonest about his true feelings, it was bound to happen.

Packing a small bag, Cartier eventually left out knowing that if he tried to explain himself to Chardonnay right now, it would only lead to another argument.

Deciding to stay in his condo for the next few days to clear his head, he decided to head to the store to grab a few things such as a new toothbrush and toothpaste along with a few other essential items.

Walking around Walmart, he adjusted his watch and looked down at his basket full of shit and laughed at himself. Shaking his head, *I always end up grabbing shit I don't need when I come to Walmart.*

Standing in the ice cream aisle, he bit his lip debating on which flavor he wanted. One thing he loved about Bluebell was that they had so many flavors to choose from; he damn near loved them all.

"Excuse me, could you pass me that butter pecan and a vanilla please?" Snapping his neck in the direction of the familiar voice, Cartier smiled when he saw it was Naomi.

He hadn't seen, nor talked to her in about a week; he was more than positive that he was the last person she wanted to see, but he couldn't lie and say seeing her there didn't make him happy. She looked good as hell standing there dressed in only a pair of tights and an oversized Howard University sweatshirt.

"Oh shit, my fault." Grabbing what she wanted, he handed it over to her, assuming she would speak or say something, Cartier frowned when she went to walk away.

"Naomi, wait." When she looked back at him, he began making his way towards her as she waited.

"What's up? You can't speak?" Cartier asked with a confused look on his face.

Giving him a blank expression, Naomi rolled her eyes. She couldn't believe he thought after the stunt he pulled they'd still be cool- as if he didn't stand her up.

"Alright, I guess I do deserve the silent treatment. But look, I was going to reach back out to you, there was just so much going on and I apologize for that." Cartier spoke.

Watching as she just stared at him, he thought she was just going to walk away until she opened her mouth to speak. "I know you're going through a lot and I'm okay with giving you the space you need, but standing me up on a date that *you* planned, with no explanation, is fucked up; I would never do that to anybody I'm so-called interested in. If this is your way of *applying pressure,* you can keep it."

"I know I fucked up and I'm sorry from the bottom of my heart, just please let me make it up to you. I swear to you I am more than what I've been showing you." Cartier pleaded. "Let me cook for you tonight at my place."

"I don't know Cartier."

"Please, I can only show you I'm truly sorry through my actions so, please just give me one more chance." He begged.

Rolling her eyes, she sighed. "Fine whatever, just text me the time and address. I'll see you later." She walked off, not giving him a second glance or anything. Cartier sighed to himself because he knew he needed to step his game up. He hoped after tonight, things between them would go back to how it was before.

It was almost eight o'clock at night and Naomi found herself sitting outside of Cartier's place contemplating on going back home or not. She was really becoming fed up with the back-and-forth shit with him. She had already put up with that for four years with a man and she wasn't about to do it again.

Looking back at his place, Naomi let out a sigh before quickly checking herself in her mirror. She shut off her car, deciding to stay. She at least wanted to give him a chance to prove himself, but this was it. If he messed up again, she was done and not looking back.

She got out of her car and walked up to his door, he greeted her holding a bouquet of white roses. "Good evening beautiful, these are for you." Taking the flowers from him, Naomi smiled as he moved out of the way, escorting her inside.

She noticed that he set the dining table with candles and roses for them both. Naomi appreciated the effort he was putting in, but it was still going to take more than this to win her over.

Cartier pulled her chair out for her. Naomi took her seat and thanked him, as he did the same for his seating at the end of the table. It was as if they were sitting side by side, but still able to face each other. "You look beautiful Naomi and I hope tonight you give me the opportunity to make things right between us."

"We'll just have to wait and see how the night goes." Naomi replied being genuinely honest.

"Well again, I thank you for allowing me cook for you. Tonight, we'll be having steak with shrimp and lobster tails, crab legs, and of course mac and cheese, and if you want, I have some baked potatoes in the oven." He explained and Naomi nodded impressed.

"You cooked all that? For me?" Naomi asked surprisingly.

Laughing, he reached over and grabbed her hand bringing it to his lips. "Yes, you deserve the best and that's exactly what you're getting from me."

"Sounds good and it smells amazing in here."

"Thank you, I'll be right back. Did you want anything to drink? I have wine, water, juice?"

"Wine would be fine." Naomi responded, followed by a laugh since that rhymed.

Watching as he walked off, Naomi took that time to look around his place. The interior was nice and very well kept, as if he barely stayed here; she was almost scared to even eat with how clean his place was.

Noticing a few pictures along the walls that seemed to be of him and his family, Naomi smiled, admiring the way Cartier's smile shined throughout the pictures. It was obvious to see that his family is one of his main sources of happiness.

Becoming slightly startled when the sound of music began playing, Naomi smiled in content, loving the sound of the saxophone that blared out of the speakers. It surprised her to know that he takes a liking to this genre of music.

Returning with her glass of wine and plate of food, Naomi felt her stomach doing back flips just from the sight of it all. It all smelled and looked so good causing her mouth to water.

When he returned with his food and drink in hand, he retook his seat and went to start eating, but Naomi popped his hand causing him to frown. "What?" He asked, confused.

"We have to say our grace first."

Growing shocked at her request he eventually bowed his head and let her grab a hold of his hand. "Lord, we come to you today to thank you for blessing us with this delicious food and we pray you blessed the hands that prepared it. We ask that it brings nourishment to our bodies and that it doesn't hurt, harm or danger to us. In Jesus name, amen."

"Amen." Cartier repeated.

Taking a sip of her wine, Naomi glanced over at Cartier who had begun eating. "You alright?" He asked when he peeped her looking and she only shrugged.

"I honestly feel like I should be asking you that." She replied.

Cartier wiped his mouth. He was a little unsure on how to answer that, he was also baffled by her statement. "I want to be, but it's a lot going on honestly. That whole entire night just keeps replaying in my head, I feel as if I should've done more to protect him." He admitted.

"You can't beat yourself up over what happened that night Cartier. You did what you could and that's all that matters. I'm sure Meech wouldn't want you blaming yourself either, so you have to let what happened go and accept it." Naomi replied.

"I know, but that's easier said than done though. We had big plans; he was so young and so full of life and just like that, his life was just taken from him." He sighed, trying not to let his emotions of what happened alter the mood.

"But despite what I'm going through, I was wrong for what I did to you. Like, I swear to you, I'm truly sorry for standing you up that night and ghosting you like that; it was just so much going on with me mentally. I often just feel so alone at times and don't want to be bothered but nothing excuses what I did either though." He expressed.

Naomi nodded, understanding exactly what he meant. "I know exactly how you feel, but shutting folks out is not the way to go. You saved my life that night, along with my friends, and I can't thank you enough for that. I know losing Meech was hard for you and my brother, I can't even act as if I know what that feels like, but I would like to be there for you and help you through this, if you let me."

Looking up at her, he reached over and grabbed her hand. "I know and I'm sorry. I ain't gon' lie though, I did really miss you and I must say, seeing you today really made a nigga happy."

"I can admit I missed you too. With us talking and getting to know one another these past three weeks, I was a little bummed out and even thought something bad happened when you stood me up at the restaurant. Sometimes I'd even ask my brother if you were okay and if he had saw you- the answer was always yes. Then I randomly see you out at Walmart. I started to feel as if I did something wrong, like you were avoiding me or something." Naomi admitted.

"I promise you it was nothing you said or did, it was all me, but I swear to continue to prove myself to you and do all I can to get back on your good side."

Staring at him, Naomi just had a gut feeling something was off, but she wanted to give him a chance. She figured this feeling was just coming from the trust issues she had caused by Dre, and so far, Cartier had done nothing to make her not trust him or think otherwise, so she let it go.

Picking up a few potatoes with her fork, playing around with the food. Naomi sighed, "Just please promise not to waste my time and be completely honest, regardless of how ugly the truth may be. That's all I ask for."

Looking her dead in the eyes, he nodded. "I promise." He replied as he grabbed her hand, placing a soft kiss on the back of it.

Naomi looked into his eyes, becoming hooked into the intense stare he had placed on her. She bit her lip, refraining herself from doing something she had no business. It seemed like every time he looked at her or even just touched her, he sent chills throughout her whole body.

"So, what do you know about this type of music?" Naomi asked, finding a loophole to break the sexual tension between them.

Although her girl down there was becoming aroused (due to her short-term of celibacy she began shortly after things between her and Dre officially ended), she knew it was still way too soon to give up the goods just yet.

Laughing at her random question, he took a quick sip from his glass, "My mom actually. We grew up listening to her play this when she would cook her big Sunday dinners or whenever she would clean the house. It had a way of relaxing her and bringing her the type of peace she needed while trying to raise us, eventually it grew on me. I honestly think I just loved the way this type of music made her feel, so I grew to love it due to that."

"Mama has taste." Naomi said before covering her mouth with a napkin as she chewed her food, catching all the good flavors he seasoned the steak with. To her surprise he could actually "cook cook"; she was truly impressed with how he went all out for her tonight.

Glancing up at him, watching him eat for a second, Naomi let her mind wonder as she took in all his features. Cartier was literally everything a woman would want in a man and surprisingly here she was, she couldn't help but to think this was all just too good to be true.

God, I pray this man doesn't disappoint me. Naomi thought.

The rest of their evening was spent with them talking and laughing. However, Naomi's favorite part of the evening was when they slow-danced to the music he was playing.

His hand was resting slightly above her butt as his other hand intertwined with hers. They danced in silence not wanting to ever let go.

The smell of his cologne traveled up her nose as she rested her head on his chest. He then pulled her in closer as she wrapped her hands around his neck, enjoying the feeling of comfort she got from him. Words couldn't express how good it felt to be in the arms of a man and finally feel a bit of fresh air.

Naomi smiled to herself taking in this moment, *if only this could last forever.*

Chapter 5

5 months later

"What the fuck is the purpose of this shit man? We already know them niggas in there! Why can't we just go in and pop shit off!!" One of Cartier's young bulls by the name of Chase spoke out, while passing Cartier the blunt.

Nassir looked over at Cartier and shook his head before turning his attention back to the trap house they had been staking out.

Chase is one of their street runners who has great potential, but they both knew he wasn't going to get too far if he didn't learn when to be muscular and when to use his logic in certain situations.

"We don't know who all in there, nigga! One fuck up and we could all be dead. How many times we gotta tell you that hot headed shit gone get you killed out in these streetz. So, sit back and chill the fuck out." Cartier replied, not hiding his frustration as he took a hit from the blunt.

This was mainly why Cartier liked either working alone or just working with Nassir, they seemed to better understand each other when it came down to planning and analyzing situations before jumping right in. Cartier learned that shit the hard way when he was younger; when doing something risky, the key is to always analyze the situation first, so you'll know exactly what you're getting yourself into.

However, these young and too eager ass niggas just couldn't seem to listen or grasp that concept, and Cartier was not about to lose his life behind someone else's reckless and careless ass mistakes.

Cartier heard Chase smack his lips and mumble shit under his breath while he finished cleaning his gun off. Cartier simply shrugged, not giving a damn if he was mad at him or not; he needed to know when to shut the fuck up and let shit play out.

Glancing over at the traphouse, Cartier watched as folks walked in and out, capturing every face. They had been staking out all of Trig's trap houses for the past few months and learned the way he moves. If the streetz never taught him anything else, it certainly taught him to always know your enemy like the back of your hand.

Throughout their stakeout he developed a lot of knowledge as to how Trig operates his business. The traffic throughout this house was very limited compared to a few of his other locations they staked out. You never saw women or him hosting parties at this location, and the men that entered and exited this house are always the same exact four.

So, they all figured this had to be his stash house.

“You gone pass the blunt nigga?” Nassir asked, snapping Cartier out of his thoughts.

Noticing he dropped ashes onto himself, Cartier laughed before handing it over to him.

Lately, he’s been zoning out, getting lost in his own thoughts.

“That bitch getting you off your game.” Cartier heard Nassir say before taking a hit from the blunt. “I've been telling you to let her ass go from the jump.”

“Says the man that ain’t took a bitch seriously since who broke his heart?” Cartier teased laughing as Chase joined in.

When they were both in high school Nas met this girl named Alana. Back then you couldn’t tell Nas anything when it came to Alana, he felt she was his Bonnie and was head over heels behind her. That all changed sadly when he found out that she was cheating and left him for a nigga that runs with Trig now.

Since that incident Cartier hasn't seen him genuinely care for another female besides Naomi, but he does feel that Sheree might be the one to heal that broken heart of his with the way he’s been talking about her lately.

“Fuck y’all niggas, but I’m serious nigga. With you starting this shit with my sister you need to hurry up and figure out what it is you plan on doing. She has already been through a lot, and I love you both to death, but when it comes to her, you know I don’t play and that’s all I’ma say about the situation.” Nassir replied, leaving it at that.

Cartier couldn’t say much back to that because at the end of the day he knew he was right. Cartier knew he had no business starting anything with Naomi because he’s still technically in a whole relationship. He also knew if she were to ever find out, she’d be done with his ass.

So, he knew he had a choice to make before somebody got hurt, and the last person he wanted that to be was Naomi.

Shit was just complicated.

After a brief moment of silence, they all tuned in and focused on the traphouse. They noticed two niggas come out the house suspiciously carrying duffel bags in both of their hands.

"I think they're about to drop off the money to Trig." Cartier said, paying close attention to them.

When the niggas finished loading up, Nassir started up their car and made sure to keep a great distance behind as they pulled off. Chase and Cartier began putting on their gear, just in case the guys noticed them, and things got out of hand.

They followed behind them for about fifteen minutes before they came to a stop at this white and brown brick brownstone on the north side of the city.

"You think this is his crib or where he just keeps his shit?" Cartier asked Nassir. He studied their movements from transporting from the car to the house before responding.

"This is most def his spot, he had his bitch answer the door and her outfit was way too comfortable for this to be a business area." Nassir responded by turning off the car. "Dumb ass nigga, I would never bring this shit to where I lay my head at."

"So, what's the plan?" Chase asked, becoming agitated, ready to pop shit off.

"We gon' get his two bitch ass goons and then send his ass a nice little message." Cartier responded, smirking to himself as he watched the woman pull off in her car.

They waited for about forty-minutes to an hour until the guys finally returned from the house, not once watching or checking their surroundings.

"Rookie mistake." Cartier thought to himself.

It was so funny to Cartier to know that Trig really felt as if he could compete and possibly take someone like him out of the game, when he had nothing but bitch-made niggas surrounding him who clearly weren't even on their shit at all.

Cartier felt like if he wanted to, he could've easily popped their asses right then and there, they wouldn't have seen it coming, but he wanted to have a little fun first.

They followed them back to their traphouse, which took almost an hour since they decided to stop at a nearby liquor store. Cartier was annoyed and beyond ready to get this shit over with.

When they pulled up, they put on their masks and exited the car, and checked their surroundings as they crossed the street. The guys were so occupied in their conversation they didn't even realize the presence of the three of them approaching.

Once Cartier gave me the signal, Nassir raised his gun back and knocked the passenger out as he exited from the vehicle.

"What th-" before the other guy could finish his sentence, Cartier already had his gun pointed and let out a shot right in the middle of his eyes.

Cartier signaled for Chase to come over. Chase helped Cartier remove his body from the car and they both quietly carried the men to their van that pulled around right on que.

Chase hopped in the back with the bodies and Cartier tapped the truck so they could pull off. Quickly running over to their car, Nassir pulled Cartier back by his sweater stopping him.

Looking back, Cartier frowned. "Nigga what?"

"Nigga this his stash house and I know his bitch ass got money stacked up in that bitch." Nassir pointed out, implying that they should rob the place.

"Nas-" Cartier attempted to speak but Nassir stopped him.

"I already know ain't nobody in that bitch. This nigga been causing us to lose money and they asses need to pay for that shit they did to Meech!" Nassir semi-yelled.

Although Cartier knew Nassir was telling the truth, he honestly didn't feel any of it was worth the risk of shit possibly turning into a bloodbath; but it was clear from the tone in Nassir's voice and the look in his eyes that nothing was going to change his mind and he knew if he didn't go with him, Nassir was still going to do it regardless.

"Fuck it, let's go."

The street was completely empty and all that could be heard were birds faintly chirping in the distance, along with stray cats and dogs roaming the streetz looking for food. With it being so early in the morning, they both knew eventually folks would start waking up for work and that people would soon be on the streetz, so they knew they had to do this quick and fast.

Walking towards the back of the house, Cartier and Nassir both hopped the fence and snuck in through the back door by breaking and shooting the door handle off.

When they entered inside Cartier made sure the coast was clear before motioning for Nassir to come in. They wasted no time ransacking the place. They came across bags full of money; stuffed inside couches, hidden under floorboards, and stashed away in cabinets.

Nassir and Cartier both couldn't believe how dumb this nigga Trig was. They would never leave their stash house unattended like this and due to his dumb decision, they were about to come up like a fat rat.

"With the way we've been finding bundles of money, it's gotta be at least a million dollars or more in this bitch," Nassir said surprised.

"Nah forreal, but let's just get what we can and get the fuck out of here before that bitch come back." Cartier told him as he began bagging up the money inside some duffel bags they had found.

After calling one of their guards who was already driving around the area to make sure nothing popped off, they loaded up the bags of money inside his trunk and quickly jogged over to their car and sped the fuck off. The neighborhood was surprisingly still quiet and settled, they saw why Trig chose this place as his stash spot and it worked out for them as well, since no one saw them enter or leave the house.

After a long three-hour drive from the city to their farmhouse also known as, "The dungeon," Cartier and Nassir were both ready to get down to business. The dungeon was where they handled a lot of their business because it was off the grid and far away where nobody really knew the location.

Pulling into their garage right beside the van, Nassir and Cartier immediately hopped out and headed straight towards the basement where their guys were waiting for them. Once they reached the basement, they saw the boys already setting up and getting the grinder ready for use, which caused a smile to creep up on Cartier's face at the thought of what was about to happen.

"Make sure y'all clean this place well and feed pieces of them to the pigs out back once they're processed through the machine and be sure to separate the parts you're going to feed them, and the pieces you don't, so we can deliver our message." Nassir instructed before heading to the back to switch out of his clothes.

Cartier followed behind him and did the same. He made sure to throw their clothes in the pit of fire they set up outside.

After changing out of their clothes, Nassir motioned for one of their guards to help unload the bags of money from the trunk. Placing each of the bags on the table, another worker immediately started taking the stacks of money out as Cartier set up their money counter.

"How much do you think we got?" Nassir questioned as Cartier began unwrapping the money and placing a few stacks inside the counter.

Taking the blunt from one of his workers who was passing it, he shrugged taking a few hits of it. "I don't know, but we gon' see."

After counting and rewrapping all the money, the money came to a total of 2.5 million dollars. Splitting the money evenly down the middle between everyone who helped with the job today, Cartier and Nassir began passing around everyone's share.

Cartier always made sure he took care of his workers because he knew without them a lot of shit wouldn't even be possible. They are the foundation of the business and for that he was going to make sure they were forever straight.

After having a short meeting with the guys to discuss a few business plans, namely, what they were about to do next with this whole Trig situation, Cartier headed inside the house to see what his aunt and uncle were up to.

The farmhouse actually belonged to his Uncle Rome and Aunt Shanda. They were once in the family business but decided to retire and moved away to live the country life, raising cattle and other livestock.

However, they still let everyone use their house for business since their home was like the perfect hiding spot. From the outside, it just looked like any old farmhouse in the country and that's what kept this place under wraps for so long; no one would ever imagine they were moving weight or grinding humans and feeding them to pigs.

Walking into the kitchen Cartier spotted his aunt facing away from him cooking, a smile crept up on his face. Coming up behind his aunt, Cartier wrapped his arms around her and placed a quick kiss on her cheek, slightly startling her.

Glancing back to see who it was hugging her from behind, she laughed as she hit him with her oven mitt. "Don't be scaring me like that, what are you doing here?" She questioned before turning back to her pot of infamous Jambalaya.

"Just handling some business TT. Let me get a bowl of that real quick though." Cartier tried to steal a piece of shrimp, but she popped his hand away.

"Are you asking or telling me?" She gave him a look, causing him to laugh.

"I'm asking, may I please get a bowl of your delicious Jambalaya auntie?" Cartier asked sarcastically.

Waving him off, she turned and grabbed two bowls, one for him and one for Snoop when she saw him walk inside. "Y'all have a seat and I'll make you some. Be sure to wash your hands first, y'all know I don't play that." She taunted.

Before going to wash his hands Cartier reached into his pocket and pulled out a stack of sixty-thousand dollars and placed it on his aunt's counter.

Glancing at the money, she laughed and shook her head before grabbing it and placing it back in his hands. "Baby, we don't need your money. Thank you though." She smiled.

"I know, but I want y'all to have it. Y'all have been really helping me out these past few months and this is just my way of saying thank you." Cartier said, leaving the kitchen before she could respond and protest.

After washing their hands and eating, they decided to catch up with the family and stay a while to make sure the boys did what they wanted. Cartier always liked to make sure a job was done before walking away, he didn't have time for any slip ups especially with Trig plotting against him.

Stretched out on the couch watching football with Nassir and his Uncle Rome, Cartier quickly fetched his phone when he felt it vibrate in his pocket. Seeing Naomi's name pop up on his screen, he smiled to himself before unlocking his phone to see her message.

Nao🩶:
Hey baby, I just finished my last client and I'm about to head back to my place to get ready for our date tonight! I can't wait to see you😘.
Sent at 3:39pm

Cartier:
I can't wait to see you either mamas, I'm still at my uncle's but I should be back in town at about 7 or 8. I'll call you when I'm outside.
Delivered at 3:41pm

Placing his phone back in his pocket, Cartier looked up to see his Uncle Rome staring at him with a confused expression. Motioning for Cartier to follow him with his head, Cartier soon got up off the couch and followed him out the back door that led to their backyard.

"What's up Unc?" Cartier asked as he stared at the side of his face wondering what he wanted.

"Do you plan on living this lifestyle forever? Or do you see more for yourself?" His uncle simply asked.

Not sure where this question came from, Cartier shrugged. "I honestly don't know yet, I mean I know what comes with this lifestyle and the risks I'm taking but it's a lot of good that comes with it as well."

Laughing, his uncle shook his head. "And what good is that? Money? Cars? Women?"

Cartier shrugged, "I mean yeah those are a few perks that come with it, but hell this lifestyle guarantees a life of no struggle and if and when I have kids, I don't ever have to worry about them going without."

"So, you plan on bringing kids into this type of life?" He questioned curiously.

Frowning, Cartier gave him a look. “I don’t know, but what’s the point you’re trying to get at Unc?”

“I’m just tryna see where ya head at, you and I both know this ain’t the lifestyle you really want, and it don’t seem like you tryna walk away anytime soon either.” His uncle replied.

“I mean I got time Unc and right now business is boomin’, but you’re right I do see more for myself, and I do want more but you and I both know walking away from this lifestyle ain’t easy.” Cartier explained.

Cartier knew his uncle meant well and only wanted better for him, but Cartier knew he wasn’t about to step away from this lifestyle any time soon. He still had other things he needed to handle and more money to make before he even considered walking away as an option.

“We always feel like we have all the time in the world, but son we all know tomorrow isn’t promised! I’ve lost a lot of people in my life due to this shit, including my own brother and the last thing I want is for you or someone close to you getting hurt. The drug game ain’t shit to play with or something you can use as a way to earn fast cash; shit is real, and it changes people, sometimes for the worse.” Glancing over at Cartier, his uncle briefly smiled at him.

“But I know one day you’ll wake up and be ready to walk away from this shit and when you do, you know where to find me.” Ending the conversation on that note, his uncle stepped back into the house to leave Cartier in his thoughts.

Chapter 6

Glancing at herself in the mirror for the fifth time, Naomi took a step back to admire her outfit and debated whether she wanted to change it or not. She was in the middle of getting ready for a date with Cartier and she was beyond nervous for some odd reason.

He didn't explain exactly where they were going, but she knew it was going to be something over the top since Cartier loved treating her to high class places and making her feel special.

Over the past five months Cartier managed to keep his word on showing her how he was serious about making her his woman. He has taken her on multiple dates, they facetime almost every other day whenever they aren't around each other, and their connection between one another has grown from all the deep and intimate conversations they've had.

When they first started to really get to know each other, it wasn't the basic, "tell me about yourself," conversation. They were genuinely curious to know how they both operated and why they are the way they are and why they do the things that they do.

The many nights they shared opening up to one other was amazing, and Naomi truly got to see a more vulnerable side of Cartier and vice versa. However, despite how deep some of their talks have gotten, there were still a few things neither of them was ready to discuss regarding their past.

Overall, though Naomi appreciated all of Cartier's efforts to impress her and show her that he wasn't playing when it came down to how he felt about her. It felt good to finally be wined and dined by a man with genuine intentions, it often felt almost too good to be true at times.

Due to all his kind gestures and smooth words, Cartier definitely managed to sneak his way into her heart, which sorta went against everything Naomi previously said about taking things slow with him. At this point, it was hard not to fall for a man like Cartier who says and does all the right things. As the days passed by, her feelings continued to grow.

Looking over towards her door to see Sheree entering her room, she smiled. "Please tell me that's the outfit you're choosing, you look cute." She complimented before she took a seat on Naomi's bed. "If I was gay, I'd hit." She joked.

Turning back towards the mirror, Naomi laughed and shook her head. "You really think so? It's far too revealing, dontcha think?" She asked as she glanced over the white long-sleeve shirt and black and white pattern overall pants that hugged her body like a glove, showcasing all her curves once again.

"You look fine, Cartier is about to be all over you tonight and if not, I damn sho' will be." She joked, making both of them laugh.

Sheree and Naomi have gotten really close during these last few months, Naomi feels like their relationship has gotten better than her and Lanay's. Of course, Lanay and her were still close and hung out, but lately things with Lanay have been off and she's been keeping her distance, so no one really knows what's been going on with her.

Once Naomi finally agreed to settle with this outfit, Sheree helped her with her make up and curled her bundles she had recently installed to perfection.

Sitting on the edge of her bed she slid on her white heels to finish off the look, before standing back up to glance at herself in the mirror once more. Turning to the side to catch the angles, Naomi smiled feeling satisfied with this look, she knew she looked good.

"I see you girl, I told you that you looked amazing. I can't wait to see what Cartier thinks." Sheree boosted.

Letting out a heavy sigh, Naomi walked over to Sheree to give her a hug. "Thanks so much for coming over to help me get ready, I would've been stuck without you."

Waving her off just as they both heard a faint knock on her front door, Naomi smiled big knowing it was him.

Adjusting her clothes and checking her hair once more, she walked to the door excitedly, but sadly to her surprise when she opened the door it was just Nassir, her smile dropped in disgust.

"Damn you not happy to see me?" Nassir asked, before forcing his way inside and plopping down on her couch.

"I have a date with Cartier tonight and I thought you were him," Naomi answered as she took a seat next to him. "But what's up?"

"That's actually what I came over here to discuss with you about."

Looking at him weirdly, Naomi shrugged. "...Okay, what? You don't want us seeing each other anymore or something?"

"Nah, I just want to know how serious you are about Cartier?" With the intense eye contact they were having; Naomi knew Nassir was being serious, which lowkey worried her since for the past few months he has shown little to no interest at all towards her relationship with Cartier.

"I can say I'm interested in seeing where things could possibly go between us. But for right now I'm really just trying not to rush into this and end up making the same mistakes I made in the past again. My feelings however are definitely starting to become involved." Naomi told him, being truly honest about how she felt.

Nassir didn't say anything for a while, she grew anxious and worried. He looked down as if he was contemplating on saying something. Looking up at her with a small smile plastered on his face, he then leaned over and placed a small kiss on her cheek, before sitting back. "You know I love you and after everything you've been through, I just want to see you happy. You know that right?"

Smiling, Naomi nodded. "I can honestly admit this has been the happiest I've been in a long time, Nas. He has managed to make me feel like myself again, but better if that makes sense."

"As long as you like it, then I love it. Just be sure to be careful with him, Naomi."

Before she could respond to his comment, Sheree had walked from the back interrupting their conversation. "I didn't know you were coming over; I was just about to call you." Sheree stated once she saw Nassir sitting on the couch.

Naomi frowned when she saw the way Nassir perked up at the sound of her voice. Peeping the way they embraced each other, Naomi almost passed out when they shared a quick kiss. She knew Sheree and her brother were feeling each other, but she was not aware that things between them had gotten a lot more serious.

"Um, excuse me? What's the tea on y'all?" Naomi questioned them both. "When did this happen?"

They both just shared a look between one another and laughed.

"You in my business—" Nassir joked childishly as he threw his arm over Sheree. Naomi rolled her eyes and joined in with their laughs. "But nah forreal, this my lil baby though."

Watching Sheree blush and smile, Naomi went to reply but was cut off by a knock at the door. Quickly hopping up, she did a quick once over before walking up to the door excitedly.

When she opened the door this time it was Cartier, and she couldn't be happier to see him right now. He was looking and smelling good, he had his hair freshly lined up, and waves were neat as usual. He wore a button-down white shirt with a pair of nice black jeans to match, along with a pair of all white AF1's. To finish the look off, he had a nice Cuban link around his neck that matched the new watch Naomi had gifted him.

"Hey beautiful." When those words rolled off his tongue as he smirked and licked his lips, Naomi felt her stomach do a backflip.

Embracing her in his arms, Cartier made sure to get a good grip of her ass and began kissing her neck. Naomi laughed and pushed him away. "Somebody's happy to see me." She flirted.

"Always, but here these are for you." Handing her a gift bag and a bouquet of her favorite flowers that she didn't even notice he was holding, Naomi smiled softly, truly grateful.

Taking the bag from him, Naomi stepped to the side to let him in before going to her kitchen to put her gift up and flowers inside a vase. The gesture was really nice. It is very rare to find a man that still does little things like this to keep their woman happy and Naomi loved it all.

Walking out of the kitchen she grabbed her purse, keys, and phone. She went to join them in the living room and saw Cartier and Nassir kinda off to the side talking, but she wasn't too sure as to what they could be discussing.

"Yeah, we're cool man." Naomi heard Nassir say, before they slapped hands and hugged whatever out.

Watching them from the side Naomi became curious as to what happened to the point where they were at odds and then it made her think back to Nassir questioning her about her and Cartier's relationship.

A part of her was thinking maybe Nassir wasn't fully accepting of her and Cartier dating, which would be understandable since Nassir had a way of trying to control her and dead any potential love interest she ever had in the past.

However, Naomi was actually surprised at Nassir's calmness towards the situation. When it was first revealed that her and Cartier had something going on Nassir didn't really react or say much, which was not like him at all. She wasn't quite sure as to where the changes of his attitude came from, but she's hoping it's here for good.

"You ready?" The sound of Cartier's voice snapped her out of her thoughts, she smiled so he wouldn't ask what was on her mind.

"Mhm." She replied as he grabbed a hold of her hand.

As they got ready to leave Nassir and Sheree got their things and followed them out as Naomi made sure to lock up.

Once they reached the parking lot, Naomi hugged both Sheree and Nassir goodbye, before walking over to Cartier's car where he stood holding her door open for her. Cartier took a hold of her hand and helped her inside before shutting her door and jogging over to his side.

Naomi always loved riding around in Cartier's cars, the first time she ever rode in one of his cars, it was obvious that he was a man that took pride in his vehicles. They were all so neatly clean and polished and had a faint smell of the cologne he wore and weed.

"Where are we going to eat?" Naomi questioned as she buckled her seatbelt.

"To the best place that serves the best gotdamn southern food in the city. You gon love it, I promise." He bragged proudly as he started the car and pulled off.

"Sounds good, I can't wait." Naomi smiled. "But anyways, how was your day? Do anything exciting?" She asked, trying to make conversation.

Shrugging his shoulders as he switched lanes, he shook his head no in response. "My day was chill, got a lot done but I ain't really do anything too exciting, just handled some shit that aint really worth speaking on, then went and chopped it up with my aunt and uncle for a bit. What about you?"

"My day was good; my clientele is building so I was busy doing heads most of the day. So, my hands and feet are killing me right now from using em and being on em all day." She sighed.

Reaching his hand over, Cartier grabbed her hand and sweetly kissed the back of it. "Don't even worry about that, I'll take care of that tonight."

Blushing hard as ever, Naomi leaned over and pecked him on the lips a few times. "You treat me so well."

"And will continue to do so," He winked before focusing back on the road.

When his phone started ringing, Naomi handed it over to him, not bothering to even look at who was calling, since for one that wasn't her business- nor did she want to come off as that type of female.

Watching as he rolled his eyes and declined the call, Naomi frowned. "Everything okay? Who was that?"

"Just some business-related shit, ain't nothing I'm trying to deal with right now." He mumbled lying. "Nor is it anything that's more important than us at the moment."

The person who was calling was Chardonnay and Cartier knew with Naomi being there, he could not answer that call, nor did he even want to. Things between them were still very complicated and right now he was not in the mood to deal with her, his main focus was Naomi.

Naomi nodded. "Is everything okay though? Is business not doing so well?" She questioned.

Although he had opened up a little to her regarding his business, she always just felt as if there was still more to him that he hadn't revealed yet. It was like it was always something about him that made her want to know more about all the aspects of his life, including the good and the bad.

Watching as he glanced from her to the road with one hand on the wheel and the other pulling at his goatee, he laughed. "Damn you the police or something now?" He teased, raising his eyebrow.

"No, I'm serious, I mean what am I supposed to think when you get a call and roll your eyes? We don't really talk about this side of you, but I am a little curious to know more about it. Like do I need to be on the lookout for somebody targeting us when we're out together? These are things I need to know, because I know what comes with this lifestyle."

Shrugging his shoulders, Cartier looked away. “There's really not much to tell and you don’t ever have to worry about anything happening to you, I won’t let that happen.”

Smacking her teeth Naomi reached over and hit his arm, “Stop lying I just like learning more about you and since we really don’t talk about it, I’m just curious to learn more about that side of you. Like honestly, I would like to know what made you even choose this lifestyle and get into this line of work? Because I mean don’t take this the wrong way, but you just seem so much better than this.” She replied hoping she didn’t offend him.

Not expecting her to say that Cartier immediately thought back to the conversation he had with his uncle earlier.

Letting out a deep sigh, Cartier knew he at least owed her a little more insight into his life. “I didn’t really have much of a choice honestly. Growing up I was kinda exposed to a lot of shit that I had no business seeing but I guess they thought that was their way of molding me into who they wanted me to be.” He started, followed by a laugh even though it was clearly forced.

“As a kid, I was always kind of a hot head and when it came to my family, I was a ride or die no matter what; I guess that impressed my family enough to the point to where they wanted to pass down the business to me whenever the time came. So, when my dad passed my uncle couldn’t think of anybody better to carry on the business, he immediately started grooming me for this shit.” He replied dryly with his jaw clenched.

Naomi noticed the change in Cartier’s body language when he mentioned his dad and how he got wrapped up in that lifestyle; it was clear there was more to be told about that whole situation, but she wasn’t going to press him to talk about it.

“But enough about that bullshit, what about you? What made you want to do hair?” Cartier asked to change the subject. Just as much as he didn’t want to talk about his past, neither did she.

“Uh well I was raised around nothing but beauticians, I basically grew up watching my grandma, my mama and aunties do hair and eventually I wanted to learn myself. From practicing on my barbies to doing my friends' hair, it started off as something I did for fun, but I soon gained a passion for it especially when I started making a little money off my talent. After I lost my grandma, I always had a dream of opening my own salon just like her, but some things transpired in my life, and I had to push that dream back.” Naomi replied, swallowing hard.

The topic of Deandre was still hard for her to open up about, especially with how things ended between them. She was still ashamed about what she did, but she knew in order for Cartier to get to know her better he had to know her past.

She just wasn't ready yet.

"Things like what?"

"Now who's the police?" Naomi teased.

Laughing, Cartier shrugged. "I'm just curious, hell I mean whatever happened had to be pretty serious for you to kinda give up on ya dream; but if you don't want to talk about it, I completely understand."

There was a moment of silence between the two, before Naomi decided to open up just a little. "After high school I ran out of the city with my now ex-boyfriend. Things were great between us, then one day it wasn't anymore, and I don't know. I personally feel during the course of the relationship, I was so busy focusing on what we once had and what we could've been- that I grew blind to what we actually were. But then I finally woke up and some things happened and here I am now back home trying to get my life back together." She said looking out the window.

Cartier glanced over at Naomi because he heard in her voice that she was hurt from whatever happened between her and her ex. Reaching his hand over he locked their fingers together then sweetly kissed the back of her hand and held it up to his chest. "You ain't gotta tell me everything that happened between you guys, but just know you don't ever have to worry about me hurting you."

Looking over at him, Naomi smiled. "I know and I really can't thank you enough for making these past few months very special for me."

After they shared a quick kiss there was a bit of a pause in the conversation. They were both trapped in their own thoughts, thinking about their pasts and what the future may hold between them.

Naomi could tell the thoughts of their pasts put them in a heavy head space. So, to lighten the mood she decided to put on some music to get their minds off of whatever they were thinking about. Connecting her phone to his aux, she put on Detwan Love's hit song, "No Chain."

As she rapped along to the words of the song Cartier glanced over at her, slightly amused and shocked that she knew this song.

Peeping him looking at her, she stopped. "What?" She laughed.

"What do you know about this? I'm honestly surprised you fuck with it. You seem like the Beyoncé, Rihanna -R&B type."

Naomi smacked her lips and waved him off. "Boy please, don't get me wrong I love me some Bey and Rih, but I can relate and listen to any type of music. It's a beautiful art and very therapeutic at times."

"That's true, like that Ghetto Angels song by Nocap, that song be hittin' home forreal. But it's cool you fuck with the different type of genres though." Cartier mumbled as he licked his lips and looked at her for a brief moment before focusing on the road.

Naomi blushed looking out the window. For the rest of the ride, they just relaxed and vibed to the music until reaching their destination.

After driving for another twenty-five minutes or so, they had finally arrived, but Naomi immediately grew confused when she saw they were parked in front of a nice pretty, yellow, and white house in Decatur.

The driveway and yard were filled with cars, and she could faintly smell the scent of barbeque dancing its way up her nose. Naomi looked over at Cartier confused because this looked far from a restaurant.

"Whose house is this, Cartier?" She asked him as he turned off the car.

"My moms," He replied nonchalantly.

Playfully hitting him on his arm, Cartier laughed as he blocked her hits. "Why are you hitting me? I told you I was bringing you to the place that serves the best southern food in the city."

"You could have told me we were coming to your moms; I would have worn something better." Naomi felt her stomach begin to turn as she unbuckled her seatbelt.

Naomi hated surprises sometimes, especially surprises like this. She hadn't met a man's family before, besides Deandre's, which didn't turn out too well at all, so she definitely grew nervous by the minute.

"Are you mad at me?" Cartier asked, giving her puppy dog eyes. "If you aren't ready for this just yet, we can leave right now." He reassured her.

Naomi looked at him trying to remain upset with a blank face, but she knew at the end of the day she clearly must've meant something to him for him to bring her to meet his mom and family.

"I'm just saying you could've given me a heads up. I'm nervous as shit now, you are about to have me in a house full of killers, kingpins, and god knows what else- and on top of that your mother!" Naomi confessed pulling down his visor, checking her hair and makeup.

"You ain't got shit to worry about, when we're all together we just a regular drama filled family, I promise."

Letting out a sigh, she nodded. "Okay."

"You wanna smoke one to relax your nerves before we go in?" He asked her, while pulling out a big ass zip of weed from his middle console.

Cartier knew that she would be surprised with him inviting her to his mom's house so quickly, but his family were just as good as him when it came to picking out a snake and separating the real from the fake.

He wanted to see what his folks thought of her and if she passed the test in their eyes, then that was all the confirmation he needed in pursuing things with her.

"Fuck it." She said, closing the visor and sitting back in her seat.

Naomi watched Cartier take some weed out of the bag and grab a pack of Al Capones to start rolling, Naomi used that time to check her phone and text a few people back.

"Now don't get to hallucinating and shit on a nigga." He joked, while breaking down the weed. "Y'all females be trippin."

"I can handle my shit." Naomi replied cockily.

One thing Cartier would soon learn about her is that she was not the average type of woman he's used to dealing with.

"Oh, you a big dawg huh?"

"Damn right." She smiled.

Cartier smirked and finished rolling the spliff and then began to light it up before taking a few hits.

Naomi watched as he inhaled then exhaled the smoke and found herself getting turned on. Here lately the sexual tension between the two have grown; Cartier could be doing absolutely nothing, and she would be ready to jump on him.

Realizing that he picked up on her staring at him, she looked away and watched some younger kids walk by the car and go towards the side door of the house.

Naomi didn't have much of a family besides her brother and parents. In fact, that's all the family she has, so seeing how Cartier's family can come together like this warmed her heart because it's something she didn't have. The only thing her family comes together for are funerals and even that's rare.

"Here baby." Looking over at him, she smiled lovingly whenever he called her baby.

Taking the blunt from him she put it to her lips and inhaled it slowly, allowing the smoke to fill her lungs. Shortly after she released and blew the smoke out. She could feel her body already starting to mellow out.

"Do you see yourself getting married and shit?" Cartier asked randomly.

Naomi glanced over at him for a moment and saw that he was serious before she gave the weed another hit.

"Honestly I never really saw that happening for me, but it is something I want one day." She answered, ashing the blunt before passing it back to him. "What about you?"

"Honestly yeah, I didn't really get to grow up with the best example of what love should look and feel like from my parents, so I want to be able to have kids and experience that family feeling."

"Your mom never found someone after your dad passed away?" Naomi questioned curiously.

"No, my father was everything but perfect and he put her through a lot and really traumatized her. Hell, if the physical abuse wasn't enough to make her give up on love, I'm sure the emotional and mental abuse played a part in it as well." He mumbled. "Like she would go on dates and shit, but she never got too serious with anybody since my brother and I were her main focus, but that's not really what I meant." He answered.

Naomi nodded realizing that he's starting to become more comfortable with her, given the fact that he's letting her learn more about him. But it honestly broke her heart to learn that his mother went through something very similar to what she experienced with a man.

"I'm sorry to hear that." Naomi said sympathetically.

She didn't know what the severity of their relationship was, but she sympathized with any woman that went through what she went through and lost herself behind a man.

Taking the blunt from him when he passed it her way, Naomi took another hit feeling a lot more relaxed than she was before.

"I'm really feeling you." Cartier confessed looking over at her with those brown sexy pair of eyes. "Like a lot."

Naomi smiled, trying to hold back her blush. "I'm feeling you too."

Leaning over for a kiss, Naomi met him halfway and pressed her lips against his while putting the blunt out in the ashtray at the same time. Gently grabbing his chin, she began caressing his goatee and deepened the kiss by sliding her tongue inside his mouth.

As the kiss deepened, Naomi had half the mind to hop into his lap, but she knew this was not the time or the place for that. When Naomi let out a moan against his lips, she immediately pulled back realizing they were at his moms, and anybody could have walked over and saw them.

Glancing over at him she looked in his eyes and saw nothing but pure lust and admiration. It was clear that he wanted her just as bad as she wanted him.

A bang on the window caused both Naomi and Cartier to slightly jump. Looking over, Cartier laughed when he saw it was his big head ass cousin being childish as usual. "Got y'all asses, get your bitch ass out the car Carti and come get in on this game nigga!" He yelled, while waving his Ps5 controller around.

Letting his window down, Cartier flicked him off. "I never seen a nigga so eager to get his ass whooped, we bettin?" Cartier questioned as his cousin leaned more into the car.

"You already kno'." He smirked, before looking behind Cartier at Naomi. "This yo new ole' lady Carti?"

Smiling, Cartier looked over at Naomi as well before nodding. "Yeah, this my baby, Nao, meet my big head ass cousin Kevin."

"How are you, beautiful?" He questioned causing Cartier to smack his teeth.

"Cut that out nigga." Cartier mumbled.

Laughing, Naomi reached her hand over for a handshake. "I'm doing alright, nice to meet you."

"Likewise baby girl, but don't let these folks scare you off. Today we're just drunk and in our element, we mean no harm with half the shit we gon' say." He told her. "But aight kinfolk I'll see you inside."

"Ight bet, give us five minutes." Slapping hands with him, Cartier soon let his window up and turned off his car.

Getting out of the car together, Cartier waited until she walked from around the car and grabbed her hand to lead her inside.

Soon as they walked inside the home, the smell of soul food danced around their noses. Naomi's mouth watered at the thought of eating. As they continued making their way through the house, the sound of folks talking and laughing filled her ears and that southern family atmosphere roamed the room.

You had folks either sitting around talking, dancing, drinking, playing cards, or dominoes- Naomi was loving it all.

When they reached the kitchen Naomi was almost blown away at how big it was. Her kitchen was something you would see in a magazine, and she had it decorated so beautifully with pictures of her family and bible scriptures all over.

"Now I just know my eyes are not deceiving me right now." Looking in the direction of where the voice came from, Naomi smiled when she saw an older woman approaching them. "I had a feeling that was you, hey baby, who is this pretty girl?" She questioned as she looked in between the two with a warm smile on her face.

"TT this my girl Naomi, Naomi this my Aunty Shanda." He introduced.

Looking at him shocked, she frowned. The last girlfriend anyone had heard about or even seen was Chardonnay and Shanda didn't even know they had called things off. "Your girl? What happened—You know what, it doesn't even matter. It's nice to meet you Naomi," Shanda greeted warmly.

Reaching her hand out, Naomi smiled back. "It's nice to meet you as well."

Pushing her hand away, Shanda pulled her in for a hug instead. "Baby you don't have to be all formal with me, we treat everyone like family over here." She replied before releasing her. "But I ain't gon' hold y'all up, I'm sure the rest of the family is anxious to meet Miss Naomi, but again I'm Shanda and if you need anything just let me know."

Thanking her, Cartier grabbed Naomi's hand and led them further into the kitchen where his mom was cooking. Naomi felt her nerves kick in and her hands started to sweat the closer they got to her.

She was oblivious to them being in there, so Naomi took that time to admire her, she was breathtakingly beautiful, and she was amazed at how much Cartier resembled her.

"Mama!" Cartier called out instantly, catching her attention.

Naomi stood off to the side and watched as she quickly washed her hands, before walking over and embracing him into a big hug. "I thought you said you weren't going to make it," She heard her say as they pulled away from each other still holding hands.

Laughing, Cartier turned towards Naomi. "I wanted to surprise you and introduce you to someone very special to me." Bringing her over to where Naomi was standing, Naomi tried to mentally prepare herself. "Mama this is my girlfriend Naomi, baby this is my beautiful and crazy mama." He introduced.

Cartier's mom held the same confused facial expression as his Aunt Shanda since the last girlfriend she had met was Chardonnay and Cartier never said anything to her about the two breaking up.

She wasn't complaining or anything since she didn't care too much for Chardonnay, but she was a little curious as to when this relationship between Naomi and Cartier began. "Hello Miss Naomi, it's a pleasure to meet you sweetheart."

"It's so nice to meet you as well, Mrs. Wil—"

"Chile, you can call me Mama Joyce." She stated as she brought her in for a hug. "I'm loving this outfit by the way."

Smiling, Naomi looked down at herself. "Thank you."

"You're welcome baby, but the food is almost ready. Carti, go show her around the house and let her meet everybody, I'll let y'all know when it's time to eat." She smiled. "Oh, and baby if you could take this pan of mac and cheese down to the basement for me, I would greatly appreciate that."

"Yeah, I gotchu ma."

Grabbing the pan of mac and cheese, Naomi followed behind Cartier down to the basement where a group of guys and girls were chilling on a sectional couch, playing NBA 2k. On the other side were a row of tables where the food would be placed.

"Hey Aunt Molly, mama wanted me to bring you this." Cartier explained.

"Thank you, baby, just sit it over there on the table with the pan of yams and greens." She instructed. "How have you been by the way?"

Walking back over towards her, Cartier smiled as he threw his arm around Naomi. "I've been good, I want you to meet my girlfriend Naomi tho."

"Hi sweetie, nice to meet you."

"It's nice to meet you as well, this food smells and looks amazing by the way." She complimented.

"Be sure to try my potato salad and tell me whatchu think." She winked.

"I will."

Walking over to where the couches were, Naomi politely smiled at everyone as they took a seat. "What up bitch ass niggas? Who got next?" Cartier asked before pulling out an already rolled blunt from behind his ear.

"What's up nigga? When did you get here?" One guy spoke up.

"Not too long ago, but aye y'all this my girl Naomi, Naomi this my cousin Duke, my older brother Quentin, my cousin Kev, Kev girl Cedes, and my annoying ass cousins Genesis and Jewell."

"Yo girl? Uh un since when? You love popping your ass up with surprises." Genesis joked as she reached over to hug Naomi.

"You just nosey, all that matters is she's my girl now."

Genesis smiled. "So, miss thang is finally out of the picture, I see."

"Yup, onto bigger and better things now." Cartier smiled before kissing the side of Naomi's face.

"Who are we talking about?" Naomi questioned.

"Nobody important, shut up G. Messy ass." Cartier mumbled.

"You know I never liked that girl, hell at least Naomi has a sense for fashion. Like, I am living for this entire outfit you have on."

Naomi laughed, "Thank you girl, but so do you! I have to ask, where'd you get those shoes?"

As they continued talking, Cartier focused on the game, not interested in hearing their conversation. Glancing around the room and smiling at his family he had gone a while without seeing, his smile instantly dropped when he locked eyes with Cedes who was giving him the death glare. Avoiding eye contact, he looked away already knowing why she was looking at him like that, and he hoped like hell she didn't start any drama tonight, especially in front of Naomi. Deciding to go upstairs to chop it with his mama real quick, Cartier let Naomi know where he was going before leaving once he saw she was in good hands with Genesis and Jewel.

Speaking to a few family members he passed along the way towards the kitchen, Cartier smiled at the sight of his mama in her element. One thing his mama always loved doing was cooking, it was one of the many things that made her happy and Cartier loved seeing her like this.

"Just the person I was looking for, have a seat real quick." His mama stated when she saw him walk in.

Taking a seat at one of the bar stools, Joyce smiled as she handed him a small plate with a piece of chicken on it. "Try that for me and tell me what you think, I tried a new recipe."

Taking a bite out of it, he nodded. "This shit good as hell mama, you gotta me run that recipe forreal."

"Okay good and I will, but first tell me about this Naomi girl. When did this relationship come about and what happened between you and Chardonnay?" Joyce asked.

Joyce was all for Cartier finding love, but something about this just didn't feel right and she needed to know what was up right now. Sighing, Cartier sat back in his seat. "I've been seeing Naomi for a few months now and things between Chardonnay and I are complicated. We decided to take some time apart from each other, but we never really broke things off completely."

Shaking her head, Joyce threw a towel at him. "You know I've raised you better than that, why would you even allow yourself to fall for another woman when you aren't even done with the previous woman in your life? What if Naomi finds out? You don't think that would hurt her son? Like are you even thinking or considering either of their feelings if they found out about one another?" His mama spat.

Joyce was really disappointed in Cartier and the way he was going about things. She didn't care too much for Chardonnay, but she would have rather him break things off completely with her before moving on.
"Mama, I know—"

"Clearly you don't! Here you are introducing this girl to your family and bringing her around, knowing you are still technically in a whole relationship with another woman. I don't care how bad or toxic a relationship is or how much you want to leave that person, until you actually walk away from that relationship, and it's understood on both ends that it's over- you do not bring somebody else into the picture, because in the end someone will get hurt!" She snapped, cutting him off, she didn't want to hear a single excuse come out of his mouth.

"Mama, I know I fucked up by bringing Naomi into this situation knowing that things between Chardonnay and I are unfinished, but I honestly couldn't help it ma', she's amazing and I love being around her. I feel she is the one for me and I do want to be with her." He admitted truthfully.

"That's beautiful and all baby, and I'm happy that you found someone who makes you happy. But the question still remains the same, what are you going to do about your situation with Chardonnay?"

Looking down Cartier shrugged, "I really don't know ma', and I know that sounds fucked up, but you know Char and I have been through a lot and at the end of the day I do love that girl shit is just complicated all around." He sighed.

"Have you and her had sex yet?"

Looking at his mama confused, Cartier frowned in disgust. "What the hell ma'? That's personal information."

"Boy hush up, we're both grown, and I know you ain't no virgin, so, answer the damn question." She demanded.

Rolling his eyes, Cartier let out a deep breath. "We haven't yet."

"Good and keep it that way until you figure out what it is you're going to do with Chardonnay! The last thing a woman wants to do is give her body to someone and then find out some fucked up shit afterwards. At the end of the day, I just don't want to see anybody get hurt, including you. You're playing a dangerous game with people's emotions and that's not right at all, you're better than that baby." She expressed before turning away to finish cooking.

Not saying anything else, Cartier let his mother's words play in his mind. Everything she said was right and he knew he was wrong, but at the moment he didn't have the answers to any of his problems. He still needed time to figure out exactly what he wanted to do. Downstairs in the basement Naomi, Genesis, and Jewel had hit it off real good, just simply talking about whatever came to mind. It was like they've all known each other their whole lives and Naomi simply loved meeting people she could easily connect and vibe with.

She felt a set of eyes burning a hole in her face as she talked, Naomi scanned the room to meet eyes with Cedes, which confused her since she hadn't said much of anything to her, she wasn't sure what her issue was.

Feeling a touch on her knee, Naomi looked over to Genesis who was shaking her head. "Girl don't mind her, she's just really protective of her friend." Genesis said, typing away on her phone.

"Who's her friend?"

"Cartier's ex Genesis was talking about earlier. They're good friends so with you being his new girl she's not too fond of you, so don't take it personal." His cousin Jewell said, chiming in on the conversation. Naomi nodded taking in all this information, it was all starting to make sense why everyone was so shocked to see her when clearly, they were used to him being with someone else.

"Noted." She mumbled.

"So where did you and Cartier meet? I ain't trying to be in y'all business or anything, but I just would like to know more about who my cousin is dating, especially since this was kinda just sprung on us." Jewell asked. Since Naomi was now aware that the family wasn't expecting her, she knew she had to make a good first impression, especially since everybody was already comparing her to Cartier's ex.

"We actually met a few months ago at my brother's birthday party." Naomi answered.

"Girl, which friend of his is your brother?" Jewell asked even more intrigued in the conversation. Jewell was obsessed with the family business and wanted to date a man that was just as ruthless as her father.

"Snoop."

"Damn, that's your brother? I'm not gonna lie, he's fine as hell." Genesis stated.

Naomi laughed, she was used to females taking a liking to her brother, but she just didn't understand what it is they saw, "Not at all." She frowned.

"Of course, you would say that, he's your brother." Genesis laughed.

"But he ain't mine and I most def agree with G, your brother could have his way with me anytime, anyplace." She joked as both her and Genesis slapped hands agreeing.

Shaking her head and laughing at their dramatics, Naomi focused in on the guys playing the game and she noticed Cartier had returned, but she really admired how relaxed and at peace he looked. Sometimes even when they're together, alone he just seems so stressed, so to see him laugh and joke around without a care in the world brought a smile to her face.

"Come eat!!" Cartier's Aunt Shanda yelled.

Everybody wasted no time running towards the food like vultures, especially the men. Naomi laughed as they were bumping kids and women out the way to get a plate, but that only annoyed Cartier's mom.

"If y'all don't back y'all black asses up and let them kids eat first and then the women. Y'all men know better." She snapped. "Acting like y'all ain't ate a meal in days."

Now front in line Naomi had one of his aunts hook her up with a little bit of everything. The food smelled and looked so good she couldn't resist. "I see we don't have a salad eater over here." One of his aunts joked as they placed some mac and cheese on her plate.

"Damn right, trust me I ain't missing no meals." Naomi joked back, making them all laugh.

"I know that's right! Here you go baby, I hope you enjoy it!" His aunt replied as she handed her plate to her. Walking back upstairs where almost everybody was seated at the dining table, Naomi took her seat next to Cartier who had already started eating. Shaking her head at him, Naomi almost popped him since he knows they need to say their grace, but his mom beat her to it.

"Don't make me slap you Carti." She threatened, before she stood up from her seat calling everyone's attention.

Laughing, Naomi nudged his shoulder as he waved her off. That was one thing his mama and Naomi were good at doing, love trying to put him in his place and if he didn't care for them as much as he did, he would not let it slide.

"Alright everyone I really can't thank y'all enough for coming out today. I love y'all so much and seeing you all here really makes me happy." She started. "But I know y'all ready to eat, so come on, gather hands and bow y'all heads."

Holding onto Cartier's and Quentin's hands, she eventually bowed her head when she saw everyone else doing it. "Dear heavenly Father, we have gathered here today to share a meal in your honor and to give thanks to you for allowing us to be together as a family, and of course for blessing us with this food. Please bless this food with your hands and make sure that it doesn't hurt, harm, or danger our bodies, Lord. Guide our mealtime conversations and please steer our hearts to the purpose you have for our lives. In Jesus name, we may ask it all, amen."

"Amen" everybody said in unison before they all started eating.

Taking a bite out of the baked mac and cheese, Naomi almost moaned from how good it was. Her favorite part of any family gatherings or cookouts was the mac and cheese and his family certainly put their foot in this.

As everyone ate and talked amongst each other, that once nervous feeling Naomi had slowly faded away. His family was so welcoming and loving, which was something totally different than what she experienced with Deandre's family. So to have Cartier express the importance of her to his family was another check in her book of reasons to like him.

"So, Naomi, how long have you and Cartier been dating?" Cedes asked her, wasting no time on getting the scope as she took a bite of her chicken.

With this being a question everyone wanted to know, all eyes landed on Naomi as they awaited her answer.

Wiping her mouth, Naomi cut her eyes at Cedes who simply smirked as she waited for her to answer.

"You ain't gotta ans-"

"We've been dating for a few months now." Naomi answered, cutting off Cartier.

Naomi already knew Cedes could care less about her and Cartier's relationship, so she wasn't even about to entertain her pettiness.

"A few months huh? And you've been hiding her from me all this time?" His mama asked, hitting him on his arm.

"I had to make sure she was the real deal before meeting y'all," Cartier responded with a mouthful of food.

“Well, I like her already.” She replied, giving Naomi a smile that she gladly returned, happy that his mom liked her.

“I second that.” His aunt Shanda spoke. “She seems very respectful and loving.”

“Dang the girl has only been here two seconds, it’s really too soon for anyone to really know if she’s a good fit for Carti.” Cedes blurted out rudely. “Plus, we all know how Cartier gets down, she could be here one day and gone the next, and a new girl will already be on his arm. Cartier switches women like he switches his damn drawls!” Cedes dissed as she took a sip from her canned mountain dew.

“Chill the fuck out!” Cartier snapped. “Kev, getcho girl man forreal.”

“Yeah baby, chill out, was all that even fuckin’ necessary?” Kevin asked before apologizing to Cartier and Naomi for Cede's actions.

“I’m just saying, I *know* you, Cartier.” She replied as both her and Cartier held an intense look between one another.

“What is she talking about?” Naomi asked quietly so no one else could hear.

Shaking his head, Cartier sighed. “I’ll explain later.”

Deciding to drop whatever issue Cedes was trying to start, Naomi continued to enjoy herself and got to know the rest of Cartier’s family in which she adored very much. They were all so funny and made her feel a part of the family already. Cedes continued trying to be petty, but eventually everyone just paid her no mind and focused their attention elsewhere. Once everyone finished eating, people eventually cleaned up their mess and went back to doing their previous activities.

Leaving Naomi in the dining area with the ladies, Cartier got up and took a seat next to his Uncle Pernell who was sitting in the living room watching basketball with his Uncle Rome and a few of his cousins.

“You finally were able to sneak away from Womanville up there I see.” Pernell joked as he slapped hands with Cartier.

“Man, every time I tried to leave, they found a reason to make me stay.” He sighed. “But what do y’all think of Naomi so far?” Cartier was genuinely curious as to what they thought about her, he felt Naomi was the perfect woman for him, but he wanted to know if they felt the same

Cartier valued his uncle's opinions very much since they both were good at reading people and knowing who was real and who wasn't. Especially with the type of lifestyle they lived, he knew he needed someone around him he could trust, and he knew if they felt Naomi couldn't be trusted, they would tell him.

"She seems like a really sweet girl, especially compared to that Chardonnay girl. She's not like that girl at all, when you first brought her around here I could read right through her and something about her was just sneaky. Naomi on the other hand seems genuine and it's clear ya mama and aunties feel the same." Rome replied before focusing back on the television.

"I agree, but does she really know what she's getting herself into? I mean what you need to make sure of is if she's even ready for your lifestyle. Not everybody can handle the life of a kingpin and it's better to find that out sooner than later." Pernell shared.

Rome nodded in agreement. He didn't like the choice that Cartier made to follow in their steps of taking over the business, but he felt if he was going to do it, he wanted him to do things right, and that meant making sure whoever he had on his side was solid and wouldn't fold on him when needed.

"I mean I personally feel she is ready; this type of lifestyle isn't new to her." Cartier stated.

"That may be true, but I'm sure it's not something she has ever had to deal with on a daily basis. It took your aunt a minute to adjust to this lifestyle as well, because it ain't easy and can be very stressful and demanding at times. I feel before you two go any further, y'all need to have this talk." Rome stated sternly.

Sitting there in his thoughts thinking about what they said and the question he never really cared to think about started to replay in his mind. Glancing over at her as she laughed and talked with his aunties, Cartier started to wonder if Naomi was truly ready to be the wife of a kingpin and if she wasn't, was she worth leaving all this behind, in hopes of not losing her?

Naomi joined Cartier's mama in the kitchen to help her cut the slices of cake, so Joyce wanted to use this as an opportunity to learn a little bit more about her privately.

"So, Naomi, tell me what are your intentions with my boy?" She asked while taking out a Sock-it to me cake and strawberry cheesecake.

"I like him a lot. But I'm not gonna lie, at first I was a little skeptical about getting involved with him, but he has managed to prove that anything he has ever told me he meant. And I'm all for a man backing his words with actions to make me feel special and he has done just that and more. In the long run, I hope to see us all grow with one another and become a family. I haven't had the best experience with men, but Cartier has shown me the difference of what it is like being with a boy compared to being with a man. I gotta say you truly raised your son properly." Naomi smiled.

"Thank you and I really love how you didn't mention anything about his money or having kids. I like the fact that you appreciate his efforts in trying, because Lord I know my baby is far from perfect but he's a good person at the end of the day and I'm grateful that you see the good in him."

"Going after a man simply behind what he has in his pockets is shallow to me. I wouldn't want Cartier doing anything for me that I can't do for myself because at the end of the day, with or without him, I know I'ma be good, plus the last thing I need right now is a baby." Naomi joked but was slightly serious.

With her just escaping that bad situation with Dre, having kids was the last thing on her mind. She at least wanted to be a little more established within her career and relationship with Cartier before ever considering having a child. If her and Cartier didn't work, she didn't want to be labeled as just his baby mama.

"But you do want kids eventually, right? I would love some grandbabies running around here." His mom laughed.

"It all depends on when your son decides to place a ring on my finger, then he can have as many kids as he wants." Naomi joked.

Slapping hands with her, his mama shook her head laughing. "I know that's right. Smart girl." She pointed before going back to slicing pieces of cake.

In the midst of them placing slices of cake on plates, Cartier made his way inside the kitchen, smiling at the sight of Naomi and his mama getting along so well.

Just as much as he valued his uncle's opinions, gaining his mom's approval meant a lot as well. So, seeing them both bond and connect the way they did told him everything he needed to know about Naomi.

"Hey baby, I'm sorry I'm holding Miss Naomi hostage." Joyce stated. "But she has been a big help today, keeping me company."

"It's all good, I was actually about to let you know we finna head out," he said, pulling his mom in for a hug.

"Boy you are always on the damn go, stay a little a while longer." She fussed.

Joyce barely saw Cartier that much since he spent a lot of time running around in the streetz, so any moment she got with him she wanted him to stay as long as he could. Her biggest fear was whenever he would walk out her door it might be the last time, which is why she hated that he chose to stick with the family business. It constantly had her thinking the worst.

"I'ma stop by and see you tomorrow, but I actually got something else planned for Naomi today." He explained.

Letting out a sigh, she nodded. "Alright, you better stop by and see me tomorrow." Hugging him, she kissed him on the cheek, then turned her attention to Naomi.

"It was so nice to meet you Naomi, you're more than welcome to stop by anytime with or without Cartier you hear me?" Going in for a hug, Naomi smiled.

"It was nice meeting you too and alright I'll keep that mind, might come show you my infamous mac and cheese."

"Please do." She smiled as they pulled away from the hug.

Making their rounds around the house, Naomi and Cartier said their goodbyes to everybody so they could leave on a good note.

Standing outside his car Naomi and Genesis exchanged numbers, while Cartier chopped it up with his uncles about business.

"Girl, please don't be a stranger, we gotta hang out sometime." Genesis told her. "You, me and Jewel."

"I promise I won't, I'll text you." Sharing a quick hug goodbye, Genesis eventually made her way back inside the house.
When Cartier noticed Naomi getting inside the car, he immediately ended the conversation with his uncles and hopped inside. "I'll call y'all tomorrow."

After they slapped hands and said their goodbyes to Naomi, his uncles eventually walked off towards their cars to leave as well.

Pulling out of the driveway, Cartier looked over at Naomi who was looking out the window smiling. “You enjoyed yourself today?” He asked.

Glancing at him, she nodded. “I really love your family," She started. “They made me feel welcomed and right at home. Your mom and aunts are so sweet.”

“I’m happy to hear that, they all enjoyed you as well.” He smiled.

“All except Cedes.” Naomi rolled her eyes before looking out the window.

“Fuck Cedes, don’t nobody care about what she thinks.” Cartier spat.

“What was her problem anyways? Like I know she’s friends with your ex, but damn can people not move on?” Naomi asked, alerting Cartier since he didn’t know Naomi knew Cedes was friends with Chardonnay.

“How did you know she was friends with my ex?” He asked, trying to see how much she knew.

“Genesis told me.”

Nodding his head, Cartier focused back on the road. “What else did they tell you?”

Naomi shrugged. “Nothing really, but it was clear everybody was shocked to see me though. How long have you and your ex been broken up?”

Cartier sighed. “We ended things a little bit before I met you.” He lied.

Cartier knew he could not fix his mouth to admit that he and Chardonnay weren’t really broken up; yes, they agreed that they needed some time apart, but they never officially broke things off.

Deciding not to ask any more questions regarding his ex, since it was clear he didn’t want to talk about it, Naomi changed the subject. “So where are we going now?” She asked.

“Wherever you want to go.” He shrugged.

"We can go back to my place." She replied softly, starting to become a little nervous for some odd reason.

When they reached her apartment and made it up to her door, Cartier was all over Naomi and she couldn't lie and say she wasn't enjoying the attention. With her back pressed up against the front door, he had his arms wrapped around her waist and stared down at her with those beautiful, intoxicating eyes of his.

"I really enjoyed you today," His voice was deep and low. He was so close; the scent of his cologne breezed its way up her nose, sending her hormones into a frenzy.

"I enjoyed you too." She replied, blushing as she looked down and began playing with her nails to avoid eye contact.

Using his hand, he lifted her head by chin forcing her to look back at him, before gently wrapping his hand around her neck and pulling her closer until their lips met.

Letting him take full control, he slipped his tongue inside her mouth while using his free hand to caress and grope her body.

Pulling away, Naomi reached for her keys to unlock her door as Cartier wiped his mouth that was covered with her lip gloss. When she unlocked and opened the door, Naomi looked back at him before grabbing him by the hand and pulling him inside.

Locking the door behind him, Cartier followed her to her room as she turned on a few lights. "Would you like something to drink?" She asked.

Taking a seat on the edge of her bed, Cartier ignored her question and pulled her in between his legs. Gripping her butt firmly in his hands, Cartier leaned up so their lips could meet, which started off as a few pecks but then soon turned into a full blown make out session. With the way his hands rubbed and groped her body, Naomi had never craved a man as much as she was craving Cartier right now. Everything he was doing was turning her on and she was ready to let him have his way with her.

Pulling away from the kiss, Cartier laughed as he smacked her ass. "I'll take that drink now."

Mushing his head, Naomi walked off as he hopped up, following her into the kitchen. Reaching inside her fridge she grabbed a bottle of wine and poured them both a glass.

Joining him on the couch, she handed him his drink and sat the bottle on her coffee table before sitting back and taking a sip, letting the coolness of the drink chill her body.

They were sitting in complete silence until Cartier's phone started to vibrate in his pocket. When he pulled it out, Naomi noticed the name "Chardonnay" flash across the screen, she wondered who she was to him to be calling this late.

When he declined the call and quickly shut his phone completely off, Naomi frowned. She wanted to fix her mouth to say something, but she decided not to ruin the night by asking questions and causing a scene.

So, she made a mental note to bring it up into conversation at another time.

"I love your place by the way, I'm usually in and out whenever I come by so this is my first time really getting the chance to look around. It's really dope." Cartier complimented as he took a sip of his wine.

He wasn't much of a wine drinker himself, but this was some pretty good shit, it was already making his body feel relaxed.

"Thank you." She smiled. "I've always been told I had a small eye for interior design."

"I can tell, I need you to come decorate my shit."

Laughing, she sat her glass down before crossing her legs underneath her thighs, while slightly turning her body to face him. "What's wrong with your place? I think it looks amazing the way it is now."

Cartier shrugged. "Just in need of a change."

"Well, if you're serious I'll help you re-decorate it." She smiled.

Sitting his glass down on the coffee table beside hers, Cartier decided to stretch out on the couch and lay his head in her lap as he stared up at her.

Naturally, Naomi began rubbing his head and the side of his face as he laid there with his eyes closed feeling at peace.

Feeling that liquid courage rise within her, Naomi soon bent her head down and placed a small kiss on his lips, which alerted him to open his eyes.

She then continued kissing different parts of his face, his cheeks, forehead and nose.

Cartier found her shyness really cute to him, everything she did was always so gentle and subtle.

Naomi softly tapped him to move up, Cartier did as she wanted, sitting upright. Naomi immediately climbed into his lap, she caught him by surprise.

At this point she was feeling bold and knew what they both wanted. She was tired of trying to act like the sexual tension between them wasn't there, her body needed this. She had been craving the touch of man for the past few months, and although she would be breaking her vow of celibacy, she felt Cartier was worth it. She pressed her lips against his and began helping him remove his shirt and unbuckle his pants. Cartier raised himself up so he could pull them all the way down. Naomi used that moment to strip out of the jumpsuit she had on, remaining only in her bra and panties.

Cartier stood up and made his way to Naomi. They laid back on the couch as he hovered over her, trailing his wet lips down her body. Kissing the exposed part of her breasts, Cartier soon reached behind her and unclasped her bra. When his tongue met her breast, Naomi gripped the back of his head as he sucked and swirled his tongue around her nipple, using his free hand to play with the other. But he didn't stop there. Cartier explored her entire body with his mouth. When he reached her legs, he raised them up and slightly spread them apart, kissing her feet to the inner part of her thighs, inching closer and closer to her vagina.

Cartier kissed the lace on her panties that covered her lips. Naomi slightly moaned and grew anxious when he began sliding them off, exposing her freshly waxed honey pot, leaving her completely naked underneath him.

The throbbing sensation Naomi was feeling became unbearable the longer she waited for him. He dipped his head low, and his tongue encountered her clit. Naomi immediately threw her head back as he began sucking and flicking his tongue on her clit.

Inserting two fingers inside her, Cartier continued teasing her clit while sliding his fingers in and out of her, slowly. Naomi arched her back off the couch moaning uncontrollably.

"Fuck," she moaned, biting her lip as she looked down to see him eating what seemed to be his best meal of the night.

With her eyes tightly clenched shut, the grip Naomi had on the back of his head pushed him down further. She moaned out his name because she felt the pressure of an orgasm coming along. Tears threatened to fall from her eyes as he continued working his fingers inside of her.

"I think I'm gonna cum." She moaned out as her legs began to shake uncontrollably and her moans grew louder.

Cartier raised up just when she was about to cum and laughed to himself before motioning for her to move. Dropping the boxer briefs he wore, his dick sprung out, ready for showtime. Naomi sat there in disbelief at how big he was.

Using one hand to stroke himself slowly, Naomi watched, becoming wetter at the sight of it. He pulled her into him, roughly kissing her while groping her ass.

Pulling away, Naomi pushed him back down on the couch before dropping to her knees. Cartier stared down at her with low hooded eyes, slightly moaning as she began sucking and licking the tip of his dick.

She licked up and down the sides of his dick as if it were an ice cream cone before orally taking all he had to offer; bobbing her head back and forth, she caressed his dick with her hands at the same time. He... lost... it.

His toes started to curl, and inaudible cuss words left his mouth as she sucked the soul out of his dick, wetting him up with her spit.

He watched her intensely as she swallowed him whole, bucking his hips, he started fucking her mouth and making his dick hit the back of her throat. Naomi gagged but she loved it. She let him have control for a little while and then pulled his dick out her mouth, spat on it and made it sloppy.

Each time she pulled it out, the spit left a trail from her mouth to his tip, which sent him into overdrive. Naomi stroked him with her hands, and bobbed her head up and down, making his dick repeatedly hit the back of her throat. Cartier couldn't control the moans and curse words that left his mouth.

Giving head was something Naomi enjoyed because she got to be in control. She knew a man's penis was the weakest thing on his body; once you have control of that, he's yours.

She loved when Cartier moaned and groaned and ruffled her hair as she gave him head, it confirmed that she was doing good. The way his body shifted to keep himself from busting was another favorite of hers as well.

He felt his dick jerk a little, and thought she would have stopped, but that only amped her up to keep sucking him off.

Cartier busted in her mouth; she devoured his dick a little bit longer, then swallowed it all, licking the cum that was on her lips as well. He thought that shit was sexy as fuck.

Raising up off her knees, Naomi leaned forward to press her lips against his as he stared at her in a daze.

Naomi pulled him by the hand and walked him over to her bedroom. Climbing into the bed, Naomi motioned with her finger for him to come here. Laying completely on her back, Cartier stared down at her, admiring her beauty and body before lowering his head to kiss her.

"I want you inside me." Naomi whispered while piercing his soul with her eyes.

Raising up some, Cartier stared down at her, "Are you sure you're ready for this? I don't mind waiting." He reassured her.

Cartier didn't want Naomi to feel pressured into having sex with him, he was honestly willing to wait until she was ready.

"I'm ready."

Watching as she laid back, basically opening her body for him to have his way with; Cartier took a deep breath, he wasn't expecting this all to happen so soon. Wanting this to be special between them, Cartier positioned himself right at her entrance before looking back up at her.

He could tell from the look in her eyes that she was nervous, so he sweetly kissed her on the lips just as he slid in.

Naomi closed her eyes and moaned out when he started sliding in and out of her. She wrapped her legs around his torso and grabbed the back of his neck as he stroked her slowly. Naomi's eyes began to water because it felt so good.

Looking down, she watched his dick slide in and out of her before throwing her head back as he started speeding his strokes up. The sound of her headboard hitting the wall filled their ears.

“Shit, this pussy feels good as fuck ma,” Cartier groaned in her ear as he stroked in and out of her.

As their bodies became one, Naomi’s eyes began to water, she was experiencing a great deal of emotions. She had never met someone like Cartier, he was everything she ever imagined in a man. He stared back into her eyes and fucked her slowly, roughly- her body was melting.

A man had never looked at her like that before, it was like he was in love; in that moment Naomi wondered if they were in fact making love to one another.

So caught up in her emotions and thoughts, Naomi didn’t realize she was crying.

Cartier looked at her and noticed her tears, he immediately stopped his motions. “Do you want me to stop, baby?” He asked with concern laced in his voice.

The last thing he wanted to do was hurt Naomi or force her into doing something she wasn’t truly ready for.

Shaking her head, no, Naomi raised her head up to kiss him as she pulled him closer. “No, keep going.” Naomi whispered.

Cartier began stroking inside of her again, he picked up the pace and made his thrusts more powerful, her breasts were bouncing to his motions. Lifting himself up slightly, he grabbed Naomi's legs and placed them on his shoulders so he could go deeper.

When he started to hit her spot, Naomi screamed out his name. A smile appeared on Cartier’s face as he listened to the smacking of her wet pussy mimic the sound of macaroni being stirred.

“Cartier, slow down.” Naomi whined as she felt her body tense up, ready to release. Cartier ignored her and continued to speed up as he too felt himself about to nut.

The sounds of their bodies slapping together, and their moans could be heard throughout her apartment; she prayed her neighbors would not file a noise complaint.

Caressing her hard nipples, Naomi bit down on her lip. She couldn't believe the way her body was responding to Cartier. It was as if she truly didn't know herself sexually until sex with him. Naomi looked at him in his eyes and he returned the stare. As each stroke happened, a spiritual connection between them intensified, they could not break that stare. She bit her lip even harder; it was turning her on to see him drool over her.

Arching her back, she screamed out in pleasure, "oh, shit daddy I'm cumming!" as her eyes rolled back and her mouth agape.

"Fuck." Cartier groaned, cumming shortly after, still inside of her. He released his nut before sliding out, but felt the urge to slide back in.

Moving from off top of her, Cartier plopped down next to her as they stared up at the ceiling trying to catch their breaths.

Turning over, Naomi stared at the side of Cartier's face as he laid there with his eyes closed. Moving closer to him, she laid her head on his chest as he wrapped one arm around her to pull her as close as possible to him.

Listening to the sound of his heartbeat, Naomi soon closed her eyes as well, allowing the sound of it to soothe her. It was clear by now she had fallen head over heels for Cartier, which was exactly what she was afraid of.

Cartier began rubbing small circles on her back. Naomi looked up at him and he looked down at her before they shared a quick kiss. "Please don't hurt me, my heart can't take any more pain." She whispered as a tear fell from her eye.

Wiping her eyes and kissing the top of her head, Cartier hugged her tighter. "I won't baby girl. Your heart is in safe hands with me. I promise." Cartier reassured her, pulling her in closer.

Sharing another kiss, Naomi soon relaxed and fell asleep in his arms. Looking down at her as she slept, slightly snoring, Cartier knew he was fucking up big time. He had gone completely against everything his mother told him, now he was in too deep and there was no going back from it all now.

Shutting his eyes, Cartier knew he had a decision to make and fast... before somebody got hurt.

Chapter 7

Sitting on her newly purchased, Alcova Tuff bed, filing away at her nails, Chardonnay looked up, slightly confused when she saw an anxious Cedes come walking into her room full speed. Noticing her strange behavior Chardonnay sat up in the bed, studying Cedes movements, wondering what was wrong.

"Girl what the hell is wrong with you?" Chardonnay questioned putting down her nail file.

She was currently in a good mood after doing a little retail therapy; the last thing she needed was to be brought down by someone else's drama.

"I got some tea for your ass bitch!" Cedes answered excitedly as she took a seat at the edge of her bed.

Chardonnay rolled her eyes, becoming slightly annoyed. All Cedes loved to talk about now was Kevin and her baby, and all the drama that came with them. Chardonnay was happy for her friend and loved her baby as if it were her own, but sometimes she wished that shit could be like the old times.

"What did Kev do now?" Chardonnay assumed.

Laughing, Cedes shook her head. "See bitch that's what you get for assuming, this is actually about Cartier trifling ass." Cedes announced catching Chardonnay's full attention.

"Wait, what!?"

"Girl yes, so look, yesterday his mom had a little family dinner; why his ass show up with some girl named Naomi, announcing her as his girlfriend to everybody!?" She started. "So, you know I had to do some digging. I asked her how long they've been dating, cause I'm thinking maybe y'all broke it off and you just hadn't told me yet- but this bitch said they've been dating for months." Cedes explained.

Sitting there confused and dumbfounded, Chardonnay felt her blood begin to boil. She had been accusing Cartier of another woman for a while now; but now that she knows for sure it's a reality, it hit her hard because she could no longer deny or try to make excuses for what was now staring her right in the face.

"So, he had her meeting his family and everything!?"

"Yeah girl, I'm sorry you had to find out this way." Cedes responded sympathetically when she noticed Chardonnay's demeanor change. She knew that the information was starting to get to her.

In efforts to lighten the mood, she spoke again. "But sis, fuck Cartier! You can officially start fucking with Rashun, who has more money and is actually in love with you. You don't need Cartier sorry ass, hell if anything you won! Ole' girl the only one that should be worried since she clearly doesn't know who she is messing with."

"You're right! But I just can't believe that nigga played me like a fucking fool again. Talking about a break." She scoffed.

"Welcome to the real world baby; to men we come a dime a dozen."

Chardonnay fumbled with her hands, processing everything; trying to figure out what she was going to do. One thing was for sure, she was done being his fool.

"It's all good, I got something for his ass." She smiled devilishly.

Trig sat on his couch, looking over at the boxes that were sent to him a few days ago. They were filled with the remains of his two men, stuffed inside fat ass pigs; to say he sat in disbelief would be an understatement. They were the only men he personally trusted with his money; for them to have been taken out just wasn't sitting right with him.

On top of all this, he also discovered that Nassir and Cartier ran through his stash house and wiped him out. Taking one last hit of the cigarette he was smoking, he angrily put it out in his ashtray before standing up. *If they didn't think they had war before, they damn sure do now.* He wasn't stopping until he got the both of em.

"Clean this shit up." He demanded one of his housekeepers before entering his kitchen.

Trig realized that every hand he played made him a rookie. *I should've known after taking out their homeboy and shorting Cartier on business, to be on guard, to be expecting them to retaliate sooner or later. I fucked up.*

Walking into his kitchen, he saw his cousin, Porsha. She was sitting at the island, freeloading and running her mouth on the phone, which angered him even more. Trig snatched her phone from her hand and threw it against the wall, causing it to shatter.

"What the fuck is you in here doing? You still don't have not one lick of information for me on Cartier; yet you're up in my shit, eating my food, and running ya dick suckers while my shit runs dry!" Trig yelled not hiding one ounce of his anger.

Porsha rolled her eyes. "Nigga, I told you I needed some more damn time. It's not easy getting this nigga to talk or actually open up about shit. So far, I just know that he's cheating with some new bitch in town, and that across town, he has a house outside of his and Chardonnay's house, and he has this trap house where he and Snoop meet up a lot in the hood." Porsha snapped back smacking on her gum.

"You know the addresses?" Trig asked, pulling and rubbing his chin hair, as a way of soothing his fumes.

"No, but if you take me there, I can show you." She answered, paying more attention to her nails than the conversation at hand, not really caring.

Trig grabbed her by the throat and stared into her eyes. "Find out who the new bitch is and get me some more information on what's going on, over there at the trap house! I don't want to see your ass until you do. Understood?"

Growing scared at the tight hold he had around her neck and the look in his eyes, she quickly nodded and stuttered in response before leaving the kitchen the moment he released her, "Y-y-yes."

Reaching inside his fridge, Trig poured himself some orange juice before returning to his bedroom. Quickly adjusting his mood- so his girlfriend wouldn't ask any questions, he forced a smile on his face.

Looking up when the door opened, Trig knew by the look on her face that she could sense something was wrong. "Everything ok?" She questioned as she sat up in the bed after hearing him yelling moments ago.

"Yeah boo. I'm cool." Trig reassured her as he climbed into the bed to snuggle up under her, she began massaging his back, this really put him at ease.

When Trig first started messing around with *Chardonnay*, it was all a scheme to get closer to Cartier and find out more information regarding his business.

However, things between them got a lot more serious, and he felt as if she was indeed the woman of his dreams; so, to save her, he canceled the plans he first had and went a different route using Porsha instead.

Once it was revealed how wandering Cartier's eyes could be, Trig honestly thought Chardonnay would've left Cartier for him, but she had deeper feelings than what he knew. Chardonnay's really a good woman in Trig's eyes, the only thing he wanted to do was love her in a way that Cartier never would.

So now, he's just patiently waiting for her to recognize her worth.

When his phone started to ring, Trig excused himself before walking into his master bathroom to take the call. "Hello?"

"What the fuck is going on man?" His right-hand Benny asked, cutting right into conversation.

"I underestimated that nigga Capone and his crew. Whole time I'm thinking these niggas laying low, turns out they were plotting on our asses." Trig whispered-yelled, trying to keep his voice at a minimum.

"So, what's the move? What are we doing?"

"Meet me in about an hour." Trig responded before ending the call.

When he opened the door and stepped out of the bathroom, Chardonnay quickly jumped on the bed.

"Was she listening to my conversation?" He thought.

Shaking off his assumptions, he joined her and pulled her into his arms as he relaxed on the bed. Enjoying the moment, a contemplating Chardonnay looked at him, debating if she should release what's on her mind.

"Who was on the phone?" Chardonnay asked, not wanting to overthink herself into an argument.

She thought it was very suspicious for him to get up and leave the room to talk on the phone. Cartier used to do that, and she soon found out it was because he was talking to other women.

"Business." Trig answered nonchalantly.

He didn't want Chardonnay involved in any of his illegal affairs because it was the best way of protecting her; he also didn't know where her loyalty lied when it came to him and Cartier, if she ever had to choose.

The less she knew about him, the better. Biting his lips, Trig thought, *this shit getting deep!*

ɱ

Naomi watched as Cartier rested peacefully in her bed. They became inseparable after having sex that night. Naomi still felt her feelings towards him growing by the day; she always wanted to be around him, even if they weren't doing anything, she just liked being in his presence.

Trailing the tips of her nails up and down his back, Naomi sighed to herself. Cartier simply wasn't like most dudes out there; he always made her feel respected, safe, and loved anytime she was around him- which was a feeling Naomi wasn't used to, so she was a little scared.

When she was with Deandre, she never felt respected, safe or even loved by him; to finally experience the love she has been wanting for so long felt surreal.

Naomi stared at Cartier as he began to wake up. He peeped Naomi looking at him when he opened his eyes, they both smiled at each other.

"You love staring at a nigga huh?" Cartier asked, pulling her in closer.

"I can't help that my man is fine." She blushed before pressing her lips against his for a quick kiss.

"Good morning baby." Cartier replied as he pulled away from the kiss.

"Good morning, are you hungry? I was about to cook me some breakfast real quick." Naomi asked, while watching him begin to sit up.

Before Cartier could fix his lips to respond, his phone began to ring. Looking at the name Chardonnay pop up again, Naomi watched as he ignored it and put his phone on silent.

"Who's Chardonnay?" Naomi asked, she was dying to know at this point since she kept calling so clearly, she was somebody to him.

"What?" Cartier asked, surprised.

"She's been calling you a lot and I just wanna know who she is. So, who is she?" Naomi asked him again.

"She's just a friend." He said, before he placed a kiss on her lips. "You have nothing to worry about, I promise."

She twisted her lips and thought maybe he was right. She convinced herself that maybe she was reaching for shit due to being in bad relationships prior to Cartier.

Things shouldn't be that way. She then instantly regretted even bringing it up. She hoped he didn't think of her as insecure or crazy.

Noticing the look on her face, Cartier kissed her lips again. "I know you've been through a lot, but I promise that you're in good hands with me, alright?"

Nodding her head, she let out a sigh. "I'm sorry."

"No need to be sorry baby, I understand. What have you got planned for the day?" He asked her as he flipped her covers back and got up from the bed and began getting dressed.

Wrapping her naked body in the sheets. "I'm finally going to see my parents, what about you?"

"You haven't seen your people yet? And nothing, just handling business and meeting up with Nas later."

"Nope." Naomi responded. "There's some issues we're having right now."

"I get it, well I hope everything goes well with your folks today." He replied with a smile.

Naomi watched him finish getting dressed and decided to run herself a shower as well to go ahead and get her day started.

When he was dressed and ready to leave, Naomi walked him to the door, so she could lock up behind him. Bringing her into a hug, Cartier kissed her passionately before pulling away, "I'll see you later baby, be sure to call and tell me how things go with your folks." He told her before leaving out.

"I will."

Walking back into her bedroom, Naomi hopped in the shower to get ready. She used this time to mentally prepare herself for a talk with her parents. She had pushed it back long enough and knew deep down that her distance and behavior wasn't fair to them.

After she was officially ready, Naomi wasted no time in heading out; before she knew it, she was parked outside her parents' brownstone.

Looking at the place she used to call home, Naomi sighed. She felt butterflies in her stomach playing a game of kickball. Naomi couldn't deny, nor say she didn't love her parents. During the time she spent been avoiding them, she missed them dearly. She was honestly just too ashamed to face them after everything that happened.

Finally mustering up the courage to go inside, Naomi got out of her car, walked towards the front door, and pulled out the gate key that they gave to her.

After unlocking the door, Naomi pushed it open, instantly feeling that wave of nostalgia come over her as she looked around. Everything still looked the exact same from when she and Nassir were kids.

"Mama? Daddy?" She called out as she continued making her way through the house.

"In the kitchen, baby." Her mom, Mary yelled back.

Naomi smiled as she stared at the backside of her mom. A rush of happiness reminded her why she had to come. Naomi hugged her tightly, her mom smiled as she turned around to face her.

Wrapping her arms securely around Naomi, her mom held onto her as they hugged in silence. "I'm sorry, mama," Naomi whispered, her eyes swelling up with tears as they began rocking back and forth.

Pulling away from the hug, her mom held onto her hands, "What are you sorry for?"

"I should've come and seen you guys, but I was too ashamed to face y'all after everything that happened, I'm so sorry for that." She sniffled.

Laughing, Mary wiped her tears away before motioning her to sit down. "We both knew eventually you'd come around when you were ready to do so; all that matters is you're here now." She smiled.

Naomi was starting to feel a lot better about being back home as Mary continued preparing breakfast. "So, what have you been up to these days since you've been back?" Her mom asked, sitting a cup of apple juice in front of her.

"Nothing mama, just working and focusing on getting back to who I was before, but better. What about y'all? How's the family?" She questioned, before taking a sip of her juice.

"We've been doing well, baby. You know your cousin June might be having a baby soon." Her mom spilled as she turned off the stove and began fixing their plates.

Almost choking on her juice, Naomi started coughing; she wasn't expecting that news at all. "She's about to have a what!?" She questioned in disbelief.

"Yup, you heard me correctly. Your aunty called me last night, freaking out about it."

Naomi shook her head; she wasn't too happy at the news of her little cousin having a baby, especially since she was still a baby herself. June was only sixteen, the last thing Naomi would've ever wanted for her at this age was a baby. Sadly, this news wasn't too surprising since her aunt hadn't been the best role model for her kids.

Despite her aunty being very successful in her career, when it came to raising her kids, they were never top priority. If it wasn't about her career or the multiple men she had coming in and out of her house, she could care less.

Mary sat Naomi's plate directly in front of her, Naomi wasted no time diggin' in. Her plate consisted of her mom's infamous pancakes (she used to make them all the time for her and Nassir), bacon, cheese grits and sausage special; the scent of it all brought back memories.

Taking a seat next to her, Mary shook her head at her daughter. "I see someone has been away from mama a little too long, eating before saying your grace?" Mary questioned, raising her eyebrow.

Realizing how rude of herself it was, she quickly apologized and wiped her mouth. After Cartier left, Naomi forgot to grab something to eat, she was starving.

"I'm sorry, mama,"

Locking hands, Mary and Naomi silently prayed over the food before diggin' into their plates. However, as they dug into their plates, Mary wanted to use this time to dig a little into her daughter's life.

She was happy to see Naomi of course, but not seeing her baby for so long constantly had her mind wondering what she was up to, and how things were; she needed answers now.

"So, what's his name?" Mary asked briefly before taking a bite of her bacon.

"What are you talking about mama?" Naomi asked, laughing.

"You think I was born yesterday or something? Chile, I know you better than you know yourself. Come up in here grinning, skin glowing with your spirits higher than the clouds. I'm not saying that isn't good, but I know it wasn't Jesus alone that contributed to your smile. She teased.

Naomi could only sigh, she hated how well her mama knew her at times, but this was one of the many things that made them close.

"Since you must know, his name is Cartier." Naomi admitted. She already knew there was no point in lying. Her mama knew any and everybody's business, any type of gossip to be heard, Mary was gon' be the first to know.

"Cartier? Cartier as in Cartier Williams, Nassir's friend, Cartier?" She asked to clarify.

"Yes mama," Naomi laughed.

Mary started to say something but decided against it. "All I'm going to say is, be careful baby, messing with someone like him you're swimming in deep water. And you know how I always say, you lay down with dogs—"

"You get up with fleas. I know mama." Naomi sighed. "But he's different, I haven't felt this loved and respected by a man in so long. He really makes me happy mama, happier than I've ever been before." She smiled.

During their conversation, Naomi's dad, Joe entered the kitchen, instantly changing the mood. Naomi hadn't been in contact with her dad much; he feels she betrayed him the moment she left and kept her relationship with Deandre private.

Naomi watched him walk over to the fridge, he didn't utter a peep to her; she knew she had to be the bigger person and speak.

"Hey daddy." Naomi said nervously.

Naomi always hated being at odds with her parents, she never liked letting them down or disappointing them. She also couldn't blame either one of them for feeling some-kind-of-way after everything that happened.

"Hello Naomi," He replied dryly as he proceeded to make his morning coffee.

Naomi sighed while glancing over at her mother who gave her a look before nudging her to go over to him.

Naomi stood up from her seat, walked over to him, and wrapped her arms around him tightly. "Daddy, I know you're upset with me, and you have every right to be, but I am so sorry. I'm sorry for cutting you guys off and waiting so long to visit you. I was too ashamed to face you. I know that I hurt you both. Even after you guys told me Deandre was no good for me, a million times, I let y'all down anyway with my decision making." She apologized, not once releasing the hold she had around him.

Naomi heard her father release a deep sigh. He removed her arms from around him. She stepped back, awaiting the moment that he'd face her. "Naomi, I was never mad at you. I was more disappointed than anything because I thought we were closer than that. The day you decided to up and run away with that boy and endure all that shit while with him, but never once call us for help, made me feel as if we failed as parents." He admitted.

"As parents, we're supposed to protect our babies from harm, but you stripped that from us the day you walked out that door and cut off all forms of communication. You could've been killed, and we wouldn't have known a damn thing until it was too late!" He snapped unintentionally.

"I worried about you nonstop for four years, so did your mama, and your brother; we spent many sleepless nights praying that you were okay, hoping you weren't dead in a ditch somewhere, Naomi. Then we finally got that call from you in jail. We learned about what he had done to you, all these years, your suffering- that hurt me more than anything because there was nothing I could do."

Walking towards her, Joe sweetly kissed the top of her head and placed his hand on the side of her face, admiring her. "I'm happy that you're back, healthy and strong. I know that you're sorry baby and I'm sorry too."

Naomi's eyes filled profusely with tears. She said nothing, she hugged him tightly as the guilt ate away at her heart and mind. Wrapping his arms just as tightly around her, they both stood in the middle of the kitchen, hugging one another and crying.

Naomi had been waiting on this moment for so long. She missed her parents beyond words and was truly happy that they finally amended things.

Her life was finally coming together, she couldn't be happier.

ღ

Standing out front, looking up towards the place he once called home, Cartier let out a sigh, suddenly realizing how much things have changed. Walking up the steps that led to their front door, Cartier knew at this moment, he had a decision to make. He decided to let go of all the petty arguments and fights between him and Chardonnay, and to work towards bettering their relationship.

He had a plan to take her out, so they could possibly sort through their issues for once; just lay everything on the table. It had been a minute since they'd gone out together; he felt this might be just what they needed in order to get back on track.

As he walked towards their bedroom, he tossed his bag on the couch, and wondered where she could possibly be, she loved watching tv in their living room.

Officially entering their bedroom, he heard the shower going. He stepped into the bathroom; there she was.

Watching her in silence, Cartier started to playback their relationship in his mind. This was the woman he planned on marrying and having kids with, but now things were so different.

"Baby." Cartier called, pulling back the shower door, slightly startling her.

Chardonnay gave him a cold look before turning her head and proceeded to shower. “I know you’re angry with me and you have every right to be, but I’m here to make things right. I at least want to try to work on things before just throwing in the towel.”

Turning off the shower, Chardonnay stepped out, grabbed her towel, and wrapped it around her body. “What difference would it make to you, Cartier? You don’t want me, and you have made that very clear; no point in wasting each other's time more than we already have.”

“Don’t be like that Chardonnay. I love you and I can’t deny that I chose you for a reason. I would hate to see us end without even trying for real. Like, give me a chance to try and make things right!” Cartier begged.

“Try!? Nigga, I haven’t seen or even spoke to you in almost six months. You’ve been running around town acting single and shit, bringing ya new bitch to meet your family and shit, and you want me to give you another chance!?” Chardonnay yelled in disbelief.

She couldn’t believe the nerve of Cartier to come back as if everything was cool and ask for another chance.

“Like, you really thought Cedes wasn’t going to tell me about your little girlfriend you had over there!?” She snapped pulling her hair into a wet bun.

Cartier sighed to himself; he knew Chardonnay was going to hear about Naomi but that was not his main concern right now. “Not to mention, I've been calling your ass and you have yet to pick up or return any of my calls, I know you weren't that damn busy.” She scoffed.

“Cedes don’t know what the fuck she even talking about! How are you gonna listen to a bitch that wants your man herself?” Cartier questioned dryly.

Chardonnay stared at him long and hard, not only confused by his assumptions, but also annoyed by his nonchalant attitude towards the situation as well.

Before Cartier could process what was happening, he felt a hard sting across his face, she smacked the shit out of him.

“I’m so sick of you and your bullshit Cartier! Like, why do you keep doing this to me?” She sniffled, becoming fed up with everything.

Holding both his face and his composure, he sighed. "Char this why I'm here, so we can finally sort through all this shit. Just come out with me today, that's all I'm asking for, one more chance. I can't change the past but I'm trying to correct all my wrongs. I'm starting with you."

"Baby, we've been through so much and you've been here by my side through everything. I'm not ready for us to end just yet, so I'm begging you to grant me the chance to fix this between us." He pleaded as he got on his knees in front of her.

When he started lifting the towel that covered her naked body, Chardonnay looked down at him before closing her eyes. She felt his tongue come in contact with her clit, she began to moan, just a little.

Clutching the back of his head, he continued sucking and licking on her clit, causing her legs to shake from standing. Cartier never let up until she came in his mouth.

Continuing to kiss her inner thighs as she held onto him, Cartier looked up at her. "You gon' give us another chance?"

Looking down at him, Chardonnay bit her lip and gave him an unreadable look then shook her head yes.

Standing to his feet, Cartier kissed her forehead and told her to get dressed, while he did the same.

Once they were dressed and ready, they headed out and arrived at the mall within thirty minutes, as usual the place was packed. Walking inside holding hands, Cartier and Chardonnay wasted no time hitting up almost every store together, buying shoes, jewelry, and clothes.

Cartier knew money wasn't going to solve or magically settle their issues, but it was a start. Cartier hadn't seen Chardonnay this happy in a long time, that alone made him sorta smile.

Peeping a new sex store, they both decided to check it out to possibly find some things they could use inside the bedroom to spice up their sex life.

Walking inside, Cartier instantly noticed a sex swing on display and decided to take a look at it. Chardonnay joined him and decided to check it out as well.

"This looks like it would be a lot of fun." She said, biting her lip.

"Fuck it, let's get it." Cartier agreed, before they walked over to the variety of vibrators they had showcased on the back wall.

Chardonnay has been asking for one for a while, so Cartier decided to go ahead and get her one. Plus, the thought of watching her play with herself made his dick hard.

There were a few other couples inside the store as well, probably just as amazed about this place as them. The store had so many things to choose from to meet any person's secret desire.

Once Chardonnay grabbed the vibrator she wanted, they made their way towards the massage and edible oil section. "I like this one." Cartier told her while testing the strawberry flavored one.

Tasting it herself, Chardonnay nodded in agreeance. "That does taste good and it's organic." She pointed out before tossing it in their bag.

After they continued shopping around for a few more things such as lingerie, they decided to head out and get a bite to eat from the food court.

"What do you feel like eating baby?" Cartier asked her, wrapping his arms around her shoulders and giving her small kisses on her cheek.

Twisting her lips as she scanned the menu, she shrugged. "I think I want some pizza babe." She replied as she looked back towards him. "What do you have a taste for?"

"You." He smirked before he started attacking her neck with kisses, causing her to laugh and blush uncontrollably.

Their moment was cut short when Cartier's name was called, and he looked back to see Genesis and Jewell making their way towards them with confused expressions on their faces.

Looking at them like a deer caught in headlights, Cartier quickly removed his arms from around Chardonnay as they approached them.

"Hey Carti," Jewel greeted, while giving him a look, implying that he needed to explain himself. "What's up Nay?"

Looking back, Chardonnay gave them a half smile before looking back at Cartier. "I'll go ahead and order for us." She told him before walking off.

Turning back towards Genesis and Jewel, Cartier sighed. "Look I already know whatcha thinking, shit is complicated right now. Chardonnay and I are just tryna work some things out."

"Okay and what about Naomi? Are y'all done?" Genesis questioned, followed by a laugh.

"It never fails Carti, you meet someone, yet somehow you always end up right back with Chardonnay ass." Jewel scoffed.

"Like I said, shit is complicated between us, right now my focus is Chardonnay." He replied, keeping it short. "Naomi and I aren't technically together; I'm just weighing out my options."

"Then what was the point in introducing her to everybody, if all you were going to do is run back to Chardonnay?" Jewel asked to understand Cartier and his weird thinking.

"It's too much to explain right now, just promise me not to mention this or bring it up around Naomi." He pleaded.

Rolling their eyes both Genesis and Jewel waved him off and walked away once they saw Chardonnay walking back towards them.

Cartier watched them walk away knowing he was fuckin' up and he knew if any of this got back to Naomi, they were over.

Chapter 8

After a long day of work, Naomi finally arrived at Sheree's apartment. She planned a girl's night earlier this week. Yawning loudly, Naomi quickly shook off her wave of tiredness as she pulled out her phone to see where Genesis and Jewell were.

When Sheree told her about wanting to have a girl's night, Naomi immediately thought of Genesis and Jewel and invited them over as well. A few weeks had passed since the family gathering, as promised, Naomi kept her word by staying in touch with them; their bond continued to grow between one another.

They shared a lot of the same interests and she even discovered that they have a younger sister by the name of Aubrey. This would be the first time Sheree and Lanay would be meeting Genesis and Jewel, but she felt they'd all get along with each other.

Just when she was about to click on Jewel's contact to call her, Naomi laughed when she looked up and saw both Genesis and Jewel twerking in front of her car with bottles of liquor in their hands.

Getting out of the car, Naomi grabbed her bag and the bottle she picked up along the way and locked up. "Y'all asses are crazy." Naomi laughed as they embraced each other into hugs.

"You know how we do." Jewel joked as they walked towards the entrance of the lobby to her apartment.

Hopping on the elevator, Naomi pressed her floor number before leaning back against the wall, yawning. "Are you tired already girl? The night hasn't even started yet." Genesis nudged her shoulder.

"Work kicked my ass today; one of our stylists called into work, so we all had to take on her clients that didn't want to reschedule their appointments." She sighed, feeling a headache coming on.

"Damn, get that money tho sis." Genesis replied, giving her a smile.

As they waited, watching the numbers go up, Naomi took some time to really admire how extravagant Sheree's apartment building was.

"You said your girl is in college, right? And she's living in a place like this in Buckhead!?" Genesis questioned, admiring the building as well.

Naomi laughed as she nodded her head in approval. Genesis wasn't one to judge people based on their pay grade, but she wouldn't be caught dead with them either.

"Mhm." She replied.

When the elevator reached her floor, Naomi stepped off first as Genesis and Jewel followed behind, looking for her apartment number.

Approaching her door, Naomi knocked twice before stepping back a little. After a few seconds of waiting, the locks soon began turning and Sheree opened the door excitedly. "Hey y'all, come on in."

Giving Sheree a quick hug, Naomi stepped aside to introduce Genesis and Jewel. "Hey girl, this is Genesis and Jewel and y'all, these are my girls Sheree and that's Lanay over there on the couch."

"Hey, y'all come on in, I promise we won't bite." Sheree joked followed by a laugh, as she grabbed the drinks, they brought to place them in the fridge.

"Unless you want us too." Lanay joked laughing. There was a little truth behind her joke; Lanay has had her fair share of being with women and men, she didn't discriminate; she basically labeled herself as bisexual.

She was all for having a good time with whoever and as good as Genesis was looking, she was already tempted.

Locking eyes with Lanay after she made that joke, Genesis smiled and looked away while Sheree shook her head. "Anyway, it's about time your ass showed up, I swear I thought you were going to bail." Sheree admitted as she closed the door and locked it.

Taking a seat next to Jewel who was sitting on her loveseat, Sheree poured them up some drinks.

"I apologize y'all, I had to squeeze in a last-minute client." Naomi said, pouring herself a glass then taking a seat next to Lanay on the couch.

"So, I see business is going good up there?" Lanay asked, pulling her eyes away from her phone.

"It actually is, I really appreciate you getting me in Sheree, for real." Naomi said, raising her glass to her.

A slight frown appeared on Lanay's face, "Bitch I helped you too." Lanay chimed in, offended that Sheree was getting all the credit.

"Thank you as well bitch." Naomi said back sarcastically followed by a giggle.

Lately, Lanay has been so distant and moody; Naomi didn't understand where the sudden change in her attitude was coming from. She had been wanting to talk to her to see what's been up, but things were crazy and busy in both of their lives; she hoped Lanay would open up once she found the right time to talk about it.

"Y'all want to play a good game of drunk truth or dare? I brought a bottle of D'Usse." Jewel asked.

"You know I'm down." Genesis replied, removing her leather jean jacket she was wearing.

Getting up from her seat, Lanay grabbed the bottle of D'usse and shot glasses for them all. Scooting the couches back, they all sat on the floor with their drinks in hand.

"I'll start, Sheree, truth or dare?" Jewell asked,

"Fuck it, I'll be the badass, Dare." Sheree laughed, becoming anxious.

"I dare you to send your man a nude picture of yourself, then text back and say that you sent it to the wrong person or take 2 shots." Jewell dared her as she laughed.

"Oop, she's trying to get you killed." Lanay joked.

Shrugging her shoulders, Sheree grabbed her phone and headed to the bathroom. Quickly undressing herself, she snapped a few pictures before sending them to Nassir and returned shortly after.

While everybody sat and waited for his response, they went ahead and did Genesis' turn.

"I'm going with truth, I'ma wimp." She laughed as she threw her hands up.

Sheree rolled her eyes, "Chicken, is it true that you're undercover?"

Genesis laughed slightly confused by what she meant. "Am I what?"

"Are you on the down low? Like do you secretly like girls?" Sheree restated. She honestly already knew the answer since she was peeping the way her and Lanay kept looking at each other, but she wanted to see if her observation was true and if she would admit it.

"Okay I'll admit, I have dipped in the honey jar before, but I wouldn't necessarily label it." Genesis replied followed by a shrug before slightly glancing at Lanay who was smirking.

Before anybody could respond, the sound of Sheree's phone filled the room. Quickly picking it up, she felt her heart drop when she saw it was Nassir calling.

"Oh shit, it's him." She stated, while laughing.

"Answer it and put him on speaker." Jewel replied, becoming slightly anxious as well.

Answering the phone, Sheree put him on speaker before sitting her phone down. "Hello?"

"Man, where the fuck you at!? Don't text my phone playing and shit! What tha fuck you mean you texted the wrong fucking number Sheree!?" Nassir yelled into the phone.

Everybody in the room burst into laughter, including Naomi. She could imagine Nassir getting all mad and worked up, especially since it wasn't hard to piss him off.

Getting up, Sheree went to continue their conversation privately inside her bedroom.

After a few more rounds and playing different drinking games, the girls were all drunk by now, ready to just pass out and go to sleep.

While Jewel was in the kitchen, throwing her cup away, she frowned when she saw Cartier calling Naomi. Holding her phone up, Jewel walked into the living room where Naomi was laying down, talking with Lanay. "Hey girl, Cartier just called you. I didn't know y'all were still talking."

Looking up at her confused, Naomi sat up. "Why wouldn't we be?" She asked, laughing as she took her phone from her to call him back.

Watching as Jewel and Genesis share a look between one another, Naomi assumed they knew something she didn't. "What's up for real y'all? Do y'all know something I don't?"

Retaking her seat, Jewel sighed. "Just the other day, we saw Cartier and his girlfriend Chardonnay out at the mall. They've been on and off for years now and that's why everybody was so shocked to see you at the gathering, but when we saw them out together all boo'd up, we figured they just finally made up again, like always. I'm sorry, I thought you knew."

When the name Chardonnay left her mouth, Naomi instantly flashed back to seeing her name on his phone, right before they had sex the first night. She then recounted all the other times she called. Feeling her heart drop, tears begin to fill her eyes, Naomi just sat there in disbelief.

Genesis felt terrible, she got up and took a seat next to her. "Naomi, I swear this is not how we wanted you to find out. When we saw them together, we figured y'all broke things off because when we asked him, he made it seem that way as well."

"He said we broke up?" She asked, barely above a whisper.

"Basically, when he spotted us, he came over, and when we asked what happened between you guys, he stated that things were complicated." Jewel replied feeling bad, but she was glad she at least knew the truth now.

Naomi said nothing else after that. In that moment, she felt beyond foolish and stupid for even believing that he was different.

Standing up, Naomi grabbed her phone and left the apartment. Clicking on his contact, she called him and listened to the phone ring before he answered. "What's up baby?"

"Hey, what's up?" Naomi asked, trying to remain calm.

"Nothing, just sitting here missing your sexy ass." He replied, sounding like he was walking, from the sound of the wind in the background.

Trying to hold back her tears, she sniffled. "I miss you too, where are you?" Naomi asked him, fumbling with her nails.

"I was hoping to be on my way to you, you at home?"

"No, I'm actually still at Sheree's for our girls' night, but I can meet you there?"

"Bet, I'll be there in ten minutes."

Hanging up the phone, Naomi walked back inside, alerting everybody. Standing up from the couch, Lanay embraced her in a hug. "You okay sis? You want to talk about it?" She asked her.

"Nope, I'll be back later." She briefly replied, keeping it short and simple as she began grabbing her things to leave.

"Wait, where are you going?" Sheree questioned, growing concerned.

Ignoring all their questions, Naomi quickly grabbed everything she needed before leaving out in a rush altogether.

The whole way to her house, Naomi cried while reflecting on what Genesis and Jewel told her. She thought about all the lies Cartier had been feeding her for the past few months; to say she was hurt was an understatement, she was crushed and couldn't believe she had been played... again. She was so ashamed that she actually believed he was different and that she went against her vow of celibacy to him.

Arriving at her place, Naomi made her way up to her apartment. She was grateful she beat him there; it gave her some time to get her thoughts and words together.

While pacing in her kitchen, a knock at her door shook her out of her thoughts.

Taking a deep breath, Naomi opened the door and walked away, not giving him a hug or anything. He was confused. "Damn, it's like that now? No hug or nothing?" He laughed. Naomi found nothing funny, she couldn't believe how he could act as if he wasn't hiding a big secret.

Cartier could tell that the vibe was off, he was lowkey confused as to what happened since Naomi seemed fine over the phone.

"I really thought you would've been different from all the other guys, Cartier." Naomi started. "I opened up to you, I let you in even though everything in me was telling me not to trust you! I should've listened to my gut, but I wanted you to prove me wrong. I wanted you to show me that you weren't like the rest of em, but I was right! You're nothing but a lying ass nigga!" She sniffled.

Cartier's heart sunk to the bottom of his stomach, he knew right then and there she knew everything. "Nao—"

"How about you go back to where this Chardonnay chick is instead, seems like that's who you would rather be with, since shit is so *complicated* between us!" She snapped as she looked over at him, watching his eyes grow wide. "Weighing out your options my ass, I'll make the choice for you! Go be with her and leave me the hell alone."

"Don't look all surprised now, you really thought I wouldn't have found out?" She laughed. "Something in me kept telling me you were hiding something and that I couldn't trust you, I should've listened and left your ass in that club I met you at."

"Nao—"

"You know what, Cartier? Save it. I don't want to hear any of your excuses! I straight up asked you who she was, and you lied to me! So, since you want to keep secrets, just be sure while you're playing house with her to lose my number and to never talk to me again. I can't even stand to look at you right now and I don't want to see you again, so just get out!" She pointed as her eyes filled with tears.

"Baby please, just give me a chance to explain." He begged.

"Explain what!? You want to explain how much of a liar you are!? Like I can't believe you would do this to me after everything." She cried.

"Naomi, I'm not with her anymore! Things between Chardonnay and I have been complicated for a while now, but I promise you we are broken up and I'm sorry for not opening up sooner regarding our issues. But I swear she is the past now, I promise." He explained.

Shaking her head, Naomi looked off. "And you expect me to believe that after Genesis and Jewel just saw you two out together at the mall!? Like, do you really think I'm dumb, Cartier!? Just please get out of my apartment. I can't do this with you right now."

Cartier knew he couldn't explain or even try to make excuses for the damage he caused. He fucked up and he knew with the game he was playing, it was bound to happen, he just didn't expect it all to happen this soon.

Watching Naomi break down and cry like this really had him feeling guilty. Chardonnay was not worth losing Naomi behind, he knew he had to clean this up and make this right.

"I fucked up baby. I brought you into my life when I still had some unresolved issues within my relationship with Chardonnay. I should have been honest with you from the jump. When we met, we were on a break, and I can honestly say I didn't expect things between us to happen so fast, but I like you a lot, Naomi and I don't want to lose you. I can't change what I did or even make excuses for it either, I was wrong. I can fully admit that, but I swear to you it's over between us."

"I don't care about what you have to say, just get out and leave me alone! I'm done with you. Don't call, text, or come see me ever again, fuck you!"

Walking into her room, Naomi slammed her door shut and locked it behind her before Cartier could stop her. Standing outside her room door, Cartier could hear her crying and that alone hurt him as well.

"I never meant to hurt you Nao." He whispered before walking away from her door and leaving out of her apartment in shambles.

Chapter 9

Nassir laid out on Sheree's couch with his head resting in her lap. He sighed to himself as he vented. "I just feel guilty because I knew about Cartier's relationship with Chardonnay, but I never said shit, and now my sister is hurting when I could've prevented that shit."

"Why didn't you say anything?" Sheree questioned.

Ever since word got around that Cartier and Naomi broke up, everyone's been doing their best to try and be there for her, but she isn't making it easy. Due to her pain and anger, she's pushed everyone away, and her attitude has become too much to deal with, so we've all tried to respect her boundaries and give her some space.

"I tried to give him time to handle it. I know how he feels about Chardonnay, but I thought the moment he and my sister got serious, he would've done the right thing, but nah this muthafucka wanna try and be a playa. Everybody knows I don't play when it comes to my sister."

Sheree nodded, understanding where he was coming from. After they both left Naomi's house earlier, they've been kicking it for the past two hours, just talking.

However, finding out that Nassir knew about Cartier's whole ass relationship prior to getting involved with Naomi shocked the hell out Sheree.

"I'm sure you don't want to hear this, but you should've just told her and let her make the decision as to whether or not she'd stay with him. You know if she were to find out that you knew this whole time, she wou—"

"I already know she would be pissed at me, and I wouldn't blame her either because we never keep secrets from each other. Knowing what all she went through with that other nigga; I should've stepped up and done better by protecting her heart." He shamefully admitted.

Kissing the top of his head, Sheree smiled. "Well, we can't change the past; all we can do now is focus on the present and the future. Just keep doing your part by being there for her, despite how she's acting now, deep down she appreciates it." Sheree reassured him.

"I know, I'll take her out or something, you know to get her out of that damn apartment and just make her feel special."

Sheree tapped his shoulder, so that he could move up. She stood up from the couch and walked into the kitchen to refill their wine glasses. “That’s a start, she would love that! Have you spoken to Cartier since all this has happened?”

“Not really, when we do talk, it's mainly about business. He knows he fucked up, so I think he’s just tryna keep his distance. One of these days, we’re going to have to face the issue and move on from it.” He shrugged as he glanced over at Sheree, watching her maneuver around her kitchen.

Sheree came back into the living room and handed him his glass before retaking her seat. “Do you think this could possibly ruin you guys' relationship?”

Staring at his glass, Nassir simply shrugged unsure at the moment. “I don’t know. Cartier has been like a brother to me and despite this situation, he has never crossed me, but I don’t know how Naomi might feel about me still fucking with him. She might look at it like I’m betraying her or some shit.”

“You’ll never know until you actually speak with her. Naomi knows how much Cartier means to you, so I don’t see her holding a grudge towards you just because things didn’t go right between them. At the end of the day what happened is solely between Naomi and Cartier- not you, Naomi, and Cartier.” Sheree told him as she took a sip from her glass.

Nassir nodded, agreeing. “You're right.”

Smiling to herself, Sheree stretched out, placing her feet in his lap. “I’m always right, now give me a foot massage.”

Looking at her like she was crazy, Nassir let out a low chuckle before placing his glass of wine on her coffee table. He then began removing her mix-matched socks. “You lucky I actually like your ass; I don’t fuck with feet.”

Sheree wiggled her toes to be childish, Nassir attempted to push her feet off him and stood up. “Ok ok, I’ll stop playing. I really do need one. I've been on my feet all day.” She whined.

Adjusting her feet back in his lap, she instantly closed her eyes and began to relax when he started massaging her feet.

Glaring over at her, Nassir couldn't help but laugh at himself. He vowed never to simp over a woman like this again, yet here he was falling hard for Sheree, as if falling in love wasn't one of the dumbest things to ever do.

He couldn't deny nor resist the attraction and connection they had between one another. With all the crazy shit he delt with running the streetz; she was his peace from all the chaos and whenever he was around her, he could just be himself.

"Yo parents know you out here fuckin' wit a street nigga?" He questioned followed by a laugh.

Opening her eyes, Sheree laughed. "Last I checked I was grown, so who I choose to date is my choice."

"Why me though?"

"I mean if you want me to go out and find somebody else, I gladly will." She joked.

Smacking his teeth, Nassir pushed her feet off him. "Shut up, you know what I meant. I'm just saying out of all the guys that actually got some shit going for themselves, why me?"

"I don't go after what a guy has going for himself or what he could possibly do for me financially; I go after how someone makes me feel and you make me feel good about myself. You support what I have going on, you respect me, and when I'm around you, I feel protected- like nothing in this world can hurt me long as you're with me." She admitted before looking at her empty glass; she knew it had to be that liquid courage.

Nassir sat there, stuck on how to respond. Luckily the sound of someone knocking saved him from looking stupid.

"*Must be our doordash finally.*" Sheree said to herself before standing up from the couch.

Nassir went ahead and finished off the rest of his glass so that he could relax his nerves. He stood up from the couch and met her halfway to assist taking the food into the kitchen.

Removing the food from the bags, Sheree grabbed some plates. "Food smells so good, my mouth is starting to water."

Laughing, Nassir fixed their plates while Sheree cleared off her dining table, so they could have room to eat. Placing their plates on the table, Nassir took his seat, just as Sheree did the same, wasting no time digging into their food.

There was a moment of silence as they ate, so Sheree decided to pick back up on the conversation they were having previously.

"So why did you choose me?" She blurted out as they met eyes.

"What do you mean?" Nassir replied, acting clueless.

Tossing her fork down, Sheree smacked her teeth. "Now who's acting slow? I'm asking why you chose me out of all people? You're attractive, you're smart, and funny at times, and you could literally pull any woman you want... but why me? What made me stand out from the rest?"

Sheree wasn't usually this outspoken, but she felt since Nassir put her on the spot, it was only fair that she did the same. She wanted to know where she stood with him as well, so she'd know if she was wasting her time on him or not.

"Honestly, it's the way you view me as a person. From the moment we met, I knew my lifestyle didn't impress you and that you weren't only interested in me because I had money. Once I got to know you, I fell for your personality and how smart you are. Being around you honestly makes me want to be a better person, simply because you see the good in me that I didn't even think existed anymore." He answered honestly.

"Wow, that actually means a lot coming from you."

Nassir smiled, "Well it's the truth."

"So, when you say I make you want to become a better person, do you not see yourself doing this forever?" She asked, sipping from her raspberry tea.

"Hell nah, I never saw myself doing this shit forever. My plan is to actually go legit eventually and leave all this behind. This was only a stepping stone for me and Cartier, to help get us where we needed to elevate, but once you go deep inside this type of life, it's like quick sand trying to get out." Nassir expressed.

Sitting back in his seat, he sighed. "Sometimes I feel like we'll never make it out."

When that last sentence left his mouth, Sheree was at a loss for words. She didn't know much about the streetz or what all came with that life, besides the basic things you hear from others. Sheree came from money and never experienced any type of struggle before.

"I can only imagine how hard it may be to walk away from something like this, but I believe the day you and Cartier finally do decide to leave the game for good, y'all will come up with something amazing." She encouraged him.

Nassir smiled, before focusing back on his food. "So, what made you go into nursing school?" He asked her, while taking a sip of his orange juice.

"Um, I've always had a passionate heart to help others and I wanted a career where I could do something that would make a difference in someone's life. Knowing that I can possibly change someone's life by a simple act of kindness and compassion brings me joy, so that's why I went into nursing." She smiled.

"That's dope, most people are only in it just for the money. I used to always read up on stories where nurses or CNAs mistreated their patients. Shit is sad."

Nodding her head, Sheree agreed. "I know, a lot of those nurses make it hard for nurses like me, who actually care. I work part-time at a hospital for my clinicals, we just dealt with something like that. We had a nurse who would intentionally let one of her patients sit in her own urine or shit longer than the allotted time frame; she caused this poor woman to form rashes and an infection, which led to her wound being open."

"Wow, that's fucked up! I wish somebody would treat my mother like that, I'm tearing that whole hospital apart." Nassir replied, chewing his food.

"Exactly, like I know we do get busy and may run a little behind, but nothing excuses that! When I found out, I felt so bad for the patient; it's like people don't realize that their actions don't just reflect them, it reflects the entire hospital. That lady was ready to sue, and she has every right to do so, but luckily the doctor calmed her down and resolved the issue."

"What happened with the nurse?"

"She was suspended without pay and the board is investigating the situation, she might lose her license." Sheree shrugged.

“As she should.”

“Yup, how is your mom by the way? Naomi told me a little while ago that she wasn't feeling too good,” Sheree asked.

“Oh yeah she’s better now. Thanks for asking!”

Finishing their food, Nassir and Sheree became lost in conversations surrounding random topics. When they finished eating, they both decided to end the night watching a movie yet found themselves making out on the couch instead.

As their sloppy kisses intensified, they began removing each other's clothes one by one, never once breaking that kiss.

Everything was moving so fast, neither of them even knew how things got to this point. Pulling away from the kiss, Sheree stood up to remove her shorts and panties before dropping down to her knees.

Nassir was so high, he just stared down at her with his low hooded eyes, watching as she spread his legs and began unbuckling his jeans. Lifting a little to help her pull his briefs and pants down to his ankles, Sheree watched in amazement as his dick jumped out at her.

Just when she was about to take him into her mouth, Nassir stopped her. “Are you sure about this?” He asked.

Nassir knew they had been drinking wine majority of the night, he wanted to make sure she wanted him with no regrets later.

Ignoring his question, Sheree softly kissed the tip of his dick before swallowing him whole and taking it to the back of her throat. Adjusting her mouth to his size, Sheree then started slowly bobbing her head back and forth, letting the sound of his low moans fill her ears.

“Fuck!” Nassir moaned out, placing his hand on the back of her head. She looked up at him and stared him in the eyes as she continued pleasuring him with her mouth. Reaching one hand down between her thighs, Sheree crept her legs open and began massaging her clit with her fingers.

Sheree may have seemed shy to an outsider but behind closed doors, she loved sex and had a very freaky side that only certain people were lucky enough to experience.

Placing both her hands on the back of her head, signaling for him to take over. Nassir began thrusting his dick in and out, enjoying the warmth of her mouth. Feeling himself about to cum, Nassir started bucking his hips faster, his dick hit the back of her throat, he was turned on by her gagging.

As he released his nut inside her mouth, they held an intense gaze into each other's eyes; in that moment, they fell for each other even more. When he released his dick from her mouth, a trail of spit followed before disconnecting the two.

Sheree stood to her feet, feeling accomplished. She reached down and grabbed Nassir by the hand and led him to her bedroom.

Sheree closed the door behind them and climbed into bed. She laid on her back and opened herself up for Nassir to have his way with her. It's been a good minute since Sheree's had sex, she didn't realize how much she missed being touched by a man until now.

Sheree admired his body; she watched him remove his pants from his ankles, every muscle flexed in his arms. There he stood, naked before her at the edge of the bed. As she stared at him, Sheree imagined him lifting her up in his big arms and roughly pinning her against the wall.

Biting the tip of her finger, Sheree grew excited as he got in the bed, hovering over her as the chain he wore dangled in her face. "You like what you see, baby girl?" Nassir questioned confidently.

Instead of responding, Sheree pressed her lips against his and slipped her tongue inside his mouth. Using his knee to spread her legs a little, Nassir carefully positioned himself at her entrance before inserting his dick inside of her; they gasped for a few seconds, in awe of the feeling.

They became lost in each other's eyes with each and every stroke, they were making love and they knew it.

ꟈ

Stepping out of his car, Cartier let out a deep sigh as he made his way inside of a local bar that Nassir agreed to meet him at to talk. Cartier had been avoiding this moment, simply because he knew he fucked up by going against the one thing Nassir demanded when it came to his sister.

He needed a drink asap to get his shit together because just the thought of it all made him anxious. Reaching the bar, he took a seat and briefly greeted the bartender before pulling out his phone and staring at the picture he had of him and Naomi together on his lock screen.

Locking his phone back, he roughly shoved it into his pocket and became frustrated with himself. He didn't have a clue as to what to do to at least get Naomi to speak to him; she had him blocked on everything and whenever he would pop up at her job, she was always unavailable to talk.

He knew he failed her by going against everything she wanted, all behind not being honest. He allowed his selfishness to interfere and ruin the good thing he had going; he couldn't be mad at nobody but himself.

"What's up man? What can I getcha?" The bartender asked as he wiped down the countertop.

"Can I get two double shots of Don Julio? Keep em' coming as well." He requested while reaching inside his wallet, placing down two fresh twenty-dollar bills.

The bartender nodded and quickly fixed up the drinks and handed them over to him. Cartier thanked the guy and immediately threw back one with no remorse. He ignored the burning sensation in his throat and tossed back the second one.

Slightly turning in his seat, Cartier glanced around the bar to look at a few people dancing. There were couples ducked off in booths, he turned back around in disgust. Thanking the bartender when he placed two more glasses down, Cartier immediately went to grab one but stopped when someone sat right beside him.

Glancing over his shoulder, Cartier smacked his teeth when he realized it was Porsha. "What tha fuck you doing here Porsha? How did you even know I was here?" He asked rudely.

"Cut out all the dramatics nigga, you miss me yet?" She asked, facing him and reaching for his hand. Cartier recoiled of course. His rejection hurt her feelings, but she knew not to allow her feelings to show.

She was there for one thing and one thing only; she wasn't leaving until it was done.

"What's not clicking' inside that brain of yours!? Like please tell me, what do you want from me Porsha? I don't know how else to explain to your ass that it's over!" Cartier snapped.

Cartier has had women in the past who didn't want things to end between them, but they all eventually got the hint that things were over and would be done with their antics by now. However, he didn't understand Porsha's obsession with him or why she kept trying. even after he had made it clear he does not want her.

"We had a good thing going Capone and I want that back. Why can't things go back to how they used to be between us?" Porsha asked while placing her hand on his thigh, in an attempt to touch his dick.

Porsha knew things were over between them, but she still had a job to do at the end of the day and Cartier wasn't worth losing her life behind.

Looking down at where her hand was placed, Cartier laughed before he grabbed her hand and gave it a hard squeeze and threw it back. "Get the fuck on and that's my last time telling you P!" He snapped just as his phone started ringing.

Reaching inside his pocket, he took his phone out to see it was Nassir calling. Standing up from his seat, Cartier walked towards the back where it was a little quieter before answering.

"What's up nigga? Where are you at?" He questioned as he stared in the direction of the bar.

"I'm about ten minutes out, got caught up with Sheree but I'm on my way."

Cartier nodded silently; his focus was now on Porsha. Porsha didn't even realize that his eyes were glued on her. She reached inside her purse and slid over Cartier's shot of Don Julio and quickly poured a powder form of a date rape pill into his drink.

Laughing to himself, Cartier shook his head. "Alright man, I'll see you when you get here." He said into the phone before hanging up.

Walking back towards the bar, Cartier leaned in close to Porsha's ear, sending a chill down her spine as he startled her. "Meet me in the bathroom." He whispered. A smile crept from the corners of her mouth. Porsha stood up from her seat. He watched her walk towards the bathroom before turning to the bartender and telling him to dump those two shots.

Pulling up his pants a little, Cartier made his way to the bathroom. When he made it inside, he saw her sitting on top of the counter. He locked the door behind him. Cartier smiled. "I gotta give it to you

Porsha, ion think I've ever met a muthafucka as persistent as you." He started as he began walking towards her.

Stepping in between her legs, he could see in her eyes where her mind was at. As he trailed his hand up her body, Porsha tried to control her breathing but just the touch of his hand against her turned her on.

Raising his hand up to her neck, he gripped it slightly and leaned in close, like he was about to kiss her. "You want me?" He asked her.

When she went to nod her head, Cartier switched his movements by slamming her head against the bathroom mirror, cracking it. "Well too fucking bad, do you think I'm fuckin' stupid!?" Tightening the grip around her neck, Porsha's eyes began to fill with tears from the pain in her head and the feeling of oxygen leaving her body.

"Cap—"

Cartier shut her up by squeezing her throat and throwing her to the floor. Squatting down to her level, he snatched her by her hair. "If you ever in your fuckin' life try some stupid ass shit like drug'n me again, I will kill yo dumb ass. This is a fair warning to stop fuckin' with me or I will make your life a living hell." He spat before releasing her hair and exiting the bathroom.

Laid out on the floor, Porsha tried to control her breathing as panic began to set in; she wasn't sure how she was going to face Trig again with no new information. She knew since Cartier caught her slipping this time that he'd always be on guard from now on. Porsha knew she needed to figure out another plan quickly.

Back at the bar, Cartier sat there shaking his leg rapidly, he couldn't believe Porsha was actually going to drug him. His mind was racing; he felt even though she was dick-crazy, she had to be going that hard for another reason.

He just couldn't put his finger on what her reasoning could possibly be.

Glancing at the entrance when the door chimes went off, Cartier sighed when he saw Nassir making his way inside. He met him halfway; they both slapped hands and gave each a quick brotherly hug before walking over to a booth near the back.

"What's up wit it nigga?" Nassir questioned as he slouched back in his seat.

"Not shit man, I just wanted to clear the air about everything that's going on between me and your sister. I know I can't fix shit I've done to hurt her and if I could take all that shit back, I would in a heartbeat. But I really want to apologize to you because I know ya energy behind her, and I broke the code." Cartier expressed. "I should've never gotten involved with her, knowing' shit between Chardonnay and I wasn't over."

Nassir respected Cartier for apologizing, but he honestly felt he didn't deserve one. "I appreciate you for feeling the need to come to me and apologize for what went down between you and Naomi, but I'm the last person who deserves it. I knew what you had going on with Chardonnay and I didn't say shit, I'm already dealing with my own guilt because I feel like I failed her twice by not protecting her heart." He started.

Frowning, Cartier leaned forward wondering what he meant by that. "Whatchu mean?" Shaking his head, Nassir looked down at his hands. "Naomi got involved with some nigga she grew up with and they ended up moving out of the city together. After she was away from home for a while, Naomi eventually cut off all ties to us; so, for damn near four years we had no idea where she lived, and we had no way to communicate with her. Here recently though when she moved back, we discovered the nigga was putting his hands on her and shit, and if that nigga wasn't already dead, I swea' to God, I would've killed his bitch ass myself."

"Dead? Who killed him?" Cartier questioned.

Nassir gave him a look before turning away, confirming that it was Naomi who killed him.

Sitting back in his seat, lost for words. Cartier felt like shit even more. He wasn't aware of the depths involving her ex and here he was doing the same thing, hurting her too. As he sulked in his thoughts, Nassir took this as the perfect opportunity to touch on his feelings between the two of them. While he spoke, Cartier could feel exactly where he was coming from. If he was inside his shoes, he'd feel the exact same way behind his baby sister. During their conversation, they were able to express their feelings and man up to their wrongdoings. Nassir nodded. "Now that we got all this shit cleared up, let's order some food. A nigga is starving."

Cartier laughed, shaking his head. "You know for a skinny muthfucka, you sure is greedy."

ന

Across town, Chardonnay was having a mental breakdown about her feelings for Cartier & Trig; she couldn't believe she was dumb enough to cheat with two men that were possibly enemies. Her love for Cartier was beginning to become nonexistent, so how he felt about things wasn't a concern of hers, but how Trig would view her was something she cared about. Choosing between the two wasn't the issue, she just hoped Trig's perception of her wouldn't change once he discovers that she's Cartier's ex.

"Hey baby," Chardonnay greeted as she walked into Trig's bedroom.

"Wassup?" Trig responded, focusing on the television. He was such a busy man; it was very rare that he actually had time to sit and enjoy a good movie or show. But when he did find the time, he made sure he watched his favorites. Chardonnay took a seat at the end of the bed and contemplated a way to start the conversation. The last thing she wanted to do was mess things up between them, so she knew she needed to choose her words carefully.

"How do you know Cartier?" Chardonnay blurted out. Trig looked at her with an unreadable look. Chardonnay felt her stomach begin to turn as she fumbled with her nails, trying to display a nonchalant attitude.

"What made you ask me that?" Trig responded, now giving her his full attention. He wasn't stupid like everyone mistakes him to be. To make it in this life, you need the survival instinct of reading people, and to read Chardonnay was like an open book for Trig. He didn't know what all she knew, but he knew that she knew something.

"I just didn't realize you two knew each other that's all. Are y'all like friends?"

"Nah, I wouldn't exactly say that. We actually dont fuck with each other. How do you know him?"

Chardonnay bit down on her lip, not really knowing how to answer his question. She didn't want to lie but she didn't want to upset him either. She knew she had to think quickly so the best thing she could say was...

"I don't, I just heard of him around town." She lied.

Trig nodded, swallowing the lump in his throat. He thought that their relationship was at a point where she didn't have to lie to him about something as little as this. Now he feels as if he must reevaluate things between them.

"Maybe I'm getting too comfortable," He thought.

Chapter 10

Naomi laid in her bed and watched Waiting to Exhale as she stuffed her face with ice cream. She sighed to herself after realizing how much she related to each woman in the movie; they were all trying to find a good man, worth loving.

For the past few weeks, Naomi had been locked away inside her apartment. She was not ready to truly face reality after what happened between her and Cartier. The whole situation took her to a head space in which she had been fighting so hard to come out of, but Cartier wasn't making shit easy.

Since day 1 of their ending, Cartier's been texting and calling nonstop. He's also been sending flowers and gifts to her house and job. Although deep down she thought his efforts were sweet, it just wasn't enough to make her forgive him. He has made a few attempts to see her, but she made sure to turn him away; she had no energy to entertain whatever lie he was going to feed her, in hopes of getting back in her good graces.

However, to keep her mind off him, she focused on work. She was done crying over men who didn't value her enough to do right; her main focus now was stacking money and working on herself as a person.

Naomi heard a light knock at the door and groaned in annoyance, she did not want to be bothered. She had half the thought to just ignore whoever it was, but once they began knocking repeatedly, she was forced to get up.

Flipping her covers back off her, Naomi quickly hopped out of the bed and power walked to the door before swinging it open, revealing Lanay and Sheree who stood there smiling. "We knew your ass was home, why aren't you dressed?" Lanay asked as she bump passed Naomi, ignoring the death glare she was giving them.

"Dressed for what? I told y'all I'm not in the mood to go out right now." She sighed as she closed and locked her door behind them.

"We know, but girl, today is a new day. It's time you get out of this house and unwind for a moment. So what, things between you and Cartier didn't work out. It's plenty more brothers out here who are willing to commit and you're not going to find them up in this stank ass apartment." Lanay frowned, scrunching up her nose. "Like seriously, when was the last time you took out your trash?"

Naomi simply shrugged as she took a seat on her couch. “I hear what you guys are saying, but that’s easier said than done.”

Walking over and taking a seat next to her, Sheree threw her arm around her. “We know getting over someone isn’t easy, it's the steps you have to take, and the first step is getting back to who you used to be. Sitting around in this apartment, watching sad ass movies, will not make this journey any easier. So, we need you to go shower and get dressed.”

“Where are we going?”

“Girl, have you not looked at a calendar? You know they have our annual block party around this time every year. I don't want to hear any ifs, ands, or buts- you’re coming. You know all our people we grew up with, including everybody and their mama, will be there.” Lanay informed. “Might even be some fine available men there.” She winked.

“And when you say everybody, you mean like Cartier?” Naomi questioned, already backing out at this point.

Smacking her teeth, Sheree rolled her eyes. “Even if he is, Fuck him. You’re not going for him; you're going to have a good time and to show his ass that his weak ass game ain't mean shit to you.” Sheree snapped.

Naomi chewed at her lip, knowing they were right; it was time to pull herself together. Plus, she only knew him for a few months, and she’s dealt with much worse; to let him have her down bad like this was bullshit.

“Fine, I’ll go! Just give me at least thirty minutes or so to get ready.” She sighed as she stood up to prepare herself.

“That’s my girl!” Lanay yelled as she playfully smacked her on the ass when she walked by her. “We gon’ make sure you have a good ass time and by the end of the night, you gon’ be like, Cartier who?”

Laughing, Naomi shook her head as she entered her room to build the strength to start getting ready. She looked at herself in her mirror. “I hope so.” She whispered.

When the girls arrived, the whole street was packed with people dancing and drinking, simply enjoying themselves. It’s been so long since Naomi had been to their annual block party, it was already starting to feel like old times. This was one of the things Naomi missed and loved about being home; it was a space where you could have a good time without worrying about something poppin' off and things going left.

Folks simply came out to have a good time and left the drama at home. The most that would ever happen would be a few fights, but nothing too serious. The only time they've ever heard gunshots was on some street related shit. Despite all of that, the love in the city was beautiful.

Walking around the cones that were blocking off the road, Sheree immediately pulled them over to a food truck that served drinks. Off to the side of the truck was their menu, scanning the list of all the drinks they had, Naomi was becoming a little indecisive, since everything sounded so good.

When the couple in front of them stepped away, the girls walked up. "What can I get you beautiful ladies?" The guy asked, mainly focusing on Naomi.

"I would like to try your jungle juice." Naomi replied shyly, followed by a soft laugh.

"I'ma make yours special, you look like you're in need of a good time." He smiled.

Not opposed to that, Naomi kindly thanked him, before stepping off to the side while Lanay and Sheree ordered their drinks.

Taking in the scene around her, Naomi smiled to herself as she thought back to the days when she and Lanay were running around there; remembering their youth made her happy.

Noticing a familiar face in a crowd of men talking. Naomi tried to get a better look, but her view was blocked when Lanay and Sheree stepped in the way with their drinks in hand. "Here goes your *special* drink." Sheree joked.

"He was ready to risk it all for Ms. Naomi. We haven't even been here five minutes and you are already got a nigga ready to lose his religion!" Lanay pointed out laughing.

Naomi ignored her comment by waving her off, not really fazed or even interested in the guy. She found him attractive, but she was not there to entertain anybody. "Girl whatever, I'm not checking for him."

"You can't lie and say it ain't no fine niggas out here though." Lanay stated as she looked around, while sipping on her drink. "These can't be the same booger eating niggas we grew up with."

Naomi laughed. "Can't be."

Walking over to a table not too far from where they parked, Naomi smacked her teeth when she noticed Cartier, her brother and his friends standing a few feet away from them, they were all talking and laughing. She instantly locked eyes with Cartier but quickly turned her head in disgust.

"Can we please go sit somewhere else?" She asked.

Peeping why she wanted to move, Lanay stood up and grabbed her hand. "No maim, we are not about to let this man have you pressed all night. Come on."

Lanay dragged Naomi where everybody was dancing and began playfully twerking on her to loosen her up. She understood exactly how Naomi felt at this moment, all she wanted to do was help get her best friend back in good spirits.

When Cardi B's hit tik tok song came on, almost every girl out there got in formation to do the dance, including Sheree. She wasn't too familiar with how the routine went, but she also didn't want to be left out, plus it looked fun. The crowd around them hyped them up and had them feeling themselves.

Once the DJ realized what type of vibe everybody was feeling, he played different types of twerk songs to keep the crowd lit. For a moment, as Naomi danced and laughed with her girls, it felt as if time had slowed down, letting her really take in this session of happiness.

Lanay and Sheree could tell Naomi was enjoying herself from the smile on her face and the look in her eyes. This was the Naomi they missed; they weren't ready to lose her.

The DJ ended up playing various genres of music, but he messed up when he played Keyshia Cole's hit song, "Love." Every woman there sang that song with their entire chest, feeling every word, especially Naomi.

All the men there just stood around laughing at the effect this song had on women, across the way Cartier watched as Naomi sung the song; he knew it was hitting a little differently now, due to their current situation.

"It's gettin' a little sad up in this bitch." The DJ spoke into the mic, laughing as he changed the song.

When Dior by Pop Smoke started playing through the speakers, Naomi bent over with her hands on her knees and began throwing ass effortlessly on Lanay. Smacking her on her ass, Naomi looked back with her tongue out as Lanay continued to hype her up along with Sheree who was recording.

A guy had eventually walked up behind her and due to the slight buzz she was feeling from her drink, she continued throwing ass on the unknown guy; never registering that Lanay was no longer behind her, she was letting loose.

Naomi felt as though she were being watched as she grinded her back side up against the guy's front side, he had his arm slightly wrapped around her. Looking around, butterflies filled her stomach as she locked eyes with Cartier.

He sat on the hood of the car with some friends, giving her an unreadable facial expression; she knew it was nothing good, nor did she even care at this point. Turning away from him she continued dancing with the guy, loving the fact that Cartier had to watch another man be all over her.

Naomi finally turned around to see who she had been dancing on and grew shocked when she came face to face with her old classmate, Jacques. The two went to high school together and he used to be one of her crushes, before she got with Deandre. However, due to Jacques being quite the ladies' man back then, the small crush she had towards him never went any further than that.

She hadn't seen him since they graduated, but she had to admit he did get finer over the years.

"Oh my gosh, Jacques! I didn't even know that was you, I thought I saw you earlier, but I thought I was tripping." She laughed as they pulled each other in for a hug.

"Shit, you were out here throwing ass, I had to come see what that was all about." He joked. "What are you doing here though? Never thought I would catch you out partying, I didn't even know your ass was back in the city."

"Things have changed, I'm not the same ole' shy Naomi you went to school with anymore." Naomi laughed.

Licking his lips, he smiled as he looked her up and down. "I see that."

She felt her nerves kick in; he was sizing her up pretty hard. Naomi blushed and looked away. "What about you though? I thought you had moved away for a minute as well."

As they began walking, he nodded. "I did, but a few things happened with my family that I had to take care of, so here I am. Besides, you know ain't no place like home either." He replied.

"That is true," Approaching Lanay's car, Naomi posted up against it. "How is your family though?" She asked.

"They're good; my mom actually passed away a few years ago, so that kind of drove a wedge between everyone, but that's what brought me back home." He said, pushing his hands inside his pockets.

Naomi instantly regretted asking. "I'm really sorry to hear that."

"It's fine, a few years ago I wasn't even able to talk about it or mention it without crying, but I'm good now though." He reassured her. "So, who are you here with? I saw Lanay pinhead ass earlier, I ain't even know y'all was still cool."

"We did fall out for a bit when I moved away, but that was all on me. We're back and we're better now." She smiled.

"That's good shit, it's good to see y'all still cool after all these years. I can't count how many niggas I don' fell out with since Highschool, I thought were like my brothers."

"Hell, I look at it like whoever's still currently in my life is meant to be there. Lanay and I have always had our differences but that's my girl and I wouldn't trade the friendship we have for nothing. She's helped me through a lot of my darkest days with no judgment and vice versa and it's been like that since day one." Naomi expressed as she looked over at Lanay who was dancing with some guy.

"That's real, you don't find too many genuine people these days, so hold onto that for real." Jaques replied honestly. "But how are your folks though?" He asked, while pulling out a blunt from his pocket.

"They're doing good, I'm surprised they're not here tonight." She laughed.

Laughing along with her, Jacques took a hit from his blunt as he looked out towards all the people dancing and drinking. “I see yo girls out there occupied with some niggas, who you here with besides them?” He asked.

Shaking her head, Naomi playfully rolled her eyes. “If you’re wondering if I have a man or not, I don’t.”

Rubbing his hands together and smirking, Jacques looked her up and down with his eyes once more before stepping closer to her. “Well maybe for tonight I can be your boo. I’m not here with anybody, neither are you, so we might as well.” He suggested, followed by a low laugh.

Smacking her lips, Naomi pushed him and laughed. “Boy you are not slick, that boat sunk a long time ago.”

“What boat?” He frowned, slightly confused by her statement.

“You know back in high school, I used to like you, but that time has passed. Plus, I know how you like to get down.” She joked.

Laughing at her statement, Jacques shook his head as he grabbed his lighter to spark his blunt. “I ain’t never knew you had a crush on me, so that’s new news for me. Besides, I’m way past that shit I was on back then. I was young and reckless.” He replied.

“Oh, I see; so those one-night stands at random hotels just isn’t doing it for you anymore, huh?” Naomi teased.

Naomi didn’t believe a single word that left his mouth. Jacques was known around the city for all the wild shit he did back then, but the moment she saw he wasn’t laughing, she stopped laughing because she realized he was serious.

“Actually yeah, I was young as shit back then doing all that. That damn sho’ ain’t me no more.”

“Well, that’s good and I’m sorry if I offended you with my comment as well.” Naomi replied just as she made eye contact with the one person she had been trying to avoid all night.

Cartier’s had his eyes on her all night, which she figured he would, but she thought eventually he would have focused his attention elsewhere, especially since she’s been purposely trying to make him jealous all night.

Naomi." Jacques called out a second time, noticing she had zoned out completely.

Shaking her head, she sighed. "I'm sorry, what were you saying?"

"I was asking if you smoke?" He replied, while holding up the Spliff he had lit.

"Oh, I'm sorry, but nah I'm okay." Naomi honestly just didn't feel comfortable smoking with him. She was cool with Jacques, but she had boundaries.

Glancing back at where Cartier once was standing with his friends, she frowned when she noticed he was gone. Although she knew she had done nothing wrong, guilt started to fill her body.

Not wanting to dwell on what was happening between her and Cartier, she decided to get another drink to help ease her mind and nerves.

ღ

Hugged up against Nassir's car, Sheree felt so protected in his arms. They've been inseparable since that beautiful night they shared with each other, and Sheree was loving every second of it. He was standing on his word by making her feel like a priority and he was putting forth a lot of effort to make things work between them.

"You look beautiful tonight," Nassir whispered in her ear.

Smiling, Sheree closed her eyes and took in the scent of his cologne. "Thank you,"

Placing a kiss on her neck, Nassir glanced over at Cartier who was posted up by himself, staring down Naomi, who was back dancing with Jacques.

Laughing to himself, Nassir shook his head. "Look at this nigga. Hold on baby, I'll be right back."

Excusing himself from Sheree, Nassir walked over to Cartier, shaking his head. "You've been over here watching my sister all night, you ain't got nothing better to do? No matter how long you stare at her, she's not coming over here." Nassir teased, taking a seat next to him on the hood.

“Man, I know I fucked up, but who the fuck is this nigga? He’s been smiling in her face all night.” Cartier asked, becoming frustrated from having to watch Naomi entertain another man all night. “She gotta be doing this shit on purpose to make a nigga jealous.

“I don't know, but from the looks of it though, it seems like it. Why do you care anyway? Wasn't you just up Chardonnay’s ass?” Quentin teased adding salt to the wound.

“Shut tha fuck up Q, you always gotta kick a nigga when he already down. Fuck this shit!” Cartier snapped, getting ready to leave, but Nassir stopped him.

“Down!? Nigga, how the fuck you think these women you out here playing fucking feel? We already talked and you know you’re my brother and I love you, but that’s my baby sister! I'm not afraid to rip your head off about her. Get your shit together man and I'm not telling you this shit again!” Nassir warned.

“What am I supposed to do? She won’t fucking speak to me!” Cartier yelled back with frustration.

“For starters, you need to handle your shit with Chardonnay first, then try and fix shit with Naomi. But anyways I’m out, you do what you got to do but just don’t keep hurting her man. Give her time, when she’s ready, she will come to you.” Nassir replied as he slapped hands with both Cartier and Quentin before heading back over to Sheree.

“Man, fuck what Nassir talking about! You better get your ass up and go say something. Just gon’ let that nigga steal your girl like that?” Quentin chips in, taking a hit of the blunt.

Cartier watched as Naomi was smiling at whatever Jacques had said to her, before becoming fed up and deciding to go on over there.

Walking over towards the two, Naomi let out a sigh when he approached them. “What do you want?” She asked dryly.

“Can we please talk for a second?” Cartier asked.

“We have nothing to discuss.” Naomi replied before turning back to Jacques, but Cartier grabbed her by the arm and turned her back around.

“Please, all I’m asking for is a chance to apologize and explain.” He begged.

Before she could even attempt to respond, Jacques stepped forward, pulling Naomi behind him. “Aye man, I don’t know what all you two got going on, but it’s clear she doesn’t want to speak with you, so just move around.”

“Exactly, you don’t know; what we got going on is between Naomi and I, so you better get the fuck out my face.” Cartier said, stepping closer.

“What the fuck you tryna do then nigga?” Jacques said, tossing his red cup to the ground, not showing one ounce of bitch in his blood.

Stepping in between the two, Naomi pushed Cartier back. “Chill out!” She yelled before turning her attention to Jacques. “I’m so sorry for all of this, can you please just give me a second.”

Stepping away with Cartier, Naomi sighed. “Haven’t you embarrassed me enough already? Why are you creating a scene right now in front of all these people?” She semi-yelled.

“I just need to talk with you Nao, how can I make things right between us when you won’t even give me the chance?” Cartier asked, pushing his hands in his pockets.

Folding her arms, Naomi shook her head. “There are no more chances Cartier; I told you that I don't want anything to do with you. You're a liar and I don't need somebody I can’t trust in my life; I’ve been down that road before and I’m not doing it again!” She snapped.

Hearing her say those words hurt. Cartier felt his eyes gloss over, he decided to speak to keep himself from crying. “I don’t know how many times I have to apologize for not being all the way real with you about my situation, but everything between us was genuine and real. I love you Naomi and knowing that I hurt you is fucking me up. Just please let me prove myself and fix it.”

Quickly wiping the tear that fell from her eye, Naomi let out a low laugh. “You’re so fucking stupid Cartier! It’s not about fixing it or about how many times you must apologize. It’s about how you’re acting like this shit isn’t a big fucking deal! You led me to believe you were a single man and the whole time you were just playing a role! I was the cause behind another woman's pain without even realizing it! This shit is not cool Cartier, and you know it! I can't even have this conversation with you right now!” Naomi screamed as her emotions began to rise, she needed him to hear her, so she continued.

"I am so fucking hurt; all I want to do is punch you in your shit! You could've at least kept it G with me and told me what it was, and then let ME decide if I want to deal with it or not! You embarrassed and played the fuck out of me! How do you expect me to look at you the same after this?"

As she yelled, it felt like Déjà vu from her and Dre; every tear she fought fell in that moment. All she wanted was real love and not to be broken again. She knew she deserved to be happy and loved correctly, she wasn't about to let a man play her again.

"Just please leave me alone." She whispered, before going to walk away but Cartier stopped her again.

"Naomi, you have to believe me when I say I'm sorry for hurting you. If you don't believe anything else I say or do, just know that I really am sorry for the pain I've caused you." He told her before letting go of her hand.

"I'm sorry too." She replied softly as she continued to walk away, leaving him there alone.

ღ

After dancing to a few songs, Lanay realized Naomi and Sheree had been gone, as well as the guy she was dancing with. Searching for them, she sighed when she saw Naomi talking with Jacques and Sheree all boo'd up with Nassir.

She decided to grab herself a drink, she figured it'd be a nice distraction, rather than sulking in her loneliness. She walked over to a booth where a few people stood ordering drinks as well.

Looking back at Sheree and Nassir as they laughed and whispered things into each other's ears, Lanay looked away in attempt to ignore that feeling of jealousy rising within her. Lanay was more than happy for her friends progressing in their love lives, but she yearned for one of her own. She hadn't had a man to call her own in almost 2 years.

The occasional hook ups she had with men were fun, but she wanted more than just sex.

When it was her turn to order, Lanay walked up and took a seat in one of the chairs they had lined around the booth. "Hey pretty girl, what can I get you?" The older black lady asked with a polite smile.

"Can I get a double shot of Hennessy?" Lanay asked, followed by a heavy sigh.

"Oou we're doing it big tonight I see, long night sweetie?" The lady asked as she started making her drink.

"Something like that." She shrugged.

"Well honey, I'm sure whatever it is, it'll get better soon. It always does." Handing her the drink, she began wiping down her counter space.

"How can you be so sure of that? I want to believe that things will get better for me and that one day I will find exactly what I'm looking for, but it's hard." Lanay opened up.

Throwing down her dishrag, the lady leaned over the counter with her elbows resting on the countertop, she gave Lanay her full attention. "Well, all depends on exactly what you're looking for, so what is it you're in search of?"

Throwing back her drink, Lanay closed her eyes as she released a sigh. "I'm looking for love, it's like I always find myself in situations that lead to nowhere, besides sex, and I want more than just that."

"I'm sure you've heard this plenty of times, but never go searching for love. Plus, we as people, especially women, must stop placing ourselves in situations that we know we don't want any parts of. If a man approaches you simply for sex and you know that's not what you want, why would you allow that man to come over and have your body, then get mad when you see it's not going anywhere?" She questioned, not really expecting an answer at all.

"One thing I've learned from men is that they will always make clear what they want by their words and actions, but more so their actions. If you choose to ignore that then that is simply on you for expecting more from a dead-end road."

Listening to her words, Lanay had to admit she was right. The last thing she expected was to be receiving advice from a stranger tonight, but she felt it was meant for her to hear every word.

"I always felt like love was supposed to be one of those things that happen when you least expect it; this can go for friendships, jobs, and relationships. It's just like you wake up one day and you find yourself given an opportunity, you take a chance on it and next thing you know, you realize you finally received everything you were wanting and more."

Letting her words sink in, Lanay thanked her as she walked away to help a few customers that approached the booth.

A few moments later the lady returned with another drink, "This drink is on the house, I hope your night gets better sweetie." She smiled.

Thanking her again, Lanay took a sip of the drink before placing it down as she looked out at the party watching everyone have a good time. She should've been out there with them all, yet instead here she was drinking and having a therapy session with a stranger.

Locking eyes with a guy who was sitting on the hood of his car, smoking, Lanay looked away, convinced they'd locked eyes by accident. However, she had to admit that the guy was fine, the intense stare down they had didn't feel as if it was just a coincidence, but she didn't want to get her hopes up either.

Glancing back over where the guy was sitting, Lanay frowned when she saw he was no longer there.

"It's clear we both have good taste, but my question is what is a woman as gorgeous as you doing over here all alone?" Startled by the voice from behind her, Lanay slightly turned her head to be faced with the same guy.

"Maybe because no man here has had the courage to approach me besides you." She shrugged.

"So, what does a guy like me, who actually had the courage to approach someone as beautiful as you, have to do to get your number?" He asked as he took a seat beside her.

"Straight forward, I see." Lanay smirked.

Laughing, he shrugged. "Only way I know how to be."

They both stared at each other before Lanay broke character. "What's your name?" She asked.

"I'm Quentin and you?" He replied, extending his hand.

"Lanay."

"Beautiful name for a beautiful woman, so where do we go from here Miss Lanay?" He asked, leaving it up to her.

Quentin was very attracted to Lanay, but he was only going to pursue this if she was feeling the same. He didn't want her to feel as if he was pressuring her either, so he wanted to leave the choice up to her and whatever her answer was, he was going to be cool with it regardless.

Letting out a deep breath, Lanay stood up from her seat before turning to face him. "Would you like to dance?"

Smiling, Quentin stood up as well. "Lead the way, beautiful."

Looking back at the lady, Lanay smiled when she held up a thumbs up for her to go for it. All she could hear in her mind was her wisdom of how love comes unexpectedly.

So, she was going to take a chance on this opportunity and go for it. She was going to be open about exactly what she wanted, and she wasn't going to settle for anything less than that.

Chapter 11

Cartier decided to leave the block party early, he rushed home with his mind racing with thoughts about Naomi. He knew at this point there was nothing he could do to prove to her that he was sorry, but he wasn't going to give up either. So, tonight he was officially ending things with Chardonnay to work on himself and get Naomi back at the same time.

When he arrived at the place he used to call home, Cartier quickly parked his car in the driveway and hopped out just as fast before he rushed to the door.

Using his key to unlock the door, Cartier stepped inside and faintly heard Chardonnay's voice coming from the back of the house, he followed it. When he realized she was on the phone talking with someone, he waited at the door before going inside to listen.

"You are so funny; I'll stop by later and drop you off a plate baby and I'll be sure to wear that red lingerie set you bought me as well." She flirted.

Frowning to himself, Cartier opened the door and cleared his throat to catch her attention. Chardonnay immediately said bye and hung up the phone as she adjusted the silk robe she was wearing.

"Nah, don't let me interrupt." He laughed. "It's clear what's going on. I'm just tired of doing all this back-and-forth Chardonnay. We are clearly not happy, nor are we made for each other. We both have done some fucked up things, I'm just tired of us hurting each other."

Chardonnay remained silent, so Cartier decided to continue expressing himself.

"But one thing I don't understand is how you got so mad when you found out about Naomi and me- whole time you had a whole nigga on the side. What was the point?" He asked.

Rolling her eyes, Chardonnay let out a scoff. "Are you really that surprised Carti?" She half laughed.

"I mean honestly, what'd you expect? All those nights of cheating; the nights I spent alone while you were out doing God's knows what. I got lonely and a part of me already felt as if the relationship was over. We became roommates who'd fuck every once and a while, I wanted more than that. I met someone and he has been the best man to me but for some dumb ass reason, I still can't seem to let you go, even though I have someone who would go to war for me and loves me deeply." She expressed, shaking her head.

"Then you ghosted me for almost five months, what was I supposed to do? Wait for you while you ran around town with some new bitch, as if you didn't have a whole girlfriend at home? So yes, I found someone in the midst of all our bullshit and things between us did get serious. Then boom, here you come ready to work things out again and because I loved you, I was willing to give us another shot. But then I realized you were never going to change, so I continued being with this guy because you weren't worth losing him behind."

"You could've just told me, instead of us wasting each other's time." Cartier replied.

Laughing, Chardonnay looked away from him. "That's the difference between you and I; anytime I put forth an effort to make things work between us, I meant it. You're the one who fell out of love with me and basically left me no choice but to move on! So, I wasn't wasting my time fighting for a relationship I didn't want to end, you're the one who wasted your own time staying with someone you clearly didn't love anymore." She snapped, becoming emotional.

Knowing she was right; Cartier didn't know what to say to that. But a lot of things he questioned back then were slowly starting to make sense now, and he knew he couldn't get mad at Chardonnay for moving on when he had stepped out on her countless times.

"Who's the guy?" He asked, curious to know if he knew him.

"His name is Rashun Howard."

Cartier nodded; the name sounded familiar, but he wasn't going to dwell on it too much. He had other things on his mind. "How long have you known him?"

"Two years, maybe a little longer; we started off as friends then things got serious between us as time passed." She answered.

Chardonnay could tell from the look on his face that there was something heavy on his mind, seemed like he wanted to ask her something; at this point, she was ready to air out whatever secret, so they could finally clear shit up, once and for all.

"What is it Cartier? It's clear that something else is on your mind, so just say what you have to say or ask whatever it is you want to ask."

"I just want to know if you aborted the baby because you weren't truly ready or if it was because at the time you didn't know who the father possibly was?" Cartier simply asked, looking in her eyes. She looked shocked by his question, but he needed to know.

Chardonnay had a good feeling that this was where he was going with all those questions. Swallowing the lump in her throat, she started to fidget with her nails, trying to find the words to best explain herself. "Both, but—"

"I honestly don't even care to hear it." Cartier shook his head, that was all he needed to know, nothing else mattered.

"So that's it?" She asked with a lil bit of anger in her voice.

"Yeah. We're done Chardonnay! Ain't no point in us keeping whatever this is going. We're bad for each other and I'm tired. We clearly found happiness in other people and I'm not tryna be in the way of that for you." Cartier answered as he zipped up his suitcase.

Hopping up from the bed, realizing that he was serious, Chardonnay stopped him from leaving. "Cartier I'm genuinely sorry, I should have told you from the beginning, but I didn't know how." She cried, laying her head on his chest.

Letting out a deep sigh, Cartier eventually wrapped his arms around her as she cried. Despite the hard demeanor they both put on to cover their hurt, the undeniable love was still there between them. It was clear that they just weren't meant to be, it was taking everything in him not to break down with her. He used to love Chardonnay deeply, the fact they were at this point hurt him, indefinitely.

"Chardonnay, stop. Baby you and I both know this is what's best for the both of us." Cartier said before removing his arms from around her grabbing his bags again.

"This is what's best for you! I swear I hate you so much!" She screamed from the bedroom.

Chardonnay was honestly more disappointed that he was leaving her for another woman. She knew this day would come with the way he stepped out, but it still didn't take the pain she felt away; it was like a slap in the face to her.

When Cartier reached the door, he removed his key off his keychain and sat it on the living room table before leaving out.

Leaving Chardonnay wasn't as easy as he thought it would be, but he knew staying with her would do more damage than finally letting go. This was all for the best. Chardonnay watched Cartier back out of the driveway, her blood began to boil from anger.

She grabbed her cell phone to make a call. She dialed the number and listened to the phone ring three times before they picked up.

"Hello?" They answered.

Sniffling, to make it seem as if she were crying, she put the phone on speaker. "Hey, it's Char, I need a favor."

"Say the word and it's done." The person replied.

ꙮ

A few weeks had passed since everything between Cartier and Chardonnay went down. During those weeks, Cartier used that time focusing on business, getting settled into his place, and orchestrating ways to get back in Naomi's good graces.

He decided to surprise Naomi with a trip to Miami. After packing up his last suitcase, Cartier carried it out to his car while making sure he turned off all his lights and locked up properly.

He spoke to her boss at the salon and discovered that she'd be off on these particular days, so he planned according to that. The only thing he hoped for was that she'd agreed to go with him. He wanted to use this as a step towards the right direction of amending things between her.

When he reached her apartment, Cartier sat outside in the parking lot, praying all would go well. He reached in his backseat and grabbed the gift bag he had for her, before stepping out and heading towards the entrance.

Entering the building going to the second floor, he knocked on her door twice. Hearing her small footsteps a few moments later, his nerves began to kick in when he heard the locks start to turn, when she opened the door, she looked surprised.

"Why are you here Cartier?" Naomi asked dryly.

"Look, I know you're tired of hearing me say how sorry I am, so I'm trying to show you and I want to start by taking you out." Cartier answered, stepping inside uninvited.

Her house wasn't the usual clean he was used to; she had clothes everywhere, balled up tissue scattered across her living room couch, and he could tell she hadn't done dishes in a while.

"Here, I got this for you." Cartier said, giving her the bag. She hesitated at first but took it anyway and looked inside.

"Aww this is cute." Naomi said, pulling out the stuffed teddy bear filled with pictures of them all over. Cartier smiled at her reaction as she proceeded to open the rest of the gift.

When she grabbed the box, Naomi slightly shook it to try and guess what was inside before opening it to see a plane ticket to Miami with a note attached that read, "*Will you go to Miami with me?"*

Naomi frowned as she looked up at him, shaking her head. "This is nice Cartier, but it won't fix things."

"I didn't say it would, but it's a step towards fixing things between us. Just give me three days babe, that's all I'm asking of you." He pleaded.

Letting out a sigh, she looked down to avoid eye contact. As bad as she wanted to hold her attitude, she did really miss him, and she couldn't ignore his efforts either. No man had ever gone to this extent to apologize after cheating, so his persistence was commendable to her.

She agreed to give him a chance and see what else he had up his sleeve, "I'll go, but like I said before, this doesn't fix things and it doesn't automatically mean I forgive you either."

Cartier smiled. "I know it doesn't, I'm just happy you agree to go with me."

"You are so lucky I had taken off work to get my mind right." She said walking towards the back.

Cartier smirked and decided to clean her kitchen and straighten up her house while she packed her things and got ready. He felt so good that she was giving him a fair shot to make things right. The last thing he wanted was to lose her.

After an hour or so passed, they were finally ready to head out. Naomi checked over everything to make sure she had what she needed, as Cartier loaded her things inside the SUV.

Their flight was set to depart at seven o'clock tonight, so they were running a little behind but luckily the airport wasn't too far from where Naomi lived. After he finished putting her bags up, they got inside the car and Cartier headed towards the airport.

The car ride was quiet but peaceful, Cartier and Naomi shared the love of music, so they vibed out to the songs that played on the way there. The closer they got to the airport the more anxious and excited Cartier became. The thought of all the things he had planned for her made him nervous, but he was ready to show her his romantic side.

His excitement intensified because she had no clue of all the special things he had planned for them in Miami. He just hoped that by the end of the trip, this would put them back on the right path and show her that he actually does love her.

Once they arrived at the airport, they grabbed their things and headed towards the entrance. After checking in their bags and going through the security check, they had less than five minutes to board their flight. When they reached their terminal, the flight attendants were already beginning to board the plane, which caused Naomi's anxiety to rise because they almost missed their flight.

Finding their seats in first-class, Cartier put their carry-on bags inside of the compartment above them before taking his seat next to Naomi.

He hired a company specializing in interior design, he checked his phone to see if they responded back to his message about the hotel. He booked them a penthouse suite in one of Miami's most luxurious beach hotels; he needed the company's decor to match the energy of the surprise he had for her.

From Decorator:
Good evening, Mr. Williams! Everything is good to go for your room. I will send you pictures shortly as we finish up.
Delivered 7:20pm

After he responded, he locked his phone and got comfortable in his seat. Naomi laid her head on her pillow and drifted off to sleep. He decided to take that time to check up on the business. Cartier relaxed and prayed that everything would go as planned during this trip.

They finally arrived at Miami International Airport; Naomi was becoming very excited to see what else Cartier had planned. They went to get their things and then meet with the car service. They saw a man with a sign holding up their names, so they approached him. He introduced himself as Walter Hughes and then helped them get everything into the car.

Although it was night, the weather was much warmer than Atlanta and Naomi loved it. She rolled down her window to enjoy looking at the beautiful views of the city as they headed to the hotel.

After a twenty-minute drive, they arrived. Cartier went inside to check in and Naomi helped the driver with their things. Once he finished, they were escorted to the room. During the elevator ride, Naomi noticed that they pushed the penthouse button. She looked at Cartier and he flashed her a smile, she tried to hide her bashful reaction.

When they got off the elevator, Cartier dismissed the staff and told Naomi to close her eyes. Naomi looked at him weirdly but did it anyway. She then felt him guiding her inside, "you can open them now."

She stood there in shock; he had rose petals all over the room, candles lit, balloons, and several different gift bags. All Naomi could do was smile at his efforts.

Covering her mouth as tears of joy began to fall, she shook her head in disbelief. No man had ever gone out of their way to please her like this, the fact that he did, said a lot.

"Really!?" Naomi exclaimed, smiling. Cartier pulled her into a hug, Naomi unexpectedly gave him a kiss, which caught Cartier off guard, but he wasn't going to decline it.

When she pulled away from the kiss and just hugged him, Cartier kissed the top of her head. "I'm so sorry I hurt you, Naomi." He whispered in her ear, clenching her tightly in return.

They finally let go of each other. Cartier finished putting away the rest of their things, while Naomi took the time to examine their suite.

Walking over to their bed, she decided to look inside a gift bag that was sitting there; the rest of them were displayed on the bed. Reaching inside, her smile reappeared as she pulled out a box from Pandora. She opened it up and saw an encrusted heart shaped, rose gold ring inside- she closed it back up, quickly.

Closing the door behind him he noticed she opened the promise ring he got her. Walking over to her he took the box from her and slid the ring on her finger. "I bought this ring as a symbol of my promise to you. Seeing you go through the pain that I caused not only broke me, but it crushed my spirit. I don't ever want to make you feel like that again, so today I promise to always be honest with you and be the best man I can for you." He expressed.

A single tear gracefully fell from her eyes, Naomi pulled him into her and inserted her tongue inside his mouth. This was exactly why she tried staying away from him for so long; he was so hard to resist.

She pulled away from the kiss and wiped the remains of her lip gloss from his lips. She decided to open the rest of her gifts later because she was dying to get inside the jacuzzi.

After getting undressed while Cartier unpacked a few of his things, Naomi grabbed herself a bottle of wine and a glass before heading out to the jacuzzi to relax for a bit.

The warmth of the water touched her body as she stepped inside, she let out a sigh as she leaned her head back with her eyes closed. "Is this what heaven feels like?" She asked herself, earning a laugh from Cartier.

"Mind if I join you?" He asked before he started to undress as well.

Opening one of her eyes, she shrugged. "Might as well, I guess we could use this time to actually talk." Naomi replied.

Reaching over to pour herself a glass of wine, Naomi took a few sips to help relax her nerves. Once Cartier was inside the jacuzzi with her, he reached down into the water and grabbed one of her legs and began massaging her foot.

Smiling at his kind gesture, Naomi tried to mentally prepare herself for the conversation she has been avoiding. "So, I'm giving you the chance to finally explain yourself. I want you to tell me everything. If we're going to do this, I just need you to be completely honest with me." She expressed.

Letting out a deep sigh, he nodded. "Well, all I can say is things between Chardonnay and I go way back before I even met you. Our relationship was never perfect, mistakes were made on both ends, which caused us to resent and hate each other during the course of our relationship. When I met you, things between her and I weren't the best and we were sorta on like a break. I admit though, I didn't expect things between you and I to progress as quickly as it did, I have no regrets besides me hurting the both of you. I should've been straight up from the jump about all of this, but I honestly didn't want to drive you away either or ruin the chance of actually getting to know you, I see now, that was selfish on my part."

Naomi nodded, taking in everything he was telling her. She knew he had a point when it came to possibly ruining a chance for him to get to know her, because she knew right off the bat that if he would've mentioned anything about a girlfriend, he would've had no chance with her.

"I can understand your reasoning behind why you didn't say anything, but at the end of the day it was still very selfish on your part. If you guys were that unhappy you should've just walked away. Trust me, I know first-hand how it is to let go of a relationship you worked so hard to build, but I would never allow myself to get involved with someone new knowing that I still have unfinished business with someone else. Like honestly, what exactly were you thinking?" Naomi questioned being totally forward with her standpoint in the situation.

Cartier looked at her, taken back a little, he knew she had every right to feel and say whatever she wanted at this moment. "I wasn't thinking. Look, I'ma be totally honest, I wasn't faithful to Chardonnay, stepping out on her wasn't new, this time was just different. I really hope you don't take what I'm saying the wrong way; all the other females I cheated on Chardonnay with, meant nothing to me. It was just sex." He replied.

"But things with you were more than that and before I knew it, I realized I was damn near falling in love with you, but a part of me always knew I couldn't give you everything you wanted because portions of me were still attached to another woman. I hate you had to find out the way you did, but I swear to you, I broke things off with Chardonnay for good. I really do want to be with you and work on building back the trust you once had."

Searching his eyes, Naomi could see he was being honest, but this was a lot to take in. "Why did you cheat so much?"

Cartier scratched the back of his head before letting out a sigh, "Like I said before, our relationship was never perfect. She began neglecting my needs as her man and then I found out she aborted our child behind my back.

When I first found out, I was told she aborted the baby because she wasn't ready, but I recently found out that it was because the baby might've been another man's child instead."

When that last statement left his mouth, Naomi's eyes grew wide. "Oh wow." Was all she could manage to say.

"Yeah, and I know nothing excuses me cheating but like I said, mistakes were made on both ends. I just think due to how long we had been together; we were so focused on what we used to be, rather than looking at what we were becoming. We needed to realize that the love we once had for each other was gone."

"I've been there before, so I can relate to that. I found myself hanging on to a dead-end relationship, simply because of what we used to be and the man that I knew he could be. I lost sight of reality." Naomi admitted.

Cartier nodded as they both stared at each other, "So, where do we go from here?" He asked her.

Shrugging her shoulders, she looked away. "I don't know yet, let's just see how the rest of this trip goes first." She answered.

Smiling at her response, he nodded his head in agreement. "I'll take that!"

"As if you had a choice." She joked.

Laughing along with her, Cartier and Naomi decided to spend the rest of their time in the jacuzzi, talking. They discussed the possibilities of what the future may hold, as well as life and all the things they learned along the way.

Naomi really enjoyed every moment of it, she felt as if she was gaining her best friend back again; if the trip continued this way, the chance of Cartier getting another shot would more than likely be granted.

Slowly opening her eyes to a dark room, Naomi instantly knew she had woken up way too early and decided to catch some more sleep. As she laid there with her eyes closed, she tried to get back comfortable, but nothing was working. After a few minutes passed, she was now wide awake, so she gave up on the thought of getting more sleep.

Reaching over to grab her phone from her nightstand, Naomi pressed her lock button to check the time. When she saw that it was only three something in the morning, she smacked her teeth, frustrated.

Glancing over at Cartier to see him still asleep, she had the urge to slap him awake so she wouldn't be up alone, but she decided against doing so and chose to go out on their balcony instead.

Carefully flipping the covers off her body, she slowly got out of the bed and grabbed her robe that was laid out on the floor. She wrapped it around her body before stepping out.

Holding onto the railing, Naomi smiled in amazement at the perfect view of the city. The wind blowing and the scenery brought her peace, she closed her eyes and took in the moment. Naomi realized she often forgets how far she's come from dealing with Deandre; from escaping that relationship, to moving back home for a fresh start and succeeding, and now having a man that'll go the extra mile for her, literally. She felt accomplished.

She thanked God for where she was now, because a year ago she would've never imagined. She honestly thought she'd be dead by the hands of Deandre by now, yet there she was, still here; she was granted a second chance at life- she decided she was going to make the best out of it.

Hearing the balcony door slide open, Naomi looked back to see Cartier yawning and rubbing his eyes. Walking up behind her, Cartier wrapped his arms around her waist, kissed her shoulder blade softly, and stared out at the city with her.

"You alright?" He asked.

She turned her neck slightly so she could his face, she nodded. "Mhm yeah, I didn't want to wake you, so I came out here and found myself reflecting on my life and all the accomplishments that I tend to ignore and take for granted."

Securing the hold he had around her, Naomi relaxed against his body and listened to the sound of the wind and his heartbeat. "I sometimes find myself doing that as well, I used to do it a lot as a kid when I would run away to escape the beatings from my dad. I found this hill, I'd sit out there for hours, just thinking about everything."

"I think this is the first time I ever really heard you mention your dad. Like, I know he passed away, but you never really say much of anything else about him." Naomi pointed out.

Laughing to himself, Cartier shook his head. "For good reason, ain't too much to say about him. He wasn't a good man." He shrugged.

Naomi smacked her lips. "What was he like? It's clear there's something between you guys that you haven't gotten over yet; you try to dismiss any topic pertaining him."

Cartier knew she was right. He took a deep breath and sat in one of the chairs they had and motioned for Naomi to sit on his lap. "Like I said before, he just wasn't a good man; he was manipulative, abusive, and money hungry. The only thing I've ever respected my father for was showing us a lifestyle where we never had to go without. He wanted to give us the life he didn't have as a kid, but I feel like along the way he lost himself and became a fucking monster. As a kid I used to look up to him, I wanted to be him but then I soon realized the man I saw was not the same man my mother witnessed behind closed doors."

"I was about seven or eight when I realized he was abusing my mama and on top of that he was cheating on her as well. That shit fucked me up bad when I witnessed him knock her down as if she was some hoe on the street. But it's crazy because despite the shit he put us through, he never let anyone fuck with us. Like, he protected us like no other and raised my brother and I to be close since family meant everything to him, but that shit used to confuse the hell out of me when one minute he's instilling love and life in us then the next minute he's beating our ass for no apparent reason." He laughed.

"Maybe your dad had a lot of demons he was running from and rather than facing them and getting help, he lashed out on y'all instead." Naomi expressed.

"You might be right, but we'll never know now. I watched my dad take his last breath right in front of me and I remember feeling so many different emotions at that moment. I was angry, I was sad, I felt helpless and then a part of me was even a little happy because I knew at least my mama or us would never have to deal with the abuse again." Cartier admitted.

"But the moment he died; my uncles wasted no time in molding me to take over whenever they felt I was ready. Most of my life, I tried so hard being everything he wasn't. I wanted to be better but sometimes I find myself making those same mistakes and then I realize I'm more like him than I ever wanted to be." He mumbled.

Cupping his face with her hands, Naomi leaned forward and pressed her lips softly against his lips before hugging him tightly. He wrapped his arms around her just as tight. "I'm so sorry you went through all of that, but Cartier you're nothing like your father. You may be strong headed like him and you may have his will power to succeed by any means necessary, but when it comes to the way you love and help others, it's like no other and that is what made me fall for you." She whispered.

"Long as you don't lose sight of that kindness and love in your heart, you will be alright."

Chapter 12

Lanay stood over the stove, making breakfast while she listened to music, setting the vibe for the mood she was in. She swayed her hips to the beat of the song, oblivious to Quentin making his way inside the kitchen. He was amused by her dancing. Wrapping his arms around her, Lanay slightly jumped before she playfully hit him.

“I thought you were in bed, sleeping,” She stated, before grabbing a spoonful of the eggs she cooked for him to taste.

Leaning up against his kitchen counter, he smiled. “I was, but my homeboy BJ called me to tell me he was on his way over.”

Nodding her head, Lanay turned back around to finish cooking. “I can leave after I finish cooking; I don’t want to impose.” She suggested.

“You ain’t imposing on me at all, I like having you here.” He told her as he walked up behind her, kissing her on her neck. Pushing him off her, Lanay laughed as she shook her head at him.

Since Quentin and Lanay met at the block party, they’ve been hanging out a lot. Things between them were kinda going fast, but it all felt right to Lanay, and she was happy.

For the past few weeks, Lanay found herself doing things for him she wouldn’t dare have done if it was another man in his shoes. She couldn’t explain it, when it came to Quentin, things were just like that.

Sheree and Naomi weren’t too fond of their relationship, since they felt as if the two were rushing but Lanay simply did not care. It had been a while since a man had treated her the way Quentin did, so she wasn’t going to allow their opinions to cloud her mind.

Hearing her phone chime, she looked over and hesitated when she saw Naomi was calling but she still decided to answer since they hadn’t talked much lately.

Lanay hadn’t been feeling the sisterly love from her girls, so she chose to distance herself from them sometimes. Don’t get her wrong though, she loves them, but she feels they just don’t understand her newfound relationship and she didn’t have time for their judgment.

Every time they’d talk, they’d complain or lecture her about moving too fast with Quentin. She knew it only steamed from their love for her, but she didn't want to hear that. Last she checked she was grown and was grown enough to make decisions of her own.

"Hey Nao, what's going on?" Lanay greeted as she placed the sausages inside the pan to cook.

Fixing her makeup in the mirror as she placed her on speaker, Naomi smiled, "Girl nothing, I just wanted to check in on you. I haven't heard from my sister in a while."

"Oh, I'm doing fine. I just been busy with work, and you know hanging with Quentin." Lanay explained.

Hearing Naomi sigh over the phone, Lanay rolled her eyes, "Well you be sure not to forget to take some time out for yourself too, Lanay."

Naomi was truly delighted for her friend's happiness, and she loved that Lanay found someone who treated her well, but her only concern was that Lanay would become dependent on him for her happiness.

"I know Naomi, but please no lecture today, okay? Can I please just go one day without hearing it from either you or Sheree." She pleaded, becoming frustrated. "How is your trip going with Cartier?" She asked, wanting to change the subject.

"It's not that we're trying to lecture you Lanay, we just want you to be careful. Quentin may be a great guy, but at the end of the day I just don't want to see you get hurt again." Naomi expressed.

Letting out a sigh, Lanay half smiled. "I know and I appreciate both you and Sheree's concerns, but I promise you Quentin is a really good guy, and he treats me even better. So, can I please just enjoy being loved on freely?" Lanay asked, followed by a low laugh.

As Lanay continued her conversation with Naomi in the kitchen, downstairs Quentin and his friend Bj sat on his couch discussing business and future plans he had in the works.

Leaning forward to flick his ashes into the ashtray, Bj sighed. "So, what are we gonna do now man?"

Sitting back in his seat, Quentin was consumed in his thoughts for a moment. He became frustrated about his plan to take over the family business, due to the fact that his brother decided to do business with their Uncle Pernell.

This put shit in a whole different perspective and made things a little harder, especially since he didn't want his plan to be exposed just yet; not until the timing was just right.

So, it was very important that he moved precisely and quietly with any decisions made.

Quentin was simply tired of being left out when it came to the family business. He felt as if the family didn't respect him, and he was tired of coming second to Cartier, when he was the oldest. The moment they revealed Cartier was the one they wanted to take over the family reign, it was like a slap in the face to Quentin, he didn't understand why they didn't think he was good enough.

"I don't know man; we're going to have to wait this shit out a little longer than expected. Once I find out who the new connection my uncle is introducing Cartier to, I plan to cut them out with my new business partner instead and go from there." Quentin explained.

Passing over the blunt he asked, "And who might that be?"

"Don't worry, just know I have a supplier that I'm meeting with in a few weeks, and I know for a fact that I can seal the deal. Once that's done, I can finally execute my plan." Quentin informed him, placing the blunt between his lips as he inhaled.

BJ was listening to what Quentin was saying, but at the same time he wasn't understanding either. Quentin and BJ have known each other damn near all their lives, and he was close with his family as well. So, witnessing this wedge between them did make him feel a certain way.

"Honestly bro, I don't understand your vendetta against your blood. Like, what's your reason behind all of this?" He asked.

"Them niggas ain't my fucking family man. Every chance this nigga Cartier got, he short handed me. I'm his big brother, his blood fucking brother and he would rather go and make money with Nassir over me?" He expressed angrily, chuckling. "Then the whole family just kisses his spoiled ass. Nobody ever gave a fuck about Quentin, it was always about Cartier and him taking over the family business, like I don't fucking exist, so enough is enough."

"I feel what you saying bro, I do. Have you ever expressed this to them though?"Before he could respond, Lanay came downstairs with two plates in her hand. She sat Bjs in front of him on the table and then she sat in Quentin's lap and placed his plate on the table.

"Damn sis, this shit looks good as fuck," Bj complemented picking his plate up and eating a scoop of her eggs.

"Thank you." She replied softly before focusing her attention on Quentin. Noticing that his body language was off, she frowned. "Everything ok?"

"Yeah, I'm cool. Thank you for the food tho baby, it looks good." He answered, pecking her on the lips and gripping a handful of her behind.

Lanay smiled and leaned into his chest to whisper in his ear, "Hurry up with your company. I have a surprise for you."

Placing a soft kiss on his cheek, she stood up, waving bye to BJ before disappearing upstairs. Quentin held his head down trying to hide the blush that appeared on his face. He never pictured himself as the type of man to ever fall in love and have a family, but he was really starting to like Lanay. She was growing on him in ways no woman ever had before.

The connection they had was out of this world, it's as if they've known each all their lives.

When Quentin heard BJ laughing, he quickly looked up at him frowning. "What's funny nigga?"

"She got you wide open bitch," Bj teased with a mouthful of food.

"Man fuck you, let's get back to this shit so I can go attend to my woman before she put your black ass out." Waving him off as they laughed together, BJ and Quentin went back to discussing his plan. Although BJ felt like there were other ways Quentin could've handled this sibling rivalry, he was going to ride for his brother no matter what.

ꦩ

Trig hit the locks to his BMW as he stepped outside into the cool air. Adjusting his jacket, he began to make his way inside of his stash house, which appeared to be a laundry mat to everyday folk.

Opening the doors, he held his mug as he scoped out the place. He was beyond heated that he had to hop out of the comfort of his home to take care of snake in his camp. Receiving a call that one of his workers had been doing some sneak shit behind his back wasn't the highlight of his afternoon.

Stomping down the steps, a smirk appeared on his face once he came into view of his main man, Beans. He sat in a metal chair with his feet and wrist covered by metal shackles so tight blood began to drip down, creating a puddle.

Clapping his hands as if he was congratulating him, everybody shared looks of confusion, "Damn man, I gotta give it to you. I ain't gon' lie, I would've never expected this shit from you. But one thing I did realize was that you always thought you were so much better than me, Beans. But you know what your problem is? You're too fucking greedy, ain't nothing but a sheisty ass nigga! I tried to give yo bum ass a chance at some real money and you do this shit to me!?" He laughed.

Licking his dried lips, he attempted to speak, "Please just give—"

Trig held his hand out to one of his workers, he placed a Glock inside it. Swiftly cocking it back, he pointed it at Beans, "Fuck all that, where tha fuck is my money?"

The look in Trig's eyes feared Beans. He never saw that look in him before. The two grew up together and attended the same high school. Off the strength of that, when Beans came to Trig looking for some fast cash, he didn't hesitate in putting him on.

However, Beans being the kind of man he was, saw that as the perfect opportunity to fund his old habits.

"I got robbed over on the north side. I was coming out the liquor store and some niggas got on my ass. But if you give me till Thursday, I promise you man, I'll have your money." He stuttered.

Trig began laughing hysterically as a few others surrounding the room, joined him. "Man boss, this clown thinks you a flimsy nigga or something." A worker joked, shaking his head.

Looking around the room, Beans swallowed hard and tried to figure out what was going on. Trig was handed an envelope, he removed pictures out of the slip and tossed them onto the floor. Exposed were photos of Beans inside a hotel room with naked women doing coke, photos of him in night clubs blowing money, and photos of him hanging around a few local dope heads giving them free drugs. Bean's habit wasn't a secret to anybody, when he came to Trig, Trig wanted to believe he had changed, so he gave him a chance to prove himself.

"So, you're telling me this ain't you in these photos, B?" Trig raised an eyebrow as he closely watched his reaction, "Now I'ma ask again, where tha fuck is my money?"

"L-l-look man I can have it. Just give me time." Beans pleaded with tears filling his eyes.

He knew how serious Trig was about his money but with him being who he was, he thought he could've received the benefit of the doubt. Unfortunately, the man he knew in high school wasn't who stood before him today.

Shooting him in both feet, he squatted down and stared at him as Beans screamed out in pain, "Nigga, you should know better than anybody in this fucking room not to fuck with me when it comes to my fucking money!"

Pistol whipping him across the face, Trig shook his head in disgust before handing the gun back over to his worker. "Y'all know what to do; kill him and get rid of the fucking body. I got shit to do." He ordered before turning on his heels to leave out. Soon as Trig turned his back, Beans began to plead and cry for another chance. Deep down, Trig hated to kill someone he looked at as a brother, but that line of loyalty had been crossed and there was no coming back from that.

Hearing two shots go off, Trig shook his head in disbelief as he made his way to the front where a few of his workers lounged around, talking. "I'm out." He told them.

"Aye wait boss, can I holla at you for a minute?" One of his workers by the name of Sergio called out.

"Yeah, what's up? Make it quick though, I got somewhere to be."

Nodding his head, they both walked outside. Trig used this time to spark the Spliff he had rolled earlier. "I've been doing a lot of thinking with this Capone situation, and I feel the best way to get this nigga is to go after something or someone close to him, like his mama or girlfriend or some shit. That nigga be on game, and I feel if we go after his weakness, that'll give us the upper hand."

When Trig heard the word girlfriend, he immediately thought of Chardonnay and was already against that idea. As far as he knew, Chardonnay was oblivious to his dealings with Cartier, he wanted to keep it that way.

"You might be onto something but remember the nigga cheats like a muthafucka, so I don't know if his girlfriend would be much of a weakness to him." Trig explained.

Sergio nodded, "I know but word on the street is that he has a new girl. I'm not too familiar with who she is just yet, but somebody told me he was about to fight a nigga at the block party a few weeks ago behind her."

"Do me a favor, find out as much information as you can on who this new girl is and let me know what you come up with. We might have found our new angle on how to take this nigga down." He smirked. "We'll talk more tomorrow though, alright, I'll call you!"

"Alright bet, be safe, nigga." Slapping hands with each other before going their separate ways, Trig checked his phone and mentally cursed because he was running late.

Getting inside his car after hearing that news, shifted his mood. In honor of his father, Trig was so ready to take down Cartier's family empire. He had so much riding on him when it came to this, and he didn't want to let his father down. He wanted nothing more than the satisfaction of watching Cartier and his family's legacy crumble and he was determined to get it- no matter what it'd take.

 က

Naomi got out of her uber, tired from a long day of shopping and running errands. All she wanted was a nice meal and a warm shower. Since this was their last night in Miami, she wanted to end it on a relaxing note and just be with Cartier.

The entire trip was perfect so far, Cartier had managed to outdo himself when it came to making her feel appreciated and loved. There were still so many more things they needed to work out, but this was a great start, so far.

Unlocking the door to their suite, her eyes lit up at the view before her. There lied a trail of roses and candles that led up to the master bedroom door. Soft music played in the background and the scent of vanilla danced up her nose, it made her smile.

Closing and locking the door behind her, Naomi sat her bags by the door and followed the trail to the doorway of their bedroom. Pushing the door open, Naomi covered her mouth when she saw he had balloons and roses in the shape of a heart on the bed with a card sitting on top.

Grabbing the card, Naomi silently read it to herself.

Hey Beautiful,
I picked out something I thought would look amazing on you. Take your time, relax, and get ready for the last surprise I have for you tonight. By the time you're finished, downstairs a car will be parked out front waiting for you. See you soon Nao.

– Cartier W.

Naomi blushed hard after reading the card then focused in on the perfectly wrapped gift box that sat on their bed. Taking a seat at the edge of the bed, she opened it and pulled out a beautiful black dress with heels and jewelry to match.

After undressing so she could start getting ready, Naomi walked inside their bathroom and was blown away again at the sight before her. He had a bath already prepared for her with rose petals scattered across the water, and candles burning around the perimeter of the tub.

Naomi could only imagine what else he had planned for her since he was already going all for her now. Stepping inside the tub, Naomi sat back and let the heat of the water soothe her body.

After soaking and bathing for about a good twenty minutes, Naomi finally got out so she could continue getting ready, she didn't want to keep Cartier waiting too long.

Naomi nearly fainted when she stepped out of their bathroom, she saw two women dressed in all black scrubs standing there with smiles on their faces.

"We're so sorry to have scared you ma'am, we are just here to do your hair and make up for tonight." One of the girls spoke up politely as they motioned over to the vanity, Naomi saw hair products and makeup pallets.

Letting out a sigh of relief, Naomi relaxed. "No worries, thank you ladies! Let me just throw on this robe really quick."

While Naomi threw on something to cover her body, the ladies continued setting up their station so they could get started.

Once they were done, Naomi had never felt more beautiful than she was feeling in that moment. Her hair was slayed to the Gods and her face was beat to perfection. She couldn't wait to see the look on Cartier's face when he saw her, just the thought of it made her a little anxious.

The ladies assisted her with slipping on her dress and heels; Naomi made sure to lotion up her body. She sprayed herself down in her favorite perfume scent. Before leaving out of their room, she made sure she had everything as the ladies escorted her downstairs.

Stepping out of the entrance doors of the hotel, parked on the curb sat an all-black Cadillac CT5 with a driver standing there waiting for her. Naomi honestly felt like royalty as she descended the stairs and watched as he opened her door for her.

"Your chariot awaits, Ms. Naomi." He politely greeted and helped her inside.

Sitting back in disbelief, Naomi looked around in amazement at what all Cartier had managed to put together for her so far. She could already tell this night was going to be amazing and she couldn't wait to see him to thank him for all of this either.

Cartier nervously awaited the presence of Naomi at the table he requested in a private area for them. Watching as the next poet walked up on the stage, Cartier smiled. He loved poetry and felt this was the best place to set the tone for the things he had in store for his night with Naomi.

Getting a text, he pulled his phone from his pocket and opened it to see it was his driver letting him know that they had arrived. Placing his phone back in his pocket, he took a quick sip of his wine.

Looking towards the entrance, his eyes lit up when Naomi entered and made her way to him. The dress she wore hugged her body like a glove and the black heels paired with the jewelry pieces complemented her skin so well.

"Damn," he said to himself.

Standing up when she approached the table, Cartier held her chair out for her before retaking his seat.

"You look really beautiful tonight; I mean you always do but damn it's like you have a glow to you." He complimented causing her to smile.

"Thank you, I honestly don't even know what to say right now. From all the gifts, this trip, and this beautiful evening you have planned for us, I'm overwhelmed with happiness. I can't thank you enough." She expressed.

Grabbing ahold of her hand, Cartier brought it to his lips and kissed the back of it softly. "I told you when I first met you that I was going to make you mine. I know I fucked up but I'm showing you and giving you everything you deserve and more. I can't take back what happened, but I'm hoping this is the first step to us moving forward and starting over. You don't have to answer right now, but that's simply what I am hoping for."

Naomi nodded her head, listening to his every word. She went to reply but when the lights dimmed and the next poet walked up on stage, Naomi's attention went elsewhere.

On stage, stood a beautiful older black woman. She had on a black dress with long sleeves that draped down to her legs. Her hair was loc'd with beads and shells that flowed down to her calves, and she sported dark shades over her eyes. Although she hadn't uttered a word yet, everyone in the building locked in on her as her musician began to beat on a conga drum. She slowly swayed her body to the beat, getting into the groove before she began.

"If a stranger were to see me smile," She started. "They wouldn't know the secrets this smile holds, or even the secrets this smile has told. When in the eyes of the world, I smile, proud and bold. Yet when I'm on my own, this fire filled smile turns ice cold."

Cartier watched as Naomi got lost in her words, he could tell she was feeling it. He heard this poet was one of the best and wanted to treat Naomi by seeing her live.

"If a stranger were to see me smile, they wouldn't know that deep down my soul is full of pain. But somehow, I still manage to smile through the toughest storms and even the rain. But only God knows how such hurt is in vain." Her musician turned over a rain stick, it continued to set the tone as she recited the rest of her poem.

"If a stranger were to see me smile, they wouldn't know that my world was crumbling. Picture this as a football, I'd forever be fumbling." Stumbling on stage as if she tripped and was trying to hold onto something, she dropped down to her knees and looked up towards the ceiling with her hands reaching out.

"In this full field game of life that I can't seem to catch or hold, I'm left to feel empty and often like a fragile piece of paper... I fold." Lowering her arms, she coddled herself on stage, still on her knees. "I also long to be whole, but there's more where that came from and so much more to be told."

Slowly standing to her feet, she raised her arms up high. "But I know I must remain the victor, the survivor, and the overachiever. I am a conqueror and a believer, and *I will* see this through!" She yelled out. "Though the smile on my face may hide the hurt, beneath this smile is a woman who has been strong since birth, and I will break this horrible curse... of pain."

She paused for a moment as she started to remove her shades, her eyes were still closed. "Pain. A word that's too familiar, so if a person were to see me smile maybe they would see something very similar."

When she opened her eyes to showcase the tears she was holding, Naomi felt her eyes begin to water as everyone snapped their fingers and blew whistles.

Naomi felt so connected to her words, they held great truth about herself. The smile she has shown the world has covered up a lot of secrets and pain. The entire time she spoke, she couldn't help but think about her and Deandre's past situation. There were many times she had to smile through the pain and cover up the lies of what was really happening between them, but she always knew her eyes told it all.

Turning her attention to Cartier, who was already staring, Naomi smiled as she grabbed a napkin to dab at her eyes so she wouldn't mess up her make-up. "I'm sorry," She chuckled.

"You alright?" He asked her.

"Yeah, I'm fine, those words just really hit me hard." She replied, picking up her wine glass and taking a sip.

"I had a feeling you would enjoy this." Cartier smiled, looking at her. "You should go up there," He urged.

Taken back by his suggestion, Naomi laughed nervously, "Boy please! Me? No. I can't talk in a room full of people and besides I have nothing written, nor am I even prepared." She rambled.

Laughing, Cartier ignored her as he stood up with his hand out for her to grab. “Come on ma. Just speak from whatever’s in your heart.” He encouraged.

Naomi hesitated, but eventually took his hand anyway. As she stood up, Cartier led the way to the host stand. Naomi’s nerves began to kick in. Standing back as Cartier talked with the guy, Naomi nervously played with her fingers, regretting her agreement to do this.

Turning back towards her, Naomi forced a smile. “What did they say?”

“After this next person, you’re up next. Guess we can get a little liquor and food in your system to help relax your nerves and give you time to think of something.” He joked as he walked her back to their table.

Retaking their seats, Naomi let out a deep sigh. “I can’t believe I agreed to do this.”

Smiling, Cartier grabbed ahold of her hand. “You’re gonna do great! Nassir told me all about how you did poetry back in high school. What made you stop?” He asked.

Naomi shrugged, “Life happened. I used to love writing poetry to free my mind, it really helped me get through a lot of my darkest days, but after a while I just stopped... didn’t have that motivation to write anymore.”

Cartier nodded, “Well let’s hope tonight, we spark that flame of motivation again.”

Smiling at his words, Naomi took a sip of her drink and focused on the next poet. Before she knew it, her name was being called to the stage.

Slowly walking up to the stage, Naomi tried to relax her nerves with each step she took. Approaching the mic, she accidently hit it and caused it to screech and ring out; everybody cringed from how loud it was.

Once the sound settled, Naomi grabbed the mic, shaking. “I’m so sorry about that, I hope everyone is having a good time tonight. My name is Naomi Banks. I’m going to recite a short poem I wrote called “ *The Unspoken Truth of Love.*” Y’all gotta bear with me though, I haven't written or done poetry in a while.” She explained briefly.

"You got this baby!" Cartier yelled out, making a few people in the crowd laugh at his outburst.

Taking a deep breath, Naomi watched as the lights dimmed. She closed her eyes for a brief moment before focusing on Cartier who was staring directly at her. "How can something we all want... feel so right, but that one thing also leave you up crying all night; it can hurt so bad. Within the same breath it can make you so damn happy but can also make you very sad." She spoke into the mic.

"Tears of pain often leave a stain in our eyes that the world can see. I love love and love loves me, but sometimes we wonder if it's even meant to be. When our hands touch, my body turns warm, but that same touch has also caused me harm. Love is something that can bring you security but can also bring you pain. It can be used in honesty and can also be used in vain. It can be conditional and either beneficial or malnutritional." She spoke as she looked out, seeing everyone tuned into what she was saying. "You see any and everything goes in this oh so confusing game. The one game all of us must once in our lives be forced to play and love... love is the name, and this is the unspoken truth of it." She finished.

As the crowd began to snap and cheer her on, Naomi wiped the tears from her eyes she didn't even realize had fallen. Thanking the crowd, she stepped down from the stage with the help of a man who sat close to the front, as she made her way back over to Cartier.

"That poem was beautiful, and you did amazing up there! The crowd loved you." Cartier complimented, pulling her in for a kiss.

Helping her retake her seat, Cartier motioned for the waiters to start making their way over to them with their food.

Sitting her plate down in front of her, Naomi smiled at the fact that he ordered her favorite dish; lemon grilled salmon, served with buttery garlic green beans, and roasted parmesan rosemary potatoes. The food smelled and looked so good she couldn't wait to dig in.

"This looks so good." She complimented as one of the waiters refilled their wine glasses.

"I'm finna run to the bathroom real quick, I'll be right back." Cartier told her before excusing himself.

Doing a small prayer over her food, Naomi wasted no time grabbing her fork and eating; just as she imagined, the food was amazing. The salmon was grilled to perfection and the green beans and potatoes were seasoned just right.

Glancing around the venue, Naomi rocked to the beat of the song that was playing before she stopped dead in her tracks. She locked eyes with the last person she ever expected to see.

A sinister chill went up her spin, she felt as if she couldn't move a muscle. She watched a smile creep on the person's face before they held up their hand in the form of a gun. Naomi's body began to tremble when they acted as if they shot her before walking off.

Cartier placed his hands on her shoulders, she jumped. He frowned and wondered what was bothering her. "You good? What's wrong?" He asked her.

"Can we go, please?" She suddenly requested as she began standing up.

Cartier was beyond confused on her sudden switch up, but he didn't question it. He flagged down a waiter and asked for the check and two to-go boxes, before focusing back on Naomi who looked disturbed.

Grabbing her hand, he made her look up at him. "Naomi, talk to me. What's going on?"

"I just really need to get out of here." She replied frantically as she went to stand up again and run towards the exit, but Cartier stopped her.

"Relax, let me walk out with you." He told her, finally deciding to just forget about the food. Cartier threw some money on the table and escorted them out of the building, still thinking about what could've suddenly changed her mood that fast.

When they arrived at the Hotel, Cartier gave Naomi the space she clearly needed, but after an hour had passed and she still wasn't talking, he became fed up and needed answers now. He was so worried because of how shaken up she was, he couldn't make out what the hell had happened.

Stepping out onto the balcony where she sat, staring out, Cartier took a seat next to her. "I promise you I'm not trying to pressure you to say or do anything you don't want to, but what was that back at the poetry club? I thought everything was going well, did I do something wrong?" He asked her. Sighing to herself, Naomi shook her head as a tear fell from her eye. "You did nothing wrong, you made tonight perfect!" She explained.

“So then what happened baby? I want to help, but I can’t help you or even try to understand what’s going on if you don’t say anything.” Pulling her into his lap, he kissed her shoulder.

Not making eye contact, Naomi tried getting her words together before she released a deep breath. “The reason I moved back home was because I was running from something I did in the past. In my last relationship before I met you, the guy I was with was not a good man. He was abusive... verbally and physically, a compulsive liar, and he cheated all the time. I felt so trapped in that relationship due to fear, until one day I just reached my breaking point.”

Cartier sat in silence although he was already familiar with what happened because of Nassir, hearing it come from her mouth just hit a little differently.

“It wasn’t in my intentions to kill him, it just happened.” She spilled out as she began to cry harder. “I had never felt so free but so guilty in my life before, until that moment. I knew I had to do something before it was too late for me. He was a monster, and it was like no one could ever fucking see it.” Wiping her eyes with her wrist, Cartier was disgusted.

After witnessing his mother get beat on as a kid, abuse never sat right in his spirit. He never understood how a man could intentionally hurt someone they claimed they loved with no remorse.

“So, what triggered you at the club? Was it the poem?”

Shaking her head, no, she played with her fingers. “After my trial, before I moved, I heard around town that my ex’s cousin and brother, Benny and Trig, were after me. As soon as I heard, I skipped town and never looked back, but tonight- I saw Benny and I already know he’s going to spread the news that I’ve been spotted; just seeing him brought back some unwanted memories.” She explained.

As soon as the name Trig rolled off her tongue, Cartier immediately became alert. “You said his brother's name was Trig, correct?” He questioned.

“Yeah why?”

Reaching for his phone, Cartier went to his camera roll to find the pictures one of his guys took as they stalked out his spots. “Is this him?” He asked, turning the phone around to show a picture of Trig dressed in a Gucci tracksuit, getting inside of a car.

Nodding her head, Naomi sat there confused. "How do you know him?"

When Cartier threw his phone, Naomi stood up off his lap, a little nervous at this point.

"Fuck!" He snapped. "I can't believe this shit."

"What is it Cartier? Who is he to you?"

Taking a deep breath, Cartier motioned for her to sit back down. "Trig used to be my supplier, but then I found out he was on some snake shit due to this ongoing beef his family and my family has had since before I was even born. I wasn't aware of this shit until my uncle explained it all to me and right now, we're kinda in the middle of a war with him." He explained.

"But if this nigga finds out we're together, this makes the target on your back even bigger. This nigga will literally go after anything I love to try and break me, so he can't find out about us." Cartier sighed.

Naomi felt her heart drop at this news, "What are we supposed to do? Benny spotted me already, he probably saw you too."

"Regardless of the fact, you might need to just lay low for a minute, the last thing I need is for something to happen to you." He told her.

"What is hiding going to do for me though? I've been spotted. The only good thing is that he saw me here in Miami instead of back home, but I can't keep running." She expressed. "Maybe it's time for me to finally face this shit and handle it."

"So, what exactly are you saying Naomi?"

"I'm saying whatever happens, I'm going to be by your side through it all, we both have issues with Trig for different reasons. I want him dead just as much as you do, so let me help you."

Shaking his head, Cartier laughed. "I know you're being serious right now, but baby no. I'm not risking anything happening to you, just let Nassir and I handle this shit."

Walking back inside their room, Naomi begins stripping out of her clothes. “I can handle my own Carti.”

“I never said you couldn’t, I’d just rather you not have to handle your own at all.”

Tossing her hair into a messy bun, she climbed into bed before grabbing her silk bonnet off the nightstand. “Whatever, just promise not to leave me in the dark on any plans you and Nassir have. I need to know everything that is happening so I’m not just out here clueless.”

“I got you, I’ma make a few calls in the morning but I swear on everything I love I’m not going to let anything happen to you.” Cartier reassured her as he climbed into the bed pulling her closer to him.

Naomi laid her head on his chest as she felt her body relax against his. She listened to the beat of his heart. “Do you ever get scared?”

Looking up towards the ceiling, Cartier sighed. “All the time, but shit being scared gets you nowhere. Plus, in this life you can’t let anybody see that you are either.”

Naomi nodded, understanding what he meant. “I used to live in fear and be scared to take risks, but when I’m with you I feel the most protected and I guess that’s what hurt the most when I found out about you and Chardonnay. You became my safe haven, and just like that, it was ruined.”

“I know I fucked up and I hate myself for it every day because you didn’t deserve any of that. All I ask for is a second chance to get what we had back, to show you the love I’m capable of giving you.” He told her.

Things grew quiet between the two as Naomi stared into his eyes. Not saying anything else, Naomi leaned closer and pressed her lips against his before slipping her tongue inside his mouth.

As the kiss deepened, Cartier adjusted himself over her. Naomi pulled away, laid back and stared up at him. “Show me how much you love me.” This was all the confirmation Cartier needed, he did exactly what she wanted, all night; he loved her beyond words.

Chapter 13

The following day, both Cartier and Naomi were packing up to leave. It was their last day in Miami together. Cartier found out that his Uncle Pernell and his auntie had taken a small vacation to their beach house out there; he decided to drop by for breakfast.

Last night, Cartier and Naomi connected on a deeper level, which made it all worth it. After doing some hard thinking, Naomi decided to finally give Cartier another chance, but they were taking it very slow this time.

Walking inside the bathroom, fully dressed, Naomi looked over at Cartier who was still half naked. "Why aren't you ready?" She asked him.

"I just gotta throw on my shirt and pants, we gon' make it on time."

"We were supposed to be there by ten, we are late." Following behind him as he left the bathroom, Cartier laughed.

"Okay, I'm coming. Give me like ten minutes."

After another hour had passed, Naomi and Cartier were finally headed to the beach house. They would've left sooner, but Cartier started getting a little touchy and eventually, one thing led to another; next thing Naomi realized, she was bent over.

Fixing her hair as they approached the house, Naomi was trying to make sure she looked good. Even though she had already met his aunt and uncle, she still wanted to look her best in their presence.

When Naomi looked out the window, she was amazed at how their house was covering at least ten acres of land. "This is their beach house?" She asked, looking back at Cartier in disbelief.

Laughing, Cartier pulled up to the gate and entered in the code before driving through as it opened. He pulled up next to one of his uncle's cars. He and Naomi got out and were greeted by one of his uncle's butler's.

"Hello, Mr. William! It's always a pleasure seeing you." He greeted them. "Please allow me to escort you both to Mr. and Mrs. Williams." He smiled before turning on his heels.

Grabbing ahold of Naomi's hand, Cartier kissed the back of it as they followed the guy inside the house. Naomi couldn't believe how breathtaking their house was; the entire interior was beautiful and so spacious and although the design was very modern it still gave off that homey vibe.

Escorting them to the deck where his aunt and uncle sat, eating breakfast, Naomi felt the butterflies in her stomach begin to play a match of kickball. "Well, if it isn't the lovely couple, finally. About time y'all made it." Pernell joked as he stood to slap hands with Cartier and hug Naomi.

Going in for a hug, Naomi smiled. "How are you doing, beautiful? It's good to see you're hanging onto this stubborn muthafucka." Laughing, Naomi looked back at Cartier who was rolling his eyes. "I'm doing alright, it's so good to see you guys again as well! This house is absolutely gorgeous." She complimented as she shared a quick hug with his aunt.

"Thank you, I wish I could take credit for it. But this was all my baby's doing, she mapped out the floor plan, did the exterior and interior designing. I just cashed the check." He joked, pulling his wife into him as they shared a quick kiss.

"Enough of all that, we don't want to see that." Cartier blurted out before he started fake gagging.

"Shut up boy, y'all hungry? I can have the cook make you guys something real quick." His aunt asked as she waved over their butler to fix them some drinks.

"Nah, I already had enough to eat this morning." Cartier smirked as he took a seat in one of the chairs.

Catching onto what he meant, Naomi's eyes went wide in shock as she playfully hit him. "Excuse him, something to drink will be fine. Could you tell me where the bathroom is?"

"Of course, I'll show you where it is, and I can even give you a tour of the house." His aunt suggested.

Giving Cartier a kiss, she gave him her purse to hold before stepping back inside the house and leaving the men alone.

"How did you manage to fix that? For a second, I really thought she was done." Pernell teased as he took a sip of his crown and coke.

"It was far from easy, hell, I was shocked she even agreed to come but I'm glad she did. We still have a lot we need to work on, so we're taking things slow this time." Cartier explained.

"Well, that's good! I'm actually glad you stopped by. I wanted to talk to you about a few things real quick before you flew back home." Pernell told him as he stood from his seat.

Motioning for Cartier to follow him, they began walking towards the beach. "You know Rome and I are planning on leaving all this to you, but I just need to know exactly where your head is at with this shit. Like, what is your end game with all this? Do you plan on doing this forever or what?"

Cartier sighed. "You sound'n just like Uncle Rome right now."

"Good, at least I'm not the only one trying to make sure you're not in over your head with this shit. It's so much more that comes with this life besides the drugs and money, look at how we're living! You really think we got all this from just drugs?"

"Nah, y'all invested and opened up businesses to make a lot of y'all money legit. Y'all also had cover ups to help move weight on the low."

"Exactly! It's time you start thinking and moving like a businessman. Especially with this shit you got going on with Trig, we don't know what type of game this nigga is playing. But one thing we do know is that he's trying to take us down, so that means more lives will be taken and more shit is bound to pop off. If cops catch wind of any of this, the first thing they gon' do when they start investigating is look into our lifestyle and wonder exactly where this money and shit is coming from." Pernell explained.

"They don't ever question a white man. They never ask where his money's coming from and that muthafucka could be embezzling money illegally, part of the damn cartel or the mob! It doesn't matter, they aren't going to question it. We're black and at the end of the day, we don't get that same luxury. When it comes to a black man with money, they already have a stereotype made up in their minds; even if the shit is true, don't make it obvious."

"What you're going through now is only the start. If you want to be successful in this business, it's time to legitimize yourself soon." He lectured, taking in the view as he paused. "Change your look, change the way you carry yourself! All that flashy shit is the number one red flag that the feds look for. There are ways to look like money without all the flashy chains, watches, and fur coats. If you let me help you, I can take you to higher heights of success."

"So, it's time you and Nassir get together and build you a team with people you can trust and work on creating your own empire." Pernell told him. "Right now, you're living in the shadows of what your pops, Rome, and I created. It's time you create a name for yourself in these streetz; show them who Cartier is and what all he is capable of."

Cartier was listening to everything his uncle was saying, and he knew was right. It was time he started carrying himself better and changing his mindset. He knew in this life; simple mistakes could cause you to lose everything and that's the last thing he wanted to happen.

"Why me though? I mean I'm honored y'all see so much in me but what about Quentin? I don't ever see y'all pushing him like this!" Cartier questioned.

"We love Quentin and we have given him chances to prove himself, but he just doesn't have what it takes. He doesn't take the time to actually think things through and he makes irrational decisions; right now, we can't take that chance. But with you, I see so much of myself in you, and I don't want you to make the same mistakes that I did. This game is like chess and I'm on you so much because all it takes is one wrong move for somebody to infiltrate your kingdom and just like that- game over, you're done."

Cartier hated to be lectured by anyone, but he knew everything he was saying was right and clearly at this point, despite what he actually wanted to do with his life; there was no way out, the family was depending on him, he knew it was time to take shit seriously.

"I hear what you're saying unc and you're right! It's time I get more focused and start changing my mindset and look at the bigger picture before me." Cartier expressed to him.

Smiling, Pernell reached into his pocket and pulled out a set of keys. Tossing the keys to Cartier he scrunched up his face in confusion as he looked at them. "What are these for?"

"This is your new start. It's not much, but it will help get you where you need to be. The building these keys belong to is all yours; show me you got what it takes to legitimize this shit." He told him before walking away, leaving him to think.

Back inside, Naomi managed to see the entire house; she was truly in love with it all. His aunt and her managed to talk about anything that came to mind. His aunt reminded her so much of her mom, so the conversation flowed naturally.

“There’s one room I haven’t shown you yet. I’d really like for you to see it.” His aunt told her as they entered the foyer.

Naomi followed behind her as they reached a door towards the back of the house that she didn’t notice before. Stepping inside the room, Naomi instantly fell in love with the decor. On the walls were pictures of Martin Luther King with Coretta, Malcolm X with Betty, and. Barack with Michelle. The room simply screamed black excellence and love; it was her favorite room in the house.

“These pictures are beautiful.” She complimented as she took a seat on the couch they had in there.

“Yeah, this is my release room, I created one in every house we own. I use this room to read, to think, and sometimes look at these strong women with these strong men, and just reflect. I often see myself in them.” She expressed.

“You know this lifestyle is far from easy, especially as a woman, and it's not for everybody.” Naomi swallowed hard; she knew where this conversation was going. “But when you look at all these great and strong men, who’s right beside them? An even greater and stronger woman. As women, we may not always be at the forefront making things happen, but what we do behind the scenes; keeping our men grounded with our love and showing our support, goes a long way. It’s what helps make these men who they are.”

“Now I know what Pernell does isn’t the greatest, but he’s made a lot of sacrifices to ensure that myself and his family were always in good hands. I love that man more than anything and I trust him with my life, and in this game, many men need that one person they know they can always count on, no matter what.”

Naomi smiled at her words as she watched her play with her wedding ring. “I know you love and care for Cartier, but I just have to ask.”

“Ask me whatever.”

“I know things between you and Cartier are still fairly new, but do you think you’re prepared or ready to be with a man in this business?”

Diana loved her family and has done her part when it comes to keeping them safe, and now that it was time for Cartier to finally start taking over the family name, she wanted to make sure he had a woman or at least someone on his side that was fully aware of what they were signing up for.

When things between her and Pernell first began, she was not ready at all; she could tell Naomi was far from ready as well.

Although Naomi knew this was where the conversation was going, her question still took her by surprise. Naomi knew what came with this life, but she never really thought much about it until last night. "I actually haven't really thought much about it." She admitted.

"Well, if you plan on being with him, I think this is a talk you two need to have. I believe you are a good woman for Cartier, but I would hate for this lifestyle to become too much for you to handle. You must be strong, very intelligent, on guard, and always aware of everything around you. There will be plenty of women that will try you and even men that will attempt to use you, just to get to Cartier. So, it's best to know the lifestyle you are getting into before committing to something like this." Dianna warned her.

"I understand." Naomi replied.

"Here's my number, when you feel you're ready, give me a call! I can teach you a thing or two."

Naomi took the paper and nodded her head. When Diane left out of the room, Naomi took a deeper look into the pictures and wondered where her place was in all this.

She came back to reality and realized how Cartier wasn't just some average Joe; she contemplated what she wanted and if it'd be worth the risk.

Back in the streetz of Atlanta, Trig walked into his new warehouse in search of his leaders, Sergio and Rell. He noticed random people roaming, women giggling who were hardly dressed in the kitchen, and workers huddled in the living room, smoking weed and playing the game. Trig ran upstairs to Sergio and Rell's offices, he was pissed.

He sighed once the door opened and took in the view. Rell was laid back on the loveseat with a bra-less, light skin woman on top of him; she was giving him the joyride of a lifetime. Serigo was sitting in the office chair, getting his manhood devoured by a brown skinned girl, propped on her knees. He shook his head to himself because he allowed his workers to get too lazy and too comfortable.

"What the fuck is y'all doing!?" Trig yelled, startling the entire room as his voice bounced off the walls.

The women quickly hopped up in search of their clothes. "I'm outside in the car, waiting on you niggas, so we can handle this business- and y'all in here, bullshitt'n over some damn pussy!? Then y'all got random motherfuckas in this house, workers just having a good ass time out front-like we ain't in the middle of a fucking war!" He snapped.

"Man bo-" Rell tried to quickly explain but Trig wasn't having it. They really were in the middle of a war, last thing he needed was his team to be slack'n right now.

"I put y'all in charge, right?" He asked, making them both nod in response. "Well then get the fuck down there and clear this bitch out, then bring y'all asses." He demanded.

Trig left the room and headed back to the car, livid at this point. Not even five minutes went by, people were exiting the house like it was on fire. He smirked and placed his shades back on his face. Shortly after, Sergio and Rell hopped inside of the car. Trig didn't say a word.

Instead, he instructed the driver to head over to one of Capone's trap houses across town.

A few days ago, Trig received an anonymous message from someone providing details on this house and how it runs. Before getting caught up, Trig had his people peep out the scene first; whoever it was, knew this place inside-out, he figured it had to be someone inside of Capone's camp.

Once Trig realized this wasn't a trap, he couldn't wait to hit back at him and get his revenge. He didn't care who was outside or inside the place, he was blowing that bitch up in flames. He didn't want the money or the product, he needed to send a message that he wasn't to be fucked with.

Finally arriving at the traphouse, Trig stopped a block away, they geared up, quickly. On que, his driver sped down the street as they lit the house up; bullets were hitting windows, cars, people outside, and everything else in sight.

They had bottles of liquor stuffed with towels drenched in lighter fluid. Trig looked back and smirked, "Light 'em up," he said to Sergio.

Just as fast as Sergio lit the bottles, he tossed them out the window. As Trig watched the house go up in flames, he felt a wave of happiness come over his body as they sped off. *"Daddy would be proud."*
Falling onto the bed, gasping for air, Lanay looked over at Quentin who was already staring at her. The session they just had together had to be one of the best. Sex between them was always good, but this time just felt different.

Closing her eyes for a moment, Lanay felt the bed shift a little, she saw Quentin getting up. "Are you leaving?" She asked, raising up a little.

"Nah, I'm finna use the bathroom real quick."

Lanay laid back down while he went to the bathroom. She closed her eyes and enjoyed where she was right now. She didn't know what it was about Quentin, but she couldn't get enough of him and vice versa.

Lanay's phone started ringing. She looked over towards the nightstand and reached to grab it, Sheree was calling. Instead of answering it, Lanay simply rolled her eyes and flipped her phone over just as Quentin returned with a rag.

"Why are you making that face? What's wrong?" He asked as he started cleaning her up a little bit from the mess he made.

"It's honestly nothing worth discussing." She shrugged.

"I still want to know, so what's up? Talk to daddy." He joked.

Lanay laughed and sat up a little, so they could see each other better. "Here lately, I haven't been feeling much support from my girls when it comes to what we have going on. They're always on my ass about how I haven't been hanging out because I've been too busy with you, but I never said anything when they ditched me for their men." Lanay loved spending time with her girls, but she had been so wrapped up with Quentin that she hardly had time, she honestly cared less about hanging with them. She just loved having the attention of a man, she wanted to enjoy it. She thought Sheree and Naomi would get it, since they were once like this too, but instead they were complaining to her about everything dealing with Quentin.

She was starting to feel like her own friends didn't want her to be happy.

Quentin picked at his beard before speaking. "Ima be real with you. A real friend would be happy for you and would understand why you'd want to spend so much time with someone you're dating. Plus, y'all grown ass women, y'all don't have to hang out and talk every day of the week." Quentin expressed.

Quentin didn't care too much for Lanay's friends, especially Naomi.

Lanay looked up at him with a smile. This was one of the reasons she liked him so much, he understood her. "That's exactly what I was saying to myself. Like, when they were up Nassir and Cartier asses, I didn't even trip on them at all. Hell, it was times I would be bored in the house, and I couldn't call them up because I knew they were with their men. But now it's like all of sudden, I'm busy and they got all the time in the world. They make it seem as if I'm putting you before them. Like right now, all I want is for them to have the same respect I had towards their relationships." She expressed.

"I personally feel like they just don't fuck with you like you fuck with them. Y'all friendship seem to be one sided, based on the things you've been telling me. Don't get me wrong though, they cool, and I know they're my niggas' girls, but at the end of the day you're my girl and I'm gone always look out for you first."

Lanay was a little stunned when he called her his girl, but she refrained from acting on it so she wouldn't ruin the moment. "Why do you think our friendship is one sided?" Lanay asked, sitting up.

"For example, boo, you helped Naomi get into that salon and she ain't really give you much credit for it but has been all up Sheree's ass like she's known her all her life. Then Sheree basically said fuck your feelings when she decided to still date Nassir; Naomi basically took her side. It's like they both met and forgot about you; they only fuck with you when it's convenient for them. So, from the shit you've told me, they're not your friends, baby." He explained.

Lanay bit her lip and dwelled on his words. Now that somebody was speaking her thoughts back to her, she felt a little dumb.

"Thanks for being so real with me," Lanay said, leaning in to kiss his lips. Quentin applied that pressure and pulled her onto his lap. Lanay giggled and pulled back.

"You're welcome."

Lanay stood up to stretch her muscles and headed to the kitchen. All the energy she put towards sex worked her up an appetite. She also wanted to feed her man before he left out for the day.

Looking up from the TV, Quentin frowned “Where you going?”

“I'm about to whip us up something to eat.”

“Shake some ass on your way in there.” He laughed.

Lanay blushed but did what he said anyway. Quentin’s dick stiffened as he watched her booty jiggle. He felt his burner phone vibrate, he removed it from his pocket and checked the message.

Unknown:
It's done. Thanks for the anonymous tip and for giving me the info.
Delivered 2:30pm

He smiled to himself, he felt complete. He had a woman he truly liked and his plans to take over the family business were underway.

Life was good for him.

Chapter 14

Trig stared out the window of his home office and watched his family enjoy themselves outside. He was currently hosting a birthday party for his niece, Journe. Benny called his burner phone and got his attention with their code U11, he knew it couldn't wait.

Sitting back in his office chair, Trig was shocked, "Are y'all fucking with me right now!?"

Benny adjusted his bag of Cheetos and held the bag up so the remaining crumbs could slide in his mouth, "I'm telling you that's her."

"How long has this bitch been in the city?"

Looking over the pictures that Benny had, Porsha's eyes flew from her face, "This the bitch that fucked over Deandre? She had to be here for a while. She's the girl I saw Capone with at the club."

Trig slightly chuckled. He felt dumbfounded and played all at once. He couldn't believe Naomi had the audacity to act like she felt so bad for his family; she claimed to be so devastated from his brother's death, but she was on the next nigga's arm.

Shaking his head, he was oddly excited in a way as well. He was about to kill two birds in one stone. He had been searching all over the streetz of Detroit for her and here she was right under his nose in Atlanta.

Breaking the silence, Benny spoke up, "You want me to make a move?"

"Nah, she saw you, which means they're on high alert right now, especially after we hit their money-making house. We laying low until we figure out what the fuck is going on."

"So, you don't need me anymore?" Porsha asked with a sound of relief in her voice.

"You ain't done shit but fall in love with this clown ass nigga anyway. Do you have any home girls or something that can get close to Naomi?"

Benny scratched his head, "What about y'all cousin, Jacques? He knows her. Tell him if he do the job, we'll bring him in."

Porsha picked up her phone, nodded, and stepped outside. Trig motioned his hands for Benny to follow her and make sure things went as planned. Although Porsha was his family, Trig didn't trust her by far. Trig pulled out his phone and hit up one of his men in Detroit. On the third ring he finally answered the phone. "Wassup bro?"

"We found her. I need you to get back to the city, how soon can you get here?"

"Let me handle a few things here and we will be there in due time." He informed him before they ended the call. Trig stood up from his desk and decided to head back out to the party. He needed to see his dad about some business, and he wanted to check on Chardonnay. He knew how brutal his family could be.

Things between them were getting pretty serious, which kind of scared him. He didn't know when shit would hit the fan, but he was prepared for the worse. He just hoped that she'd hear him out once it did.

ന

Cartier leaned on his car and took in the view of his abandoned club. He never saw himself as the owner of any club, but he didn't turn down money opportunities either. He had to show his uncle that he could hold down the family name and get away from the rep of his father.

"You ready?" Terry asked. Terry was hired to design and reconstruct the building.

"Yeah," Cartier answered, as he switched keys for the building and walked towards the entrance. Cartier slid the key in and opened the door. The smell of garbage and dust instantly hit his nostrils.

"Do you know how long this place has been down?" He asked, scanning the place.

"Almost a year."

Terry nodded and they walked in. The layout of the place wasn't too bad. The first floor had an employee entrance right off the bar that had lockers and bathrooms. The main area had plenty of tables and booths with a big center stage that had three different walkways filled with stripping pools. Towards the back were private rooms and the strippers' dressing rooms and showers. Upstairs had the VIP lounge, bathrooms, and private rooms with a security locker room, office, and meeting room. *This place is nice.*

"I want to keep this same layout but updated," Cartier told Terry. He started to write things down in his notepad.

"Do you have a color scheme or anything?"

"Hm, I'm not picky. Just make sure the look is upscale and modern."

After they went over a few more things, he got the team on the job of getting the place up and running. Cartier stepped out for a moment to get some fresh air. He sat on the hood of his car and looked at the beautiful sun and admired the view of the city that the club sat on. He added a mental note to himself to make sure he mentions to Terry to add on a part of the club that will accommodate this view.

His mind started to wonder about the conversation he held with his uncle in Miami. He needed to sit down and thoroughly reconstruct his team. It was time he stopped treating the game as a hobby and see it for what it really was, a business. Breaking him from his thoughts his, phone started to ring.

"Hello" Cartier answered, not checking to see who it was.

"Aye nigga. Meet me down at the spot." Nassir said then instantly cut the line before he could respond. He knew it had to be serious.

Sighing to himself. He slid his phone inside his pocket and walked towards the building to wrap up things with Terry.

Cartier parked behind Nassir's car, got out, and hit the locks on his keypad walking towards the front door. The door was unlocked so he walked in to see Nassir, Quentin, and Tyrik all sitting in the living room, appearing to be deep in thought. He knew something had to be wrong if Tyrik was in the meeting.

Tyrik is the older brother of Chase. He only came around to gatherings at times but even that was rare. The only time they really saw his face is when Chase got himself into a lot of trouble.

Placing his keys inside pocket Cartier sighed, "What the fuck going on now?" Cartier questioned as his blood began to boil.

“We need to handle this nigga Trig and soon. He brought too much unwanted attention to our business, and he sent us a lil message through one of our street workers.” Quentin responded.

“What message?”

“That he's taking shit over. He even bought them out.” Nassir mumbled, putting his hands on his head. “That's not even the worse part.”

Cartier sighed. “I have enough shit on my plate as is. It seems like every time I fucking blink, another problem occurs. What else?”

“They burned down the trap house on the 64th.” Nassir said. The whole room grew quiet. Nassir really didn't want to be the one to inform Cartier that another one of their blood brothers had fallen but it's what came with the business. He continued “Chase was in that house, he gone.”

“I told y'all we underestimated these niggas.” Quentin hissed, pulling out a rolled blunt.

Cartier grew angrier by the second, he couldn't believe what had taken place. He felt responsible for it all. Chase looked up to him. Everything Chase knew about the streetz was instilled into him by Cartier. Despite his hotheaded temper, Cartier saw a lot of himself inside Chase.

Being lost in his own thoughts he didn't even realize the tears that soaked his face. Nassir stood up and comforted his brother. He placed his hands on his shoulder and gave it a light squeeze.

“We gone make it through this shit nigga, hold your fucking head up.” Nassir said, attempting to feed him the reassurance he no longer had in himself. He in fact prayed that they would but one thing he knew for certain was no matter where the ball fell, he was riding with his brother until the wheels fell off, even if they'd have to get out and walk.

Tyrik watched the moment and wiped his eyes to hide his tears that struggled to come out. Although he didn't agree with the lifestyle his little brother led, it warmed his heart to know that the people in the streetz that took him under their wing truly cared for him.

He felt like a failure, his role as an elder brother was to protect him and guide him into the right direction but Tyrik was too focused on living his own life to even give a damn. What he did know was he was gone to get back at the people who were responsible for his brother's death. He wasn't gone rest until the job was done.

Cartier roughly wiped his face and began to talk, "We have to come up with a plan to get these niggas. I wanna wipe out the entire Howard family but to do that we need to get at these workers that switched up first and see what all they know."

Cartier was furious; not only did he lose a fallen soldier, but his team was switching up on him. He treated his workers well. He made sure their pockets were full and their family was protected. All he asked for in return was loyalty, trust, and hard work.

He knew he had to lead by example and follow through with his rules. He couldn't just let their previous workers think they could trade up for higher pay and consequences weren't to be given. It's all about loyalty. Trig definitely wasn't getting away with burning his shit down either and killing his brother. This was the perfect opportunity to display the changes he was putting into effect.

"Let's get them niggas." Tyrik said hopping up from his seat.

"Hold on. Before we do anything, we plan this shit out right!" Quentin said, looking around the room to make sure everybody understood him.

"Wow, look who is starting to think strategically." Nassir stated smartly, waving him off.

"Nigga I'm serious! We not about to just go to the projects and just start airing that bitch out. We need a plan"

"He's right" Cartier said. "We need to start moving more like a team. I want to hit these bitches so hard they think it's swat busting down the door."

"So, what are we gonna do?" Tyrik asked.

Cartier gestured for everybody to sit around the table to explain the plan. He didn't like to move loud because not only does it attract attention, it leaves a lot of room for mistakes.

"Once the sun settles and night takes over. We gone go out there where they be hanging and dealing. Tyrik, since you are a new face, I need you to get bummy. Start hanging around there now and pretend like you looking for your next fix. That way, their focus is on you."

Tyrik nodded, listening to Cartier's words. "I can do that."

Looking at Quentin and Nassir he began speaking again. "Que, I need you to shoot through the back of the townhouse. You've always been good at sneakily breaking a lock. Hit that patio door."

"Nas, me and you going front and center through that apartment. Tyrik, while you outside, if you see anybody trying to flee the scene or set off a warning, handle it. Everybody cool?" Cartier explained making sure everybody understood.

"But how we gone snatch them niggas without causing attention? Won't somebody call one time?" Tyrik asked.

Nassir smirked. "Nah, we own the projects. Ain't nobody calling anybody."

Laughing Tyrik shook his head "Y'all some cold mo'fuckas."

After they finished strategizing, they all headed out to lay low and prepare for the night. Anytime Cartier gets his hands dirty, he must smoke to relax his nerves, so that's what he did. You'd think taking a person's life would be something you'd eventually adjust to, but the things it does to you, he wouldn't wish on his worst enemy.

Chapter 15

Cartier pulled up in line at Wendy's and pulled out his phone as he waited for the car ahead. Going straight to Naomi's number, he decided to see if she was hungry before pulling up on her. After a few rings, her beautiful, soft voice finally played through the speaker.

"Hey baby." She answered, sounding slightly out of breath.

"Wassup? What you over there doing?"

Holding the phone up by her shoulder as she prepared the food, she responded "Nothing, cooking. What time were you stopping by?".

"Actually, now. I was calling to see if you wanted some food but since you are cooking, I'm heading that way now." Cartier answered, smiling.

"Haha okay, see you in a min babe."

Cars began to honk at him, so he placed his phone inside the cup holder and pulled out of the drive-thru to head towards Naomi's place.

After a quiet fifteen-minute drive, he finally arrived and parked his car next to hers. He grabbed his phone, weed, and rellos, then got out and walked towards her building.

He approached the stairs and waited for an elderly woman to exit before walking in after her. He jogged up the steps and once he reached her door, he knocked a few times. Shortly after, she opened.

Her hair was placed in a cute, high ponytail. She had on the earrings and necklace that he bought her. She wore a nice pair of gray, stretchy shorts that hugged her curves and a black cami with black fur slides that rested on her manicured feet.

"Mama, I'ma call you back." Naomi said, cutting her call short.

"You look good." Cartier complemented as he stepped inside. She closed the door behind him and locked it. The smell of food instantly greeted Cartier's nose causing his belly to grumble a bit. He couldn't wait to see what she made.

Cartier was a good cook himself, but it was just something about a woman's touch that he couldn't grasp.

"Thank you, you not too bad yourself."

Cartier laughed at her nonchalant remark and removed his shoes, so he could take a seat on her couch. She walked back in the kitchen while he started to break down this weed. Cartier's phone started to buzz and another message from Chardonnay flashed across the screen. Not bothering to even open it, he slid it over and cleared it from his notifications. Lately, she's been attempting to reach out to him, but he felt she had something up her sleeve, so he wasn't going to entertain it. His life was stressful enough without her shenanigans.

Teasing, he asked "What are you burning in there?"

Naomi looked over to him and laughed. "Boy fuck you... I'm making some roast with gravy, mashed potatoes, and mixed veggies."

Licking the blunt to seal it he said, "I can't wait to taste it."

A few moments later, she came from the kitchen with a nice plate and a glass filled with ice. She left out to get hers and sat a Kool-Aid pitcher in front of them. She noticed that Cartier had already touched his food, she shook her head.

"Boy get my hand and let's say grace." She held out her hand for him to take. He silently mocked her while her eyes were closed before seriously doing the same. Once she was finished praying, Naomi grabbed her fork and started to dig in her food, she basked in all the good flavors of that roast.

"This shit good as hell mamas." Cartier complimented with a mouth full of food. Naomi smiled and finished eating. He returned the smile and watched as she ate.

Naomi had been nothing but a breath of fresh air since she came into his life. He truly admired doing little things like this with her, it was when he felt the most peace. He knew having a woman in this line of business would be tricky, family equaled weakness in the streetz. But somehow, she was worth it.

"You really like it?" She asked, pouring herself a glass of Kool-Aid and drinking some.

"Yeah, you know I love your cooking. It's not as good as mine but it's the second best."

"Whatever, so what's going on with you babe?" She asked curiously. She placed her phone on the table and looked up at him to provide her full attention.

"Whatchu mean?"

"I mean since the minute you came in here you've been having that look like something's on your mind" She pointed out.

Cartier smirked. He found it crazy how she could read him like an open book. He felt like she saw things in him that other people didn't take the time out to learn. He felt connected to her.

"Ima be honest with you ma. We gotta go and kill a few niggas tonight. They used to run with us. As hard as I may seem, taking a person's life, especially one that mean something to me, ain't easy." He confessed as he felt a bit of weight come off his shoulders.

The streetz was something everybody perceived to be a life full of thrill, money, and a good time. Nobody ever talked about the dark side of it. The parts that keep you up at night and paranoid.

Naomi got up from her seat and sat at the end of the couch, Indian-style. She motioned for him to lay his head on her lap while she caressed his hair and face. "Tell me what happened."

"Kj and Chris betrayed the family. They ratted us out to Trig, now we gotta take them out tonight. Because of their fuck up, it caused the loss of chase."

"I've been having a hard time coping with this shit. We just lost Meech a few months ago and now this shit. I swear every day the thought of leaving this shit alone haunts my mind, constantly. Like, is this shit even worth the fucking hassle it brings you?"

Kj and Chris were the roots of his business. They were the first ones to own a hood and run a product for him. They had been loyal to him since day one, which didn't make much sense to Cartier. *What would make them trade up now?* He thought.

Naomi sat there, chewing at her lip. "Things get bad before they get better. I will never tell you what to decide with your life but what I can say is, do what makes Cartier happy and whatever it is you choose. I'll support you."

"Far as this betrayal baby, I hate to say it, but you know the risks of the game and sadly this is one of them. You and Nas will figure something out and come out of this."

Hearing those words from her meant more to him than she knew. He looked up at her and smiled. She leaned down to kiss his lips. He inserted his tongue inside her mouth and moaned against her lips. Naomi allowed him to take control.

Due to their busy schedules, after they returned from Miami, their sex life became non-existent. Each opportunity they had; they took it with no regrets. He pulled her onto his lap and removed her shirt as he began placing kisses all over her neck. Naomi bit her lip and tilted her head some to give him full access to her.

When Cartier touched her body, it always felt as if he was meant to be there. Till this day, the way her body and mind respond to him is still surreal.

He unclipped her bra, moved down to her breast, and tongue kissed the left one as he massaged the right. Naomi stared at him lustfully with anticipation building up, she missed her man and couldn't wait to receive her fix.

Moving on down, he nibbled at her shorts and removed them with only his teeth. Placing her thong to the side he pulled her closer and devoured her watering entrance. Staring into her eyes as he worked his magic, Naomi returned the stare as her body trembled.

The moment he sucked on her clit; it drove her wild. Moan after moan, Naomi closed her eyes as she could barely hold her stance. Feeling her knees buckle, she was about to give in until he raised her up by her ass.

Leaning forward, she gripped the couch as he sat back and finished his meal. Rolling her eyes, Naomi wanted all of him then and there. She enjoyed his way of making her feel sexy and loved but right now she wanted nothing more than for him to bend her over and fuck her brains out.

Her walls tightened as she released herself onto him as she screamed out his name. Cartier smirked and licked his lips as she sat beside him.

"I swear you're trying to suck the soul out of my body," Naomi blushed, attempting to return the favor but he removed her hands.

"What?"

"I just want to feel you."

Removing his jeans, he hovered over her as she slid down and opened herself up to him. Greeting her entrance, he slid inside of her and looked into her eyes. Naomi blushed and quickly looked away, she was still shy with him at times and the way he looked at her made her quiver. She wrapped her legs around his torso, he continued to maneuver in and out of her. Biting his lip, he watched how she responded to him with each stroke, in awe. He loved pleasing her and making her feel good, that alone provided him with pleasure which was something he wasn't used to. Sex was usually selfish for him, he only cared about his own nut.

Their bodies intertwined in a lustful, loving connection. The sounds of their love making filled the apartment as the rain fell from the sky.

Near midnight, Cartier made his way to the projects. His mind had been cleared and he was in better spirits than before. Bobbing his head to the music that played through the speakers, he observed his surroundings carefully. Atlanta can be a beautiful city but once the sun settles and night arises, you never know what could be prying at you.

He pulled inside the parking lot next to Quentin's car. They made sure to park in an unnoticeable area so that KJ and Chris couldn't make a run for it. He stepped out of the car and made sure to lock it as he pulled his hood over his head.

"Y'all niggas ready to do this shit?"

Throwing the bud of his cigar on the ground, Quentin nodded. "Yeah bro, let's get this shit over with."

Nassir started putting on his gloves and pulled his bandanna over his lips. "Tyrik got most of their little niggas distracted so we can move in now."

Cartier signaled for Nas to follow him as he creeped across the parking lot with his gun in his hand. Putting his back against the building, Nassir did the same on the opposite side of the door. Looking at each other they both counted down before kicking in the door.

Quentin headed for his access point while holding a devious grin. He had a plan of his own in effect, the thought of it sealing precisely, excited him.

The true reasoning behind KJ and Chris' betrayal was all of Quentin's doing; he offered them a once-in-a-lifetime opportunity, them being all about the paper, he knew they'd take it. He had them lure Chase to the trap house and tipped off Trig. Unfortunately for KJ and Chris, he never planned on paying them. He didn't trust them and couldn't leave room for exposure.

While Cartier was planning to beat information out of them, Quentin was planning to seal their lips forever.

Jumping from the loud noise, Kj tried to run out the patio door but was greeted by the barrel of Quentin's gun. "Aht aht I wouldn't do that little nigga."

Nassir laughed. "Where ya going? The party's just now getting started."

Cartier shut the rundown door behind him and snatched the plugs out of their game system. Holding his nine to Chris's temple, he began speaking. "Who's all in here?"

"It's just us." He lied, silently hoping his baby mama and sister remained quiet upstairs.

Cartier tilted his head towards the steps. Nassir followed his command and jogged up them. Moments later, he reappeared with the two women, holding them by their hair.

"You still lying, I see." Cartier laughed, taking the butt of his gun and cracking Chris in the nose. "See, you about to start talking or it's going to get real bloody in this bitch."

Kj squeezed his eyes shut and muffled words under his breath. "Chris, fuck this shit man let's just tell him."

Quentin stood there debating how he'd cover up his actions. Watching how KJ nervously shook his palms, he gently nudged him, so it appeared as if he was attempting to reach for something. He placed his finger on the trigger and pulled it back with ease to watch his brain splatter. Blood... flew... everywhere.

The high yellow girl covered her mouth after letting out a loud scream, she was shaking in fear. Nassir gripped her hair even harder as she sobbed. "Bitch, shut yo ass up before you end up with the same fate as him."

Cartier gave Quentin a *what the fuck* look and he simply shrugged. "I wasn't taking any chances."

"L-l-look man I don't know shit alright? Some nigga just came up to us with a opportunity on scoring some big money and we took it. That's all it was. I don't know shit about what you and Trig got going on." Chris blurted out.

Cartier stood there and watched him closely. He knew he wasn't telling something, and he was determined to find out what that was.

He focused his aim from Chris to his sister. He pulled the trigger and watched the bullet go through her chest as her body flew back, now hitting the bloody floor. Chris's body began to tremble. Cartier held a vengeful grin. He knew that he was starting to make him sweat.

Long ago, his uncle taught him how to play mind games and how to get a person to squirm. A lot of people made the mistake of moving too fast due to not being patient. If you had the proper scare tactics mixed with brutality, you could make the loyalist man sing like a bird. All you needed was their weakness.

"You're running out of time, Chris."

"Man, fuck this shit!" Quentin spat, stepping over KJ's dead body. He let off his rounds, sending several bullets to Chris' chest. Swiftly turning, he gave his baby mama the same fate.

Bursting through the door, each man aimed their weapons as Tyrik appeared in the doorway. "Damn, I was coming to see if everything went smoothly. We gotta move quickly though, I hear sirens going off not too far from here."

"One of these bitches must've called them." Nassir said.

Quickly running out of the townhome, they all headed for their vehicles and disappeared in the quiet streetz, just before police arrived on the scene.

Cartier sat in disbelief as his mind raced faster with each minute. He knew Quentin could be reckless and impatient at times but what occurred tonight just didn't sit right with him. Pushing sixty-five down the expressway, he couldn't wait to arrive at the meeting point to get some sort of explanation from Que. Cartier arrived at the location, jumped out of his car, and headed straight towards Quentin. He walked up on him, pushed him back, and sent a right hook flying in his direction.

"What the fuck was that bullshit you pulled back there?"

Tyrik and Nassir sat on the hoods of their cars watching the two. It was nothing more neither of them could do. The two needed to have this moment to express themselves.

Holding his jaw, Quentin stood up. "Either way, we were killing them so miss me with all that dramatic bullshit."

Tyrik smacked his lips and waved Quentin off "Fuck that B, that nigga did this shit on purpose."

"So, how the fuck did you think we was gon' get answers if you killed em first?" Cartier asked. "This is why I don't do business with you. You too fucking hardheaded."

"I ain't gotta explain shit to you bitches." Quentin spat while charging towards Cartier. They both flew into the grass.

Tussling and throwing punches, the two looked like high school boys, scuffling. Seeking an advantage Cartier sent blow after blow to his face, decorating his knuckles with red. Quentin tried to block each blow by holding up his hands but it was useless.

Cartier was the better fighter. On top of that, the two were fighting for different reasons. Cartier was fighting for his respect and wanted his brother to finally understand that he was the boss. Quentin was fighting for vengeance. He wanted his brother to pay.

Watching the scene unfold, Tyrik and Nassir finally decided to step in. If it went on any longer, they were going to kill each other. Prying them apart, Tyrik held Cartier down until he stopped fighting to break his hold.

"Stop Cartier. It's over bro" Tyrik said. Although he sympathized with him, he didn't want to watch the fight get any uglier.

"I'm cool."

He sat on the hood, sighed, and looked up at the full moon in the sky. He felt like the walls around him were slowly caving in, he didn't know who to trust nor did he have any solution for his list of issues.

Thinking back to his conversation with his uncle Rome, he figured he was right. The streetz were already becoming a weight he no longer wanted to have on his shoulders. He thought maybe it was time for him to step away and do something he actually had a passion for.

Disrupting his thoughts, Nassir joined him, "You good?"

"Hell nah, what the fuck we gone do man! Shit around us is falling the fuck apart. My brother on some iffy shit, our niggas is dying left and right; money's good but is all this bullshit coming with it really worth the headache?"

Nassir stuffed his head in his pockets, searching for words. "I don't know, we're gonna figure this shit out though. We always do."

Cartier noticed Tyrik's long face. He Hopped off the car and walked over to him.

Tyrik sat in the truck waiting and while he did that he thought about his brother. He couldn't believe his life was taken away from him at the tender age of 22. All he wanted was to seek revenge and live in his brother's truth. He felt he owed him that much and he wasn't resting til the deed was done.

Standing outside the driver's side window, Cartier leaned on the car, "For what it's worth, I'm sorry about Chase man."

"As bad as I want to C, I can't blame this shit on you. Chase wanted this life and knew what all came with it man. I just wish he wanted different, nah mean?" Tyrik admitted, watching the cars fly by on the freeway.

"Yeah man, I do." Cartier responded, shoving his hands in his pockets as he headed to his car.

Cartier was beating himself up about what took place with Chase. Everyone kept reassuring him those things weren't on him, but he didn't feel that way. Instead of encouraging and teaching him wrong, he should've done the opposite.

Cartier inhaled and exhaled deeply. He pulled out his phone and dialed up the one person he knew could take his mind off things, Naomi.

ღ

"I can't believe I let your ass convince me to see that scary ass movie." Naomi giggled, taking a seat across from Jacques.

After Cartier left her apartment, she laid in the bed, watching movies, until Jacques hit her up with plans. She wasn't up for sitting in the house.

“Aye you can't lie, that shit was good though.” He said, taking a bite of his coney dog.

“Mhm." Naomi shook her head, sipping from her slushy. “Thanks for getting me out of the house. This was pretty cool.”

“Yeah, it was. I had to catch you while I could. Since the block party, you went all hide-n-seek on a nigga.”

“Well, you know I took my man back.” Naomi informed him, dipping her fries in ketchup. Jacques' smile fell a little, but he still had business to do, and he couldn't allow Naomi to get in the way of that.

When his cousin, Porsha, hit him up with an opportunity in exchange for getting put on, he had to accept it. Money has been tight for him, and he knew Trig had it raining from trees. Who wouldn't want a piece of the pie?

Popping a fry in his mouth, he looked up at her. “What's going on with you two?”

Smirking, she responded. “We good, I mean, he had his little moment of fuck boy behavior but he's a good man.”

“Fuck boy behavior?”

Naomi sighed. She didn't know if she should release her tea to Jacques, but she wanted a males' perspective of things. “When we first got together, he was already in a situation with another woman. They were on the verge of ending things, but he wasn't honest with me about it. I found out from his cousins."

“That's not a good man, Nao. A good man will keep shit real with you and let you know what it is, then let you choose if you'd like to deal with it or not. You know how wild I was in high school; I'm just speaking from experience.”

Naomi was deep in her thoughts. Jacques didn't want her to shut down on him before he could press for more information, so he spoke again.

“Where you living at now? You still on the north end of the city?”

Relieved from the change in conversation, she shifted in her seat, "Nah, I have my own spot in Overlook Ridge. My parents still live on the same block though. Where are you at?"

"A little bit of everywhere, you know how I am." Jacques joked.

Naomi laughed. "I knew it was too good to be true. You still playing the field huh?"

"Not purposefully, I'm just trying to find the one." He answered looking Naomi in her eyes.

The two shared an intense stare down as they held gazes. Jacques knew what he was doing, he always had a woman falling victim to his hazel eyes. It was one of his best features, aside from his muscular frame. She broke the stare after realizing she held a gaze with him longer than she should. She excused herself to the bathroom.

When she entered the bathroom, she let out a sigh of relief once she discovered it was only her inside. She pulled out her phone to FaceTime Sheree. Nervously waiting, she stood there with her eyes shut, hoping she'd pick up.

"Girl, what's wrong with you?" Sheree's voice finally boomed through the speakers.

Opening her eyes, Naomi saw her best friend standing in the mirror, fixing up her hair. "Okay bitch where is you going?"

Blushing, she responded, "Me and Nassir are going out tonight. Wassup sis?"

Rolling her eyes at the mention of his name she asked, "Is he around you?"

Although her brother apologized to her several times, she was still a little salty about his betrayal. Out of all people, she never suspected him. Of course, she forgave him, but she just needed some space to let it go.

"No and you need to stop acting like that. You know he loves your spoiled ass!"

"Mhm I will. Girl why am I out at the movies with Jacques- and before you start, it's not a date, we just hanging as friends. So, we get to talking about me and Cartier and if I'm not mistaken, I think he was just flirting with me. I didn't even say anything though, there was just a pause in conversation, and we shared this intense ass look before I excused myself." Naomi confessed, feeling terrible. The last thing she wanted to do was hurt her relationship with Cartier, especially after what they just went through.

"Girl, take your ass home before I come get you myself. He know what the fuck he doing, don't let him! You and Cartier have a good thing going, don't allow Jacques to ruin that for you. If he was a good man, he wouldn't even disrespect your relationship like that." Sheree said. "I think your brother outside text me when you get home or I'm popping up."

Naomi sat there feeling queasy. She knew Sheree was right but somehow, she just couldn't shake the feeling of being cool with him. Besides the hidden crush she used to have, they were childhood friends. She didn't know if she was okay with kicking him to the side so soon over an assumption.

"Okay girl. I love you, enjoy your night."

"I love you too."

They ended the call; Naomi slid her phone back in her pocket. She decided to clean her hands to make it seem as if she really used the bathroom before exiting. While walking to the table she put on the best apologetic look that she could.

"I'm sorry Jacques, but can we end this early? I have to get home." She informed him.

He looked up from his phone and nodded. "Yeah, that's cool. Everything okay?"

"Yeah, I'm fine. It's just a friend's emergency, you know how we women are behind our man troubles."

Standing up and pulling out his wallet, he placed a tip on the table before grabbing his jacket. "Yeah, I do. Y'all be plotting to key a nigga car and everything."

Naomi playfully rolled her eyes. "Not me and my girls. We are too damn good to allow anybody to have us stoop us that low. Don't get me wrong, I've been there before but once you step back and look clearly at the situation, it's not worth it."

Walking to the car, they indulged in conversation about the scorned heart of a woman. From the lifetime movies to the snapped tv shows, they discussed it all. Naomi was so wrapped up in conversation and pleading her case for women, she hadn't even realized they arrived at her place.

Turning off the engine, Jacques sat back in his seat and held his laughter in at Naomi. "So, you telling me just because a man is busy and doesn't disclose that, women will automatically assume he's out with another woman and somehow we're the issue?"

"Yes! Hear me out though, what else are y'all out doing in the whew hours of the morning?"

Scratching his head, he failed to come up with a logical answer. "Alright, I see your point. Unless he's working, there really isn't much of a reason."

Naomi clapped her hands cheerfully; she finally took him down in the debate. Unbuckling her seat belt, she gathered her purse and keys before getting out the car.

Jacques stared at her and debated on the words to use for how he felt. "I apologize if I overstepped with you tonight. That wasn't my intentions. I'm just excited about hanging out with my old friend. Sometimes my flirtatious jokes may slip. It's inappropriate of me, I apologize on my part."

"You're fine. Just keep that flirtatious shit to yourself. View me as one of the guys that just looks better." she said, laughing.

"I got you. You mind if I come up to use the bathroom real quick?"

"Come on."

The two exited the car and Jacques made sure he hit the locks as he followed her to her building. He looked up at the number and made a mental note to remember it's building five B. He walked in front of her, held the door open, and looked in her direction. He was confused as to why she didn't move. Following her eyes, there stood Cartier in the doorway, even more disoriented.

"Naomi, what were you doing? I came over here to ask you to come over to my place; what I'm looking at right now ain't looking too good. To add to that, you haven't been answering my calls either. Wassup ma?"

Jacques could see Naomi was oblivious to choking up an answer, so he decided to help her out. "Man, it's not even like that, I ca-"

“I honestly don’t care to hear anything you have to say man. I was talking to my woman; your words are irrelevant to me.” Cartier said, interrupting Jacques’ words.

Cartier knew Naomi was smart enough not to do something as loose as cheating on him and jeopardizing what they had; he just didn’t understand why she still kept entertaining this Jacques character when anybody with eyes could see he wanted her.

Looking at Jacques with apologetic eyes, she said. “I'll talk to you later.”

He nodded, removed his keys from his pocket, and headed to his car. Naomi sighed, relieved that this didn’t escalate into something else. She then grabbed Cartier's hand, went inside her apartment building, and headed to her front door.

As she unlocked the door to her place she began explaining. “Baby, listen. Nothing’s going on between us. Me and Jacques are just friends from back in the day and we went out together tonight, that's all. I apologize for not picking up, I wasn’t paying my phone any mind.” Naomi explained.

Cartier sighed and decided to let the issue go for now. He already had enough on his plate. The last thing he wanted to do was argue with Naomi tonight. “I'm going to choose to trust you and your word, but I don't trust him. I came by to see if you wanted to spend the night with me for the funeral, I really need you.”

“Of course.” Naomi said, kissing him on the lips. “Give me a minute to pack my hoe bag.”

Cartier laughed as he watched her disappear in the hallway. Although he would never admit it to her, he silently hoped he could trust her word despite his gut feeling.

Chapter 16

Naomi looked over herself as she finished her last curl. Pulling out her lip gloss, she applied them to her plump lips before massaging them together. She turned off her wand curler and glanced inside the bedroom to check on Cartier.

He sat at the end of his king size bed, holding his tie as his mind drifted off. Frowning, Naomi turned off the light to the bathroom and sat next to him on the bed.

Over the past few weeks, he's been having nightmares about Chase. Last night, Cartier woke up around 3am crying and fighting in his sleep. He had sweat covering his forehead and his breathing was rapid. Naomi held him all night to get him to go back to sleep. When she woke up this morning, her shirt was covered with sweat and tears.

"What are you thinking about?" Naomi asked, breaking the silence that filled the room.

"I can't do this again, Naomi... I'm not strong enough to handle this shit."

She stood up and lifted his chin, so that he could look up at her. "It's okay to not be okay. I'd be worried if you felt like everything was fine. You don't have to be strong all the time, Cartier. I got you but what I won't allow you to do is quit."

He watched her as she put on his tie, a small smile crept upon his lips. "Thanks mamas."

Sharing a quick kiss on the lips, they gathered their things to leave.

Inside of the car, Cartier stared out the window and watched the rain fall. To say he wasn't slipping into a depressive state would be a lie; he was far from his usual self. Burying another brother at the hands of the streetz was something he didn't want to get used to. All he had left was his family, Naomi, and Nassir. He wanted to keep them close and safe because without them, he would lose his mind.

In attempt to escape his thoughts, he allowed the music Naomi played to flow through his ears. "I can only imagine what was going through his head when he made this."

Naomi glanced at him and focused back on traffic. She smiled at hearing his voice. He's been so quiet today, she was starting to worry, "Me too. Drake has the kind of music that makes you sit back and really think about things."

"Man, tell me about it. Him and Pac music really got me through a lot of dark nights." He mumbled before pulling out his phone and placing it on his ear. "Yes mama."

Mama Joyce frowned. "Boy, where is y'all at? Don't make me come over there and pull you out of that damn bed, Cartier. I know you are a depressed baby, but you are attending this funeral."

He laughed and responded. "We actually down the street mama."

"Mhm okay. See you in a moment."

He ended the call, sniffled, and wiped his eyes. He noticed the sky was clearing up. He smiled and thought about Chase, *My boy happy.*

They pulled into the parking lot of the gravesite. Cartier put on his shades; he wasn't really in the mood to be social. Naomi turned off the engine to the car and looked at Cartier with concerned eyes. "You ready?"

Dryly, he responded. "Yes."

They opened their doors and held hands as they followed everyone to the chairs. The funeral was decorated very nicely; well put together. Cartier made sure Chase's mom had everything she wanted for her son and even paid for all the cost. He felt that was the least he could do. Squeezing Naomi's hand tighter as they began approaching the casket, Cartier felt his eyes glossing over and palms began to sweat. This was the moment he hated the worst at funerals. He investigated the casket and allowed his tears to fall as he got one last look at his brother. Chased lied there lifelessly. His body was pale and burned up, Cartier's stomach turned. He hung his head low while all the moments they shared together resurfaced in his brain. Another tear fell. He touched his chain, displaying his initials, and laughed as he sniffled. "See you on the other side nigga."

He turned to face Tyrik and his mom. They pulled them both into hugs and gave their condolences; seeing the looks on their faces made Cartier feel even worse. He looked down at the grass as he walked. Him and Naomi took their seats next to his mom. Quietly sitting, they watched as everybody came and said their final goodbyes.

The sounds of heels clicking across the pavement alerted everyone. Turning their heads in its direction, Chardonnay swayed her hips as she headed to the casket. Leaning forward, Nassir whispered in Cartier's ear, "Why did this bitch even come?"

Cartier only shrugged, not really caring to find out either. He didn't have time for Chardonnay and whatever trick she had up her sleeve. Draping his arm around Naomi's shoulder, he waited for the service to start. After the service, everyone went back to the hall that rested inside of the funeral home for family gatherings. Everybody was talking, eating, and even smiling; lifting each other up during this tough time. Some people even hit the dance floor and reminisced through the sweet sounds of old Sokol music. Naomi sat at the table with Nassir, Sheree, Quentin, and Lanay, while Cartier walked around mingling.

Chewing some of her food, Sheree covered her mouth, "I don't know who made these greens, but they put their foot in this."

"You better slow down before it makes your ass even fatter," Lanay warned, sipping from her water.

"I could use just a little more," Sheree giggled.

Scoping out everyone, Naomi's eyes landed on Ariana. She seemed to be a little out of place and alone. Naomi felt bad for her because she knew what it was like for a man's family not to mess with you. She experienced that firsthand with Deandre's family, so she knew the look all too well. The two locked eyes, Naomi signaled for her to come over.

Approaching the table, Ariana made sure to greet everyone. "Hey y'all." She waved.

"What's up Ari? How are you feeling?" Cartier asked, giving her a quick hug.

"I'm numb right now but I know eventually I'll be okay. I just wanted to come and speak before I left. Y'all please keep in touch with me, I'ma need y'all more than ever now." She expressed as tears started to fall from her eyes.

Tyrik got up and threw his arm over her shoulder and escorted her to the limo so they could take her home.

"I feel so sorry for her, I can only imagine what she's going through right now." Naomi spoke out, thinking about how much she would be affected if she lost Cartier. As they all sat around and continued talking, things went silent when Chardonnay started making her way over to their table. "Oh, don't let me interrupt the conservation, I just came to pay my respects." She stated, but Cartier wasn't buying that.

"Well, we appreciate that, thank you for coming." He replied dryly.

Chardonnay laughed and rolled her eyes when she looked over at Naomi who was already staring. "Damn, not you giving me the cold shoulder-like you weren't the one out here running around playing house with this bitch."

Cartier stood up and immediately pushed Naomi behind him. "Really Char!? You wanna pull this shit today of all days!?" He yelled.

"Do you really think I give a fuck? You never once gave a fuck so why should I?" She asked. "Oh, I know what it is, you just don't want miss clueless over here to know the real you huh?"

Chardonnay knew exactly what she was doing and to her surprise, it was working. She was starting to become okay with the fact that things between them were over, but the wound still did sting. However, her only motive today was making sure she stirred the pot well enough for it to boil over.

"Chardonnay, you need to leave." Cartier gritted out.

"Don't worry, I'll leave." Looking over at Naomi, Chardonnay scoffed. "I wonder how it feels to know you were the second option since I no longer wanted his ass. Bitches like you are so fucking pathetic, I really hope you don't think you won, bagging a man like Cartier. The same way you get them is exactly how you lose them. Hopefully you're smarter than me to leave but then again, I highly doubt you will." She laughed, realizing she struck a nerve.

"First of all, Chardonnay, you don't even know me, so I advise you to stop while you're ahead. Leave." Naomi replied.

"And if I don't? What exactly are you going to do about it, bitch!? I been owed your stupid ass an ass whooping since the moment I found out you was fucking my nigga." Chardonnay taunted.

Although Cartier was trying to keep the peace, nothing was working. Naomi had gotten from around Cartier, both her and Chardonnay were now fighting.

Cartier carried Naomi away while someone carried Chardonnay, who had a busted lip and nose, away. She yelled out inaudible curse words, trying to fight her again. Cartier could not believe this was how the day had to end, nor did he ever expect things to pop off between Naomi and Chardonnay.

Chase and Tyrik's mother, Noni, picked up on the drama that occurred. They decided to showcase the video she put together of Chase throughout his entire life. A giant projector screen was displayed at the front of the funeral. Everyone's attention turned to the screen as it began to play. In response, laughter and cries spread throughout the room. Chardonnay held one last glare at Cartier before she made her grand exit from the building. He watched as she was escorted out. Cartier shook his head and remained waiting on Naomi to exit the women's restroom.

"What the fuck was that shit man?" Nassir asked, approaching him with Tyrik beside him. "It started to turn into an episode of bad girls club up in here."

Cartier sighed followed by a slight chuckle. "Man, your guess is as good as mine. I can't believe Chardonnay ass came up in here with that bullshit."

Tyrik laughed. "That jawn is nuts."

"I told this mothafucka when he first started fucking with her ass that she was crazy." Nassir said, sipping from his glass.

"Fuck y'all niggas man" Cartier spat. "How are you holding up Rik? You need anything?"

Tyrik was far from okay but beyond the mask he held on, nobody would know. Instead, he held his famous smile and said, "I got a lot of shit on my mind but I'm gon be good."

Tyrik excused himself after hearing someone call his name. Cartier and Nassir were left to talk for a moment. Stuffing his free hand inside his pocket, Nassir decided to touch on the topic of business, briefly. "On a more serious note, are you ready for this meeting we're about to have in a few weeks?"

"Hell yeah. The supply we have isn't going to hold us over for long. We need a new shipment real soon, so I'm hoping this deal with him goes through smoothly."

Nassir nodded, understanding where he was coming from. Since being fucked over by Trig, business had been fluctuating up and down. The new supplier will give them more opportunities and a possibility of expansion outside of Georgia. Cartier watched closely at everybody interacting, one person stood out to him in the crowd of people. A woman that appeared to be in her early thirties. She had her hair neatly tucked away in a ponytail and her attire was business casual. By the way she flowed through the crowd, he could tell this wasn't an environment she was familiar with.

"Aye, don't stare but check out ole girl over there in the black pants suit. Does she look like a fed to you?"

Trying to play it smoothly, Nassir swiftly scoped out the room. Making contact with her eyes for a brief second, he shook his head. "Nah, she must be one of Ms. Noni prissy ass office friends. Stop being so paranoid all the time nigga, relax."

Cartier wasn't buying it and made an intelligent decision to keep his eyes and ears out for her. The sound of the bathroom door opened and out came Naomi and Sheree. Naomi appeared to be her usual self but inside she still was furious, she couldn't believe Chardonnay had the audacity to come for her. She wasn't expecting them to be the best of friends considering the situation, but she didn't expect this either. It was her mistake for thinking she was able to put differences aside and be a grown woman about things. The home videos finally ended and the song that could get any black person out of their seat made its way out of the speakers. *Before I Let Go* by Frankie Beverly and Maze.

Snapping her fingers to the sound of the beat, Naomi smiled at Cartier. "Come on, you have to dance with me baby."

Returning the smile, he took her hand and guided her to the dance floor. Everyone joined together on the floor, dancing and laughing. Cartier watched as Naomi swayed to the beat of the song, gracefully. She looked so at peace and joyful. He was pleased to finally see her back enjoying herself and not allowing the scene with Chardonnay to destroy the celebration of his brother's life.

He held her in his arms, they swayed together, snapping their fingers. He snuck a quick kiss on her neck before continuing to enjoy their moment

Chapter 17

The sounds of laughter and loud voices caused Naomi's eyes to flutter open from her sleep. Noticing the once sunny bedroom now dimmed, she knew she must've slept more than she intended to. She propped herself up and cleared her eyes of the eye boogers that rested in the creases of her eyelids. She moved the blanket off her and stood up to stretch her muscles.

She walked to the bathroom, sat on the toilet, released herself, and made sure to clean up before flushing. Naomi frowned once she noticed how tore up she appeared.

After freshening herself up, she left the bedroom to join Cartier downstairs. Feeling the warmth the carpet provided between her toes, Naomi smiled when she came into view of the living area.

The loveseat was occupied by Nassir and Sheree, Quentin sat between Lanay's legs at the end of the couch, and Cartier sat on the other end, playing a game of Call of Duty with Nassir.

Naomi walked into the living room, sat next to Cartier, and rested her head on his shoulder. Checking out the game, she noticed that Nassir had the leading points per usual. He's a die-hard fan of Call of Duty; any game ever released, he owned it.

Noticing Naomi's presence, Lanay frowned at the site of her. "Damn you don't see anybody else?"

"I'm sorry, hello to you too, Lanay." Naomi responded, looking over in her direction.

"Girl, don't mind her, she's on her period today." Sheree teased before directing her attention back to her phone.

Lately, the tension between the girls had been very thick, for their own good reasons. Lanay felt like her friends didn't understand her or cared for her relationship; however, they did but they knew Lanay couldn't see clearly what they were trying to convey- which was they wanted her happy, but with herself first.

"Nigga, unlock that door in the back. I just used my damn points on these perks!" Nassir shouted with his eyes glued to the screen.

Smacking his teeth, Cartier waved him off, "I got this. Just focus on not getting your ass down."

Naomi watched them play like it was a movie. She knew nothing about gaming, but she enjoyed watching it. Cartier ran towards the closed door with a swarm of zombies, high on his tail. Before he could press square to unlock the door, he noticed Nassir's radar go off, indicating that he was down.

"Fuck." Cartier spat, unlocking the door anyway. He attempted to turn around and go pick up Nassir but failed to do so. Before he knew it, zombies surrounded him, attacking him from every angle.

Nassir dropped the controller and pulled out a blunted that rested behind his ear. "That was a good ass game though."

Quentin pulled out a zip of weed from Lanay's purse, shook the Ziplock bag, and held it up. "Match muthfuckas."

Cartier shut off the game and grabbed the remote to put the tv on YouTube. Pulling up the search bar, he typed in Polo G, and went to his song Rapstar. "Fire that shit up. I got some rellos."

Watching as everyone indulged in their own activities, Naomi smiled. These types of moments reminded her of the old days when she was a teenager. Of course, she didn't know Sheree, Quentin, or Cartier back then but her, Nassir, and Lanay used to throw intimate kickbacks all the time, just enjoying their people with no drama.

"We should have a kickback y'all. I mean we could all use a day off from the bullshit that's going on around us. Invite over some family and friends, have some good fun, and music." Naomi suggested.

Sheree finally pulled her head away from her game of Homescapes and nodded. "That would actually be cool. I could use a night of fun."

Cartier draped his arm around Naomi and pecked her on the lips. "Let's do it then, ma. Y'all can head over to Walmart and grab the food and drinks, while we stay here and set up."

"Okay. Let me throw on something real quick and we can go y'all." Naomi announced before disappearing upstairs.

She walked into the bedroom, went to her overnight bag, and stripped out of her pajamas. She threw her clothes in his laundry hamper, slid on her black leggings, one of Cartier's white tees, and her Adidas slides.

Grabbing her keys off the dresser, she headed back down the stairs. "I'm ready."

The girls stood up and said goodbye to their men before heading for the door. Naomi felt her body being pulled back, she turned around to see Cartier standing there, counting out money with a blunt resting between his lips. She bit her lip and enjoyed the view. It didn't matter if Cartier was doing something as simple as cooking; she was turned by his existence alone.

"What are you doing?"

He ignored her questions and handed her fifteen hundred dollars. "Take this to get everything y'all need."

Naomi smirked at his offer but pushed his hand away. "Cartier, I don't want your money. I can pay for it, boo."

"I know you can but as your man I want to provide it for you. So, allow me to do that."

She nodded, pecked his lips, accepted it all, and followed the girls outside. Lanay nudged Naomi's shoulder on the way to the car. "You and Cartier seem like y'all getting serious."

Naomi's eyes trailed around. She hadn't noticed it, but Lanay was right. Lately they've been spending all their free time with each other and things like spending the night over each other's places became normal for them. Without realizing it at first, she went against everything she promised herself she wouldn't do.

However, she didn't care. Things with Cartier weren't like her relationship with Deandre. She wasn't going to allow a good man like him slip through her fingers, so yes, she was moving a little fast with Cartier.

"Yeah, that's my baby," She admitted proudly. "What's going on with you and Que?"

Sliding in the backseat, Sheree added in her two cents. "Exactly, ever since I saw y'all together at that block party, you two have been inseparable."

Naomi placed the keys inside the ignition and turned on the car. She adjusted her mirrors and seat, then hooked her phone up to the aux and instructed Apple Music to play her playlist.

"I'm feeling him, y'all. I know y'all don't like him or the idea of us but he's good for me. I'm happy." Lanay blushed looking out the window as Naomi backed out of the driveway. "I mean, at first I never thought I could find a man like him. But Quentin, he's different. He gives me a feeling no other man can."

"I'm happy for you Nay. You deserve this, don't get me wrong. I just also worry that you depend on him for happiness and that's not good. Don't forget about self-happiness, that's all I'ma say." Naomi told her truthfully.

"That's all. I understand wanting to be all up under your man. Hell, if I could be in Nassir's skin, I would be, but if he left me today- a bitch would be salty, but I'd survive without him tomorrow." Sheree added.

The rest of the car ride was silent, not a tense silence but a peaceful one. Everybody was wrapped up in their own minds and enjoying the music that played.

Finally arriving at Walmart, they all exited the car before Naomi locked it. Headed for the entrance, Naomi was grateful there wasn't a crowd. She wanted to get in and out. Walmart had a way of making her pick up many things she didn't even come for.

Grabbing her cart, they all walked over to the fruit and veggie area. "What should we cook?" Sheree asked.

Naomi felt her phone vibrate in her pocket, she pulled it out to check it. Jacques' name flashed across her screen with a message.

Jacques:
Hey Naomi. I apologize for everything that went on yesterday and I hope I didn't fuck up shit between us. Would you like to go out with me and a few of my friends for a game night?
Delivered 5:24pm

Naomi stared at the message and thought of a way to respond. She wasn't so confident herself on Jacques' intentions with her. but in her eyes, he was only a friend. That's all that mattered.

Naomi:
Don't sweat it. I know you didn't mean anything by it. I have to take a rain check on the invite though. I'm having a kickback today at my boyfriend's place. If you would like to swing by let me know. It's around 6:30.
Sent 5:27pm

She put her phone back in her pocket and quickly caught back up with the girls.

"Girl, tell Cartier you will be back." Lanay teased.

"That was actually Jacques."

Frowning, Sheree snapped her neck in Naomi's direction. She wasn't a big fan of Jacques. She just felt something was off about him. "Jacques? What did he want?"

Shrugging, she looked over the sugar cookies that were on display, getting distracted already. "He just wanted to hang out, but I told him I couldn't. I offered for him to slide by if he had time."

"Why the hell would you do that? You know Cartier does not like that man." Sheree said. "Especially after last night!"

Looking between the two, Lanay shook her head. She felt out of the loop a lot; hell, she's the one that introduced them, but they bonded harder with each other than her. "What happened last night?"
"She hung out with his high yellow ass and intentionally, unintentionally flirted. I think the boy is trying to break them up." Sheree admits.

Playfully rolling her eyes, Naomi ignored Sheree's comment. "Me and that man are only friends, everybody will see that."

She was becoming annoyed with everybody's talk about Jacques. They acted as if men and women couldn't be friends. She knew that last night was a little inappropriate, but her heart was with Cartier, she wouldn't risk losing him for nobody.

"Mhm." Lanay mumbled as she shook her head.

Continuing their shopping they settled on cooking rotel, wings, and nachos for the menu. They made sure to pick up dominion, uno, and playing cards as well. Tonight, was going to be a night to remember for some but the exact opposite for others.

They arrived back at Cartier's place. Naomi peeped the horn and on cue, the guys came outside to grab the bags, like the gentlemen they were. Following them inside, Naomi was surprised at how well they cleaned and set everything up.

Naomi checked the time and allowed the girls to start cooking while she headed upstairs to change into something more fitting to the occasion.

She turned on the water and started stripping out of her clothes while the water warmed up. She noticed that Cartier had his outfit laid out on the bed. A smile appeared on her face when she noticed he was going to wear the necklace she made him for Chase; it was encrusted with gold and had angel wings with chase's names carved nicely inside.

She decided to match her man's fly, so she picked out something that was grey and black also. She chose her distressed jeans; they hugged her curves just right. She also grabbed her cami top; it was black and laced up the back. She set out her accessories, walked back in the bathroom, and stepped inside the shower.

She applied Dove soap on her towel, lathered it up, and began washing her body as she hummed the lyrics to a song. She was so caught up in her self-care, she didn't realize Cartier stepped inside of the shower with her.

She felt the familiar feeling of his tool poking her ass, she jumped. She turned and saw him smiling at her, she playfully splashed water on him. "You play too damn much."

"You enjoy it." He mumbled, snaking his arm around her waist and pulling her closer to him.

Giggling at his touch, she stood there for a moment and enjoyed being in his arms. A moan escaped her lips when she felt his lips touching her skin followed by his tongue. Naomi knew that they needed to head downstairs to entertain their guests but at that moment, what guests? She wanted him too.

She faced him and pulled him into her; that was all the confirmation he needed to enter her body.

After their steamy love making session, they finally showed their faces downstairs. It was now going on 8:30 pm, everybody was there. Naomi saw Jewell inside the kitchen, she walked over to her.

"Hey girl, how have you been?" She asked, grasping her attention from the plate she held.

Chewing her food, she sat her plate down and pulled Naomi into a friendly embrace. "Hey girl! I ain't been nothing but the same ole, same ole.

I was starting to wonder where you were. I haven't seen you sin—"Jewel froze not wanting to touch on what happened at the girls' night. "It's just good to see you girl."

"You too. Is Genesis here too?"

"You know she is. She's there mingling with Cartier's friends, asking to get a friendly ass whooping by him. She knows how protective he is." Jewell said, picking her plate back up and wasting no time in popping a chip inside her mouth.

Naomi shook her head and laughed. She walked over to the cups and made her a cup of jungle juice. She heard the sound of cheering; she glanced over to the pool table and saw the guys in the middle of a heated game.

She made her way over to the table, stood next to Cartier, and sipped from her cup. "Who's winning?"

"I'm whooping his ass!" Tyrik chanted, hitting a ball and sending it flying straight into the corner, earning a score.

Shaking his head, Cartier took a sip from Naomi's cup before handing it back to her. "You're not doing shit."

"Let me hit one." Naomi offered.

She knew nothing about playing pool in real life but if you challenged her in the app, she was a beast. She figured it couldn't be that hard. Watching Tyrik miss his next hit, Cartier shrugged and decided to let her have one play.

"Can you play ma?"

"Nope."

Laughing, he flashed his intoxicating smile as he pulled her into his embrace. He placed her into the proper stance and helped her aim for one of the balls.

"Slightly pull back." He said gently, pulling his hands back in sync with hers. Once they released it, the ball gilded nicely into the middle hole of the table.

"Ou okay!" Sheree cheered.

Naomi smiled and watched Cartier go ahead and hit the next one. She continued sipping from her cup and watched them play for a moment. Next, she joined the girls who sat in the living area with snacks, drinks, gossip.

“Girl, fuck that, the brotha is fine. He can wear me out any time.” Genesis said, checking out a guy over by the pool table.

“What y’all over here gossiping about?” Naomi asked, taking a seat beside Sheree.

“That’s these two. I’m too busy checking my damn phone to see where my man is!” Jewel responded by scrolling through her phone while sipping some juice.

“I don’t blame her though. He is nice looking.” A familiar brown skinned woman added.

She appeared to be in her mid to late twenties. Her hair was styled in a curly pixie look, colored with a dark purple. She had a nice big boned shape with beautiful almond brown eyes.

“What’s your name?” Lanay asked her.

“I’m sorry. I’m Keisha, Tyrik’s girl.”

“Oooh yeah okay. I remember you from the funeral. You look so different with the short look.” Naomi greeted, flashing her a smile.

Everybody started back their regular chatter amongst each other, Keisha blended in with them just fine. It was as if they already knew her. Naomi’s phone chimed. She picked it up and saw a text from Jacques.

Jacques:
I’m outside.
Delivered 9:15pm

Naomi stood up and made her way to the door. Opening it, she saw him coming up the pavement holding a bottle of Remy Martin in his hand. Pulling her into a friendly embrace, he greeted her.

“Wassup Nao.”

“Wassup.”

They closed the door behind them. Jacques bopped his head to the music playing, feeling the vibes. "What y'all cook? A nigga is starving."

She showed him to the kitchen, sat his bottle down, and told him to help himself. She decided to make herself a small plate too, so that it wasn't only alcohol resting on her stomach.
He slightly leaned on the counter and picked up one of his wings to bite into. "I stopped by your shop earlier, but your ass wasn't there. I was trying to get you to hook a nigga up with some twist."

"Some twist? Hm, I can see you rocking that look. We gon have to set you up an appointment."

He wiped his face with his napkin and nodded. "Bet. How shit going with you and your man? I hope I didn't stir the pot too bad."

"No, you good. Cartier just going through a lot right now and he only remember you as some nigga trying to push up on me at a party. In due time, he will see you as one of the guys." She explained.

"Speaking of him, are you sure he's cool with me being here? He staring pretty hard."

Naomi followed his eyes, and he indeed was staring from over by the pool table. Cartier wasn't the type of man to make a scene, he was real laid back and chill, so Naomi silently hoped that this night didn't take a turn for the worse.

Focusing her attention back to her plate, she shrugged. "I'll talk to him."

Naomi suddenly lost her appetite from her nerves picking up. She started to regret even inviting Jacques from the start. She thought he'd understand her inviting him and see that there was nothing there; the way his face looked told a different story.

Naomi began washing her hands. Sheree walked over, looking like she'd seen a ghost. "Girl, Cartier is walking over here." She whispered.

Approaching Jacques, Cartier slapped the plate from his hands and made an entire mess. "I know I didn't invite your ass so what you doing in my place? Better yet, how do you even know where I lay my head at?"

Jacques showed no signs of fear, he stepped closer to him. "You better chill that shit out nigga. Your girl invited me. Now, since we at yo crib,

I'm gonna let you knocking my plate out my hand slide- but that's the only warning."

Cartier allowed everything he said to go in one ear and out the other. The only thing that stuck was him saying Naomi invited him. He glanced over at Naomi with an expression she couldn't read but she knew it was nothing good. "What the fuck he mean, you invited him?"

"Cartier, I told you me and him are just friends, it's not like that..." Naomi attempted to explain but she didn't even know what to say. In that moment, she realized if the roles were reversed, she would've responded the same way, if not worse.

Cartier angrily chuckled. "Every time it comes to this nigga, it's never like that huh?"

Naomi stared at him, not responding. Cartier sucked his teeth and sent a punch flying in Jacques' direction. He knew his actions weren't really called for. He was behaving out of emotion, but that liquor made shit hit different.

Eating the punch he threw, Jacques defended himself and sent one back. After that, the two were fighting all throughout the kitchen like wild animals. Glass was flying and blood was being shed. Naomi held her hands over her mouth as she watched the scene unfold before her.

What have I done? was all she could think.

"Aye, y'all chill the fuck out!" Nassir shouted pulling them apart with the help of Tyrik and a few other people.

Cartier tried to walk back up on Jacques after they had been pulled apart. Tyrik pushed him back even further, blocking his access. In a rage, Cartier looked Tyrik in the face and shouted, "Get this nigga up out my shit before I lose my fucking mind in here."

Tyrik nodded. "I get it bro, trust me. Just calm your ass down for a second."

Genesis stood up from her seat and walked over to assist Tyrik with Cartier. She's seen Cartier this angry before when he used to fight his dad, so she knew how to get him calm.

Back in the kitchen, Nassir returned inside after making sure Jacques left. Grabbing Naomi by the arm he pulled her to the side. "What the fuck was that Nao!?"

She rolled her eyes and folded her arms. "We are just friends, Nas. Y'all are really blowing this up. I invited him in hopes of getting everybody together, not to have WWE showdown."

And that's the truth. Naomi honestly had good intentions but after placing herself inside his shoes, she realized how this may have come across.

"That's just something you don't do Naomi. You didn't ask this man if he could even come inside his house. Not only that, once he arrived, you failed to even introduce him to the man of the house. Get your shit together, sis."

"I know. I fucked up." She admitted.

"Nao, if you want to be with Cartier, you need to learn and understand how to do that. I know you fucked up from Dre, but we all have shit we're dealing with. If you don't pull it together and stop doing wild shit, you gone lose him." Nassir lectured. Although Naomi wasn't feeling it, he was right. She knew inviting him over wasn't the best idea, she didn't know why she did it anyway.

"Ugh, way to make me feel even shittier than I already was." Naomi sobbed, running into the arms of her brother. She hated when Nassir of all people chewed her out, whether she deserved it or not. He had her spoiled in that way, but she knew he was right. She spent so many years hurting, now that she's free of it, she's the one causing damages.

"It's gonna be okay. You just have to start thinking and making better choices. Have you talked to mama?" He asked, pulling back to look her in the face.

"Yeah, I can't believe she has cancer. She looks so healthy on the outside."

"I know. I'm stopping by there tomorrow; you should come too." He said, kissing her on the forehead before walking off to the patio, where Que and Cartier had gone. Naomi sighed, wiped her face, and went upstairs to the bedroom.

Sheree sat in disbelief; she couldn't believe what began as fun became such a nightmare. Sitting on the couch with the girls while the guys sat outside calming down Cartier, Sheree finished the rest of her cup and debated if she should check on Naomi.

"You okay?" Genesis asked her, breaking her from her thoughts.

Sheree nodded. "Yeah, girl I'm fine."

Taking a hard sip from her cup, Lanay rolled her eyes. She was getting tired of being in the environment of her friends. It was always something happening. She started to think maybe Quentin was right, she probably did need a new scenery of friends for a bit.

"Naomi ass knew what was going to happen. There isn't any sense in sitting around, moping about it. She should've never invited his lame ass to begin with."

Genesis rolled her eyes. "Girl, all that attitude is unnecessary. Isn't Naomi your girl? You should be worried about comforting her, not down here low key shading her out."

"Agreed." Keisha added.

Lanay glanced around the room and gave everybody a scoff. "I've known Naomi longer than all you bitches; I know when she's tripping. Anything I say about her I can say to her. Don't try to check me boo."

"What the fuck is your problem!? Ever since you've been sniffing up Quentin 's ass! You been changing by the fucking day." Sheree snapped.

She was becoming fed up with Lanay's distance and shady comments. She loved her friend, but she didn't like the person that she was becoming over a man. She knew it had been a while since Lanay had one, so she tried to be patient in hopes of her coming around, but the chances of that happening were slim to none.

"Girl, this ain't about no damn Quentin. See that's the bullshit I'm talking about. You and Naomi asses are just jealous. Y'all want me to be fucking miserable. Which ain't gone happen because me and Que are real serious."

"Lanay, you sound fucking delusional as hell. Let me go befo--"

Before Sheree could finish her sentence Lanay grabbed a handful of her hair and yanked her back. Sheree instantly reacted and sent punches flying in her direction. Lanay ate each one and tried to choke Sheree lifeless, but before she could get to her, Quentin snatched her up.

"Let my fucking hair go, bitch." Sheree yelled, growing angrier by the minute. Lanay wasn't hearing it though, she wanted blood.

"Bitch, fuck you" Lanay responded gripping even tighter.

"Aye man, get your girl." Nassir said starting to become annoyed himself. He knew Sheree could defend her own, but he wasn't about to let Lanay pull her hair out either.

"Baby come on. She's not worth it." Quentin said. His words went in and directly out. He noticed her death stare and turned her face to his and repeated his words- "Baby come on. She's not worth it." Lanay immediately released her.

Sheree wasted no time trying to charge at her, but Nassir picked her up and disappeared upstairs. He knew if he allowed her to stay down there a second longer, the two of them would destroy the entire place. Back downstairs, Quentin decided it was time for them to leave. Gathering their things, he and Lanay made their way out the door.

Naomi sat on the bed, deep in her feelings; the entire night went to shit, it was supposed to be *different*. All she wanted was a night of fun to free everybody from their own individual issues that they hide from the world. Instead, things turned into a brewing spill over. Fidgeting with her hands, she silently laughed at herself.

She honestly understood Cartier's anger. Although she wanted nothing more than a friendship from Jacques, she knew that she enjoyed his company a little more than she should.

The sound of the bedroom door opening and closing broke her from her thoughts. She looked over to see a now calmer Cartier. He sat at the end of the bed and sighed.

"Naomi, you know how I feel about you. You everything a nigga thought didn't exist for me. So, losing you is something my mind can't comprehend. When I saw you with him, that's all I thought about. What were you thinking mamas?"

Hearing his words made Naomi feel even worse. She crawled over to him and rested her head on his shoulder. "I wasn't thinking. I apologize baby. I thought maybe if you saw us hang out that you would know there was nothing going on between us."

"You may feel that way, but he doesn't. You can't honestly tell me it ain't true."

As badly as she didn't want him to be, she knew he was right. "I will keep my distance."

Cartier pulled her into his lap and kissed her lips. "I don't want to control you. I'm not that type of man. All I'm asking for you to do is respect me enough to be honest. If he does come on to you, cut that little friendship lose."

Naomi nodded and listened to his words. She closed her eyes and enjoyed the silence and peace that filled the room.

Chapter 18

Cartier sat at the head of the wooden table, every right-hand man he had was in attendance. It was finally time for him to strap up his boots and put his foot down. He stood up and adjusted the suit he wore. Part of being a businessman was looking the part; he didn't want to be viewed as your typical nickel and dime hustler anymore.

He reevaluated everything; he moved his cooking houses, supplies, and money to spots that blinded in, and made sure his team no longer appeared as street-men. Everyone dressed as if they were clocking in at a corporate office. With all the new changes and structures, business was going exceedingly well. The only issue that was still at hand was something every leader despised, war.

Rubbing his temples, Cartier let out a deep breath. He was conflicted on what to do about the issue he had with Trig. Part of him wanted to be ruthless and act off emotion, but he knew that would bite him in the ass.

"I say we just get this shit over with, honestly. What's the big deal if we just get rid of him?" Nassir spoke out, breaking the silence that filled the room.

Tyrik shrugged his shoulders in agreement with Nassir. He didn't understand this "Beat around the bush" way of thinking. "I'm with Nas on this one."

"Handling business that way only makes room for error to take place, dry up money, and cause a lot of bloodshed. We don't need that..." Cartier trailed off as his mind started to race ahead of him. "That's it."

"What?" Quentin questioned.

"Trig is so fucking shady; I'm more than sure we aren't the only ones he's fucked over. We do business with his connections and make them offers they can't resist. Not only would we have a wide variety of products, but we'd also rule out his entire family. We wouldn't be shunned if everybody they feed is in our pockets." Carter explained. "It would be like a kingdom ruling out the mayor."

Quentin sighed. He was beyond tired of these meetings and listening to his brother's plans. "Honestly bro, you should just let me handle this shit for you. I mean it's not like you wanted this life anyway."

Cartier shot Quentin a look of confusion. He didn't understand where his energy was stemming from. Over the past few weeks, he's noticed Quentin's odd behavior. He always knew his brother felt some-type-of-way about him running the family business, but he never thought that was the wedge that sat between them.

Sitting up in his chair, Cartier shrugged. "Why would I do that?"

Picking up on the direction of the conversation, Nassir sighed. After what occurred last night, he wasn't up for anymore drama. "Don't start this shit. Let's focus back on what we got our black asses out of bed for."

"Nah Nas, let his ass speak." Cartier replied.

Quentin smirked, pulling at his goatee. "Well, fuck it then. Ever since dad passed away, Uncle Pernell and Rome have been grooming your spoon-fed ass for this position, like you earned it. Nobody even tried to see my fucking potential! They just handed it to you on a sliver fucking platter and your ungrateful ass still don't even want it."

Quentin was tired of holding in how he felt to salvage his brother's feelings; it was time he showed up for himself. He knew it was a bad business move to show division in front of the team, but in the heat of the moment, he didn't care.

"You sound like a weak ass bitch! That shit not on me. Okay, so what!? The shit is over with. Whatchu keep whining about it for?" Cartier snapped.

He didn't understand where his brother was coming from and at that point, he didn't really care. He felt his issues were misguided and had to be with their uncles; it wasn't his fault that the family saw his potential and chose him instead.

Quentin stood up angrily causing his chair to fall back. He headed towards Cartier like a bull seeing red. Cartier picked up on his movement and got up from his chair as well. The two both stood there, heated as fuck, their faces were inches apart.

Everybody in the room grew silent and watched the scene unravel before them. They knew this moment was bound to happen; the tension between them was no secret, and their energy towards one another always spoke when they didn't.

"What you on nigga!?" Cartier yelled angrily.

"What the fuck you wanna do, C?" Quentin responded as he pushed Cartier back some.

Nassir smacked his lips and jumped up from his seat to stand in between them. "Man, sit y'all asses the fuck down and let this shit go."

Quentin walked to his seat and snatched his keys before heading for the door, "Fuck him" he said before slamming it with no remorse.

"What the fuck was that?" Gunz asked, looking around the room in search of an answer.

Nassir sighed and rested his hands on the back of his chair. "Give us a minute y'all. I'll update everybody on everything later." Nassir told the team.

Without any protest, everybody left the room. Nassir then looked at Cartier with a *what the fuck* look. He knew that brothers fought but the scene that unfolded before him today wasn't your typical family dysfunction. They looked as if they wanted blood; it was apparent they hated each other.

Cartier looked out the window in deep thought. His hands rested inside his pockets. He tried to soothe his mind, but he was uneasy. "Man, something ain't right with Que, and I'ma find out about it."

"Nigga, that's yo fucking brother! Y'all niggas grew up in the same house and came from the same pussy and ball sack. Do you really think he a fuck you over?"

Cartier knew his accusations were a bit far-fetched due to no real evidence to back it up, but he was a believer in coincidences. He also trusted his gut, which was telling him that something wasn't right.

Cartier shook his head. "Nas, wake the fuck up! You can't tell me that nigga ain't been moving funny lately."

"All I'm saying is, y'all brothers. This is not the time for that bullshit, especially without any solid proof. Tighten up man." Nassir expressed.

Nassir was all about family and loyalty. He hated to see the two coming for each other's heads over something he felt could be fixed with a simple conversation. He decided to give Cartier some space, so he grabbed his keys and left the room.

Cartier clenched his jaw. He needed to get away for a moment and he knew the perfect spot.

When he'd get too frustrated or overwhelmed, he'd just go to his mom's house, so that he could sit and vent to her about whatever was on his mind. She gave him feel that warm, heartfelt feeling he yearned for.

He got in his car and connected his phone to play the 2000s Drake the entire way there. During this time, he could especially relate to a lot of lyrics that Drake spoke.

He arrived at his mom's house around sunset and made sure to lock his doors before heading up the driveway. He walked up to the side door and already smelled her home cooking; it put a smile on his face. He pulled out his spare key to unlock the door to his second home.

"Ma, it's me." He announced, closing the door behind him and walking into the kitchen. Mama Joyce sat at her dining room table, sipping a nice glass of lemonade as she waited for her fried chicken to cook.

"Hey baby, what brings you by?" She asked, standing up to give him a hug. Once he was in her embrace, he felt all his problems and emotions just falling out. He held her tight and tried to control his breathing.

Mama Joyce stood there, caressing his back. Seeing him like this made her nervous. Life for Cartier was finally starting to look up, she prayed it was news that she could handle. She hadn't seen him this worked up since Chardonnay aborted their baby.

"Cartier Maurice Williams. What's going on with you?"

Cartier released her and took a seat. "Excuse my language mama. Shit is starting to get too real for me. It's like I can never catch a break. All I'm trying to do is make enough money to make sure my people are set forever, but it seems like every time I make a step towards progression, I'm going back ten."

"That's life, son. Nothing about it will ever be easy. You get over one bump just to drive into another. Stop talking in circles and tell me what happened."

"Que coming at me sideways about running the business, I found out Naomi killed her abusive boyfriend, his crazy brother is after her- who happens to be Giovanni's son." He tried to explain between tears. "On top of me having to fix all the problems in the business. I'm lost and ready to quit."

He began to feel a little better after letting it all out. He used the tissue his mom gave him to clean up the only mess he could actually fix right now. Besides Naomi, his mom was the one person he could be vulnerable with. He always made sure to show no signs of weakness because if you allowed a person to see it, it'd be the very thing they use against you to take you down.

"Look at me!" Mama Joyce demanded. Following her instructions, he did just that. "I didn't raise you to be a man that quits just because life has gotten difficult. I raised you to be the kind of man that can handle a punch, even if it makes him stumble or fall. You will figure things out baby. As far as you and Que, I will talk to him. Y'all are brothers! I didn't raise y'all that way."

Hearing the sound of her chicken grease pop, Mama Joyce hopped up and cut her stove off. She took the chicken out to drain it of its excess grease and then started to grab plates and silverware. "Boy you almost made me burn my food. I know you want a plate, make yourself comfortable."

"Yeah, I'm hungry." Cartier giggled, wiping some of his fresh tears. He pulled out his phone and read a message from Naomi.

Nao🩶:
I miss you baby. I'm sitting over here, bored, trying to find something to binge watch on Netflix. You want to come over?
Delivered 6:55pm

Cartier smirked then responded to her message.

Cartier:
I miss you too mamas. Let me chop it up with my old lady for a minute, then I'm on the way to you.
Sent 6:57pm

"Naomi?" Mama Joyce asked, placing a plate filled with fried chicken, baked macaroni, collard greens, and cornbread in front of him.

"Yeah, how did you know?" Cartier asked, waiting for her to sit, so they could bless the food.

"Boy, please. That girl has your nose wide open. I saw the look on your face." She laughed, bringing him a glass of lemonade before taking her seat. "Let's pray."

He held his mom's hand and closed his eyes as she prayed over their food. He hoped she didn't take too long giving God his good graces. His stomach was starting to rumble, and he couldn't wait to devour his plate. There was nothing like mama's cooking.

"Amen" They both said in unison.

"So, how are you and Miss Naomi doing anyway?" Mama Joyce asked packing her fork with greens before placing it in her mouth.

"We are doing okay. We better than before."

She nodded. "What changed?"

Cartier picked up his chicken and bit into it, enjoying every minute of it. As he chewed his food, he decided to vent some more. "Naomi has this friend. She went to school with him, and I know he has feelings for her but I'm not sure how Naomi really feels about him. Last night, we had a get-together and she invited him over. I got jealous and allowed my anger to get the best of me. After that, we had a conversation about it and came to an agreement. I told her she could stay his friend, just respect me. As much as I hate to admit it, part of me wanted to really tell her to end the friendship. Do you think she has something there?" He asked, hoping his mom didn't confirm his suspicions.

"She's going to answer it for you. Watch her actions, no woman will keep anybody around that hinders her relationship, unless she's doing something with him, or she has feelings for him. Especially if he's disrespecting it." She expressed. "But the fact that she had enough courage to invite him over says a statement on its own. Naomi seems like a very respectful girl; I doubt she would have a man in your face that she's involved with."

Cartier nodded, not really knowing what to think of the advice. He sat and enjoyed conversing with his mom for a while before he left to go see Naomi.

Getting out of the car, Cartier entered the store around the corner from Naomi's house. He walked inside and headed straight for the chip aisle. He grabbed himself a bag of hot Funyuns and a Strawberry Kiwi, Clear Fruit, his all-time favorite munchie snack. He headed to the counter and sat his things down. He pulled out his wallet and said, "Let me get 4 packs of your al Capone's Cognac."

The girl behind the counter nodded. "Your total is 10.89."

Cartier pulled a twenty-dollar bill from his wallet and handed it to her. He grabbed his bag and headed for the door. "Keep the change."

Cartier didn't mind paying more than what was needed. He loved giving people tips, he felt you never know how much they need that extra 5 or 10 dollars. It all adds up.

Before he could even open the door to his car, he felt a hard collision to the back of his head. He dropped his bag and turned around quickly to place hands on whoever threw the punch. His attempt failed due to another person hitting him in his side and then knocking him to his knees.

Holding his stomach, he went down. Cartier grew angry. He's never been caught slipping like this and whoever was doing it, he wanted names. From the bellboy up to who called the shots. After several hits and kicks, the three men finally stopped when they felt he had enough. They quickly sped off.

"Oh my God! Should I call the police!?" The store clerk asked, frightened by what she just witnessed.

Releasing a mouth full of blood and spit, Cartier slowly stood up. "I'm good shorty, don't call."

Cartier picked up his bag and tossed it on the passenger side before speeding off. His wounds hurt and there was soreness but that was all. He's gotten worse beatings from his father. What angered him most was who thought they had the balls to pull this shit off. He pulled up to Naomi's house, turned off his car, and held his torso as he slowly walked to her door. He knocked, faintly. Moments later, she came to the door with a smile, but it quickly faded when she saw the condition he was in.

"What the fuck happened!?" She questioned, pulling him inside and locking the door. She ran to the bathroom to grab her first-aid kit and towels. When she returned, she quickly attended to all his wounds.

Naomi knew that Cartier kept a lot of things from her to keep her safe, but she didn't want things to be that way anymore. She felt like she was woman enough to handle shit too, she didn't want Cartier to face it all alone.

Sure, he had his friends and all but there's nothing like your woman being your partner.

The room was silent, nothing was said at all. They only shared glances here and there. Naomi was a little hot from the situation, even though she didn't know anything; she pissed that her man came in, tore the fuck up. She wanted whoever was behind this to feel her wrath.

Noticing the look on her face, he knew she was irritated. He smirked at how cute she looked trying to hold an attitude, it amused him. "I got jumped by some niggas at the corner store. Stop worrying though, I'm good."

"No, you are not good, Cartier. Look at your face! Do you know who these niggas was?"

"Nah, but I'm definitely gonna find out." He answered. He struggled to smile as he watched her clean the towel. "Thanks for being here for a nigga." Naomi looked at him through the mirror that rested above her sink and smiled. "Even though you get under my skin, so bad, I will always be here for you."

Lanay smiled as she chewed her popcorn. She never thought she'd get the chance to experience the love she feels with Quentin. Despite her questions about his vendetta with his family, he's everything she could ask for. When it came to his love and loyalty for her, it wasn't questionable, so that's all that mattered.

Smiling, she accepted a stuffed animal that Quentin handed to her, he won. "Thank you, baby,"

"Anything for my queen." He said, intertwining his hand with hers as they walked away from the booth.

The two were on a date out at the county carnival. It was filled with children, teens, and parents enjoying a good time. It was nearly dark, the lights from all the stands and rides made it even more of a sight to see. Staring at her feet, Lanay looked over at Quentin, noticing his mind was in a different place.

"How are things with you and your brother?"

Quentin twisted his lips, unsure of how to answer the question. His mom sat them both down and let them hear it. It ended with them sharing a brotherly hug, but Quentin wasn't all the way sold on him being genuine. He loved his little brother with every bone in his body, but his pride wouldn't allow him to shake the grudge he held.

"It's complicated," was all he could say- which to him was exactly how things were.

In efforts to be encouraging, she kissed his cheek. "Y'all will figure it out. Families fight all the time but come together even stronger."

Quentin nodded. "How are you and the girls?"

Taking a seat on the benches in front of them, she shrugged. "I don't know. We haven't spoken since everything went down. They haven't reached out to me." Quentin sat beside her, biting his lip. At this point, he felt he and Lanay were strong enough for him to confess his true plan to her. He wanted to give her the benefit of knowing what was going down beforehand, so that he wouldn't have to worry about division when shit got deep. Plus, he could also use her help, if she was willing to give it. He looked into her big brown eyes and smiled. "I want to tell you something important, but I need to know that I can trust you with this shit, despite however you may feel about it."

Lanay played around with her hands, silently hoping that he wasn't about to confess that he cheated on her. Usually, that's how things went for her. Her great mood was starting to diminish.

"What is it, Que? Please don't tell me it's another woman."

Taken back by her accusation he frowned. "What? Nah, I told you that you are the only woman for me Lanay. I wasn't playing when I expressed my feelings to you..." He paused and took her hands into his. "I'm planning on taking down my family's business."

"I know the shit sounds pretty fucked up but hear me out first. I want to finally show them that I have more power than what I'm given credit for. Everybody thinks I'm just some street ass nigga without any knowledge but I'm more than that. I wanted to grant you with the respect of knowing beforehand and ask if you would like to help me?" As the words rolled off his tongue, she got pissed off. She felt stupid once again for falling for another man's charm, foolish for thinking there was actually something between them, and dumb as hell- because to him, she was just a part of his plan. Thinking back to moments they shared, she figured it made sense. He was only grooming her to become weak to him.

She threw the teddy bear he won for her to the ground and attempted to storm off, but he grabbed her arm. "What?"

"So, you just gon walk off in the middle of our conversation?"

Lanay wiped her eyes from the tears she allowed to fall. "Here I am falling head over heels for your black ass and all you saw me as was an opportunity. Is that why you gave me the advice to cut Sheree and Naomi lose? You sorry as hell, Quentin!"

"What!? Girl I fucking love your crazy ass. I wouldn't be doing all this romantic, soap opera shit with you if I only wanted to use your ass. Hell, I wouldn't even be giving a fuck!" He expressed, regretting even bringing the conversation up. "Look, I'm sorry for offending you. We can just forget this conversation even happened, ok?" Lanay's eyes smiled when she heard him say he loved her. She felt silly for jumping the gun so quickly, but she couldn't help it. That's all she was used to.

"Baby, I'm sorry too. I'm just really falling hard for you. I assumed that you were using me because I'm so used to it. As far as your plans with your family, I don't agree with it all the way, but you're my man. You ride with me when I need you to, so I'm riding with you. What do I have to do?" He took a seat, pulled her into his lap, and wrapped his arms around her waist. "I just need you to listen in on any information Naomi and Sheree says about Nassir and Cartier. I don't care if it's good or bad."

"You know y'all friendship will probably end once I come out about my plan, right?"

Lanay sat in deep thought for a moment. She honestly didn't care to lose Naomi and Sheree anymore. She felt they didn't care for her so why should she lose sleep over them? Quentin's shown her more love, support, and loyalty than people she's known for years. She shrugged. "I don't care. Our friendships are already sinking anyway but I need something in return for this."

"What's that?"

"You give me my ring and my baby. I'm not doing all this shit for your ass without being your one and only." Lanay answered. She loved Quentin but she wasn't a fool. If she was going to go this far for him, she needed him to go even further for her.

He kissed her lips and smiled. "That was already in the works."

Chapter 19

Once Cartier arrived at his hotel suite, he wasted no time rushing inside his room to relax for a moment. Their flight was long, he needed to rest before he went into this meeting. While Nassir and Quentin got dressed to meet the new supplier with Cartier, Cartier sat on the edge of his bed to take a call from his private investigator.

Placing the phone to his ear, he laid back. "What's the news?"

"For starters, Trig isn't his real name. It's Rashun Howard, the son of Giovanni Howard. He had three kids, Rashun, Deandre and Aubree. Your father and Giovanni were friends back in the day. A man named Trumaine Capell, better known as Godfather, was the guy that put out the hit on your father. Giovanni executed the hit."

"Wait what? Why would he take out my dad if they were friends?"

"The Godfather was a pure and high-end supplier. Giovanni wanted a piece of that pie." Lewis explained.

Cartier sat in disbelief, soaking in everything. His father's murder was portrayed to be a petty business deal; it provided him a little comfort to know that it wasn't true. However, he still held hate in his heart towards him; he was still a terrible husband and father. He put the streetz before his own family and that was something he could never understand.

"There's more." His private investigator said as he continued. "Your girlfriend dated Deandre. He was a cheater, and he was also abusive. In the case files that I read, one night, she killed him while he was attacking her. Back in Detroit, there's a hit out for her head, ordered by Rashun; He wants her to be brought to him alive. Rashun is also involved with your ex, Chardonnay. I don't know what's all going on there but give me a week or so and I'll find out."

Cartier sat straight up and nodded. "Yeah, thank you man."

Hearing all this new information was overwhelming for him. He knew he needed to hurry up and jump on this issue with Naomi and Trig. He wasn't allowing anybody to snatch or even get close to her. He was willing to break whatever code and start a war behind her, she was worth it to him.
He thought about Chardonnay and shook his head. He felt she had no knowledge of the situation she was in with her new boyfriend. Chardonnay wasn't a street-smart girl; she only knew the high-class way of living.

He stood up and headed to the bathroom to get ready for the meeting. So much for gaining a peace of mind. They rolled out.

“Are you for real?” Quentin asked, processing the information that Cartier informed them with.

He couldn’t believe that everything about the events of his father’s death was a lie. The new information didn’t really change his perspective on his father, since he always chose Cartier over him. Everybody saw him as the black sheep of the family.

Looking out the car window, he had a vengeful look. *I’m proving everybody wrong real soon. I was born to run these streetz,* he thought.

Cartier stopped at the red light, sat back, and nodded. “Man, I wish I could be playing about this shit.”

“Shit getting deeper and deeper. Have you told Naomi yet?” Nassir asked, passing Quentin the blunt.

Nassir really didn’t know how to feel about Quentin and Cartier’s family issues; he was more concerned with what he just learned about Naomi. He made a promise to himself to keep her protected and he was willing to die behind doing so.

He knew the streetz weren't a walk in the park, he wasn’t a fool. He felt there were a lot of things going on that they didn’t know about, and he questioned if the answers were worth knowing. Either way, he had his people’s back.

“Hell, she told me about it. I guess she didn't want to bother us with it. You know how her ass is, but listen y’all, we don’t really know how deep this shit go. We have to be very mindful of who we share information with.”

Approaching the address he was given, he arrived at a spacious mansion resting on the street of Forest View Ave. They all sat in amazement, scoping out the place. It was well secured and armed.

Looking around at all the other beautiful homes that filled the street, Quentin smirked. “He’s eating well.”

He rolled down his driver side window and waited for the guard to walk over. The man appeared to be in his early 30s with a solid form. “State your business.”

"I'm here for a business meeting with Perseus."

He leaned forward, checked out a view of everyone and everything in the car, looked back at the other guard, and signaled for him to allow them access.

"Y'all, when we get inside, allow me to do all the talking and keep shit professional. Pernell said this man is really legit and he don't work with people he feels is a liability."

"Nigga, I know how to be professional." Quentin said, giving his brother a smug look.

Nassir shook his head at them and looked over at Cartier. "I got you bro."

They all approached the door, it swung open before anybody could knock. Stepping inside, the cool air greeted their skin, they had goosebumps. Cartier's nerves sped rapidly as he scanned the room, analyzing every detail. He activated his game face and silently prayed that this deal would go smoothly.

"What chu mean I can't carry my pistol?" Quentin scoffed.

Holding his arms out as far as they could reach, Cartier looked over in his direction. "Que give him the gun. Everything is all good."

Que hesitated but handed over the gun and allowed them to continue their search. He didn't like the way things were going already but he needed to get an earful of the negotiations and identify the man.

"Once the meeting is over, y'all can have them back." A henchman said, sternly. "Follow me." They followed him through the kitchen and down to the basement, where they walked through a doorway that led to his private office. They all took seats in the chairs and sat patiently waiting for him to enter the room.

During the wait, Cartier took the opportunity to scope out the room with his eyes. One thing he learned from working the streetz was to always know the person you're dealing with. The fact that he knew little to nothing about this man made him uneasy, but he trusted that his uncle wouldn't send him inside a snake pit without informing him.

He noticed pictures of his family on the walls. To an outsider, you would think they were your normal American family. He also noticed various cameras and hidden doorways his office had as well. Cartier figured he didn't trust his employees, or he had a safe somewhere behind these walls.

"Gentlemen." Perseus said, entering the room with a fat Cuban cigar dangling from his mouth. His attire was very formal, so he was either returning or leaving out for some fancy party. He took a seat in his chair and observed all three of them for a moment. "Can I offer you a drink? You look so serious."

"Actually, that wouldn't b-" Quentin attempted to say but was cut off by Cartier.

"No, we're fine. We're just ready to get down to business." Cartier interrupted.

Surprised by the decline, he spoke again, "A man about his business. I can respect that, I'm actually glad you didn't take a drink anyway."

"Why is that?" Cartier asked.

Perseus sat the glass bottle on the table and said "This is a bottle of liquid cocaine. This is how I smuggle my product. This bottle here is a whole kilo."

Cartier was nonetheless surprised. He admired him. It was smart and less risky. Who'd ever think a bottle branded as tequila was really cocaine?

"How would we get it back to powder?" Cartier asked.

"My people will show you. Fellas, I'm a legitimate businessman. Everything I do is carefully calculated, and precise. I've been in this industry for 20 years now with no run-ins with the feds, I would love to keep it that way." Perseus said, ensuring to make eye contact with everyone in the room. "I take it you the boss man?" He stared at Cartier for confirmation.

"Yes sir." Cartier said, looking him directly back in the eyes. When it came to doing business, not only did he have a natural sense of it, but he operated in a way most men in his generation didn't- which is what made him the perfect heir; looking a person in their eyes is the way to their soul.

"Give us the room." Perseus said, snapping his finger. His guards led Nassir and Quentin out to wait in the formal living room. Quentin wasn't too pleased with him asking them to leave but he knew when to use his mouth and when to use his brain.

Perseus sat at the end of his desk and looked at Cartier. "Your uncle told me a little bit about you and off the strength of him, I'ma give you a chance. I can be a great partner to you but don't fuck me! You don't want to see how that'll end for you."

"I can be a good partner for you as well. I'm loyal and consistent." Cartier pitched.

The two shared an intense stare down, looking for any form of dishonesty or uncertainty in each other's eyes. Neither could find any.

"How much can you front me?" Cartier asked getting right to business. Perseus chuckled. "How much can you handle? I have no limit on stock. It's what you can afford. My price is 32,000 a kilo. Do you have that kind of money son?"

He thought about his savings and nodded. "I'll take 50."

Cartier knew not to gamble such a high amount with all his savings, but he needed this connection. Perseus had the purity and quality that would drown his pockets. He had finally run out of the product he had from doing business with Trig and to hold him over, his uncle gave him the last of what he had before retiring; he needed the restock badly.

He held a lighter to the end of his cigar, inhaled it, and blew out smoke. "I tell you what kid. We make our first exchange- Saturday afternoon. Do you have an operation for how you get your product back to Atlanta?"

"My family owns a trucking company that's been solid for generations. People will know its legit, I have a truck that can get here tomorrow."

Perseus nodded his head in approval "Don't fuck me." He repeated as they shook hands sealing the deal.

Cartier stood up and headed for the door. He felt good about the legitimacy of the supplier; he was nothing like Trig. He knew he could trust him to be about his business.

He just hoped that his team would be ready for the adjustments. It was time for a whole new era of business.

Chapter 20

Naomi, Sheree, and Lanay all sat in the nail salon, getting their nails and feet tended to. Lanay finally reached out to the girls and apologized, so they all decided to drop the beef and have a nail date. They had been friends far too long; petty things should never wedge them apart.

However, they didn't know she only apologized to get information out of them for Quentin. Most would think she easily betrayed her friends behind a man but in Lanay's eyes, she truly believed they were never her friends.

Naomi smiled as she listened to everybody's gossip, she felt so relaxed; she needed this girl time and nail trip. Lately, stress has been her best friend. Since Miami, she's been having nightmares about Deandre, and she didn't know how to shake it. What she did know was that Deandre's dead and she wasn't going to allow him nor his family to haunt her new life.

"I'm tellin' you, it be them street niggas who love them some back door action." Lorenz stated as he shaped Lanay's nail.

"Uhn un, not mine." Sheree quickly defended.

"With a man as fine as yours, it's only a matter of time before he falls for a bad bitch like me." Lorenz joked.

Everyone fell into laughter. Lorenz was the owner of Runway Nails. He was the best in the city and could do all different sorts of designs; everybody loved him. He wasn't one to always take, take, and take. He gave back to his community by hosting different events and fundraisers. They loved supporting black owned businesses, plus -this place was just the spot.

For example, a few weeks ago, word got around about a family who lost their house due to a fire. Lorenz hosted a fundraiser that ran 7 days long; any nail set and design for only $30. All the proceeds went to the teenage girl from the family, so that she could attend prom. He also gave her a free mani/pedi; that's how kindhearted he was.

"No, seriously though. Y'all know how long they will be out of town?" Sheree asked, looking from Lanay to Naomi.

Naomi shrugged. "Cartier told me just a few days. While they're away, we should have a girls' night. I miss bonding time like this."

Lanay rolled her eyes at that suggestion and sighed. She wasn't really up for it, but she didn't want to miss out on any tea. "Maybe, I have to see."

"Girl, what else are you doing?" Naomi asked, playfully.

Before Lanay had time to respond, Sheree hopped out of her seat and raced towards the bathroom. Exchanging looks, Naomi and Lanay followed her in concern.

Once they entered the bathroom, they saw Sheree hovered over the trash with her insides pouring out; everything she ate that morning was shooting out inside the trash bin. Naomi instantly went to her side and caressed her back. Lanay frowned at the site but hesitantly held her hair up.

Naomi watched her closely as she thought about all the little things she noticed lately; she was always sick and not really drinking. A lightbulb went off in her brain, she smacked her lips and felt silly about how she missed it.

"Sheree, are you pregnant?" Naomi asked.

Sheree stood up, took a paper towel to wipe her face, and then went over to the sink to drink and spit out some water. "6 weeks" she mumbled.

"Okay, I'm confused. Why don't you sound happy about it? Ain't that all your ass talk about?" Lanay asked, secretly excited about the new information she just discovered.

"I'm not. I'm not ready and I feel so fucking stupid about it." Sheree responded, trying to hold back her tears. She paused, took a few deep breaths, and continued. "Plenty of women get pregnant. Once they tell their man, he's an ass. I have a good man; I just don't want to give him a child right now."

No longer able to hold it in anymore, Sheree released her tears. She felt selfish and ashamed. Many women would kill to fill the shoes she was in. Naomi pulled her into a hug and allowed her to release her emotions. Lanay joined in.

"It's gonna be okay and you will figure this out." Naomi said, attempting to reassure her.

“Yeah girl, Naomi is right. Nassir loves you; he will respect and support your choice.” Lanay added in. Although she secretly hoped that this was Sheree’s karma for being a bad friend and messing with Nassir anyway.

They sat in the bathroom for a brief moment to comfort their friend and gather in their thoughts.

ɱ

Jacques got out of his dodge charger, looked around, and scoped his surroundings before entering the abandoned building. Ever since he started doing Trig’s dirty work, his guilty conscience had been messing with his mind. He found himself always under the impression that somebody was watching.

Little did he know, somebody was, indeed. Inside the building, Trig sat patiently waiting for him. To occupy his time, he was sending thirst traps back and forth to see who would crack first. He had to admit, she was definitely taking the lead. Noticing Jacques' arrival, he stood up and locked his phone before placing it in his pocket.

In a rush as usual, he cut all small talk and jumped right into the point of their meeting. “What did you get for me?” He asked.

“Well, for starters, she lives in Overlook Ridge. I don't know the exact apartment door, but I definitely know the building. She and Capone don't live together and right now, I don't think their relationship will last long at all.” Jacques explained.

“Why not?”

“The nigga can’t keep his Johnson to himself. She mentioned some back and forth shit he had going on when she first got involved with him. Also, a few days ago she invited me to a kickback at his place. He wasn't feeling the idea of me being there, so he stepped to me, and I had to piece his ass up.”

Jacques hated the idea of spying on his childhood friend's life but if taking down her boyfriend was his way in the door, then he was all for it. However, his eagerness was his greatest weakness. It was no secret that Jacques wasn’t built for the fast life and Trig knew that; he was simply using him for his advantage and that only. He knew flashing money in his face and feeding him false intel was what he needed to get him talking and that's just what he did.

Trig stood there for a moment, gathering up his thoughts. He smirked at the thought of things in Cartier's life not being so picture perfect. He found it funny that Cartier always portrayed shit to be that way, perfect. "Anything else?"

"Nah, I can get you something more, just give me a few days." Jacques said as he contemplated if he should say what was occupying his mind. "When will you get me off this petty ass task and put me on in the streetz? I'm ready to make some real money."

Trig chuckled. "In due time, you're exactly where I need you right now."

Jacques clenched his jaw and decided to remain silent. He wasn't pleased with his answer, but he had to do what he had to; he needed the money that Trig was gone provide him with.

ღ

Naomi laid across her bed, smiling into the phone as she conversed with Cartier. It was his last night in Cali, and she couldn't wait to see him. Throughout his absence, all she thought about was reuniting with her man. Ever since he came to her apartment after being jumped, it triggered her worries. She was always concerned about his well-being. She knew he could hold his own, but he was also human. He bled just like everyone else.

"Do you ever plan on completely leaving the street life alone?" Naomi asked, flipping over and staring at the ceiling.

"I don't know Nao. I want to but my gut keeps telling me this shit is only the beginning." He sighed, thinking about all the information he just received from his private investigator.

"What is it?"

"Can I trust you ma? I mean really trust you with anything? I don't want you to get me misunderstood but lately I've been feeling like everybody around me is not loyal. I wanna believe that you are but sometimes a nigga wanna hear it."

Naomi stared into the ceiling and could tell by the sound of his voice that he was being genuine, and that he was opening his heart to her. Although she didn't know Cartier that long, she felt that he was it for her. She knew the answer to his question before it even rolled off his tongue. She was in love with him and wanted to bask in his love until the end of time.

On the other side of the phone, Cartier sat there, awaiting her answer. He was more than willing to truly open himself up to Naomi and give love a second chance, but the question that rang in his head was, was she truly ready herself? Especially considering all that she had been through with Deandre. He wanted her to experience a love she never knew before, give her the world, and show her how a woman is supposed to be cherished. In return, all he asked for was her loyalty.

Before he could dwell on things any longer, she broke the silence that sat between them.

"I'm loyal to you, Cartier."

Hearing those words not only warmed his heart, it also gave him the reassurance he needed. He prayed that Naomi took it seriously. He'd give her whatever she wanted in this life, as long as she remained loyal and honest with him.

"I hired a private investigator to help me find out more about Trig. Turns out, our fathers were best friends, kinda like me and Nas. My father did a shady deal on the wrong person, and he put a hit out on his head. Since Trig's dad wanted to do business with that motherfucka, he took out my dad to show him his loyalty, and that's not even the worst part mamas. Chardonnay is Trig's new girl." He explained. He didn't even care that he and Chardonnay had a relationship but what he did care about was how much he possibly knew and what all she could've told him.

Naomi sat there, not really knowing what to say. "You think she knows?"

"Chardonnay a smart one, so if she didn't at first, it hasn't taken her long to put the pieces together."

"Cartier, you should tell her anyway just in case. He could be using her." Naomi told him. She didn't really care much for Chardonnay, but she believed in sparing peoples' pain, if it were possible.

"Yeah, you're right about that ma. Anyway, I miss your annoying ass. When I get home, I need a hot plate of food followed by some of your loving."

"I miss you too and you know I got your big head ass." Naomi said, smiling into the phone. "I feel like we need another trip. When we were away in Miami, despite the mishap, we were so stress free and relaxed."

“Yeah, I know what you mean. This business has been stressing a nigga out. I can't do it just yet but in due time, we will. I have to get things rolling with my club first. It's almost finished.”

“I'm so proud of you baby. No matter what you’re up against, it never knocks you off your square. Our kids will be happy to have a daddy like you.” Naomi expressed allowing her feelings to guide the conversation. She couldn't lie, hearing the news about Sheree’s pregnancy had her thinking about what the future held for her and Cartier.

Cartier sat up in bed. “Our kids? Are you trying to tell me that you’re pregnant?”

Naomi laughed. “Boy no. I was just saying. I think about our future sometimes, that’s all.”

“I don’t know, with the way you be wearing a nigga out in the bedroom, it might occur faster than we think.” He teased before yawning.

“Are you tired? I'll let you go.”

“I'm good. I love talking to you.”

Blushing, Naomi stood up and turned off her bedroom light before making herself comfortable. She laid in bed and caked on the phone with Cartier until the sun rose.

Chapter 21

Slowly stroking in and out of Sheree, Nassir stared in her eyes, in awe as he enjoyed the feeling of being connected to her. As the calm music of Keith Sweat played in the background, setting the mood, Sheree couldn't help but dwell in her guilty conscience.

Since Sheree confessed to him that she was pregnant, she felt that's all their life was now. If they weren't arguing about whether to keep the baby, they were using sex to not talk at all.

She had originally showed up to finally tell him that she was going through with the abortion, but once she saw the surprise he had for her, she couldn't bring her mouth to say it; he had candles lit, slow jams playing, and varieties of snacks on the coffee table.

They sat and enjoyed each other the way they did before they even knew a baby was coming. Their undeniable chemistry filled the air- that and a boost of wine lead to what they were doing now; making sweet love to each other.

Caressing his back, she squirmed from how deeply he was reaching inside of her; he was definitely activating the button that drove every woman crazy over her man.

Nassir stared at her and admired her features. It had been so long since he made love to a woman, even to this extent was new for him. Memories of them filled his mind as he thought about how far they came; meeting her at his birthday bash that day, he would've never guessed that they'd end up here.

Sheree laid there, holding back her tears of guilt and pleasure. She felt something had to be wrong with her because Nassir was everything she ever asked for in a man, yet she didn't want to produce his seed. The way he was making love to her body, she had never experienced before; if this was what it felt like for a man to truly love you, she didn't want to let it slip through her hands.

From the way he whispered, "I love you" in her ear to the way he kissed and maneuvered inside her, so effortlessly, it was like she was the only woman in the world to him. She wanted this feeling forever. She wanted to hold the honor of having Nassir as her man. She was in true ecstasy.

Nassir noticed her staring at him, so he pulled her closer and went in for a kiss. The way her plump lips felt against his enhanced their chemistry. She slid her tongue inside his mouth at ease and their tongues wrestled in luster. They leaned back, but their lips never parted. Sheree took over and made her way onto his shaft. She sat there for a moment, got used to the way his size was filling her up, then she winded her hips and rode him as if her life depended on it.

Enjoying the way her titties bounced in his face, Nassir's hands found their way to her hips as he guided her, he was about to *cum*. Sheree moaned and screamed out his name as she picked up her pace with each bounce.

Seconds later, they shared an intense orgasm, their juices mixed, once more. Sheree covered her breast and fell to the bed, gasping for her breath. As they laid there catching their breaths, the sound of the door erupted throughout the apartment.

Rolling over to face her, Nassir wrapped his left arm around her waist as he closed his eyes. Sheree smiled as she stared into him. "I'm loving this affection, but you not gone answer your door?"

"Nah, whoever it is can wait." He mumbled.

Banging out the door once more, Cartier pulled out his phone, prepared to call him. "Open the fucking door nigga, I know your ass up in here!"

"Shit!" Nassir cursed to himself before sitting up to throw on some clothes. Sheree giggled at him and snuggled under the covers.

Nassir crawled out of bed and quickly put on his boxers and Nike shorts. He was filled with annoyance, all he wanted was a well needed nap as he laid under his woman. *I swear this nigga about to hear my damn mouth if this shit ain't important.* He thought.

Just as he was about to walk out his bedroom door, Sheree spoke. "Hurry back so we can take our nap baby. You know I hate sleeping without you."

"Iight, stay in here. It'll only take a second." He said, closing the door to his bedroom and walking to the front.

He went to open the door and saw a bubbly Cartier with duffle bags in his hands. Cartier sat the bags on his couch, walked into his kitchen and opened the fridge. He helped himself to a Gatorade and walked back into the living room.

“Nigga, this shit better be of importance.” Nassir stated, folding his arms.

“Oh, I see yo ass in here beating some cheeks huh?” Cartier noticed how messed up Nassir’s clothes appeared and the sweat that dripped from his forehead. He didn't want to cock block his homeboy, so he decided to cut things to the chase. “I’m dropping off your cut of the sales. Since we been doing business with Perseus and my uncle, shit been going amazingly well.”

Nassir opened the duffle bags, revealed were hundred-dollar bills wrapped in stacks of ten thousand. His once irritated mode shifted into pure happiness.

“Now this what the fuck I’m talking about, when is our next shipment? Is we out?”

“Shit, damn near and it's only been a few days since we've been back. The streetz are loving this shit. But look, we need to discuss some things about Trig and nem, and then I'll leave you to it. “Cartier said, gulping down some of his drink.

Nassir sat on his love seat and looked at him with a serious expression, “What's the word?”

In other news, Quentin sat across the office from his new potential supplier. He kept a hard mellow demeanor on the outside but on the inside, he was a kid screaming with excitement. Quentin will have everything he needs to get up off the rocks and start his own family business with Lanay, if shit with this deal goes as planned.

“So, does your uncle know that you’re here?” Trumaine asked, leaning back in his chair as he sat, analyzing things.

“Nah, and I would actually like for things to stay that way. At least for now.” Quentin answered, looking him directly in his eyes.

Trumaine returned the stare and gathered his thoughts for a moment. He knew from the sound of things that something wasn't right. He hoped that Pernell wasn’t stupid enough to send his unequipped nephew in there to set him up, as if he was an amateur to the streetz.

However, the look Quentin held in his eyes said differently. He was like an animal hunting for its prey. Willing to do anything to eat- that alone is what intrigued Trumaine.

"Why am I under the impression that you're here to set me up?"

"Because of who I'm connected to by blood and I can't help that. I can help who I choose to be loyal to. Honestly, godfather you're big time and I wanna work with big time. Yeah, I know shit seems a little fishy, but I'm not included in that. I'm trying to build my own business and not with my family. I can prove my loyalty to you." Quentin expressed pitching his sale.

Trumaine picked up his glass of scotch and sipped from it before he watched the brown substance twirl inside it. "I'm listening."

"For starters, I know you're doing business with Giovanni's son, due to a deal you two made back in the day to eliminate my pops. Unfortunately for you, Trig isn't the brightest fish in the sea- so you're hoping to replace him with somebody who wouldn't mind not only taking him down, but also filling the big shoes he couldn't fit; that's where I come in. Not only would I solve that issue for you, I'd also hand you my family's operation to sweeten this deal."

Trumaine sat up from his seat, surprised by his offer. He wasn't entirely convinced because he was well aware of the rules of the game, and he didn't get this far in life by trusting everyone but something inside of him was willing to give Quentin a fair shot.

He nodded, more than impressed. "I see somebody did their homework. What's all in this for you?"

Quentin smirked, satisfied that he was finally getting exactly what he wanted. "I told you before. I want in on your product. I'm not gone lie, if the roles were reversed, I'd hesitate too. Front me a key and let me prove to you how much money we both can make doing business together."

Trumaine held an unreadable facial expression but inside he was burning with excitement. He just landed the key to infiltrate the William's family once and for all. He extended his hand and said, "You got yourself a deal son."

Chapter 22

"Hey daddy." Chardonnay said sweetly into the phone as she walked upstairs to Trig's bedroom.

"Wassup baby girl, how are things looking down there?" He asked.

Chardonnay sighed and plopped down on her couch, "Things are going well. Cartier and I aren't together anymore but I've still been getting well needed information about him through Trig."

"Who's Trig?"

"My new boyfriend. I'll let you know if he's meetable or not. Now, it's too soon to tell." Chardonnay explained, searching for the remote.

"Mhm, just don't lose focus baby girl. This is a very important mission." He informed her.

Chardonnay rolled her eyes. She loved her father, but sometimes she wished he'd let business talk go for at least a moment. "I know, I have to go. I'll call you in a few days with the information you requested."

They ended their call, Chardonnay let out a relieved sigh. She couldn't wait to get him off the phone so she could occupy her time with things she didn't mind doing. The minute she closed her eyes to rest, Trig came in from the hallway.

"I knew I heard you, who was that?" He asked, with nothing but a bath towel wrapped around his waist.

"My father, nobody important."

Trig laughed and walked over to her. "Damn babe, I'm sure your pops is important. Come take a ride with me."

Chardonnay's eyes lit up; usually they're always laid up in the house together to keep a low profile. So, him suggesting for them to go out in public-together, was a big step. "Trust me, you don't know my father. Anyway, are you serious baby? I mean, don't get me wrong, I'm excited, but we agreed to keep things out of the public."

"Well, one day I'm going to have to meet ya old man myself." He said, opening his closet doors. "Yeah, I'm serious though, let me get dressed and we can head out."

Trig had a white Audi with all-black interior, he and Char sat in it and listened to the music that flowed from the speakers. Chardonnay was very confused as to why they were at some abandoned parking lot on the outskirts of town. She assumed that he was taking her out to dinner or something along the lines of that. If it wasn't about business, it was about sex, and she was becoming highly agitated about it all.

Glancing over at Chardonnay, Trig noticed the distasteful mug she held while staring out the window, consumed by her thoughts. "What's wrong with you, Char?"

"It's nothing, Trig." She mumbled, refusing to make eye contact with him.

He smacked his lips. "Don't start that shit man. I know when something's wrong with yo ass, so just tell me what's wrong."

"You are what's wrong with me, okay!" Chardonnay snapped, rolling her eyes. "Everything between us now is just sex and business, I'm getting fed up. I'm more than just some booty call or bitch to hold your stash. What happened to you, Rashun?"

Trig released a small chuckle before using his hand to turn her face to his. "I apologize for making you feel less than what you truly are to me. Shit, I'm in love with yo ass girl. Business just been wearing a nigga out, sometimes I get too involved with my work. I wasn't aware that I was making you feel this way."

Chardonnay smiled before she pecked his lips. This was what she loved so much about him. Most guys would've added more fuel to the fire and disregarded her feelings, but with Trig, it was different; he always took responsibility and valued her feelings.

Trig reached under his seat and revealed a Smith and Wesson 9mm, he handed it to Char and then pulled out his Glock. He then went into his glove compartment, pulled out his bandanna, and began cleaning off the bullets before restocking the clip.

Although he wanted Chardonnay far away from this lifestyle, he couldn't keep that vow. It was as if she was meant to be in it; her street knowledge and skills were impeccable. So instead of holding his defense of being against it, he decided to welcome her with open arms. He preferred she got her hands dirty with him rather than the next person.

"What is this, Rashun?" Chardonnay asked in confusion. She didn't know where they were, and she most certainly didn't understand why he was handing her weapons.

"Remember what I showed you right?"

Chardonnay nodded her head and placed the gun inside her purse. A few months ago, he confessed to her the depths of his lifestyle. He wanted her to be able to defend herself in case something ever happened, so he taught her how to use several weapons. He knew his lifestyle could be very heinous, so he needed his woman to be prepared for anything.

Moments later, a chevy impala pulled inside the parking lot and parked next to them. Chardonnay looked over to Trig and wondered what he was up to. She didn't like him being secretive, but she knew he wouldn't put her in harm's way.

A guy with a dark complexion, appearing to be in his mid-twenties, stepped out of the car. He pulled a white hood over his head and sat on the hood of his car. Char and Trig unlocked the doors and walked towards him.

"Wassup Trig." He said in a low tone.

"Wassup Murder. This my girl, Diamond." He said, making the introduction. Char played it nice in front of this *Murder character*, but she was definitely going to address the issue of him calling her by another name.

Slightly chuckling to herself, she realized how silly she sounded. This man had her head over heels; here she was becoming offended, thinking he had mistaken her for another woman, when he was really only looking out for her protection.

"Nice to meet you." She stated.

Murder gave her a quick smirk after putting the pieces together and said, "Likewise."

"So, let's get to the point, what happened?" Trig asked. He already knew the answers to his question, but he wanted to see if Murder was truthful. Anytime he had a meeting with somebody, he always checked their background to see what the streetz put out about them.

Murder wasn't new to the streetz. He knew how to put in work and get the job done, which was why he wanted to work with Trig. Trig's name was getting bigger in the streetz, Murder wanted a piece of the pie; he no longer wanted to spend half his day on the corner and only come home with enough money to make things stretch. He yearned to live comfortably.

Murder sighed then spoke, “Honestly, shit not looking too good. We don't have the supply to be pulling in as much as I’d like and I wanna work with some real money.”

Trig nodded, understanding the position that he was in. “So, what do you need from me?” Trig asked, looking him directly in the face.

“Put me on your team.”

Trig chuckled, “Are you sure you're ready for something like that? You’re a corner boy, working with me would be a big promotion. Can you hold down your own team and still be able to pay me for the supply?”

Murder chewed at his lip, thinking. He knew how much weight they were pulling. He wasn't used to pushing that much, but he had what many people lacked, determination. “Yeah.”

Chardonnay giggled to herself and decided to speak. “It’s not going to be that easy. We don’t know you, which means your word means nothing. We need a little more reassurance than just your word of mouth.”

Murder smacked his lips and waved her off. “Ya girl tripping.”

Trig looked over at Chardonnay. It turned him on how well she knew her business, he winked at her before focusing his attention back on murder. “She’s right, unless you can come up with some reassurances, we can't afford the risk.”

Murder looked between the two and made a facial expression, he was in deep thought, “Alright, I can respect that. Before I decided to go into business for myself, I learned about Capone’s new operation. I know about his cooking houses down to who he lays in bed with. Shit, that nigga own brother barely fucking with him.”

“You not fuckin with me?” Trig asked, stepping closer to him. He knew Murder’s information could be creditable but that’s all it was. If he couldn't be loyal to the hand that fed him, he damn sure wouldn't be loyal to him.

Murder held up his hands and returned the stare. “I wouldn’t even play you like that.”

The two men extended hands and sealed the deal.

"Iight, I just hope this shit is worth the pay. I'll have the information in a few days." He said before making his way back to his car.

Chardonnay smiled, feeling empowered; she thought that maybe she should be his wing woman more often. She felt good being the Head Bitch In Charge; being on the arm of Rashun Howard was a bonus to her. Watching him conduct business turned her on.

"I knew you had it in you, mamas." Trig complimented as he started up the car.

"Mhm, so what you're saying is you trying to make me your number two or something?" She asked while putting on her seatbelt and sliding the nine back under her seat.

Trig looked at her, eyes infused with lust and admiration. He loved a woman that could take charge and besides, he didn't trust a man to be his number two. Nine times out of ten, the most loyal person ever to be in ya corner was a woman, especially if she was yours. "To be honest, that's not a bad idea at all. I know ain't nobody gon' have my back like you do and vice versa."

Chardonnay smiled as she leaned over to kiss him on the lips. She sat back in her seat, looked out the window, and reflected on the meeting she had with Cartier a few days ago.

She turned to Trig and touched his hand, which caused him to look over at her. "I have to be honest with you, if we're gonna continue to be serious about each other. I should've said something sooner, but I wasn't sure how you'd react."

"What is it?"

"Cartier, well you know him by Capone, is my ex-boyfriend and I met with him a few days ago. I'm guessing he found out about us, he tried to give me a warning about you. He said something along the lines of you're using me to get to him." She blurted out.

Trig nodded after studying her body language and facial expression, he wasn't mad, nor did he feel a way about her holding in the lie. It'd be very hypocritical of him because he knew he held lies for his own reasons as well. "Why did you lie to me about him?"

“I didn't want you to look at me differently. I also didn’t want to be another source of beef for y’all. I thought if I told you then, things between us would change. I know I'm wrong for lying to you and I'm sorry for that.”

Trig read her eyes and knew that she was being genuine, which was something he always wanted from her. “I haven't been all the way honest myself either, baby girl, but it was only to protect myself and what we had. Capone was right. I met you intentionally at first, to try and use you to get closer to him, but after we really started hanging out, I knew I couldn't bring myself to hurt you like that. I caught feelings and I love what we have going on, ma.”

Chardonnay shifted in her seat, unsure of what to say or how to feel; she knew that she wanted him, so did he, so that's all that mattered to her at this point. She leaned in and pecked his lips.

Trig pulled the car over to the side of the road and stared at Chardonnay. He wanted her to be by his side and lead with him, but he needed her to make a choice; it was either him or Cartier.

“Look ma, I want you and I want to be with you. But being my woman means I need to trust you and trust that you’re all for me. So, who’s it gonna be?” He asked, looking her directly in the eyes.

Chardonnay sat at a loss for words, it wasn't a difficult choice for her because he stated everything she needed to hear. “I want you, what Capone and I had is long gone. I want to be with you, not him.” She answered.

Trig smirked and pulled her into a kiss. It warmed his heart to know that she didn't need time to think or consider. She chose him. He put the car back in drive and handed her his cell phone.

“Babe, call your favorite place to eat at and make us reservations.”

ꟹ

Sheree sat in the waiting room growing nervous by the minute. She hated what she was doing but she knew it was for the best. Her leg shook uncontrollably, and she grew impatient every second. She knew she needed to calm herself but how could she, she was getting ready to pull the plug on her own baby.

“First time?” Another mom asked her, noticing her body language.

Sheree smiled weakly and nodded.

"Trust me, it gets easier to cope with as time goes on. You will be fine. Doing what's best for you is never a wrong thing and don't let nobody tell you differently. Especially those protesters." She said in attempt to reassure her before directing her attention back to her magazine.

Sheree took a deep breath and pulled out her phone to check the time. She couldn't believe she was really about to go through with this. No one even knew she was there; she figured the less people- the easier it would be. Before she had any more time to dwell on her difficult decision, her name was called by a nurse.

She picked up her purse along with the clipboard that held all her information and followed the nurse to the back. With every step she took, surprisingly, her nerves slowly faded away, which warmed her doubts. She knew if this wasn't the right choice that her body wouldn't allow her to make it.

"Here you are, give me just a moment and I will be with you shortly." The nurse stated, headed around the corner.

Sheree walked in and sat her purse in one of the chairs that was set aside for your support person. She then climbed up on the examination table and sat there, reading the room. There were various posters about abortions, pregnancy options, and numerous numbers to hotlines.

Sheree snapped from her daze when she felt the sound of her phone ding. Looking down, she unlocked it to reveal a message from Nassir.

Nas😊:
Wassup baby girl. I apologize for earlier; I've been doing some thinking and you're right. I shouldn't pressure you into doing something with your body that you aren't ready for. Call me later so we can talk.
Delivered 10:55am

Guilt instantly started to fill the pit of Sheree's stomach. *Why does he have to be so damn perfect?* she thought. Sighing to herself, she began to respond to him.

Sheree:
Thank you, I'm glad you had time to think about where I was coming from. I'll call you when I get home, it's a lot we need to sit down and discuss.
Sent 10:58am

Sheree heard the nurse knocking before she entered, she felt relieved. It was time to begin the process that could potentially end her relationship.

In the end, she hoped that he'd understand and forgive her.

Nassir pulled up to one of the cooking houses. While he waited for Gunz, he sat and scoped out the scenery. He smirked at how well business had been doing ever since they conducted it with Pernell and Perseus.

"Wassup fool." Gunz greeted, approaching the car with a cup full of noodles. Him and Nassir slapped hands with each other then Gunz spoke again, "I see you riding through this bitch extra secure."

He was referring to the henchmen that occupied the car with Nassir. Nassir knew in this game you could go out at any moment, so he never really lived his life precautious, until it came time to get his hands dirty. He knew the chances of bullshit dying down tripled, so he wanted to be prepared for whatever.

"Hell yeah, what's been going on around here?" Nassir asked, getting on a more serious note.

Gunz is one of the overseers of the trap houses; each one had a manager that made sure things ran smoothly. Normally, you wouldn't catch Nassir or Cartier at the location of them, publicly; there'd always be a middleman in communication, but Nassir decided to start scoping business more closely since snitches were becoming more frequent.

"Shit, niggas putting in work as usual. Money been looking real good since the boss man dropped off that new product." Gunz said before looking around to make sure nobody could hear what else he was about to say. "So, lately, I been seeing an unmarked vehicle parked a few houses down, scoping out the place."

Nassir's smirk faded and his intuition kicked in. He didn't suspect the feds because they were on the payroll and Pernell would've definitely got word out. His only other suspect had to be Trig.

"Word? What kind of vehicle?"

"A black Ford Fusion." Gunz responded, searching around for it as they spoke but fell short.

Nassir sat for a moment, gathering his thoughts. He didn't want to raise too much awareness without knowing exactly what was going on, but he now needed the block to be even more precautious.

"Alright, don't worry about the shit too much, man. Next time you see that car though, hit my line. I'ma hit up Capone and find out what's what." Nassir responded turning over the key. Gunz nodded and slapped hands with him again before disappearing inside the house.

"Anything you need us to do?" The henchmen on his passenger side asked.

"Actually, there is. I'm about to set y'all up in a house on this block; I need y'all to monitor what's going on without being seen. Nah mean?"

"Yeah, we got you."

Chapter 23

Cartier sat and studied the faces of the crew that gave him a beating at the liquor store a few weeks back. He knew they had to be new to the city or way in over their heads to even make a bold move like that. Everybody in the city knew his family name and knew that blood came with it. So, letting disrespect slide wasn't something he was about to do.

"These niggas slipping- getting drunk off they ass and probably high, flashing money and shit, just to get some pussy." Nassir laughed, watching things unfold.

"Aye, I think I know the motherfucka in that blue shirt. He was over by the block a few times. He had to be watching shit." Tyrik stated.

After the death of Chase, Tyrik fell headfirst into the game. Cartier didn't know what made him have a change of heart, but he did know that pain could change anybody. So, in honor of Chase, they decided to cut him in and surprisingly, he was good at it.

"Come on, we're finna move in now." Cartier announced, opening the car door.

The three of them crept down the dark street and held their guns to the side as they made their way behind their car. They were so into the women and attention, they fell oblivious to their surroundings, which made it even easier for them to attack.

"Damn this you? This a nice ass ride." Cartier smirked, removing his hood. Turning around to face the voice, Jerome's eyes widened as if he saw a ghost. He soon straightened it up to appear hard, it was tough to keep his persona. He couldn't believe that Cartier found out who they were. He was ensured that he wouldn't. *Fuck, I shouldn't have gotten mixed up in this shit!* He thought.

"Yeah, this me, who the fuck are you, nigga?!" He questioned keeping his cool.

Cartier laughed, cocked his gun back, and sent several shots to his car. He hit his tire, windows, and door. His friends tried to rush behind Jerome, in attempt to scare Cartier, but what they didn't know was that Cartier was fearless and that this time, he wasn't alone.

Tyrik walked behind Cartier with a nine in each hand, ready for war. Nassir then came around on the other side and cocked his as well, everyone looked over at him. The women that were with them were now scared as fuck, they held onto the men that they were in attendance with.

"You know who the fuck I am. Let's cut the bullshit and get right to it. Who sent y'all niggas to jump me?" Cartier questioned, looking directly in his eyes.

Jerome smacked his lips and waved Cartier off, "I ain't telling you shit without some reassurances."

"Man, fuck these niggas. We can pop shit off now." A guy in Jerome's crew by the name of Lucky said.

"Well, do something bitch!" Nassir said, pressing the barrel of his nine behind the man's head.

"Do y'all niggas really think y'all in the position to be making fucking ultimatums? I ain't got time to be fucking around with you bitches. Who the fuck sent you!?" Cartier asked, growing angry and impatient. He had bigger shit on his mind, so he was more than ready to nip this little snag and get back to other issues.

Jerome looked over in his car and realized that he sat his gun in the seat. He mentally cursed himself and tried to come up with a move, fast. He figured either way, Cartier would kill him; the last thing he wanted to do was go out like a snitch.

Cartier shot the girl on Jerome's arm directly in her head, her body fell to the floor instantly. Jerome pushed the other girl beside him in Cartier's direction and reached for his gun.

Shots began flying back and forth, bodies dropped, instantly. Cartier squatted behind a car with Tyrik beside him and sent off shots towards Jerome's car. Bullet after bullet.

"All we want is a name!" Nassir yelled, shooting on the other side, hitting a few of the men that were out there.

Jerome hated to leave his team, but he needed to get out alive and the only solution he had was to ride out. He started up his shot down charger and floored down the street, making a left at the stop sign.

Cartier cursed under his breath, they all ran to the car and sped after him. He pushed down on his gas, going well over the speed limit to catch up to Jerome. He knew that whoever set him up was either was someone he knew or someone that held power. Either way, he was getting to the bottom of it tonight.

"Bruh, we gotta catch up to this nigga fast. We dropped all those bodies back there so the streetz are about to get hot in about 15 minutes." Tyrik stated.

"Don't worry, I got this."

Cartier was now pushing 85, he caught up to the back end of Jerome and smashed into his rear. He drove him straight into some brick building. They all jerked back from the collision. Cartier was barely fazed; all he saw was rage. He unbuckled himself and jumped out the car to pull Jerome from his. He snatched out his nine and held it to him.

"I want a name." He said coldly.

Jerome groaned in pain as blood leaked from his nose. Cartier used the end of his gun to slap him across the face. Jerome yelled and then spit out a mouth full of blood, struggling to speak. He mumbled out, "Chardonnay."

Cartier felt his body tense up. He knew things between them were over, but he never suspected her of all people to betray him like this. He tried to be a good person to her because of the damage he caused her, but she crossed a line with him that she could never come back from; Chardonnay was now on the other side.

Cartier cocked his gun back and sent shots straight to Jerome's body. Watching as the metal pierced his skin, he smiled in satisfaction.

"Come on man, we gotta get the fuck out of here!" Nassir yelled, shaking Cartier from his gaze.

The sound of police sirens filled the quiet streetz. Tyrik sent a match flying to the truck. They all got inside a stolen car to get away from the scene.

ღ

Trig sat in his unmarked car, studying Naomi. He knew in order to perfect his plan that he needed to know a lot more about her life. So far, he learned about the nature of her and Cartier's relationship and now he's learning her routine.

He watched her walk back inside the salon from her lunch break. Trig ashed the blunt he was smoking. “Man, how much longer do we have to do this shit!? Let's just snatch her ass up.” Benny sighed, running his hands through his freshly done braids.

“Not much longer man, but come on, we got a few moves to make. We'll come back later.” Trig replied. Benny started up the car and pulled off.

Benny was anxious to do some real work- instead of sitting around, watching Naomi all day. He was more than ready for this problem to be over with. He needed his old boss back.

He wasn't understanding the obsession he had at this point, he was lowkey becoming fed up with it.

“Have you heard anything new from Jacques?” Benny asked, stopping at the red light.

“Nah, he's been really lowkey, lately. Matter of fact, before we head to pick up this money, let's go pull up on him.”

Benny nodded and headed straight to Decatur. They pulled up to Jacques' newly renovated home. Since Jacques had been working for Trig, his pay increased indefinitely, so he started to splurge.

Turning off the engine, they got out the car and headed to knock on the door. Moments later, Jacques opened. He stood there, chest bare, with a pair of basketball shorts on.

“What's up?” He stepped aside to allow them in.

“I see the money is treating you well?” Trig asked, looking over his new home. He had very few furniture and moving boxes laying around.

“Yeah, but this is only the beginning. What made y'all stop by?” Jacques said, cutting straight to the chase.

“Damn, nigga what's the rush?” Benny asked, becoming suspicious. He looked around the place in search of anything out of order.

“It's just-”

With nothing on but only a silk robe, appearing in the stairway, Paris folded her arms. “Who's at the door baby?”

Since his best friend, Paris, was in town, he had been hiding out with her inside his new spot. He didn't want to consume his mind with silent battles he never told. "Go upstairs P, I'll be there soon."

Trig laughed. "Now it makes sense. That's why your ass has been hiding out these past few days."

Jacques grew quiet. His real reason for staying hidden was that he didn't know if he could follow through with kidnapping Naomi anymore; by the look on Trig's face, he felt like he knew it.

Trig waited for Paris to head upstairs. As soon as her feet hit the wood above them, he took the pistol from Benny and smacked Jacques across the face with it. The hard impact immediately caused swelling and a busted lip.

Trig watched him hold his face and stared into his eyes. "You holding out on me, nigga?"

"Nah man. I know better than to do some foul ass shit like that. Who do you mistake me for?"

Trig nodded. He didn't get this far in the game by believing the words of a man, if no fact was able to verify it. That meant Jacques' word meant nothing to him.

"I need that job done, tonight, it's been a change of plans. I don't want to hear any of your excuses. Just get the shit done. I'll be having two of my men join you, in case you get any funny ideas." Trig informed him.

Before Jacques could even respond, they hit the door- leaving him with his thoughts and a leaking lip.

Chapter 24

Naomi shifted in her sleep. Her eyes fluttered open in response to an unfamiliar sound. She laid there, attempting to make out what she heard but fell short. She turned over to check her phone and frowned once she realized it was only three in the morning.

She knew she needed to go back to sleep since she had an early eight o'clock appointment, but after the dream she just had, sleep was the furthest thing from her mind.

Flipping the covers off her body, she got out of her bed and walked into her bathroom. She turned on the water and quickly splashed a little on her face, before resting her arms on the counter with her head hung low.

"It's just a dream, Naomi." She said to herself.

She heard another unusual sound, which startled her again. Naomi's fingers began to sweat, and her heartbeat picked up. She knew her nightmare had her nerves overworked, the last thing she needed was for her fear to be true.

She grabbed her pocketknife; it was hidden away in her bathroom drawer. She tiptoed to the front of her apartment, hoping there was a logical reason for the sounds that haunted her ears.

Approaching her living room, her eyes grew wide as she saw three masked men tearing her place apart. She covered her mouth quickly, so that no sound could seep from it. She wondered what they could've possibly needed in her apartment, what was of value to them?

Thinking quickly, she chose the only choice she had. She slowly crept behind the closest man to her, unlatched her pocketknife, and stuck him directly in his back, repeatedly.

One of the men noticed the commotion and quickly grabbed her by the arm. He squeezed her hand until it forced her to drop the knife on to the floor. Naomi tried her best to fight him back, but it was useless.

She fought to escape his hold by kneeing, she used her 10-second window to scoop up the knife and draw it back, she stabbed him in the shoulder. Winching out in pain, the man backhanded her, causing her to lose balance and fall back onto the floor. She felt her lip throb as blood poured out of it.

"Come get this bitch. Her ass just fucking cut me." The mysterious man snapped, waiting for one of the last guys to take over while he attended to his wound.

He caught her by surprise; she felt strong arms wrap around her neck and squeeze the life out of her, second by second. A wet rag drenched in a strong chemical, covered her airways and blocked access. Naomi struggled to remove it. She also struggled to fight off whoever was on top of her, but his weight paired with her strength was no match. Moments later, the toxin became too much for her lungs to bear.

The fume soon developed a scratching couch in her throat. She knew that there was no use in fighting anymore. It was too late. *Is this how I go out?* She thought as she slipped in and out of consciousness. Her vision was becoming blurry and using her voice was beyond useful.

Before she could make another movement or utter a word, her vision was taken over by darkness.

She was out cold.

"Shh, it's okay," were the last words she heard, from the voice of a man she was all too familiar with... Deandre.

MEET YOUR AUTHOR

ALEXIS TAYLOR

Alexis Taylor is a young, bold, and new Author from Flint, MI. She's been tucked away and gaining flight to rise within her community.

Currently, she's paving the way for writers who aim to take their talents to the next level, while on the verge of launching many projects of her own.

Alexis enjoys the thrill that a good novel can bring, because her writing knows no bounds.

She invites you all to join her on this journey, so that you may find bits and pieces of your own literary freedoms.

COMING SOON...

The Streetz 2 & 3
Dysfunctional Relationships
Breaking... Healing... Loving
&
The Family Business!

Don't forget to stay connected! Follow your Author for release dates, book signings, and so much more!

Facebook: Alexis Taylor
Facebook Like Page: Alexis's Novels
Instagram: @lexthewriter_
Twitter: @lexthewriter_
TikTok: @lexthewriter_
Wattpad: @AlexisNovels

www.ingramcontent.com/pod-product-compliance
Lightning Source LLC
Chambersburg PA
CBHW020249030826
48979CB00030B/2725/J

* 9 7 8 1 7 3 5 7 9 0 1 5 2 *